Sometimes Your Best is Not Enough

"Captain, what the hell do you think you're doing?" Ferrol snarled. "You've got your window—get going."

"We're not leaving you here alone," Roman told him flatly. "Missile crew, shift your aim aft to—"

"Don't be a damn fool," Ferrol cut him off. "Sir. You can't beat the shark, and you know it. Get back to the Cordonale and bring back a warship or something useful."

"Sorry, Ferrol, but we're not taking applications for martyr today," he said. "The shark isn't going to get either of us."

"The shark doesn't give a damn about *us*," Ferrol shot back. "It's the space horses it wants. We cut Quentin loose and let it run, and we'll be perfectly safe."

"Maybe. But maybe not; and we can't take the chance."

For a long second he thought Ferrol was going to argue. But—"Yes, sir," the other gritted out. "Wwis-khaa, you heard the captain."

"Main drive ready," Yamoto announced. "Laser crew reports difficulty in aiming through the vultures."

"Acknowledged," Roman said. "All crewers; stand by." The alert warning warbled, and for a brief moment Roman's mind flashed back to the *Dryden*. A genuine ~~~~~~~~~~~~~~~~~~~~~ with genuine weapons ~~~~~~~~~~~~ them.

The moment p~~~~~~~~~~~ with jury-rigged w~~~~~~~~~~~ facing an enemy ~~~~~~~~~~~ never dreamed of.

All they could do was their best.

fighting ship, the Dryden, with
...and a trained crew to handle

...be refused. He was on the Amity,
...ny refugee weapons and an unskilled crew.
...the Starforce's planners had

WARHORSE

TIMOTHY ZAHN

BAEN BOOKS

WARHORSE

Copyright © 1990 by Timothy Zahn

Parts of this book appeared in substantially different form in the May 1982 and March 1984 issues of *Analog Science Fiction/Science Fact*.

A Baen Books Original

Baen Publishing Enterprises
260 Fifth Avenue
New York, N.Y. 10001

ISBN: 0-671-69868-0

Cover art by David Mattingly

First printing, April 1990

Distributed by
SIMON & SCHUSTER
1230 Avenue of the Americas
New York, N.Y. 10020

Printed in the United States of America

Chapter 1

Two hours earlier, the C.S.S. *Dryden* had killed its rotation, moving for the first time in fifteen days back to zero-gee. An hour earlier, the last course change had been implemented, bringing the ship into as close a direct vector with the target planet of Arachne as possible. And now, with five minutes remaining on the clock, the bright red mass-line had finally appeared at the center of the helmtank and was beginning its leisurely stretch toward the edge.

They were almost there. Almost to Arachne . . . and the Tampies who would be waiting for them.

Captain Haml Roman gazed at the mass-line a moment longer, wishing one last time that someone else's ship could have been tapped for this mission. Appearances and assurances apart, the outcome was about as much in doubt as Arachne's orbit, and it soured his stomach to have to be part of the charade. But neither the Senate nor the Admiralty had ever been in the habit of asking his opinion on such matters. Probably just as well.

Four minutes to go. Reaching over to his intercom board, Roman keyed for his passenger's cabin; but even as he did so the door to Roman's right slid open and Ambassador Pankau floated onto the bridge. "Captain,"

1

he nodded, giving himself a push that sent him gliding across the bridge in Roman's direction. "We have an ETA yet?"

"I was just about to call you, Mr. Ambassador," Roman nodded back, wondering distantly how Pankau managed to maintain that stiff dignity of his even while floating like a child's balloon across the room. "We'll be making breakout in just under four minutes."

Pankau caught the back of Roman's chair to stop his momentum and set his feet firmly into one of the velgrip patches in the deck. "How long to Arachne from there?"

"Shouldn't be more than a few hours. Maybe less, depending on how close in we get before breakout."

Pankau snorted gently, but he was clearly experienced enough to know the uncertainties were beyond Roman's control. At thirty hours per light-year, the Mitsuushi StarDrive chewed up an astronomical unit every 1.7 seconds, and even with computer control a ship was lucky to make breakout within a half-million kilometers of its projected target. "Do your best," the ambassador said, almost grudgingly. "And then I want a minimum-time course to Arachne. No point dragging this out any longer than absolutely necessary."

At the exec's station Lieutenant Commander Trent threw Pankau a sour look, one which the other fortunately missed. "Understood, Mr. Ambassador," Roman said, keeping his own voice and features firmly in polite/ neutral mode.

Pankau nodded curtly and fell silent, and together they watched the steady lengthening of the mass-line. It was almost to the edge of the helmtank when, abruptly, the bridge lights dimmed and half of the main status board went from green to red and then to dark blue.

The *Dryden* had arrived.

"Lieutenant Nussmeyer?" Roman invited, keying on the main display. The screen came to life, blazing with stars and, off center to the left, the red-orange globe of Arachne's sun.

"Dead on target, sir," Nussmeyer reported, peering at his helm display. "We're just over seventy thousand kilometers upslope of Arachne."

Upslope; which meant that the sun's gravity would be helping, instead of hindering, their approach. "Very good, Lieutenant. Plot in a minimum-time course at—" he glanced at Pankau. "Keep it under 1.5 gees."

"Aye, sir. Approximately ninety minutes to orbit, then."

"Very good. Execute."

The acceleration alert began its warbling, and Roman listened to the clicks and creaks as the bridge began swiveling into position for forward linear acceleration. The number and decibel level of the squeaks had been on the rise lately, and he sent up a quick prayer that the equipment would hold out at least until they could make port again. Trying to handle even a relatively small warship like the *Dryden* from a misaligned bridge could get nasty very quickly. "Will you be sending any messages before we make orbit?" he asked, looking again at Pankau.

The other was squinting at the main screen, which now held the small crescent shape of a planet dead center. "Probably depends on whether the Tampy delegation's still topside or whether they've gone down and sent their ship home," he said. "Can you get any more magnification on that thing?"

Roman turned back to his console, feeling an odd stirring of anticipation as he keyed the screen for full mags. If the Tampy ship was indeed still standing by . . .

The small crescent jumped in size to fill the entire screen; stabilized and enlarged again to become a flat strip of mottled planetary edge. The camera started a slow scan. . . .

And there it was, silhouetted against the lighted section: a small, dark rectangular/cylindrical shape, trailing behind a similar but much larger cylinder. The Tampy ship . . . and its accompanying space horse.

The screen's scale came on, locked and stabilized, and someone on the bridge gave a low whistle. "Nine hundred twenty meters long," Pankau read, a touch of awe seeping through the professional coolness in his voice. "I don't think I've ever seen a space horse quite that big before."

"The average is supposed to be eight hundred," Roman agreed. Even preoccupied, he could hear the underlevel of schoolboy excitement in his voice.

Pankau obviously heard it too, and Roman could feel the ambassador's gaze shift from the screen to him. "Your first space horse, Captain?"

It was, fortunately, difficult to blush in zero-gee. "It's the first one I'll have a chance to see close up, yes," Roman conceded. "I *have* seen them from a distance, of course."

Pankau grunted. "It would be rather difficult for the commander of a bordership to totally avoid them." His eyes shifted back to the main screen and his lips puckered. "I suppose I ought to go ahead and talk to them. At least let them know we're here."

Roman nodded. He reached for the comm laser control; remembered just in time and keyed the radio instead. The Tampies had never developed the laser themselves, and had shown complete disinterest in acquiring the necessary technology from the Cordonale. "It's all yours, Ambassador," Roman said.

Pankau cleared his throat. "This is Ambassador Pankau, aboard the Cordonale Star Ship *Dryden*," he called. "Whom do I have the pleasure of addressing?"

The response was immediate; clearly, the Tampies had already noted the *Dryden*'s arrival. "I hear," the alien voice replied.

The whiny, grating, set-the-teeth-on-edge alien voice. Roman clamped his teeth together hard, trying to remember that the Tampies didn't do this on purpose.

"I am Ccist-paa; I speak for the Tamplissta," the other continued. "I greet you."

"And I you," Pankau said, his tone and manner showing none of the reflex irritation Roman felt. But then, Pankau was far more used to putting up with Tampy voices. "I come with open hands and goodwill, and bring the Supreme Senate's desire that our differences here be resolved as quickly as possible." He hesitated, just the barest fraction of a second. "Can you tell me if there's been any change in the situation in the past fifteen days?"

There was a hint of resentment in Pankau's voice, a feeling Roman could well understand. Irritating voices and mannerisms were something professional diplomats learned to live with; lack of adequate and timely information was something else entirely. Running on the Mitsuushi for fifteen days, cut off from access to the Cordonale's network of planet-based tachyon transceivers, everything the *Dryden* knew about the trouble on Arachne was two weeks out of date. The Tampy mission, in contrast, would have been in contact with their own colony here up until the time they'd had to leave their home port . . . which had probably been no more than a few hours ago.

And in this case, the time-lag turned out to be significant indeed. "There has been change," Ccist-paa said with what sounded like a wheezing sigh. "Some of the humans of the Arachne settlement have attacked the Tamplissta of the Tyari."

Pankau clucked his tongue gently. "Any fatalities?"

"No humans were injured. Two Tamplissta have died."

Roman grimaced. It was a pattern that was repeating itself more and more frequently these days on the half-dozen worlds that the Cordonale shared with the Tampies: simmering confrontations boiling over into sharp episodes of violence . . . and always the Tampies who got the short end.

"I'm sorry," Pankau said. "We'll reach your ship in approximately ninety minutes. I'd be honored if you would allow me to transport you to the surface."

"The honor is mine," Ccist-paa said. "However, there

is no need. My lander is capable of providing me with transport."

"Ah," Pankau murmured. "In that event . . . perhaps you'd be kind enough to give *me* transport."

There was a short silence from the Tampy end. "We have no filter masks aboard," Ccist-paa said.

"I have one of my own." Pankau hesitated, glanced down at Roman. "It seems to me that, in the light of recent events, it might be good for us to discuss this matter in private before we talk to the settlers themselves."

Another pause. "You are welcome to ride in my lander," Ccist-paa said, without any trace of emotion Roman could detect. "If you will come alongside, my lander will join with your ship."

"Thank you,"Pankau said. "I'll look forward to seeing you."

"Farewell," Ccist-paa said, and a moment later the aliens' radio carrier cut off.

Roman keyed off the *Dryden*'s own radio. Behind him, the rising drone of the ship's main fusion drive became a dull roar, and weight began to return. "Drive activated, Captain," Nussmeyer confirmed unnecessarily.

"Very good," Roman nodded. "Start calculating the intercept vector to the Tampy ship whenever we're close enough." He looked up at Pankau. The other's face suddenly looked older; but then, it might have been merely the effect of returning weight. "I hope you were prepared to deal with an outbreak of violence," he commented quietly.

Pankau made a face, his eyes still on the main display. "What else *is* there when humans and Tampies get together?" he said sourly. He looked down at Roman, his gaze intensely thoughtful. "It doesn't bother you to be moving your ship in close to a space horse?" he asked, his tone oddly challenging.

Roman cocked an eyebrow up at him. "Not really. Should it?"

The searchlight gaze continued for a moment, then seemed to flicker out. 'There's a lot of misinformation floating around concerning space horses," Pankau said obliquely. "False and embellished stories, general paranoia—that sort of thing." Straightening his shoulders, he stepped off the velgrip. "I'll be down in my quarters, preparing my pack. Let me know when we reach the Tampy ship." He hesitated. "Or if anything . . . unexpected . . . happens."

Roman glanced at Trent, saw the exec looking steadily back at him. "I'll do that, Mr. Ambassador."

"Tampy lander away," Trent reported. "Trajectory . . . right on the money."

"Acknowledged," Roman nodded. "Stay on it, Commander—make sure it stays that way."

The other threw Roman a glance before turning back to his displays. "You think Pankau knows something we don't?" he asked over his shoulder.

Roman shrugged. "I'd guess he's just being cautious. On the other hand, there *has* been at least one incidence of violence down there already."

Trent snorted. "And since Pankau's instructions are probably to give the Tampies whatever they want . . . ?"

Roman shrugged again. *Ours is not to reason why*, he quoted silently to himself. Though that didn't mean any of them had to like it.

Ten kilometers away, their orbit just below the *Dryden*'s, the Tampy ship was pulling slowly away. "Keep us with him, Lieutenant," Roman instructed Nussmeyer, studying the velocity readouts on his tactical display. A kilometer ahead of the alien ship floated the dark mass of their space horse. . . . "On second thought, let's do more than just catch up," he corrected himself suddenly. "I want a closer look at that space horse. Slow approach, parallel course, and keep us about two kilometers away."

The background hum of quiet conversation abruptly cut off. Nussmeyer looked at Trent, and Trent looked at Roman. "Something, Commander?" Roman asked mildly.

Trent's lip twitched. "The Tampies aren't going to be pleased if we spook their space horse."

"That's why we're staying two kilometers away," Roman told him.

"What if that's not far enough?"

Roman cocked an eyebrow and glanced around the bridge. "We're not exactly going to be sneaking up on it, gentlemen. The Tampy Handlers should certainly be able to hold onto it, or at the very least figure out that they can't in time to warn us off. Besides, space horses aren't *that* skittish."

Trent's expression was stony, but he turned back to his work without further argument. Roman watched his back for a moment, then shifted his attention to the helm. "Lieutenant?"

"Maneuver plotted and fed in," Nussmeyer reported, his voice a little strained. Like Trent, he clearly wasn't happy about this; unlike the executive officer, he wasn't in a position to argue about it.

"Very good," Roman said. "Execute."

Through the hull plates the whisper of the drive on minimal power could be felt, bringing with it an equally faint echo of returning weight. Slowly, the *Dryden* moved forward and planetward, passing the Tampy ship and the kilometer of nearly invisible webbing.

And within a few minutes, they were paralleling the space horse itself.

It was something of a cliche—a twenty-year-old cliche, at that—that no camera or holo could truly capture the awesome majesty of a space horse. Roman had heard it probably a hundred times since joining the Starforce; but it was only now that he finally understood why everyone who'd seen one close up seemed so insistent on repeating the standard line.

The creature was *huge*, for starters. Nine hundred twenty meters long, built roughly like a cylinder with rounded ends and a slight taper from front to rear, the space horse totally dwarfed the small Tampy ship trailing it. The delicate webbing linking the two was essentially invisible, even on the telescope screen, but as the fibers caught the sunlight there were occasional glints from it that added a fairy tale sparkle to the scene.

It was the things that *didn't* show up on long-range scans, though, that Roman found most fascinating. The space horse's skin, for one: though in holos it invariably turned out a flat gray, it was in fact strangely iridescent, in a way that reminded him of silk. The sensory clusters, located in axial rings at either end of the cylinder, were likewise far more delicately colored than holos could adequately capture, with colors ranging from a pale blue to a dark burgundy to a surprisingly bright yellow to an utterly dead black.

"Getting an absorption readout now," Trent reported into Roman's thoughts. His voice, still disapproving, was nevertheless beginning to show some grudging interest. "The skin seems to be soaking up about 96 percent of the sunlight hitting it, holding to that same percentage over the complete electromagnetic spectrum."

Roman nodded. Space horses were supposed to be able to absorb radiation of virtually any wavelength—one of the power sources that kept the huge beasts going. "Any idea what that shimmer effect is?" he asked the other.

"Probably a diffraction effect caused by the dust sweat," Trent said. "Or so goes the theory, anyway. Let me see if I can get some kind of direct reading on that."

He was reaching for his console when the *Dryden*'s alarms suddenly began to trill.

"Anomalous motion, Captain," Nussmeyer snapped. Unbidden, the main screen shifted to a tactical display, the laser targeting crosshairs swinging up over and past the bulk of the space horse.

"Easy, gentlemen," Roman said, flicking over to the indicated screen even as his muscles tensed with anticipation. The anomalous-motion program had originally been designed to detect slow-moving ambush missiles;

but this close to a space horse . . . "I doubt we're being threatened here."

"It's a meteor, sir," Trent identified it even as the telescope screen locked and focused on the object.

"As I said," Roman nodded. "Nothing to do with us."

"Maybe, maybe not," Trent countered darkly. "It occurs to me that the Tampies could just as easily have something besides space horse fodder in mind for that rock. Like having the space horse telekene it through our hull."

Roman frowned at him, a vaguely unpleasant sensation creeping into the pit of his stomach. Unthinking prejudice against the Tampies had been growing steadily across the Cordonale in the past few years, and he'd long since resigned himself to its existence. But to find it here on his own bridge . . .

"Lieutenant Nussmeyer," he said quietly, "do you have a vector on that meteor yet?"

"Bearing toward the space horse, sir," the helmer reported, sounding a little uneasy himself. "Projected intersect somewhere in the front-end sensory ring."

Trent's lip twisted. "Means nothing," he said, stubbornly defiant. "Sir. The Tampies could be planning to throw it at us at the last second, once our guard is down."

Roman cocked his head slightly to the side. "In that case, Commander, make sure our guard doesn't *go* down."

Trent held his gaze a second longer, then turned back to his displays without another word. Reaching again to his own controls, Roman turned one of the telescope cameras onto the space horse, keying it to track with the meteor's projected intercept point. Trent's paranoia aside, he had no doubt as to what the space horse wanted the rock for . . . and like the space horse itself, it was something he very much wanted to see. The display shifted slightly as the intercept vector was updated, came to rest on one of the sensory clusters: eight impressively colored organs, each a few square meters in area, grouped around a large expanse of otherwise unremarkable gray skin.

For a moment nothing happened . . . and then, without warning, all the organs darkened in color and the blank central region abruptly split open, its edges ridging upward in an odd puckering sort of motion. From off-camera the meteor appeared, to drop neatly into the opening. The edges smoothed down, the split vanished, and the organs resumed their original colors.

"Secure from alert," Roman ordered, and as the trilling was silenced he looked over at Trent. The other's back was stiff, angry looking. Probably had hoped the Tampies really *were* attacking the *Dryden*.

Had hoped to have his prejudices justified.

"I'd like you to run a complete analysis on the event we've just recorded, Commander," Roman said into the silence. "Concentrate on the meteor movements—vector changes, interaction with local gravitational gradients, and so on. There's a great deal we don't know about space horse telekinesis, and it's a blank area we very much need to get filled in."

Some of the tension went out of Trent's back. "Yes, sir," he said. "I'll get the programs set up right away."

The tension level in the bridge faded noticeably, and Roman permitted himself a moment of satisfaction. A smart commander, he'd once been told, never rubbed a subordinate's nose in an error when it wasn't absolutely necessary to do so. In this case, it wasn't.

Trent might be bigoted; but even bigots sometimes needed to save a little face.

Ambassador Pankau returned twenty hours later . . . with an agreement that was fully as much a charade as Roman had expected it to be.

"The Arachne colonists will be moving their power plant about thirty kilometers further downstream," Pankau said, handing Roman the tapes and signed papers to be filed into the *Dryden*'s official records. "Aside from that, they won't have to give up all that much."

Roman could feel Trent's eyes on him. "What about the settlement itself?" he asked Pankau, accepting the papers. "If they're moving the power plant, won't they have to move with it?"

Pankau grimaced. "Some of them will, yes. Not all."

"And what," Trent put in, "will the Tampies be giving up?"

Pankau turned a quietly official glare on him. "It just so happens," he said evenly, "that on this one, the Tampies turn out to have been right. The power plant *was* interfering with the local migration pattern of at least four different species of birds and animals."

Trent snorted. "Any animal that can't adapt its life around one lousy power plant *deserves* extinction," he growled. "It's not like the damn ghornheads are actually useful for anything."

Pankau kept his temper, but Roman could see it was a near thing. "The ghornheads may not be, no; but the same can't be said for the mrulla. Which keep the rodunis population down to manageable levels in the fields, and which in turn follow the ghornheads around like adoring puppies." He didn't wait for comment, but turned back to Roman. "Ccist-paa also tells me they're having trouble with human poachers grabbing space horses from their Cemwanninni *yishyar* system."

" 'Their' system?" Trent muttered, just loud enough to hear.

Pankau looked back at him, his gaze hardening. "Yes, *their* system. Like it or not, Commander, the Senate has relinquished all human claims there. The Tampies can make real use of a space horse watering hole; we cannot. Playing dog-in-the-manger is hardly the action of civilized people."

The words came out, Roman noted, with the automatic fluency of a practiced speech. Probably one Pankau had had to deliver a great many times. "I think we all understand the Senate's rationale," he put in before Trent could say something he might later regret. "There are equally valid reasons, I think, why renouncing *all* claim to a system is, in general, not a terribly good idea."

"Well, there's nothing that can be done about it now," Pankau said, his tone slightly sour. "At any rate, Captain," he continued, gesturing at the papers in Roman's hand, "you and the *Dryden* now have official Tampy permission to enter the *yishyar* . . . and as soon as you drop me back at Solomon you're to head out there and see if you can catch this troublemaker."

Arachne to Solomon to the *yishyar*. This just got better and better. "I appreciate your attempts to soothe the Tampies, Ambassador—"

"My job is *not* to soothe Tampies, Captain," Pankau cut him off, his voice frosty. "It's to carry out the orders and wishes of the Supreme Senate of the Terran Cordonale—and in this case, the Senate's codified wishes are that unauthorized human ships stay the hell out of Tampy space." He eyed Roman coldly. "Or are you suggesting that I don't have the authority to send you on such a mission?"

That much, at least, wasn't in question. Roman had seen Senate cartes blanches before, and was fully aware of the range of powers such papers held. "I don't question your authority at all, sir," he told Pankau. "But we're talking a pretty long tour here for a ship the size of the *Dryden*. Two weeks to get you back to Solomon, six weeks or more from there to the *yishyar* system, plus the six-week return trip. That's three months right there, plus whatever time we have to spend waiting at the *yishyar* for your poacher to show up."

"Are you suggesting your crew can't handle a few weeks in deep space?" Pankau asked, his tone challenging.

"No, sir," Roman said evenly. "I'm suggesting that it would save us a couple of those weeks if you'd ask Ccist-paa to take a side trip to Solomon and drop you off."

Pankau seemed a little taken aback. "Ah. I see."

"Unless, of course," Roman said, looking the other straight in the eye, "you don't think *you* can handle a few hours in a Tampy ship."

For a moment he thought the professional facade was going to crack. But Pankau had better control than that. "That will hardly be a problem, Captain. If you'll set up the radio . . . ?"

Ten minutes later, it was all arranged. An hour after that, Roman sat at his bridge station and watched the space horse Jump.

It was about the only thing about space horses that was, at least visually, totally unspectacular. One instant the space horse and ship were on the displays; the next instant they were gone.

"I wish to hell *we* could do that," Trent muttered.

Roman gazed at the display, at the empty spot where the Tampy ship had been. "You and everyone else in the Cordonale," he agreed soberly. Totally unspectacular . . . until you stopped to think about what had actually happened. Instantaneous travel, over interstellar distances . . . and with no known distance limit except the ability of the space horse to see its target star. The whole concept sent a shiver up Roman's back. "Maybe when the *Amity* project gets started we'll pick up some insights on how to tame and control them."

Trent snorted. "Fat chance. Sir."

Roman eyed him. "You don't think humans and Tampies can learn to work together aboard the same ship, Commander?"

"I don't think it'll ever come to that, sir," Trent said bluntly. "In my opinion, *Amity*'s nothing but a smoke screen the Tampies and pro-Tampy senators dreamed up to try and look like they're doing something about the shared-worlds problem. The Starforce's never going to finish fitting out the ship; and even if they do, odds are the crew will be so badly biased that the results of the test voyage will be completely fraudulent."

"And if neither happens . . . ?"

Trent looked him square in the eye. "*Then*, sir . . .

no, I don't believe humans and Tampies can work together. Not without killing each other."

Roman grimaced. "You leave the Cordonale very few options."

"Appeasement, or war," Trent agreed quietly. "And even a Senate as spineless as this one won't appease them forever."

Roman looked at the display, at the place where the space horse had been a minute ago, wishing he could argue with any of Trent's assessment. But he couldn't. And even if he could, it was clear the other's mind was already made up.

As were many other minds across the Cordonale.

"Just be sure to keep an open mind, Commander," he warned the other. Even to his own ears the words sounded lame. "You never know when an alternative may present itself. Until then . . . we have a mission to carry out. Let's go track us down a poacher."

Chapter 2

"This," Stefain Reese growled to no one in particular, "is starting to get ridiculous."

A wave of tired irritation rippled through the general boredom that had settled in around the *Scapa Flow*'s bridge crew. From his command chair Chayne Ferrol watched his men glare at Reese or pointedly ignore him, according to individual preference, and stifled a curse of his own. Like everyone else, he was roundly sick of Reese; unfortunately, political necessity dictated that *someone* remain on speaking terms with the man. " 'Haven't caught anything in five hours?' " he quoted the old fisherman's joke. " 'Don't worry—*I* haven't caught anything in *eight* hours.' "

The attempt at humor was wasted. "Save it, Ferrol," Reese snorted. "I've heard that tired old joke at least five times in the last twenty-two days, and it wasn't funny the first time."

With an effort Ferrol hung on to his temper. "Mr. Reese, we made it very clear to you at the outset what it was you were letting yourself in for. Even a *yishyar* system doesn't play host to more than a few space horses at a time, and there are four hundred billion cubic kilometers of asteroid belt out there for them to

16

feed in. You can't expect one to Jump right in on top of us the first day here."

"And yet we've had at least fifteen of them Jump in close enough to register on the anomalous-motion program," Reese countered. "You didn't go after any of *them*, either."

At the helm, Malraux Demarco stirred. "There's a hell of a lot of difference between picking up a target blip and sneaking up on it," he bit out. "None of *us* is exactly crazy about floating around out here watching the rocks go by, either. Try not to forget that you *asked* to come along."

"Yes, well it wasn't exactly my idea," Reese shot back. "The Senator wanted me to come and observe—"

The slap of Ferrol's hand on his armrest echoed briefly through the bridge, cutting off the growing argument in mid-sentence. "What?" Reese demanded, throwing a defiant glare in Ferrol's direction.

For a long minute Ferrol just stared at the other, watching as the angry defiance faded into discomfort and then into the first twitchings of genuine fear. "You are not," he said at last, the words quiet but icy cold, "to mention the Senator in connection with this ship, its crew, or its mission. Not here, not anywhere else. Ever. Do you understand?"

Reese swallowed visibly. "Yes," he said.

Ferrol let the silence hang in the air a moment longer before turning back to Demarco. "Did we ever get anything more on that blip Randall picked up and then lost?"

Demarco shook his head. "The computer's equipment check came up negative," he said. "It may have been a space horse that Jumped in for a snack and immediately left." He paused. "Or it may have been another ship."

Ferrol nodded. The latter was his own gut-level conclusion. "You think they spotted us?"

Demarco shrugged. "Two and a half hours should have been plenty of time for them to have recalculated their position, looped around on Mitsuushi and come roaring in on us," he pointed out. "Given that they haven't, I expect it was just another poacher who spotted us and got nervous."

"Or else an unusually patient Starforce captain who wants to catch us with our hands on the goodies," Ferrol said. "We'll have to keep our eyes open."

"That's all you're going to do?" Reese asked.

Ferrol looked over at him. "What do you suggest, Mr. Reese?" he asked mildly. "That we turn tail and run home empty-handed—and without even knowing what it was we ran *from*?"

Reese clenched his teeth. "I was suggesting you might want to take some practical precautions," he gritted. "Like putting some shielding over the Mitsuushi ring, for instance."

"We have any Mitsuushi shielding, Mal?" Ferrol asked Demarco.

"That'll block a warship's ion beams? Not hardly."

Ferrol looked back at Reese. "Any other suggestions?"

From the expression on Reese's face the suggestion he was toying with would have been a ripe one. But even as he took the necessary breath to make it—

"Anomalous motion, Chayne!" Demarco snapped. "It's—God, it's practically on top of us. Bearing twenty-three mark six, fifteen mark two; range, fifty-six kilometers."

"A warship?" Reese demanded, his voice half an octave higher than normal.

Demarco threw him a look that was pure strained patience. "No. A space horse."

"If a rather puny one," Ferrol added, studying his own readouts. It *was* small, come to think of it. In fact, unless the computer had completely scrooned up the distance calculation—

And abruptly, a shiver ran up his back. "That's a *calf*, Mal."

Demarco peered at the display. "I'll be damned."

Ferrol licked his upper lip, his heart beginning to

thud in his ears as he keyed the general intercom. A space horse calf. Young, impressionable . . . and maybe, just maybe, trainable. "Captain to crew: we've got a target. Starting our approach now." He paused. "Look *real* sharp, gentlemen. I want this one."

At the helm Demarco teased the drive into operation, and Ferrol felt Reese's eyes on him. "If you have something to say, Reese, say it and then shut up."

Out of the corner of his eye he saw the other gesture toward the cylindrical creature now centered on the main display. "You hoping a calf won't have the same fear of human beings that adult space horses do?" he asked.

So the man had operational brain cells, after all. "That's the way it works with other animals," he said shortly. "It's called imprinting."

"If the calf is young enough," Reese agreed cautiously. "Whatever 'young enough' means in this case."

"You want a debate, go back to the Senate," Ferrol told him absently. "Right now, we have more important things to do." He took a deep breath. "Okay, Mal; let's go."

They approached at a fraction of their usual stalking speed, with the result that it took them nearly an hour to drift into netting range. Excessive and unnecessary caution, perhaps—at no time did the calf show any signs at all of nervousness, much less panic—but they had the time to spare and there was no percentage here in taking chances. Besides which, there was no way to know whether a calf on the verge of spooking would exhibit the same signs of distress that an adult space horse would.

"Net guns ready," Demarco announced. "Range to target . . . 1.4 kilometers. Plates at full charge."

Ferrol consciously relaxed his jaw muscles. This was it. "Stand by, primary gun. Ready . . . fire."

Beneath him, the *Scapa Flow* bucked once as, on the

tactical display, the missile shape of the coiled net appeared, dead on target for the calf, its tether lines snaking along behind it. Ferrol held his breath, his eyes on the calf. *Just a few more seconds*, he mentally urged it. *Stay put just a few more seconds.* On the screen the missile shape was disintegrating, unwrapping into an almost insubstantially thin mesh as it neared the calf. *Just a few more seconds . . .*

And, too late, the calf noticed the object hurling toward it. The missile—or what was left of it—jerked as it was telekened to a halt . . . but the strands of the mesh were far too thin for the creature to get an adequate grip on. An instant later the net hit, wrapping itself solidly around the calf—

"Stun it!" Ferrol snapped.

The *Scapa Flow* bucked again, far more violently this time, as the netted calf tried to pull away from its captor; but even as Ferrol was slammed back into his seat cushions he heard the muffled *crack!* of the *Scapa Flow*'s huge capacitors. On the screen, the net flared briefly with coronal discharge . . . and the calf stopped moving.

Across the bridge, Reese swore reverently under his breath. "You did it. You really *did* it."

Ferrol wiped a hand across his mouth. "Assuming we haven't killed it, yes. Mal?"

Demarco spread his hands. "Who can tell with a space horse? Nothing obviously wrong with it, though."

"Good."

A flashing light caught Ferrol's attention: the *Scapa Flow*'s middle hull, now highly positively charged from the capacitors' discharge, was threatening to arc to the outer hull. "Shorting to outer hull," Demarco announced, reaching for the proper switch.

"Hold it a minute," Ferrol ordered, the hairs on the back of his neck tingling with unpleasant premonition. Shorting the middle and outer hulls together would leave the outer hull positively charged until it collected enough solar wind electrons to neutralize the imbalance

. . . leaving the Mitsuushi inoperable until the process was complete. "Give me a full scan of the immediate area first," he told Demarco. "Look for indications that the ship we tagged earlier might be skulking around out there."

Demarco gave a curt nod and busied himself at the scanners. Ferrol waited, trying to ignore the flashing arc-danger warning, and after a minute Demarco straightened up. "Looks clear," he reported. "Of course, he could be hanging way back somewhere with a Mitsuushi intercept loop already programmed in."

Ferrol chewed at his lower lip. A distinct possibility . . . "All right," he said slowly. "Short to outer hull; then isolate the middle hull again and start the capacitors charging again. Better charge the backup set, too."

Demarco threw him a puzzled look, but nodded. "Right." Another *crack!*—"Charge drained to outer hull," he announced. "Outer hull now isolated . . . charging commencing."

"Good," Ferrol said, shifting his attention back to the space horse calf and keying for the air lock ready room. "Townne, you and Hlinka better get moving—I want the space horse secured for travel in half an hour."

"Acknowledged, Chay—"

"Anomalous motion!" Demarco snapped. "Five thousand kilometers out, coming straight toward us."

"What?" Reese gasped. "God, Ferrol—"

On Ferrol's board the laser comm light went on. "Unidentified ship," a quiet voice came over the speaker, "this is Captain Haml Roman aboard the C.S.S. *Dryden*. You're ordered to shut down your drive and prepare to be boarded."

"I see I was right," Ferrol commented into the brittle silence. "It *was* an unusually patient captain. I guess you'd better belay that securing party, Townne."

"My God, Ferrol," Reese breathed. "You're not going to surrender, are you? God, if I'm caught here—"

"Shut up or leave the bridge," Ferrol cut him off

evenly, his eyes flicking across the readouts. The warship wasn't moving very quickly, but even at its current speed it would be within reasonable boarding range in ten minutes or less, with boarders knocking at the hatches five minutes after that. The *Scapa Flow* wouldn't be going anywhere on Mitsuushi before then, either: the outer sensors indicated the *Dryden* had its ion beams playing across the *Scapa Flow*'s hull, charging it and its attached Mitsuushi ring to uselessness.

Or rather, *trying* to charge it. At the moment, the earlier discharge from the capacitors had the hull already holding just about all the charge it could, with the *Dryden*'s beams largely being deflected uselessly off into space. A situation entirely to Ferrol's liking . . . and one his opposite number on the *Dryden* might well have missed. "Capacitor status, Mal."

"Main set shows three minutes to full charge," Demarco reported. "Another four on the backups."

Ferrol nodded, keying a countdown on his board timer where he could keep an eye on it. This was going to be tight. "Let's see if we can stall him a little," he said to no one in particular.

He tapped for comm control and the *Scappa Flow*'s brand-new Domino III voice refractor, feeling a flicker of grim satisfaction at his own foresight in persuading the Senator to shell out the cash for the latter. With the Domino subtly altering the tones and frequency levels of his voice, the ship out there could analyze it forever without getting anything they could match up against a voiceprint file. The Senator had maintained the gadget was a waste of money; Ferrol had convinced him otherwise.

A light went on: the *Scapa Flow*'s laser had locked onto its target. "Captain, this is Professor John English aboard the research ship *Milan*," he said, putting just a touch of professorial stuffiness into his voice. "We're doing some highly delicate work here, and we'd greatly appreciate it if you'd keep your distance."

"Would you now," the other came back. "May I ask what sort of work that might be?"

"We're banding space horses, of course," Ferrol told him. The *Dryden*, he noted, hadn't slowed its approach in the slightest. Not that he'd really expected it to. "Trying to learn their movement patterns and social habits. Though I presume a mere civil servant like yourself wouldn't have heard of our project."

"We don't get the more esoteric scientific journals out on border duty, no," the captain said with a dryness that showed he didn't believe a word of it. "Going to strap thirty-six square kilometers of tachyon transceiver to it, are you?"

"Our version is considerably more compact," Ferrol said, improvising easily. "It's an experimental system, capable only of transmitting random blips of tachyon static. We hope that a modified version may someday be adapted for direct ship-to-ship or ground-to-ship communication."

"Certainly a worthwhile goal to shoot for. As long as we're on the subject of ships, perhaps you'd care to explain why yours isn't listed on our registry."

"Oh, we're probably too new," Ferrol said, keeping the bulk of his attention on the capacitor countdown timer and the scene on the main tactical display. The *Scapa Flow* was almost exactly broadside to the *Dryden*'s approach vector, a fairly lousy position to be in. "We registered only a couple of months ago, just before we headed out," he added. "You really ought to make it a point to have your registry updated more frequently."

"Ah," the other said. "That must be it. No doubt the procedure will be simplified once you get your miracle micro tachyon transceiver under better control. I don't suppose that along with your registry papers you'd happen to have written permission from the Tampies to be out here poking around their *yishyar* system?"

"Of course we do," Ferrol said, trying to sound simultaneously haughty and injured. "*And* a Senate directive, *and* a release from the Starforce, *and* a half-dozen other pieces of official pontification. It's astonishing sometimes how much paper it takes to run even a simple scientific expedition. Let me dig everything out of storage and have the computer send you over some copies." He touched the cutoff switch. "Mal, when I give the word, swing us around so that the calf's between us and the *Dryden*. Don't worry about straining the tether or netting—we're not going to be keeping them, anyway."

"Got it—hold it a second," Demarco interrupted himself. "Another blip just popped into view. Directly astern . . . looks like a damn Tampy ship."

Ferrol hissed between his teeth. "Same orders," he told Demarco. "Back behind the calf when I give the word."

"We'll still be in full view of the Tampy ship there," Reese pointed out, his voice tight. "In fact, we'll be broadside to it—"

"Doesn't matter," Ferrol cut him off. "They're too far back to reach us with an ion beam, even if they have one, and they're not likely to use anything heavier."

Reese frowned at the tactical display. "Why not?"

"Because they might hit the calf, of course," Ferrol growled. "Besides, I don't think they'd risk doing anything that far out of official character, not with the *Dryden* sitting there watching." He released the cutoff switch, throwing a glance at the timer as he did so. A minute and a half to go. "Just one moment longer, Captain," he called. "We've got the stack of papers here and are copying them for transmission."

"Of course you are," the other said, almost soothingly. "Well, it's been fun, Captain, but I think we've run this one pretty well into the ground. Shall we go ahead and call it quits, or are you really determined to waste more time sending over a set of forged documents?"

Ferrol felt his lip twist. If there was one thing he hated, it was having to put up with a condescending sense of humor. "Are you officially notifying me that I'm under arrest?" he countered.

"Consider yourself notified. You didn't really expect that spun-sugar story of yours to get you very far, did you?"

"It was worth a try. You'd be surprised at the number of people whose brains go into coma-mode when they see official-looking paper." Ferrol snapped his fingers and gestured to Demarco. The other nodded, and abruptly the drive roared to life, pushing Ferrol back into his seat.

He expected the *Dryden*'s captain to react with surprise or even anger at the sudden maneuver; but if the other was even annoyed it didn't show in his voice. "Whatever you're planning, Captain, let me assure you that it won't work," he said calmly. "Our sensors show your outer hull and Mitsuushi ring are carrying a heavy positive charge, and we both know you can't possibly outrun us in normal space."

"I trust that after we've been officially arrested my people will be taken aboard your ship," Ferrol said, ignoring the other's comment. The *Scapa Flow* was beginning to move now; another minute and the *Dryden*'s ion beams would be at least partially blocked by the quiescent space horse calf still wrapped in the *Scapa Flow*'s netting. "I'd just as soon your melted-face chummies out there don't get their hands on my ship, either."

"You have something against Tampies?"

For a moment the memories flooded back; ruthlessly, Ferrol forced them down. He couldn't afford emotional distractions right now. "Let's just say I know what they're capable of," he said shortly. "Despite Senate propaganda to the contrary."

The *Dryden*'s captain seemed to digest that. "Interesting comment," he said after a moment. "Perhaps we can delve into the subject in more depth on the trip back. As it happens, the Tampies out there aren't connected with this at all."

Ferrol snorted under his breath. "Not that it matters," he said. "Even if they're not just out here to monitor your poacher hunt, it's a sure bet that it was the Tampies who gave you the original orders."

The pause was brief, but it was long enough for Ferrol to recognize that his gibe had hit a nerve. "Our orders came from the Senate, Captain," the other said evenly.

"You really ought to be on *our* side," Ferrol told him. "As long as the Tampies have a monopoly on ownership and control of space horses, you and I and the whole Cordonale are going to be stuck dancing to their tune. The only way to break that hold— "

"Prepare to receive boarders, Captain," the other interrupted him. His voice was no longer bantering.

Well, Ferrol thought, gritting his teeth, *it was worth a try.* And perhaps more to the point, it had gained the *Scapa Flow* the rest of the time it needed. The ship was in position; the timer showed fifteen seconds to full charge. Slapping the laser cutoff, Ferrol keyed for all-ship intercom. "Mitsuushi in twenty seconds," he announced. "And brace yourselves—this could be rocky." He shifted his attention to Demarco. "The minute you have full charge on the capacitors, fire them both down the tether," he instructed. "If I'm right, we'll have the Mitsuushi back for only a few seconds—don't miss the window."

"Ferrol, what—?"

"Shut up, Reese," Ferrol cut him off, his eyes on the tactical display. The *Dryden* was driving laterally now, swinging around the space horse calf to where it would again have a clear shot with its ion beams. A leisurely maneuver—at current solar wind fluxes it would take another hour or more for the charge on the *Scapa Flow's* hull to be neutralized, and the captain over there knew it. Mentally crossing his fingers, Ferrol wedged himself tighter into his chair and watched the timer cross to zero. "Go," he ordered.

The double *crack*! rocked the ship; and the sound was still echoing in Ferrol's ears as the main display lit up with a brilliant flash. "We just lost the netting and tether!" Demarco shouted as the hull-stress alarm began its warbling. "The current must have vaporized them."

"Get ready!" Ferrol shouted back, his eyes on the surface charge indicator. Ahead of the *Scapa Flow*, two capacitors' worth of free electrons combined with those from the vaporized netting fibers, the whole mass of them rushing at Van de Graaff speeds toward the most electron-deficient object anywhere around them—

The hull-stress alarm tone was moving up the scale, but Ferrol hardly heard it. On his screen the Mitsuushi sensors showed the positive charge dropping like a rock straight toward—

"Hull's neutral!" he barked at Demarco. "*Go!*"

And an instant later the space horse calf, the *Dryden*, and the stars all vanished.

They'd made it.

Ferrol took a deep breath. *I'll be damned*, he thought. *It worked.* "Status?"

"Mitsuushi's clean but shaky," Visocky's voice reported from the engine room. "If we don't make breakout in an hour the equipment'll do it for us. All that charge the capacitors dumped on the middle hull has to be bled off sometime soon, too."

Ferrol nodded. "We'll make breakout in three minutes, alter course and go another ten. At that point we should be able to take as much cleanup time as we need without worrying about unexpected company."

He switched off, and turned to find Reese looking at him. His expression—"You have something to say, Reese?"

"We're heading home now, I take it?"

"There's not much point in doing anything else," Ferrol told him. "Eventually, the pro-Tampies will ease up on this *yishyar* patrol; until then, there's not much we can do. Unless you want to start scouring systems at random?"

"Not really." Reese glanced at the blackness on the main display. "That was a hell of a chance you just took.

I may not know all that much about starships, but I *do* know that triggering what amounted to a major lightning bolt between the space horse and the *Scapa Flow* could have taken out both the hull's micro seams *and* the Mitsuushi ring in the bargain."

Ferrol gazed at him. "You're absolutely right, Mr. Reese. You *don't* know much about starships."

Reese's eyes hardened. "You could have shunted the capacitor charge directly to the outer hull," he said, his voice edging into accusation. "You didn't need to vaporize the netting and tether line."

"I wanted the extra electron cloud between us and the *Dryden* in case they tried bringing up the ion beam again," Ferrol said, keeping his voice level. "Besides, shunting directly to the hull would have carried its own set of risks."

"And besides," Reese said softly, "you hoped the extra jolt might kill the calf?"

The bridge had gone silent. The charge, Ferrol knew, might indeed have killed the calf. The thought twisted his stomach . . . but he was damned if he was going to show that kind of sentimentality in front of Reese. "*We* captured that space horse," he told the other, biting out each word as if he really meant it. "If we don't get it . . . neither do the Tampies."

Reese took a careful breath. "I see," he said stiffly.

"I doubt that," Ferrol told him. "But frankly, I don't much care whether you do or don't . . . and you're excused from the bridge for the remainder of the voyage."

His face rigid, Reese unstrapped and made his way back to the bridge door. "The Senator will hear about this," he warned.

"I don't doubt it," Ferrol said. "At this point, I don't much care about *that*, either."

The door closed behind him, and Ferrol turned back to the main display with a tired sigh. It was, perhaps, the beginning of the end. Even the *Scapa Flow*'s backers no longer truly understood how thin the razor-edge was that the Cordonale was balanced on. Even they were starting to be lulled by the Tampy protestations of peace and friendship.

Or else they'd lost their nerve. Either way . . .

Either way, there was going to have to be some serious discussion when the *Scapa Flow* reached home.

Some very serious discussion indeed.

For a long moment the bridge was silent, with the kind of silence Roman usually associated with sheer stunned disbelief.

At least, that was what he himself was feeling. Disbelief . . . and a deep and personal chagrin.

The poacher had beaten him.

He took a deep breath. "Lieutenant Nussmeyer, did we get anything like a departure vector through all that?"

"Ah—I believe so, sir, yes," the other said. "Though if he's smart he won't stay on that course for long."

Roman focused on Nussmeyer's profile. There was something that looked suspiciously like awe in the other's face. "And you expect he *is* that smart, I gather?"

Nussmeyer flushed slightly. "Sorry, sir," he said. "I just—" He waved a hand helplessly. "You can't help but admire a man who takes a gamble that big and pulls it off."

"I can't?"

Nussmeyer flushed again and fell silent . . . but even as Roman looked around the bridge he saw that it was a losing battle. The poacher's crack about their orders coming from the Tampies had subtly but noticeably shifted their sympathies in his favor—that, along with the Tampy ship's damnably bad timing in showing up when it did. It was just as well, Roman thought darkly, that there was no chance anyway of tracking the renegade down. It wouldn't be an operation his crew could tackle wholeheartedly.

Damn the Tampies, anyway. Abruptly, he reached to his console, keyed the radio. If the Tampies *were* here to keep tabs on his hunting— "Tampy ship, this is

Captain Haml Roman aboard the C.S.S. *Dryden*," he
identified himself, his tone harsher than he'd intended
it to be. "Your presence in this part of the system is not
exactly conducive to our mission of hunting poachers.
Would it be at all possible for you to shift your own
operations elsewhere?"

"I hear," the whining alien voice came promptly.
"We conduct no operations here, Rro-maa; we bring a
message for you from your people."

Roman blinked. That wasn't exactly the reply he'd
been expecting. "I see. Go ahead, we're ready to receive it."

An indicator came on briefly and went off. "Farewell," the Tampy said, and a moment later vanished
from the displays.

The message was short, but no less a bombshell for
all that. Roman read it twice before raising his eyes
from his screen. "Lieutenant, lay in a course back to
Solomon," he ordered Nussmeyer. "Head out as soon
as the Mitsuushi's ready to go."

"Trouble?" Trent asked.

"I'm not sure," Roman shook his head. "The message
just says that we're to return, that the refitting for the
Amity project has been finished."

Trent's forehead furrowed. "That's it? So what do
they want from us?—a flyby to send it off?"

"Not really," Roman said. "Mostly, what they want is
me . . . to be *Amity's* captain."

Chapter 3

The courier ship that had brought Roman from Solomon to the Tampies' Kialinninni system had been an old one, right on the edge of being retired or possibly a bit past it; and if appearances and the occasional creaking from the bracing struts were any indication, the shuttle now arrowing him toward Kialinninni's sun and the Tampy space horse corral was of similar vintage. A continual and sobering reminder that the *Amity* project was looked upon with scorn or even suspicion by a significant part of the Senate and Starforce . . . and that it was that faction that controlled the appropriations. "I hope," he commented, "that the *Amity*'s in better shape than this thing."

The pilot chuckled. Like the shuttle he, too, was unspectacular: a middle-aged lieutenant who'd apparently reached the peak of his capabilities years before and had just sort of stayed there. Unlike the hardware, though, there was something more beneath his surface; some quietly flickering flame of excitement or optimism that official contempt and slashed budgets had been unable to dampen.

Roman had seen such borderline-religious faith before among the more rabid pro-Tampy supporters. He had yet to decide whether he found it encouraging or frightening.

"Not to worry, sir," the pilot assured him. "The *Amity* is a beauty—brand-new, top-line in-system freighter, modified down centerline and out. You'll have better equipment and accomodations than most anything flying. Certainly better than anything *I've* ever flown on."

Which might not, of course, be saying much. "Glad to hear it," Roman said, eyes searching the view out the shuttle's control bubble. "Can we see it from here?"

"Just barely, sir," the other said, touching the wrap-around viewport. "That's *Amity* over there—that line of reflected sunlight right at the edge of the corral."

Roman frowned. "*That's* part of the corral? I assumed that was the corral over there." He pointed thirty degrees further to the left, where the edge of a cylindrical space station was visible in the dim red light. Beside it, the shapes of three space horses could be seen, with a small ship trailing behind each. Couriers, almost certainly; the Tampies had consistently refused the Cordonale's offer of tachyon transceivers to handle their interstellar communication.

"Oh, that's just the central part of it," the lieutenant explained. "The Focus, they call it. It holds the administrative offices, quarters for on-duty Handlers, and the medical/scientific study center. The corral enclosure itself extends a good three hundred kilometers further in both directions." He grinned. "Plenty of room for even space horses to get their exercise."

Still frowning, Roman studied the indicated area. Sure enough, now that he was looking for them he could see a few space horses drifting individually around in what looked for all the world like empty space. "What keeps them in, netting mesh?"

"Mainly, sir. It's a double thickness of netting, wrapped around a geodesic support framework that keeps it from losing its shape."

Roman squinted at the dim red star. "So what keeps them from simply Jumping out? The fact that they're at a low gravitational potential this close in to the star?"

"That's part of it, sir," the other said. "Jumps are between equipotential surfaces, and practically any star the space horses can see from here is a lot bigger and hotter. That's why the Tampies put their corral in this system—the sun is cool but very dense, and any Jump from the enclosure would put the space horse pretty close to its target star. But there's more." He did something to the navigational display, and a schematic of a section of netting appeared. "Those nodules—at the framework intersections, here and here—those are the ends of lightpipes. The other ends are connected to lenses pointed outward at particular stars."

"Uh-*huh*," Roman said as understanding came. "So the space horses can look in and see a normal stellar spectrum, but because they aren't actual stars there's nothing there for them to lock onto and Jump to. However the hell it is they do that."

"Right, sir," the lieutenant nodded. "Also, the fake starlight tends to mask the real stars behind them—sort of an extra bonus. Simple but elegant."

Roman felt his lip twitch. *Simple but elegant*—the standard stock phrase used by pro-Tampies to describe Tampy technology. *Simpleminded and primitive* was the equally standard anti-Tampy retort. "Well, it obviously works," Roman conceded. "How'd you learn all this stuff, anyway?"

The other's forehead creased slightly. "I asked the Tampies, of course. They're extremely eager to teach us their ways."

"Provided one genuinely wants to learn?"

The other threw him an odd look. "Well, yes, sir," he said. "You don't think they'd force their viewpoint down our throats, do you?"

"They do a fair job of it on the shared worlds," Roman said, moved by a strange impulse to play devil's advocate. "Passive resistance is still resistance."

It was as if someone had flipped a switch on the lieutenant's personality. "Yes, sir," he said, his tone abruptly stiff and formal.

Roman let the cool silence hang in the air a moment longer. "You know, Lieutenant," he said, keeping his voice conversational, "a person who can't understand both sides of an argument hasn't got a chance of cutting through all the emotion and rhetoric and finding common ground."

"There may not *be* any common ground on this one. Sir."

"There's always common ground," Roman said bluntly. "And it can always be found if someone's willing to search for it. *Always.*"

He watched the other's profile, saw the stiffness and anger fade. "Understood, sir," he muttered. He glanced over at Roman, and a tentative smile brushed his lips. "In this case, I take it, that someone is you?"

A half-crew's worth of human beings: thoroughly— perhaps even violently—polarized in their feelings for or against Tampies . . . who would be making up the other half of the crew. "Perhaps," he said. "Peacemaker is certainly one of the two possible roles I've been cast for here."

The lieutenant frowned. "What's the other?"

Roman grimaced. "Scapegoat."

The woman was tall and slender, in her mid-forties, with graying dark hair, piercing eyes, and an air of confidence about her as she glided easily to the center of Roman's office. "Lieutenant Erin Kennedy, Captain," she identified herself. "Reporting for preflight interview as ordered."

"Welcome aboard, Lieutenant," Roman nodded to her. "Or should I say 'Commander'?"

Her eyebrows twitched. " 'Lieutenant' will be fine, sir," she said. "I was told that the reduction in rank wouldn't be mentioned in my file."

"It wasn't," Roman told her. "It happens that one of my friends served on a ship where you were exec some years back, and your name stuck with me." He cocked an eyebrow. "I presume the demotion was voluntary?"

"Yes, sir," she said. "I was originally slated to be *Amity*'s exec, but at the last minute I was bounced—one faction of the Senate battling with another, I gather, and my supporters lost. That left me the choice of either accepting a demotion to second officer or not coming at all."

"I see." Roman eyed her thoughtfully. "And riding with the *Amity* was that important to you?"

"Yes, sir," she nodded. "But not for the reason everyone else signed on."

"You don't particularly care one way or the other about Tampies." It was a statement, not a question. Kennedy's psych profile had put her almost dead-center neutral on her feelings about Tampies, a glaring anomaly among *Amity*'s emotion-churned majority.

She shrugged, an infinitesimal movement of her shoulders. "Not really, sir. Though it might be more accurate to just say that I know enough for the things I like and the things I dislike to balance out."

In many ways an echo of Roman's own feelings about the aliens. Fleetingly, he wished Kennedy hadn't lost in her bid to be *Amity*'s exec. "You see yourself as a peacemaker between the Pros and Antis, then?" he probed gently.

She smiled faintly. "And get shot at by both sides? Not me, sir. Actually, the main reason I wanted to come was for the hands-on experience of flying a space horse. With commercial shipping companies already experimenting with space horse-and-Tampy rentals, this looks to be the direction interstar travel is going."

"Perhaps." Or perhaps not; the handful of companies who had actually tried hiring space horses instead of using Mitsuushi-equipped ships had indeed raked in substantial profits . . . and had lost customer goodwill in roughly equal measure in the process. At the moment it was considered a toss-up as to the direction the private-sector experiment would ultimately go.

Just one more burden, Roman thought sourly, resting on his and *Amity's* shoulders. "Space horse experience, at any rate, I think I can safely guarantee you. Have you had a chance to look through our voyage plan yet?"

"Of course, sir." She seemed surprised he would have to ask. "I've also read the initial survey reports on the four planets we'll be looking over. Alpha, Beta, Gamma, and Delta, the reports designate them."

"The designations weren't my idea," Roman assured her dryly. "I would have picked something with a little more class."

She smiled again. "Yes, I've had some experience with bureaucracies and report factories myself, sir," she said. "One question, if I may: everything in those reports came via the Tampies?"

"Right. We'll be the first humans to visit any of the four systems."

"So everything in them—such as it is—is written from the Tampy point of view."

"It's something to keep in mind when we get there," Roman agreed. "Any other comments on either the plan or the reports?"

She considered. "Not really, sir. I did notice several places where the timetable or even the mission plan itself seemed a bit vague. May I assume that was deliberate?"

"You may indeed," Roman nodded. "I wanted to leave us enough room to play things by ear. Don't forget, Lieutenant, that this is the first time something like this has been tried. You're going to be helping to make history here."

Or at least a footnote to history, her look seemed to say. "Yes, sir," she said instead, her voice suitably neutral.

"We'll be examining the voyage plan at regular intervals once we're actually underway," Roman continued.

"I'll look forward to your input then, and at any other time you have a comment, of course. So." He glanced at his desktop display, checking to see if there were any other questions he'd wanted to ask her. "How's your organization of piloting staff and helmers going? Any problems cropped up yet?"

"Nothing significant," she shook her head. "Certainly not when you consider the potential for psychological clashes aboard."

"Yes, some of that's already surfaced back in engineering," Roman said grimly.

"I've heard," she nodded. "I don't think you'll have to worry about anything that bad in the helmer staff. I've had to handle worse conflicts on some of the warships I've served on."

"Good," Roman said. "Then unless you have any questions, I'll let you get back to your duties."

"Yes, sir," she said. "Are we still scheduled for an 0800 departure tomorrow?"

"Provided the Tampies are all aboard and have the space horse tethered to us by then," Roman said, suppressing a flash of annoyance. The Tampies, he'd discovered to his mild chagrin, had their own idea as to what constituted top speed, a level that was considerably below human expectations. "You can assume we're on schedule unless and until you hear anything to the contrary."

"My people will be ready whenever you need us."

"I'm sure they will. Thank you for coming by, Lieutenant. Dismissed."

She glided to the door and exited, and Roman turned with a sigh to his desktop display. A hundred twenty-three interviews down; just one more to go . . . but this last one was likely to be a beaut.

Amity's exec. The man who Senate infighting had succeeded in putting in as second in command, despite the record and obvious competence of Erin Kennedy. The man who, unlike the rest of the ship's officers and crew, had arrived barely twenty-four hours before the ship's scheduled departure, too late to help with any of the pre-flight preparations.

The man who'd brought with him a personal file and psych profile that practically simmered with Tampy-hatred.

It was, unfortunately, the kind of politically-twisted logic that Roman should have expected. The Senate's anti-Tampy faction would have demanded that Roman's own pro-Tampy inclinations be balanced by an opposite bias in *Amity*'s executive officer, and it was clear from Kennedy's own comments that such a demand had indeed been made and yielded to. Still, for the past few days he'd dared to hope that they might have given up that concession at the last minute; that the continuing border troubles would have convinced them that they could safely give *Amity* a fair trial without the need to stack the deck. Clearly, they hadn't been interested in taking that chance.

And coming at the last minute like this, there wasn't a lot Roman could do about it. Keying the man's file onto his display, he scanned it one last time to refresh his memory, then touched the intercom switch. "Is the exec there yet?" he asked the yeoman manning the outer desk.

"Yes, sir."

Mentally, Roman braced himself. "Send him in."

The door slid open and a young man stepped through, moving with somewhat less certainty and grace than had Erin Kennedy before him. Less experience with ships in low-rotation mode, Roman noted automatically, filing the datum away for possible future reference. "Welcome aboard, Commander," he said. "I'm Captain Haml Roman."

"Lieutenant Commander Chayne Ferrol," the other identified himself, his voice formal, stiff, and cool. "I'm looking forward to serving with you, Captain."

Ferrol had argued long and hard with the Senator and his friends about this assignment—had brought up a hundred reasons why it wouldn't work, a hundred more why he didn't want to serve under the man who'd come within a hair of nailing him and the *Scapa Flow* three months earlier. They'd assured him there would be no problem, convinced him he was the only man for the job . . . but now, standing there under Roman's unblinking gaze, Ferrol wished he hadn't given in. Those eyes were far too intelligent, far too discerning, and for that first awful moment Ferrol was sure the captain somehow knew exactly who he was. He braced himself for the accusation as Roman opened his mouth— "We're looking forward to having you aboard, Commander," the other said.

The tightness in Ferrol's chest eased, and he began to breathe again. *So much for paranoia*, he thought, annoyed with himself for jumping so easily to conclusions. "Thank you, Captain," he said. "My apologies for arriving at the last minute like this."

Roman waved the apology aside. "I imagine the fault lies with those who sent you." His eyes dipped to his desk display. "You'll forgive me if I say that at twenty-four you're a bit young for your rank."

"The commission is honorary," Ferrol said. That was technically supposed to be a secret, but Roman could hardly have failed to figure it out. "I have, however, had six full years in the merchant fleet, two of them as captain of a small ship of my own. I think you'll find me fully capable of serving as *Amity*'s executive officer."

"Oh, I'm sure you are," Roman said mildly. "It's just that your file is oddly vague on these details, and I wanted to get some of them cleared up. The size of your former command, for instance."

"It was a small interstellar tug with a crew of fifteen," Ferrol told him.

Roman nodded. "I know the type. Close-knit crew, everyone friends, captain basically God—and everyone likes it or quits at the next port. There are a lot of people who think that's the ideal starship size."

His voice was casual, almost bantering . . . but his eyes were anything but. "It would probably save time, Captain," Ferrol said evenly, "if you'd just go ahead and ask me why I'm here."

Roman cocked an eyebrow. "Oh, I know why you're here, Commander. What I want to ask is why you hate the Tampies so much."

Even eight years later, the memory of it was still a hot needle beneath his skin. "You have my file there," Ferrol said, forcing his voice to remain calm. "You should be able to figure it out."

Roman studied him. "I gather you're referring to the Prometheus treaty."

"Treaty?" Ferrol snorted. "That was hardly a treaty, Captain. It was an act of war." He nodded curtly at Roman's desk display. "Read the official papers sometime, Captain, if you can manage to dig them out of the Starforce's snowpile. Read the fairy tale about how the Tampies decided one day that *they* wanted Prometheus—never mind that we'd just spent three years working damned hard to build a colony there. Read how the Senate meekly agreed and sent the *Defiance* to forceably take us off." His voice was starting to shake, and he took a careful breath to calm it. "I doubt you'll be able to read that having their life's goal kicked out from under them was what ruined my parents' health and killed them two years later. Official papers don't usually bother with trivialities like that."

"I'm sorry," Romans said.

Even through the blur of emotion Ferrol could tell the other meant it. "I'm not after sympathy, Captain," he growled. "And before you get the wrong idea, I'm not after revenge, either. What I want is for the Cordonale to understand the Tampies the way I do."

"And that is . . . ?"

Ferrol locked eyes with him. "There're two small facts that the official version conveniently leaves out. First, that it wasn't the *Defiance*'s crewers who forced us out of our homes and off our world. It was a Tampy task force. A very efficient, very cold, very *military* task force. And second . . . that they forced us out a full *four days* before the date that's on the treaty."

For a moment Roman was silent. "You're saying," he said at last, "that the Tampies jumped the gun?"

"I'm saying," Ferrol corrected grimly, "that they took unilateral action against us . . . and that the Senate backed off and let them get away with it."

Roman rubbed his thumb and forefinger together gently. "Is it possible you could have been mistaken as to the timing involved? After all, you were fairly young at the—"

"I was almost sixteen," Ferrol cut him off. "Quite old enough to know the months and days of the week, thank you—*and* to know how to translate local dates into Earth Standard ones." He glared at the other. "There's no mistake, Captain. The public image the Tampies portray of themselves as peace-loving, passive friends of nature is a lie. I know it, the Senate knows it . . . and the rest of the Cordonale deserves to know it, too."

"And how far do you intend to go to prove it?" Roman asked bluntly.

Ferrol took a deep breath, dragging his anger back under control. "You mistake my intentions, sir," he said evenly. "I'm not here to goad the Tampies into showing their true character. I won't have to—being locked up in close proximity to a shipful of humans for three months ought to do it for me." He locked eyes with the captain. "I'm here only to make sure that that evidence doesn't somehow get itself snowbound."

"I see," Roman nodded. If he was offended by the implied slur on his integrity, he made no sign of it. "Then there's just one more question I have to ask: given your feelings about the Tampies, are you certain you're willing to trust your life to them?"

Ferrol frowned. "In what way would I be doing *that*?"

Roman frowned in turn. "You didn't know? The *Ami-*

ty's a modified in-system freighter, without a Mitsuushi StarDrive. All interstellar travel will be via the space horse . . . and the systems we'll be going to are all well beyond normal Mitsuushi range."

Something cold settled into the pit of Ferrol's stomach. "I wasn't told that, no," he murmured. All travel via their tame space horse . . . and only the Tampies able to control or communicate with the giant creature. "That seems . . . a bit foolhardy, sir," he managed.

"Perhaps." Roman was giving him an all too understanding look. "Under the circumstances, if you'd like to resign the post, I'll certainly understand."

Ferrol glared back, a flash of anger burning away the fear. That grandfatherly expression, reducing him to a child again—"Thank you, sir, but I'll be staying."

Roman seemed to measure him with his eyes, then nodded. "Very well, Commander," he said gravely. "Welcome aboard the *Amity*. We leave at 0800 tomorrow; I'll want you on the bridge two hours before that."

"Understood, Captain."

"I'll see you then. Dismissed."

It was a long walk from the captain's office aft to the officers' section, a walk made all the more difficult by the subtly shifting weight and Coriolis effects Ferrol had to contend with. It was a standard enough procedure, certainly: altering a ship's rotational speed was a quick way to simultaneously test the spin jets, flywheel, and structural integrity. But he wasn't in the mood to be lenient with standard procedures. Even ones that worked.

In politics, lying was apparently one of the standard procedures. It often worked, too.

They'd lied to him. Deliberately. A lie of ommission, but a lie nonetheless—and what really killed him was that part of the blame had to sit squarely on his own neck. Not once had it even occurred to him to ask whether the *Amity* would have a Mitsuushi backup.

Damn them.

He reached his cabin and went in, privacy-sealing the door behind him and flopping down on the bed. Beneath him, the cabin's tiny port showed a dizzying panorama as the stars swept past in time to *Amity*'s rotation; but it was to the side bulkhead that he found his attention drawn. A normal, everyday bulkhead . . . except that, by an accident of room assignments, Ferrol's cabin was at the edge of the human half of the ship.

Beyond that wall—six centimeters of metal and soundproofing away—was the Tampy section.

Tampies. Misshapen faces, stupid-looking tartan neckerchiefs, infuriatingly whining voices, strange and vaguely nauseating odors. Bio-engineered "technology" which just barely deserved the name. High-minded ideals, noble-sounding words . . . and quietly ruthless actions. Memories flooded back, sharp and clear, and for a teetering moment the fears of Prometheus loomed over him like thunderclouds.

But this wasn't Prometheus . . . and he was no longer a helpless sixteen-year-old.

No longer helpless at all.

Rolling over, he reached down and pulled open the closest of the underbed storage drawers, withdrawing a thin black box from beneath a pile of shirts. He wouldn't have put it past Roman to have had his luggage examined . . . but, no, the indicator built into the lock showed it hadn't been touched. He tapped in the proper code, heard the gentle *snick* of the lock, and lifted the lid.

He pulled out the compact needle pistol first, making sure it pointed away from him as he laid it arm's length away on the bed. The spare clip came out next, along with the special permit for him to carry the gun. Beneath the hardware was the false bottom; and beneath that was the envelope.

The gun was a conversation piece. The envelope was his weapon.

There was a single line of instructions on the front of

the envelope, written in the Senator's small and geo-
metrically precise script: *To be used when deemed necessary*. Ferrol gazed at the words, letting the Senator's
calm strength and infinite confidence flow from the
handwriting into him. No, this wasn't Prometheus and
helplessness. This was the *Amity* . . . and the chance to
turn the Tampies' quiet undeclared war right back on
them.

If he was lucky. Somehow, Ferrol thought he would
be.

For a long minute after Ferrol left, Roman sat quietly
in his chair, gazing at the door and listening to the
sound of his heart pounding in his chest. He'd expected
anti-Tampy from the other, of course—virulent anti-
Tampy, even.

He hadn't expected absolute ice-packed hatred.

Even now, with Ferrol gone from his sight, the memory of the emotional turmoil he'd sensed in the younger
man made him wince. Ferrol's pain and anger were as
fresh as if he'd been thrown off Prometheus only yesterday, the emotions kept alive for eight years by the
certain knowledge that the Senate had lied through its
collective teeth about what had happened to the colony.

About that, at least, he was right. Roman *had* seen
the official documents.

He dropped his gaze to the intercom, feeling tempta-
tion tugging at him. A single touch of a button—a short,
probably very painful, conversation—and Ferrol would
be gone. The Antis' time bomb gone from his ship, the
faction itself absolutely furious at him—

And their revenge would be to scuttle *Amity*. And
with it perhaps mankind's last chance to stay out of war
with the Tampies.

Roman closed his eyes tiredly. No, it was too risky.
For now, at least, the only prudent course would be to
play along with Ferrol. Give him all the leeway he
wanted . . . and hope that whenever he made his move—

whatever that move was—that there would be a chance to block him.

And until that happened, Roman still had a ship to run. Putting Ferrol out of his mind as best he could, he keyed his display to the status report menu and got back to work.

And tried not to notice how remarkably similar his wait-and-see plan was to the pro-Tampy Senators' own method of dealing with the problem.

Chapter 4

At precisely 0812 the next morning, the *Amity* cast off its moorings on the Tampy corral. Trailing a kilometer behind their space horse, Pegasus, on deceptively thin tether lines, the ship headed out into deep space.

Roman had already known that the view from outside a space horse ship was impressive. What he hadn't expected was that the ride was even more so.

It was quieter, obviously; but the reality of it far outstripped the expectation. Over the years Roman had grown accustomed to the many levels of noise a ship's fusion drive was capable of putting out, from the dull but still permeating drone of standby to the steady thunder of full acceleration. It was a sound that never ceased as long as the ship was under power, and to be pulling a steady 0.6-gee acceleration without even a whisper of that familiar noise was awe-inspiring and just a little scary.

No drive noise also meant no deck vibration, of course; less obviously, it also meant none of the gentle rolling motion that came of the computer sensing and compensating for slight imbalances in thrust between the different drive nozzles. It was, in fact, for all the world like sitting in a full-size simulator back at the Academy.

"We've cleared the far edge of the corral enclosure," Kennedy reported from the helm. "Signaling the Handler to increase acceleration to 0.9 gee."

Roman nodded acknowledgment. He'd rather expected Kennedy to take the helm herself on this leg of the trip, and he hadn't been disappointed. Clearly, she was serious about getting space horse experience. "What's ETA to the scheduled Jump point?" he asked her.

"One hour twenty minutes," she told him as their weight began a smooth increase. "That is, if we stick to our current minimum-energy course."

"We're in no particular hurry, Lieutenant," Roman told her. "Besides, I want to put Pegasus through a variety of maneuvers during the voyage. Minimum energy, minimum time, straight-line—you know the list."

Ferrol half turned from his station. "I trust you're not expecting the space horse to run into some kind of limit," he offered. "I've heard of them pulling five gees without any noticeable strain."

Roman shook his head. "I'm not looking for limits, Commander. Just differences." He turned his attention to the man at the scanner station. "Lieutenant Marlowe, how's the signal from the contact feed repeater?"

"Coming in strong, sir," Riddick Marlowe confirmed. "I've got it going to two separate recorders, as per orders."

Roman nodded and turned back, to find a thoughtful frown on Ferrol's face. "Comment, Commander?" he invited.

Ferrol hesitated, then shook his head minutely. "No, I'm wrong," he said, almost as if to himself. "If recording the traces from an amplifier helmet was all there was to it, someone would have compiled a library of them long before now."

Roman nodded. "Agreed. It's apparently not just a matter of getting a list of the right commands—the direct and immediate touch of a Tampy mind seems to be necessary for proper space horse control." He cocked an eyebrow. "You have an interest in space horse control?"

"Of course," Ferrol said. "And so should anyone else. If humanity's ever going to expand farther than a few dozen light-years from home, we're either going to need our own space horses or a *lot* of redesign of the Mitsuushi."

"Or else a long-term rental agreement with the Tampies," Kennedy put in.

Ferrol's eyes flicked to her. "Renting is fine in its place," he said evenly. "I don't think full-scale colonization fits in that column."

"Certainly not if they'd want to sit over the colonists' shoulders and complain about their development schemes," Marlowe agreed, almost under his breath. "Sometimes I swear the Tampies think of us as a bunch of eight-year-olds, with them as our mothers."

Kennedy chuckled. Ferrol didn't. "You may have a point, Lieutenant," Roman told Marlowe. "Bear in mind, though, that occasionally we do indeed *act* like eight-year-olds."

"Agreed, Captain," Marlowe shrugged. His eyes flicked to Roman's face, as if trying to gauge his new commander's tolerance to bridge chatter. "I'd argue in turn that most of the time that kind of behavior comes about because we have a sense of humor, something the Tampies don't seem to know anything about."

"Perhaps," Roman conceded. Whatever form the Tampy sense of humor took—if they had one at all—it had so far managed to remain hidden.

And speaking of Tampies and things hidden . . .

Unstrapping, he got to his feet. "Commander, you have the bridge," he told Ferrol, making one final check of the instruments. "I expect to be back before we Jump."

"Acknowledged, sir," Ferrol said. "May I ask where you'll be?"

"Port side," Roman told him. "It's about time I paid a courtesy call on the Tampies."

*　　*　　*

There were four connections between *Amity*'s human and Tampy halves, each equipped with a standard air lock. Beside the lock was a rack of filter masks; choosing one, Roman put it on, making sure the flexible seals fitted snugly around nose and cheeks and jaw. He'd heard stories of what Tampies in an enclosed space smelled like, and it would be embarrassing to gag on his first visit. The air lock went through its cycle, replacing most of the human-scented air with a purer oxygen/nitrogen mix, signaling ready after perhaps thirty seconds. Taking a careful breath through the filter mask, Roman keyed the door to open.

Beyond it was another world.

For a minute he just stood there, still inside the lock, taking it all in. The lighting was muted, indirect, and restful; the air cool and dry, with wisps of movement that reminded Roman somehow of forest breezes. Various art-type items—small sculptures as well as flats—were scattered at irregular intervals across the walls and ceiling. Irregular; yet despite the lack of symmetry, the whole arrangement still somehow managed to maintain a unified, balanced look. Every square centimeter of wall and deck space not otherwise used was covered with soft-looking green carpet. The latter, at least, Roman recognized from *Amity*'s spec sheets: a particularly hardy variety of moss which had been adopted by the Tampies as a low-tech air filtration and renewal system. But even here, expectation was incomplete—instead of something with the faintly disgusting appearance of terrestrial mosses, the Tampy version looked far more like just some exotic synthetic carpeting.

The pro-Tampy apologists often claimed that the aliens' aesthetic sense was not only highly developed but also entirely accessible to humans. If this was a representative sample, Roman thought, that claim was an accurate one.

"Rro-maa?" a grating voice came from outside the lock.

This was it. Steeling himself, Roman stepped out onto the moss—it yielded to his feet just like carpeting, too—and turned in the direction the voice had come from.

And for the first time in his life was face-to-face with a Tampy.

It was, actually, something of a disappointment. What with the conflict between races that had slowly been building over the past ten years—and with the contentions of people like Ferrol that the Tampies were a looming threat to humanity—Roman had apparently built up a subconscious image of Tampies as creatures who, despite being shorter than humans, nevertheless projected an aura of strength or even menace.

The short part he had right; but the rest of it was totally off target. The Tampy whose misshapen face was turned up to him was thin and delicate-looking, his narrow shoulders hunched slightly forward in a caricature of old age, his hands crossed palms-up at his waist. His skin was pale—a sickly, bedridden sort of pale—and the cranial hair tufts poking out at irregular intervals looked for all the world like bunches of fine copper wire.

The overall image was one of almost absurd frailty, and in that first moment it seemed utterly incredible to Roman that such creatures should even be taken seriously, much less considered a threat.

And then he remembered Prometheus . . . and the half-comical picture vanished in a puff of smoke. No, the Tampies were indeed creatures to be taken seriously.

Belatedly, he focused on the yellow-orange tartan neckerchief knotted loosely around the Tampy's neck. That particular color combination belonged to—"Rrinsaa?" he tentatively identified the other.

"I am," the Tampy acknowledged. "You are Rro-maa?"

"Yes, I'm Captain Roman," Roman nodded. "I wasn't expecting to be met here."

The Tampy made a quick fingers-to-ear gesture—the

aliens' equivalent of a shrug, Roman remembered. "Do you wish to see all?"

It was, actually, a tempting offer. If the rest of the Tampies' decor was as unusual and imaginative as that in the corridors, it might well be worth taking the complete tour. But that would have to wait for another time. "No, thank you, Rrin-saa," he said. "For now, I'd just like to see your command center."

"I do not understand."

"Command center. Control room?—where you keep track of the *Amity*'s movement and issue any necessary orders."

"I do not issue orders, Rro-maa," Rrin-saa said. "I do not rule."

For a moment Roman was tongue-tied. "Ah . . . I'm sorry. I thought you were the one in charge of this half of the ship."

Rrin-saas's mouth opened wide, as if in parody of a human smile—the Tampy equivalent of shaking his head. "I speak for all," Rrin-saa said. "I do not rule."

"I see," Roman said, although he didn't, exactly. Anarchy, or even rule by consensus, didn't seem a good way to run a starship. "But if you don't rule, who does?"

Fingers to ear. "You do, Rro-maa."

"Uh . . . *huh*," Roman said. It was slowly becoming clearer . . . "You mean that since your people agreed to put a human—me—in command of the *Amity*, then I'm to give you all your orders?"

"That is correct."

It couldn't be entirely correct, Roman knew. At the very least, they'd arranged their own billeting and duty rosters without any input from the human half of the ship, and almost certainly such simple housekeeping operations would continue to be so handled.

Which implied *some* sort of chain of command . . . which Rrin-saa didn't seem interested in talking about. "Where are the repeater instruments from the bridge, then?" he asked.

"With the Handlers."

Roman nodded. "Take me there, then, if you would."

The Handler room was just aft of the bow instrument packing, in a mirror-image position to *Amity*'s bridge. Sitting in the center of the room, a Tampy sporting a green-purple neckerchief sat humming atonally to himself, his eyes wide open but paying no attention to Roman or Rrin-saa. To the left, arranged in random patterns against the inner wall, were the repeater instruments; to the right, a second Tampy sat pressed against the outer wall, his face turned at a painful-looking angle to stare forward out the viewport, his head engulfed by a large multi-wired helmet. The wires of which went to a basket-mesh case, inside of which—

Roman forced himself to look . . . and actually, it wasn't too bad. Provided he remembered that the hairless, piglet-sized creature was supposed to look that way; and that it was safely asleep, not dead; and that its wired-up brain neurons had as much sheer computing capability as the Cordonale's best mainframes.

The Tampies' computer, he knew, used basically the same arrangement. Not so simple, but still elegant.

"Sso-ngii," Rrin-saa said, raising both hands toward the helmeted Tampy. "He speaks with Pegasunninni."

"Pega—? Ah," Roman interrupted himself. Pegasunninni would be the Tampies' name for the space horse: Pegasus, with the proper identifying suffix tacked on. "And the other is Hhom-jee?" he added, hoping he was pulling the proper neckerchief color scheme out of memory.

"That is correct," Rrin-saa confirmed. "He is resting."

"Ah," Roman said again, eying the humming Tampy with interest. Tampy sleep was both more physically active than the human equivalent and also came at semi-irregular intervals around the clock. A far cry from the normal terrestrial circadian rhythm, and one that had helped to poison quite a few of the early attempts at interspecies cooperation. Human workers could never quite believe the Tampies weren't simply goofing off, and Roman would bet that the human habit of going into a coma for a straight thirty percent of the day had been equally annoying to the Tampies. Though no one knew for sure; the Tampies had never discussed the matter. "I gather he's here to take over when Sso-ngii needs sleep?"

"That is correct," Rrin-saa said. He repeated his earlier two-handed gesture, this time toward Hhom-jee. "There is one other who talks to Pegasunnninni."

"Yes, I remember that there were three Handlers listed on the crew roster." Roman nodded toward Sso-ngii and the hairless caged animal. It wasn't so bad the second time. "I'd like to take a closer look at the amplifier helmet, if it wouldn't disturb him."

"Do not approach."

Roman paused, halfway into a step. "Why not?"

"He speaks with Pegasunnninni," Rrin-saa said.

"And . . . ?"

"You are a predator," Sso-ngii said.

Roman started; he hadn't realized the Handler was paying any attention to the conversation. "Is that why we haven't been able to control space horses? Or even to keep them alive in captivity?"

"I do not know," Sso-ngii said. "I know that humans sometimes have bothered space horses; that is all."

Roman pursed his lips. "Um."

For a moment he hesitated, at a loss for something to say or do. He turned away from Sso-ngii; and as he did so, the repeater instruments caught his eye, and he stepped over for a closer look. They were labeled in Tampy script, of course, but his crash course in things Tamplisstan had included some of that, and it took only a minute to locate the ones he was interested in. "I'd better be getting back to the bridge," he told Rrin-saa. "We're getting close to our scheduled Jump point."

"I understand," Rrin-saa said. "Rro-maa . . . this voyage is of great importance to the Tamplissta. We understand you; you do not understand us. This failing of harmony cannot continue."

Roman nodded. "I agree," he said. "We'll work together on this, Rrin-saa. With luck . . . maybe we can find some of that understanding for my people."

"That is the Tamplisstan hope. For if not . . ." He touched fingers to ear, and left the sentence unfinished.

"I understand," Roman said.

If not, Ferrol would likely get the war he wanted.

They still had nearly half an hour to the scheduled Jump position when the captain finally returned to the bridge. "Captain," Ferrol nodded, unstrapping from the command chair and standing up. "Still running on schedule; twenty-seven minutes to Jump. I gather from Kennedy's course plan that we weren't going to decelerate to zero vee before the Jump."

"Correct, Commander," Roman said. "Space horses routinely Jump while in motion, sometimes with rather high velocities relative to their departure star."

A fact which Ferrol had probably had a lot more experience with than the captain. He'd lost several space horses that way before he'd figured out how to sneak up without spooking them. "Yes, sir. I presume you'll want to at least kill our acceleration first?"

Roman started to speak; paused. "That's a good point," he said thoughtfully. "Any idea whether or not space horses *can* Jump while accelerating?"

Ferrol frowned, searching his memory. He remembered at least one out in the Tampies' *yishyar* who'd been going damned fast when it Jumped away from his net. But whether it had actually been accelerating when he lost it . . . "I'm not sure," he told Roman. "I don't remember reading anything about it one way or the other. I don't know why they couldn't, though."

"Neither do I. Let's try it and see."

And if the Tampies would rather we didn't find out for sure? Ferrol wondered sardonically. But there was no point in asking the question aloud. The official line was that the Tampies were honest and open and eager to share all knowledge with their beloved human brothers; and if there was one thing guaranteed about this voyage it was that the captain would be an expert at tracking along the official line. "Yes, sir," Ferrol said. "Shall I inform the Tampies?"

For a moment he thought Roman would take him up on his offer. But—"Thank you, Commander; I'll do it." He seated himself in the command chair, made a quick sweep of the displays.

Across at the scanner station, Marlowe looked up. "As long as you've got them anyway, Captain," he said, "you might want to double-check that all this dust isn't going to block Pegasus' view of the target star."

"There shouldn't be that much dust this far off the ecliptic," Roman frowned, reaching over to call up the appropriate readouts.

"That's what *I* thought, sir," Marlowe nodded. "But there is. We seem to be heading into it, too—the density's been slowly increasing."

Ferrol peered over Roman's shoulder as the numbers came up. "It won't be a problem," he told the other. "That's nothing but Pegasus' own dust sweat."

Roman looked up at him. "I didn't realize dust sweat got that dense."

Ferrol shrugged. "We're working Pegasus pretty hard here, sir, whether it shows the strain or not," he pointed out. "And there's an awful lot of surface area out there for it to sweat through."

"And of course under acceleration like this the whole mass of it falls straight back on top of us," Roman nodded understanding. "Interesting. One of the many things about space horse transport no one's really thought about. I'm sure we'll be finding more of these tidbits over the next few months."

I can't wait, Ferrol thought. Leaving Roman's side, he returned to his own station, listening with half an ear as the captain discussed the Jump/acceleration question with the Tampies. No, they didn't know whether it was possible, either, but the Handler was willing to try it.

Oh, of course they don't know, Ferrol thought, a touch of bitterness clouding his vision. It was only the first thing anyone considering space horse warfare would think to investigate; but, no, the Tampies hadn't done that.

And of course Roman would accept it all at face value. Roman didn't think about space horse warfare, either.

"Commander?"

Ferrol remembered to smooth out his face before turning around. "Yes, Captain?"

For just a second Roman seemed to study him, as if he'd somehow divined Ferrol's train of thought. "I'd like us to get a sample of that dust," he said. "Please inform the survey section, then stay on the intercom and monitor the operation."

Ferrol glanced at the chrono. "You want the sample taken before or after the Jump, sir?"

Roman pursed his lips thoughtfully. "Good point," he nodded. "The composition may be different at different times. Let's take one each before *and* after the Jump; and then have them continue to take two samples per day for the rest of the voyage." His eyes shifted to the main display. "Given their meteoroid diet, it might be instructive to see just what they consider to be waste products."

"Especially if some of it turns out to be gold or platinum or iridium?" Kennedy suggested.

Roman nodded. "The possibility *had* occurred to me, yes," he agreed.

Ferrol turned his face back to his board, keying the intercom for *Amity*'s survey section as he allowed his lip to twist with contempt. The eternal and single-minded goal of profit. Ancient Rome, he'd read somewhere, had also been hard at work trading with its enemies . . . just before those same enemies destroyed it.

Those who don't know history, he quoted bitterly to himself, *are condemned to repeat it.*

Amity was listed on paper as a research/survey ship, and its overlarge scientific contingent turned out to be better at their jobs than Ferrol had really expected. They had the first sample into the ship, onto the lab table, and through a preliminary analysis ten minutes before the Jump . . . and Ferrol found quiet satisfaction in the fact that the dust, while loaded with strange and exotic silicates, contained not a single scrap of gold, platinium, or iridium.

Chapter 5

Roman touched a button and watched the preliminary analysis of the dust sweat display itself across his screen. Silicon and iron, mainly, with trace amounts of calcium, magnesium, and aluminum. Nothing particularly useful, singly or together. "Have they got a molecular structure analysis yet?" he asked.

"Still working on it," Ferrol said, head cocked toward his intercom. "Got some really complex molecules in there, but nothing of any obvious value."

"Well, have them map and store everything they can isolate, anyway," Roman instructed.

"Yes, sir," Ferrol said, and relayed the order.

Suppressing a grimace, Roman turned his attention back to the main display. He hadn't been expecting them to find any gold nuggets, of course—after twenty years of contact with Tampies, the dust sweat must have been analyzed dozens of times, by people far more interested in making money from space horses than he was. But it would have been nice. "Lieutenant? Jump status?"

"One minute to Jump, sir," she said. "Handler's signaled ready; all ship systems show green."

"Marlowe?"

"All inboard and outboard sensors on and recording,"

Marlowe reported. "If there's anything that can be seen during a Jump, we'll get it."

Roman nodded. "All right," he said, automatically bracing himself. "Let's do it."

Several months earlier, Roman had discovered that a space horse Jump was completely unspectacular to watch. Now, he discovered, it was equally unspectacular to experience.

There was no sensation. None at all. One second they were pulling 0.9 gee through the Tampies' Kia-linninni system, with a dull red sun off their port stern; the next second, they were doing exactly the same thing except with a dazzling white sun directly ahead. "Marlowe?" Roman asked.

"Nothing, Captain," the other said, shaking his head. "No glitches or transitions on any of the inboard sensors. Outboard scanners . . . no transitional data on any of them, either."

"What's the time-quantum on the sensors, the standard half picosecond?" Roman asked.

"Better than that, sir," Marlowe told him. "The manual claims 0.05 picosecond; I'd guess it closer to 0.1, myself."

A tenth of a picosecond or less. Zero time, by any reasonable definition. "Thank you. Lieutenant Kennedy? We have Alpha located yet?"

"Working on it, sir," Kennedy said. Her voice was its usual unawed self, as if Jumping space horses was something she did every week. "Computer's got the ecliptic plane identified, and it's calculating from the Tampies' data where the planet ought to be. It'll be a few more minutes."

Roman nodded, keying his intercom as mention of the Tampies brought a sudden idea to mind. "Captain to Handler. Sso-ngii, are you able to speak?"

There was a short pause, and then the screen lit up with the Tampy's image, his twisted face almost lost between the amplifier helmet and the red-white neck-erchief. At least the sleeping animal wasn't in view this way. "I hear, Rro-maa," Sso-ngii said. "What is your wish?"

"Does Pegasus know where the planet is we're heading for? Can it sense it, I mean, from here?"

The Tampy's face was unreadable, as usual. "I do not know," he whined. "I know space horses can see many distant stars and solid objects within telekene range; that is all."

"Yeah," Roman grunted, annoyed despite the fact he'd half expected that answer. One of the more maddening Tampy characteristics was their steadfast and muleheaded refusal to ever speculate aloud unless and until they had absolute proof one way or the other. Pressing Sso-ngii on the subject would do nothing but pull increasingly obscure facts about space horses from him; and while that might be a useful exercise some day, at the moment Roman couldn't be bothered. "Well, then, just stand by," he told the Tampy. "We'll have the location in a few minutes and feed the direction back there. Until then, you might as well have Pegasus stop our acceleration."

"Your wishes are ours."

Roman frowned at the screen, wondering if the Tampy was being sarcastic. But that was hardly likely. "Very good. Execute."

He broke the connection; and an instant later grabbed reflexively at the arms of his chair as the *Amity* made a stomach-lurching transition to zero-gee.

Belatedly, the deceleration warning went on, and Roman swore under his breath. Textbook fusion-drive deceleration/cool-down was a five-minute process; once again, old reflexes had betrayed him.

"Captain?" Ferrol cut into his embarrassment. The other's voice was bland enough . . . but as Roman turned to face him he could see that the exec was privately enjoying his discomfiture. "Survey section reports they've taken the next dust sweat sample," Ferrol continued. He cocked an eyebrow. "Assuming, that is, you still want them to bother analyzing the stuff."

Roman eyed him. "Have you received any orders to the contrary, Commander?" he asked mildly.

The skin around Ferrol's eyes tightened a bit. Perhaps, Roman thought, he'd been hoping for an overreaction. "No, sir," he said, matching Roman's tone.

"Then I'd say you could safely assume I still want the dust analyzed. Wouldn't you agree?"

"Yes, sir," Ferrol said, the first stirrings of awkwardness starting to appear at the corners of his lips. He was now on the defensive, and didn't like it a bit. "I just thought the order might be worth checking on, after the negative results of the first sample."

For a moment Roman just looked at him, watching the discomfort grow. "This is a research ship, Commander," he said at last. "Its mission is to collect data; on Tampies, Tampy-human interactions, unexplored planets, space horse travel, and space horses themselves. *All* data, whether it looks to be immediately useful or not."

"Understood, sir," Ferrol said, his discomfort starting to edge into a simmering of anger.

"Good," Roman nodded. He held the eye contact a second longer, then turned back to Marlowe. "Progress on the search for Alpha, Lieutenant?" he asked.

"Another minute, Captain," the other said promptly, his voice the cadet-precise monotone of someone trying hard to keep himself inconspicuous. "We've got the theoretical position calculated, and we're searching that immediate area with the scopes."

Roman nodded and keyed his own displays to monitor the search. *Thus are drawn the battle lines*, he thought darkly. Ferrol had no real reason to care whether or not the survey section was wasting its time with Pegasus' dust sweat, and he and everyone on the bridge knew it. The question had been nothing less than a challenge to Roman's command authority, or his judgment, or both.

Or in other words, despite all of his high-sounding statements the previous day, Ferrol wasn't going to be content with simply letting *Amity*'s crew make up their own minds about the Tampies on merit alone. He was going to make this into a personal confrontation between himself, the anti-Tampy realist, and Roman, the pro-Tampy military/political hack.

And if Marlowe's reaction was anything to go by, Ferrol had at the very least managed to sour the atmosphere on the bridge a bit. A subtle but genuine form of damage.

"Got it, Captain," Kennedy announced. "Bearing 96.4, 15.3. Distance, six hundred thousand kilometers."

"Send the direction to the Tampies," Roman told her. "Straight-line path, once we've come around, and have Sso-ngii keep acceleration at 0.9 gee."

He would have thought Ferrol would be willing to quit while he was ahead. He was wrong. "Shall I compute turnover point for them, sir?" the other spoke up. "Their excuse for a computer may not be able to handle the calculation."

"Let's find out, shall we?" Roman countered. "Lieutenant, just give Sso-ngii the location and let the Tampies do the rest." He cocked an eyebrow to Ferrol. "If they can, that is."

They could, and did . . . and just under five hours later Pegasus eased the *Amity* smoothly into geosynchronous orbit around Alpha.

If Ferrol had won the first round of his private duel, the Tampies had clearly won the second.

Roman had seen a fair number of planetary landscapes over the years, either in person or in holos, and he'd found that in almost every case his first impression was of the wild and exotic color combinations alien plant life always seemed able to come up with.

It was a rule that Alpha had proved a glaring exception to. The wide prairielike field the landing party was busy poking around, as well as the forest beyond it, were done entirely in black, white, and shades of gray.

"It's really rather amazing," Ells Sanderson commented, and even through the muffling of his filter mask there was no mistaking the excitement in his voice. "The predominant black-and-gray plant coloration makes considerable sense as far as photosynthesis goes—allows more energy to be collected, including more of the infrared than straight chlorophyll-variants can utilize."

"Pretty dull as far as looking goes, though," Roman commented. "Are all the animals and insects naturally color-blind?"

"It's one of the things we'll be checking," Sanderson said. "Though you bring up an interesting point: namely, how pollination takes place without brightly colored flowers to attract the insects."

"Maybe it's not done by insects at all," Roman suggested. "Couldn't the pollen be airborne, or transmitted by animals that brush by?"

"The anthers of most of these plants are wrong for that," one of the other scientists put in. Steef Burch, Roman tentatively identified the voice. "Besides which, I can see various insects doing flight patterns through and around clumps of specific plant types."

"We're taking some proximity air samples," Sanderson added. "That should tell us if the flowers are putting out chemical cues."

"Sounds good." Roman scanned the multi-split screen that showed all of the lander's fixed cameras and the landing party's portable ones, chose one of the two that showed the analysis table that had been set up a dozen meters from the lander's air lock. He keyed for it, and Sanderson's close-up of dull gray foliage was replaced by a close-up of a small gray-brown creature that looked like a nightmare blend of aardvark face, turtle shell, short monkey legs, and lobster claws, the whole thing strapped to the table by a covering of mesh net. "Dr. Peyton? How are the animal studies going?"

"Ttra-mii and I are doing just fine," Miki Peyton said in the vaguely distant voice of someone absorbed in her work. Peyton's file had put her as marginally anti-Tampy, a fact that had worried Roman more than once as the lander was heading down. The Tampies would be watching this part of the work closely, making sure there was nothing that could be construed as mistreatment, and the last thing Roman wanted was someone who might go all twitchy under the aliens' lopsided gaze. But Peyton had been the head of the group who'd designed and built this particular analysis table, and she'd made it more than clear that she personally was going to be there for her pet project's official debut. The risk of friction down on Alpha hadn't been worth risking civil war on the *Amity* for, and Roman had reluctantly given in.

But so far it seemed to be working out all right. He just hoped Ttra-mii would have the sense to look but not touch.

"We've got the preliminary layer scans done now," Peyton continued. "Is the data coming through clearly enough up there?"

"Dr. Tenzing?" Roman invited.

"Coming in very clear," the voice of the survey section's chief came promptly over the intercom. "We've already started sifting through it."

"Good. Ttra-mii, how's your hand?"

"The damage is not serious, Rro-maa," the Tampy whined. "As I said before, the inner skin was not broken."

Which ought to eliminate any risk of infection or poisoning, even if there was anything in the lobster-clawed creature that could affect Tampy physiology. "Keep the analyzer on it, anyway," Roman ordered him. "Dr. Peyton, have you figured out yet how the creature did that?"

"You mean how it could pinch Ttra-mii through the net at a distance further than its claw-arm could physically reach?" she asked dryly. "Not yet; but at least I've proved that what happened wasn't actually impossible. This thing has no bones."

Roman frowned. "None at all?"

"None at all," she confirmed. "And very little cartilage, either. Most of its skeletal framework seems to be nothing more or less than an organic type of bi-state memory plastic, which can apparently be rigid or flexible as the need arises."

Roman eyed the creature on his display with new respect. "Interesting. Is this something unique to this particular species, or do you expect it to be the Alphan norm?"

"We'll know in a minute," a new voice broke into the conversation. "This is Singh, Captain; Llos-tlaa and I are just about to net you a rabbit."

Roman scanned the split screen, found Andrey Singh's chest camera and switched to it. Sitting on its haunches among the squat gray ground shrubbery was a creature that bore not a shred of resemblance to an Earth rabbit. "That's a rabbit, is it?" he asked Singh.

"Well, it looks like it would fill that niche in the ecosystem, anyway." A hand clutching a net gun appeared at the edge of the screen as Singh eased toward his prey, and across the way Roman could now see Llos-tlaa, similarly armed, moving in from the opposite direction. "Easy, friend," Singh murmured soothingly under his breath. "We're not going to hurt you, just take a painless look at your insides." He carefully raised the netter—

And the creature abruptly changed into something else and leapt away.

"Bloody *hell*!" Singh gasped, the view swinging dizzyingly as he spun around to watch the new creature's bounding escape. "It can't *do* that."

His last word was almost swallowed up by the hoarse sputter of a rapid-fire needle gun. Across the field, the creature jerked in mid-jump and slammed unmoving to the ground. "Hold your fire!" Roman barked. "Who was that?"

There was a moment's hesitation. "It was me, sir— Garin," the head of the landing party's four-man guard detail spoke up. "I figured the scientists would want the thing caught for study— "

"There was no need to kill it!"

Roman jumped. The scream was high-pitched, almost shrill, its tones rich with grief and agony and a sense of frustration and reproach. His eyes skated across the split screen, seeking the creature still netted to the analysis table, his first horrible thought that the scream had somehow come from it. "Who said that?" he demanded.

"Forgive me, Rro-maa." —And in those three words the shrill pitch of the voice dropped down the scale back to the normal Tampy whine. "I was angered."

"So I gather, Llos-tlaa," Roman said, his own anger at Garin's unauthorized killing vanishing in the shiver running up his back. Nowhere in any of the briefings had there been any hint that Tampy voices could do *that*. "Garin, unless you're under a deadly and *immediate* threat, you will not fire again without orders. Understood?"

"Yes, sir," Garin growled, his tone just short of surly.

"That goes for the rest of you, too," Roman reminded the other guards. "Dr. Singh, is there enough of the rabbit left to study?"

Singh was leaning over the creature now, and the close-up view of the needle-riddled body made Roman slightly queasy. "We can try, Captain," he said, working the edge of his net underneath it. "Interesting—you notice it became a rabbit again when it died?"

"Actually, in a sense it was never anything else," Ferrol spoke up from across the bridge. "I think the landing party ought to see this."

"We've got something, Dr. Singh," Roman told him. "Switch for reception from here."

Ferrol had taken the transmission from Singh's camera, scrubbed it through the computer, and run it at slow motion. It made the rabbit's transformation easier to follow . . . but no less astonishing.

"It's like the skin is *flowing*," Singh muttered. "Like some kind of high-stretch elastic or even a semi-fluid."

"And you can see the skeletal structure changing beneath it, too," Peyton put in from the analysis table. "I was right—it's exactly like a bi-state plastic. The muscles must be doing something similar—if they weren't, the legs couldn't lengthen like that without losing strength."

"Muscles, and organs, too," Singh pointed out. "Notice how the lung capacity has already nearly doubled?"

"It's becoming a running machine," Burch breathed, sounding awed.

It was, too. If the creature's first appearance had reminded Singh of a rabbit, the new form that leaped slow-motion out of the camera's range reminded Roman of a racing greyhound. "Opinions? Anybody?" he asked.

"It's pretty obvious we've stumbled on something unique here," Tenzing said. "We'll have to do more study to see whether this shape-changing ability is only used for fight/flight situations or whether each creature actually fills two entirely different ecological niches, sharing time between them."

"Ah, yes," Burch offered, half under his breath. "A planet called 'Werewolf.' "

"Let's just leave it at 'Alpha,' shall we?" Sanderson said shortly. "I think there's plenty here to occupy our attention without wasting brainpower on names. Especially when that'll be the Tampies' job, not ours."

There was a moment of strained silence, an awkwardness Roman could feel as well on the bridge. Caught up in the excitement, everyone seemed to have forgotten the bottom-line reality of the situation. Four hundred thirty light-years from Earth, Alpha was far outside the range of Mitsuushi-equipped ships. Whatever they found down there—whether a site for a future colony, marketable plant and animal life, or even just exotic and exciting biology—it would be the Tampies, not humanity, who would gain from their work.

"They're not content with just stealing us blind anymore," Ferrol muttered, just loudly enough for Roman to hear. "Now they've got us delivering the loot for them."

"That's enough, Commander," Roman growled . . . but the damage was already done. "Dr. Singh, I'll want you to do a complete microbe check on the rabbit, with an eye toward whether it'll be safe to bring it back to the *Amity*. As long as it's already dead," he added, to forestall any potential argument from the Tampies, "we might as well make full use of it."

"If our pre-exit air and soil checks didn't show anything dangerous, the rabbit isn't likely to be carrying anything," Sanderson reminded him.

"I know that," Roman said. "Do the checks anyway."

"A-*ha*," Peyton cut in abruptly. " Got it, I think. Ells, do a quick electric field reading on a couple of the plants out there, will you?"

"Okay," Sanderson said, his part of the split screen tilting abruptly as he and his chest camera knelt down.

"What, you suggesting an electric sense?" Burch asked, sounding doubtful.

"Why not? You were the one who commented on the high density of ions in the air when we took the first readings, if you'll remember."

"Yeah, but it's nothing like the density you get in seawater, which is where you usually find electric senses," Burch pointed out. "Terran sharks, et al."

"Space horses can also sense electric fields," Ttra-mii said.

"Interesting," Burch said, a bit tartly, "but hardly relevant to a discussion of animals that evolved inside atmospheres."

"Regardless, there's clear and definite evidence of an electric sense in this animal," Peyton said. "Ells? Anything?"

"Looks like you may be right," Sanderson agreed. "The fields are definitely there, with different intensities and oscillation frequencies for different species."

"Oscillation frequencies?" Tenzing echoed. "You mean the fields aren't static?"

"Far from it. The three plants I've checked have cycles ranging from about nine seconds to nearly a minute."

"Organic electric oscillators," Singh murmured. "Elegant, indeed."

"Elegant and a half," Sanderson agreed. "Not to mention potentially useful, if we can figure out the mechanism."

"Well, pick out a good sampling and bring them aboard," Tenzing told him. "Do bear in mind, though, that we've only got the one lockbox lab per planet, and you'll be poking around down there for two more weeks. You fill the lab to the ceiling and those of us who have to work in there will spend the next two months cursing your ancestry."

Sanderson murmured slightly reluctant-sounding agreement, and Roman suppressed a smile. *Just like kids in a toy store*, he thought.

"Captain?" Marlowe said abruptly. "I've got something."

His tone . . . "Got it," Roman acknowledged, keying for scanner repeater. An infrared view of the landing area taken from *Amity*'s belly cameras . . . and in the woods beyond the prairie, circled by flashing markers—

"Dr. Sanderson?—hold it a minute," he called toward the intercom. "You've got what looks like three large animals approaching from almost due west."

The background conversation abruptly vanished. "Confirmed, Captain," Garin said a moment later, his voice taut. "Still no visual contact, but we've got them on scanner. Bearing . . . directly toward us."

He paused, and in the silence the *snik* of needle guns being put on full automatic was clearly audible. "Alert status is still yellow, Garin," Roman reminded the guard leader. "Let's not panic until we see what we've got here."

"Acknowledged, sir," Garin said, his voice tight but under control.

"The animals have picked up speed," Marlowe reported. "About a minute to visual contact."

Across the bridge, Roman heard the hiss of exhaled

breath. "Comment, Commander?" he invited, keeping his attention on the view from Garin's camera.

"Shouldn't we be getting them out of there?" Ferrol asked, his voice tighter even than Garin's. "At least have them get into the lander where they'll be safe?"

"It's too late for that," Kennedy spoke up. Her tone, Roman noted, seemed more interested than worried. "They're too spread out for everyone to get back in time. Besides, if they have to fight, they'll do better out in the open where they have a clear field of fire."

"*If* the Tampies let them shoot," Ferrol growled.

"That's enough," Roman said, punching for a tactical display. The landscape below appeared, with the lander and each of the eight humans and two Tampies marked with colored crosses. Garin and the other three guards, he saw, had deployed themselves in a rough semicircle facing the point where the three approaching animals would emerge from the woods. Well-trained, armed with probably the deadliest small arms in the Cordonale's arsenal, Roman had little doubt that they could cut the approaching animals to ribbons if it became necessary.

Which meant the big question would be whether it *was* necessary . . . and whether the Tampies would see it the same way he did.

"Ells, the analysis table's instruments are going crazy," Peyton spoke up. "I think it's picking up the animals' electric fields."

"Can't be," Sanderson said, his voice frowning. "Those instruments are short-range—they're not designed to scan anywhere but the table."

"*I* know that," Peyton snapped. "So argue with the instruments, not me."

"Perhaps," Llos-tlaa suggested, "Gga-rii can confirm this with his sensor equipment."

"Don't bother me, Tampy," Garin bit out, and in his camera view Roman could see the tip of the other's needle gun. "I've got more important things to worry about at the moment."

"Do it, Garin," Roman ordered. "If those animals are

radiating strongly enough to be picked up by the analysis table, it's something worth knowing."

For a second the muzzle remained where it was. Then, abruptly, it dropped from view. "Yes, Captain," Garin said, the words coming through obviously clenched teeth. "Checking now . . . no, there's nothing there. Must be a malfunction in the table."

"It is *not* a malfunction," Peyton insisted. "Check again, especially at the high-frequency end—fifty hertz and up. There's not all that much power to it, I don't think. Directional, maybe, or else it's the high ion concentration that lets it penetrate this far."

She'd barely finished her sentence when there was a sudden crackle of displaced branches from the forest; and even as Garin snapped his needle gun up again the bushes ahead were shoved violently aside and three creatures stepped out onto the plain.

If the small animal that Garin had gunned down earlier had been a rabbit, these new ones were huge dogs. Dogs with hairless, elephantine skin and flat muzzles; with large paws whose curved feline claws were visible even two hundred meters away; with long shark-like mouths full of white teeth.

And even as the landing party froze in silence, the dog in the center took a step forward, paused . . . and changed.

Slower than the rabbit had, and far more awesome because of that. The chest and flank elongated as first the front legs and then the rear stretched to half-again their original length. The extended legs seemed to thicken, as if new muscle was reforming there, and the belly flattened. The wrinkled skin, stretched over all the expansion, smoothed out, becoming sleek and shimmery. The muzzle remained the same, but the sides of the head swelled outward, in an odd way that reminded Roman of a bird fluffing out its feathers. The whole operation took perhaps ten seconds . . . and at the end of it the dog had become a wolf.

A wolf the size of a large grizzly bear. Rearing up

briefly on its hind legs, it raised its head as if uttering a soundless cry. Then, bringing the front paws back down again, it swung its head around slowly, studying the invaders of its world. Its eyes fell on Peyton and Ttramii, still standing beside the analysis table and the dead rabbit awaiting their study. It raised its head again, uttered its soundless cry . . .

And started toward them.

Chapter 6

"Aim for its legs," Garin snapped, the muzzle of his needle gun tracking the wolf-creature as it loped forward. "We'll try to cut it down without killing it, if we can."

"Do not shoot," Llos-tlaa spoke up.

"Rehfeldt, switch to explosive; backup aim at the head," Garin continued, ignoring the Tampy's protest. "Boschelli, Wehrmann—oh, *hell*," he interrupted himself as the two remaining dog-creatures started into wolf transformations of their own.

"Gga-rii—" Llos-tlaa tried again.

"Shut *up*," Garin snarled. "That tears it—explosive needles, full-auto; legs first, then heads. On my mark—"

"*Do not shoot!*"

Roman jerked in his chair, swearing under his breath, his ears ringing with the sheer intensity of emotion in the Tampy scream. Not grief and frustration this time, but desperate urgency and an almost overwhelming sense of righteous anger. "Hold your fire, Garin," he ordered when he'd found his voice again. The wolf-creatures had covered perhaps a quarter of the distance to Peyton and Ttra-mii now, and were coming on at the same casual lope, completely oblivious to both the Tampy scream and the lethal armament pointed their direction. "Llos-tlaa, why shouldn't they shoot?"

73

" 'Cause the scitte-head bastards would rather roll over and die than bruise any of their precious woodland chummies," Garin bit out before the Tampy could answer.

"Llos-tlaa?—*answer* me."

"There is no need for killing, Rro-maa," Llos-tlaa said, his voice pitched normally but trembling right on the edge of another scream. "Ppey-taa and Ttra-mii must move away from the table, but then the creatures will not attack."

"Bull scitte," Garin said. "Guards, on three: one—"

"I said *hold your fire!*" Roman snapped. "Peyton, Ttra-mii—do as Llos-tlaa said. Move away from the table; try not to make any sudden motions."

"Captain, they're skating on damn thin ice down there," Ferrol put in, his voice taut. "Even explosive needles'll have only so much stopping power against something that size—if they get within five meters they're going to do damage no matter how fast they're killed."

"More so if they decide to charge," Kennedy agreed. "Recommend the guards take out the nearest one immediately, try to scare the other two away."

Roman squeezed thumb and forefinger together. The wolf-creatures were less than sixty meters away now. "Llos-tlaa, why don't you think the creatures will attack?"

The wolf-creatures covered an additional five meters before the Tampy spoke. "There is no sense of the predator in them," he said, and Roman had the distinct impression he was groping for words. "There is none of the hunting posture to them."

Or in other words, Llos-tlaa didn't know why he thought what he did. Great. "Sanderson? Opinion?" Roman called.

"They went through a fight/flight transformation, didn't they?" the other said tautly. "Do they *look* like they're running away from anything?"

No, they didn't, Roman had to admit. On the other hand, Tampies were legendary for never speculating in new situations . . . which implied that Llos-tlaa somehow knew what he was talking about, even if he couldn't put it into words.

But if he really *was* merely reacting to the crass thought of killing something . . .

Thirty meters away . . . and he could put off the decision no longer. "Garin, proximity lock on the lead creature's head," he instructed. "Set for eight meters; explosive needles. Rehfeldt, Boschelli—same orders on the other two."

"Eight meters is cutting things pretty damn fine, Captain," Garin grunted.

"It'll have to do," Roman told him.

"Rro-maa—"

"Quiet, Llos-tlaa."

"Rro-maa, it is not necessary," the Tampy persisted. "They are not interested in us."

"Then who the hell *are* they interested in?" Garin snarled.

Llos-tlaa's hand appeared on his camera view, pointing. "They seek the analysis table."

"They—*what*?"

And on the tactical display, the lead wolf-creature came to a sudden but smooth stop . . . at the rear of the analysis table.

"It wants the dead rabbit on the table," Peyton breathed. "That's all."

"Can't be," Singh objected. "That's not a carrion-type physique. More like—oh. *Oh*."

"What?" Roman demanded. "Singh? *What*?"

Singh snorted, gently, under his breath. "We were wrong, Captain," he said, an undertone of relief and growing amusement in his voice. "The transformation didn't have to be just a fight/flight reaction; there's a third reason for animals to want to look as big and powerful as possible. Namely—well, you can see for yourself. There he goes."

And even as they watched, the wolf-creature reared up on its hind legs and flopped onto the table, its forelegs straddling the CAT-scanner at the front. Getting an awkward-looking grip with its front paws, it reared its head up again and its entire body started to tremble . . .

"I'll be scrooned," Burch said, a touch of awe in his voice. "It's *mating* with the table."

"All those electrical fields," Singh said. "Remember, Miki, that you picked up a surge as they started toward you?"

"They were keying on the electronics in the scanners," she sighed, her voice almost a moan. "They must have thought it was a female. Oh, my poor table."

And a moment later the analysis table, never designed for such treatment, abruptly gave up the ghost. Its legs collapsed, sending the wolf-creature sprawling to the ground amid a minor fortune in delicate electronic equipment. There was a flicker, almost unseen, as the table's self-contained generator shorted to ground and burned out. "Everyone stay sharp," Garin ordered. "They could still charge us."

Roman held his breath . . . but the worry was for nothing. Even as the wolf-creature scrambled out of the wreckage, his feet stamping last-minute damage into the scattered equipment as he got his balance, he and his companions were already starting the reverse transformation back to their smaller dog-forms. One last time the lead dog-creature swung his head around, again ignoring the humans and Tampies, and then together the three of them turned and loped back the way they'd come.

"Well, *that's* something you don't see every day," Burch commented, trying too hard to be casual. "You'd think the others would have been mad that they didn't get their turn."

"Maybe when the table's electric fields went off the animals' sex drive went with it," Singh offered. He'd been closer to the creatures than Burch had, and his voice had an honest tremor to it. "Or maybe they were just there as friends of the groom."

"Not funny," Peyton growled. She was kneeling by

the ruined table now, sifting through what was left of the equipment. "Well, that's the end of the animal studies, at least for today."

"The animal studies and everything else, I think," Sanderson said. "Dr. Tenzing, I suggest we gather a few plant samples together and then come back up to the ship. No one's going to get much more done down here today."

"I agree," Tanzing said. "At the very least, we have to devise a way to either shield our instruments or else distract the local fauna away from them. I'll instruct the lander crew to start their pre-flight checklist. That is," he added, as if suddenly remembering this wasn't a university expedition with himself in charge, "if that's all right with you, Captain."

"Perfectly, Dr. Tenzing," Roman assured him. He had, in fact, already come to the same conclusion. "Lieutenant Kennedy, so instruct the lander crew."

"Yes, sir," Kennedy said, and busied herself with her intercom.

"One other thing, Captain," Tenzing spoke up again. "We're going to need a couple of the *Amity*'s electronic engineers to build whatever we come up with to keep the animals away. Can you have someone assigned to us?"

"I'll do better than that," Roman told him. Barely a full day out of port, it was already becoming clear that the politicians who'd set this whole thing up had assumed that the scientists of *Amity*'s survey section would be operating more or less independently of the larger ship community, with their own equipment, living areas, and chain of command. The first two Roman was willing to concede them; the last, he wasn't. "It seems to me, Dr. Tenzing, that we need better communication and coordination between your people and mine. Accordingly, I'm going to assign one of my officers to act as a liaison. Assist you in getting whatever you need from ship's stores or personnel; making sure your work and procedures stay within standard ship safety limits—that sort of thing."

There was just the briefest pause. "I see," Tenzing said at last. "I was under the impression that—well, never mind. A liaison would probably be a good idea, at that. You have someone in mind?"

"Yes," Roman said, unconsciously bracing himself. It was a gamble—indeed, something of a long shot—and he knew there was a good chance he would live to regret it. But he knew, somehow, that he had to make the effort. "I'm assigning Commander Ferrol to the job."

He looked up to find Ferrol's startled eyes on him. "Sir, with all due respect—"

"The job's yours, Commander," Roman told him evenly. "I suggest you get to the hangar and prepare to receive the landing party. Make sure their samples are properly sealed, and that they stay that way until they reach the lab."

Ferrol took a deep breath. "Acknowledged. Sir."

"Very good, Commander. Dismissed."

With a grimace, the other left the bridge, his back very straight.

So that's how it's going to be, is it? Ferrol thought darkly as he headed aft toward *Amity*'s hanger. *He puts human lives at risk because the Tampies tell him to— comes within a chip-skin of complete disaster—and when I try to put his priorities straight, I get sent to Coventry.* He wanted to stomp, but the ship's slow rotation was already being brought to a halt, robbing him of even that minor satisfaction. Insult piled on top of injury, particularly since the lander wasn't even due for at least another hour. Briefly, he thought about the needle pistol and envelope hidden in his cabin . . .

No, he told himself. He had to let the mission run its course; had to let *Amity*'s crew demolish this last feeble attempt to prove that humans and Tampies could be anything but bitter enemies. A draw would only lead to more stalling on the pro-Tampies' part.

In fact—it suddenly occurred to him—that might

even be what Roman was going for with this harassment. Trying to push him into making his move in hopes of that draw, or even of a pro-Tampy backlash.

Ferrol smiled tightly. *Sorry, Captain, but it's not going to be quite that easy.* He would do all that he was told, be a model exec . . . and wait.

The hangar crew proved ready to receive the lander. With things under control there, and with no particular interest in hanging around waiting for the landing party to make its appearance, Ferrol headed to the survey section's lab complex for a quick check of the lockbox facilities. The scientists and techs there also seemed prepared, though he found he was forced to take their word for most of the technical details; and by the time he returned once more to the hangar the lander had arrived.

"Dr. Sanderson," he greeted the party's leader as the latter emerged, awkward in the zero-gee as he aimed his feet toward the nearest velgrip patch. "I'm Commander Ferrol; I believe we met yesterday."

"Yes," the other nodded vaguely, his mind clearly on other things. "We've got the sample boxes back in the hold—can you get some people to help us carry them to the lab?"

From behind Ferrol the rotation alarm sounded. "If you'll wait a few minutes, Doctor," he told Sanderson, "we'll have enough gravity to use one of the carts over there."

"Yes, all right," Sanderson said, moving to one side as the rest of his team began filing out of the lander. "I'm going ahead to get things ready; Steef—Dr. Burch—will show you how to unpack and load the boxes."

Ferrol swallowed the retort that came to mind. "Yes, Doctor," he said instead.

Sanderson nodded again and took off toward the hangar door without another word, and Ferrol headed around to the aft hold door. Unsealing it, he stepped high over the rubber-edged sill and went inside.

The landing party had indeed been busy down there.

Packed beneath the cargo netting were nine fifty-liter sample boxes, wedged in together with the remains of the ruined analysis table. Ferrol's lip twisted at the sight of the latter; he was looking forward to seeing how the captain would phrase this one in his log. Unfastening the cargo netting, he guided the mesh as it retracted onto its spool. A movement of air brushed the back of his neck, and he turned—

To find a Tampy standing not thirty centimeters away.

Face to face with a Tampy, for the first time since Prometheus . . . and in an instant all of his careful mental preparation for this moment collapsed. The lopsided face seemed to press in on him—the slight rasp of the alien's breathing echoed in the enclosed space—the whiff of bitter-sour body odor curdled his stomach—

And as the red haze of memory and anger faded from before his eyes he saw that the Tampy had disappeared. And that there were the sounds of confusion and shock from outside the lander. And that the knuckles of his right fist were tingling . . .

Damn.

He stepped to the hold door, just in time to see Burch and Llos-tlaa helping the other Tampy back to his feet in the low gravity. A reddish splotch was already becoming visible to the left of the other's twisted mouth. Burch looked up at Ferrol, a disbelieving look on his face. "What happened here?" he asked.

Ferrol took a careful breath, his muscles starting to tremble with adrenaline reaction. *I need to apologize,* he knew; but even as he opened his mouth to do so the words seemed to stick in his throat. To say he was sorry—sorry!—for hitting one of the race that had stolen his home—

"It is all right," the Tampy grated, raising a hand to stroke his jaw where Ferrol had hit him. "I am not hurt. It is all right."

Ferrol clenched his teeth, a hint of the blind rage returning to haze his vision. Of course the Tampy was "all right"—he'd say the same from a sick bay bed if he had to. The Tampies were on *Amity* to score points, and proving how good they were at turning the other cheek was the obvious way to twist Ferrol's unthinking reaction back against him.

And he was damned if he was going to add to their warm charitable glow by pretending he was sorry. "Next time don't sneak up on me like that," he told the alien shortly. "Dr. Burch, whenever you're ready I'll give you a hand with these boxes."

Burch threw a look at Llos-tlaa. "Ah . . . right," he said. "Sure." With a slight hesitation, and clearly keeping a cautious eye on his coworker, he left the Tampies and joined Ferrol in the hold.

They worked together in silence, removing the boxes from the hold and stacking them outside on the hangar deck. Peyton appeared halfway through the job, but with the cramped conditions making it no more than a two-man job her contribution consisted mainly of fetching a cart from the hangar bulkhead and repeatedly warning them not to step on what was left of her analysis table. Full weight had returned by the time they finished loading the cart, and with Ferrol at the controls they headed toward the lab complex.

They were halfway there before Burch finally spoke. "Why'd you hit Ttra-mii?" he asked, his voice forced-casual.

"I don't like Tampies," Ferrol said.

"How come? If you don't mind talking about it, that is?"

"As a matter of fact, I *do* mind," Ferrol said.

He glanced, looked over in time to see Burch swallow. "Ah," the other said, a bit lamely.

"There's a lot of really interesting stuff down there to study," Peyton spoke up, clearly trying to steer the conversation onto safer territory. "Were you monitoring us, Commander?"

"I did the computer-scrub on the rabbit's transformation," Ferrol reminded her.

She reddened slightly. "Oh, yes."

A pang of guilt poked a small hole in Ferrol's conscience. There was no reason to make this so awkward for Burch and Peyton—it wasn't the scientists he was angry with, after all. On the contrary, it could easily be *Amity*'s survey section who would have the best chance of ultimately seeing through the Tampies' facade of peaceful friendliness. Giving them the impression that all anti-Tampies were violent coma-brains would only make it that much harder for them to accept the truth when the facade finally broke. "Those memory-plastic skeletons look particularly intriguing," he commented. "You think you'll be able to duplicate the material?"

"Oh, sure," Burch assured him. "If there's one thing human biotechnology has gotten down pat, it's the duplication of interesting molecules and biochemical systems."

Peyton snorted gently. "Though there's always the tendency to forget that the whole is more than just a collection of commercially useful parts. The Tampies are right about *that*, at least."

Burch threw her an annoyed look. "Philosophies of life aside, it *is* the commercial results that pay for trips like this, of course."

"And there should be plenty of that to go around," Peyton said with a sigh. "Between the memory-skeletons and the organic electric field oscillators we should bring back more than enough to keep the Senate budget watchdogs happy."

"Even though the Tampies get to keep everything we can't find in the next two weeks?" Ferrol murmured.

Burch hissed gently between his teeth. "Even then," he said. But he didn't say it like he believed it.

Peyton steered the conversation back to the wonders of Alpha's ecology and animal life after that, and neither the Tampies nor their philosophies were mentioned again before Ferrol helped load the samples into the lockbox lab and took his leave. But it was enough. There would be no need for him to plant seeds of distrust or discontent among the scientists, he saw now— those doubts were clearly already there. His job now was to simply help water those seeds . . . a job a man on liaison duty would have ample opportunity to carry out over the next two months.

Heading down the corridor back to the bridge, he permitted himself a smile. No, he wouldn't need the envelope or the gun just yet. In fact, he might not need them at all. The way things were going, Captain Roman might wind up doing the bulk of Ferrol's work for him.

Unless, he thought . . . and for a moment the smile slipped. Could that be exactly why Roman had given him this liaison job in the first place? To nurture anti-Tampy sentiment among the scientists?

Could Roman in fact be secretly on Ferrol's side?

No, Ferrol told himself firmly. *Utterly impossible.* The Senator had seen Roman's psych profile, and Roman couldn't possibly have fooled the Starforce's soul-sifters that completely. He was pro-Tampy, all right, and he'd given Ferrol the liaison post either as punishment or else from some misguided idealistic belief that frequent contact with Tampies would somehow mellow his hatred of them. The fool.

Still . . .

Ferrol had intended to spend his off-duty time the next few days trying to get access to the crew psych files anyway. Assuming he was able to get in, it wouldn't hurt to take a look for himself at Roman's profile. Just to make sure.

Chapter 7

Ferrol had fully expected some kind of official response from Roman over his flooring of the Tampy in the hangar—anything from a blistering reprimand to temporary confinement to quarters or even a complete stripping of rank and imprisonment. To his surprise, though, the captain never even mentioned the incident. Perhaps the popular image of Tampies as cheek-turning forgive-and-forgetters had rubbed off on him; or perhaps he was afraid of making a martyr out of *Amity*'s leading anti-Tampy figure. The latter wasn't an unreasonable fear, to Ferrol's mind—emotional reactions and their manipulation could be tricky things to handle, and Roman didn't seem the type to have cultivated such a talent.

Or else Burch and the Tampies, for reasons of tact or point-making, had simply never reported it. It was, he eventually decided, as good an explanation as any.

They spent another two weeks circling Alpha, watching from orbit as the landing parties poked around the planet's desert, forest, and Alpine environments, oohing and ahing at everything in sight. The "Lorelei sticks"—as Dr. Tenzing dubbed the oversized electronic tent stakes *Amity*'s techs came up with—worked beautifully, their oscillating electric fields either decoying Alpha's predators away from the landing parties or else leading them directly to net traps, whichever Sanderson's people wanted at a given moment. By the time Pegasus pulled them out of orbit toward deep space the first lab was, as predicted, loaded literally to the ceiling with sample boxes.

The Jump to Beta system went off perfectly, as did the subsequent fifty-hour drive through normal space to the target planet itself. This time Ferrol kept close track of the acceleration/deceleration profile; to his mild surprise, Pegasus held solidly to the 0.9 gee Roman had ordered, never varying more than half a percent from that acceleration. It was a striking and sobering example of just how strong and efficient the Handler/space horse bond really was . . . an efficiency that was going to be a serious problem for humanity when the war finally came.

The second target world on their list, Beta, was about as different from Alpha as two planets could possibly be, but no less interesting for all that. Circling close in to a bright red-orange star, its life had evolved into exceptionally specialized forms inhabiting exceptionally specialized ecological niches. Specialized to such a degree, in fact, that the landing parties could often cross up to half a dozen distinct variants of a plant in a five-kilometer walk, with virtually no interpenetration between the types. Half of the samples they tried transplanting aboard ship died before *Amity* even left orbit, and few of the others lasted much longer.

It was an ideal pot for stirring up human/Tampy conflicts in, and the results were all Ferrol could have hoped for. With their carefully cultivated image as "Lord Protectors Of Nature" on the line, the Tampies were forced to continually protest the disturbing of such fragile ecological structures. There were sharp words from both sides, and frustration all around, and by the end of the first week there were no longer any Tampies heading down to the surface with Sanderson's landing parties.

Oddly enough, the boycott didn't seem to make any

lasting dent in the scientists' own pro or anti attitudes. All the comments Ferrol overheard in his role as liaison indicated a generally tolerant understanding—even sympathy—for the aliens' point of view. In retrospect, he realized he should probably have expected that kind of reaction—even on Prometheus he'd noticed that the colonists who'd worked most closely with the Tampies were sometimes the most easily taken in by the aliens' big nobility act.

But if that kind of emotional infection had been what the pro-Tampies in the Senate had been banking on, they were in for a disappointment ... because even as the scientists began mouthing Tampy philosophies and worrying aloud about bruising the grass they walked on, relationships between the Tampies and the rest of *Amity*'s crew began a quiet but steady slide downhill.

The signs were there even before the Jump from Alpha system. There had been a fair amount of traffic between the two halves of the ship the first week— some of it simple curiosity, the rest probably an attempt by the pro-Tampies among the crew to stimulate friendly contact. But as curiosity was satisfied, and as Rrin-saa and the other Tampies continued to press Sanderson's people with holier-than-thou warnings against disturbing nature, the number of crewers playing tourist or goodwill ambassador dropped off nearly to zero. The Tampy boycott of the Beta landing parties did nothing to improve that, and by the time Pegasus pulled *Amity* out of orbit a spate of anti-Tampy jokes were beginning to make surreptitious rounds in areas of the ship not frequented by the scientists or senior officers.

By the time *Amity* left orbit around the third planet, Gamma, the connecting doors were being used solely for occasional ship's business, and the jokes were being told openly around the crewer mess tables.

And by the time the last samples from Delta were aboard, it was clear that the hopes of *Amity*'s pro-Tampy supporters had come to exactly nothing.

* * *

"Hhom-jee reports Pegasus is ready to Jump," Ensign Connie MacKaig reported over her shoulder from the helm.

Ferrol nodded. "Tell him to go ahead whenever he's ready," he instructed her.

"Yes, sir."

She turned to her intercom, and Ferrol took a deep breath. It was over. Over. Roman could sit down there in his office all day sifting through the final crewer questionnaires if he wanted to, but there was no way in hell that the results could add up to anything other than total failure. He knew it, Roman knew it, and anyone who'd been paying any attention at all to the ship's atmosphere these past few weeks knew it.

Ahead, the bridge displays flickered in unison as Delta system's orange sun vanished and was replaced by the yellow dwarf of Solomon system. "Jump completed," MacKaig announced. "Range to Solomon . . . 3.5 million kilometers."

Ferrol did a quick calculation. About eleven hours round trip at the 0.9 gee the Tampies seemed to prefer. "Inform Solomon that we've arrived, Ensign," he told her, "and have the Handler take us in. The usual 0.9 gee acc/dec profile will do."

"Aye, sir."

And with this little side trip finally over, it would be time to get back to the *Scapa Flow* and pick up where he'd left off. Assuming, of course, that the Starforce patrols in the Tampies' *yishyar* system had faded away . . . and assuming the Senator let him go back.

Ferrol grimaced at the memory. The Senator had made no secret of the fact that he hadn't liked the way Ferrol had handled his ship's near-capture by Roman and the *Dryden*, and had gone so far as to suggest that Ferrol was getting too reckless. The discussion had been tabled by the whole *Amity* thing, but now that that was over it was bound to be rekindled. And if he couldn't convince the Senator that he was still trustworthy—

"Commander?" MacKaig spoke up, her voice suddenly tight. "Solomon reports a tachyon message waiting for us—Level One Urgent."

War. The word came unbidden to Ferrol's thoughts, and for a split second his blood seemed to freeze. The war had come, and he was trapped on a Tampy-crewed ship . . . "Sound yellow alert," he ordered, fighting down the tremor in his voice. "I'll get the captain."

And as the alert warble sounded, and he fumbled with his intercom, the word again ran through his mind.

War.

Chapter 8

". . . Although I feel the experience was worthwhile, I don't think I would enjoy working with the Tampies again. There are just too many differences, too many ways for us to irritate each other."

The words flowing across the display ceased, and Roman braced himself. That was the last of them. Now came the moment he'd been dreading: the computer's scorecard. Tapping the appropriate key, he watched as the results appeared. Twenty-eight favorable, ninety-seven unfavorable, as compared to an original pre-flight score of sixty to sixty-five. Nearly twenty-six percent of *Amity*'s crew had switched from pro- to anti-Tampy.

Damn.

He leaned back in his chair, gazing out at the shadowy bulk of Pegasus just visible at the edge of the viewport. So it had failed, this grand experiment in familiarity breeding respect—failed beyond the ability of even the most grimly optimistic to argue. Virtually all of the originally pro-Tampy crewers had had their enthusiasm toward the aliens dampened, to one degree or another, while at the same time every single one of the anti-Tampies had had their prejudices strengthened.

I should have taken firmer control, he told himself; but deep down he knew it wouldn't have made any difference. There was no way he could have forced friendship between the races on his ship, and it would have been useless to even try. Rrin-saa's words about *Amity's* importance echoed in his mind, and for a moment he felt a brief stirring of anger toward the Tampies. Certainly some of the blame rested with them—they hadn't made the slightest effort to tone down their opposition to the way human beings interacted with the rest of the universe. In fact, they'd more than once gone borderline hysterical about it.

He was still staring blackly at the final data when the office was abruptly filled with the soft but pervasive warbling of ship's alert.

For a pair of heartbeats he just sat there, mind wrenching away from interstellar politics and back to his immediate responsibilities. He reached for his intercom; but it came on even before his hand got there. "Captain here," he said.

"Bridge, sir," Ferrol said, his face and voice tight. "We've got a tachyon message coming in from Solomon— Urgent One level."

A chill ran up Roman's back. There was only one reason he could think of why anyone would need to shoot *Amity* a message of such priority . . . "Acknowledged," he said, keying the proper acceptance code into his terminal. "Bring it in," he instructed Ferrol. "Pipe it back here to me and to the bridge crew— nowhere else."

For an instant his eyes and Ferrol's met, and there was a brief spark of mutual understanding. If the simmering fires on the human-Tampy frontier had indeed exploded into full conflict, both men wanted some time to think before breaking the news to *Amity's* Tampies. "Yes, sir," Ferrol said, dropping his gaze to his keys. "Here it comes."

Ferrol's face disappeared from the screen, to be replaced by—

TO RESEARCH SHIP *AMITY*, SOLOMON:
FROM COMMANDER STARFORCE BORDERSHIPS
EXTENSION, PREPYAT:

:::URGENT-ONE:::URGENT-ONE:::URGENT-ONE:::

PROCEED IMMEDIATELY NCL 1148; EMERGENCY RESCUE
OF SCIENTIFIC RESEARCH STATION ON THIRD PLANET.
NCL 1148-B PREPARING TO GO NOVA.

"Holy hell," someone on the bridge muttered in the
background.
"Quiet," Ferrol's voice growled back.

FURTHER DATA ON SYSTEM AVAILABLE FOR FEED FROM
SOLOMON STARFORCE STATION. ABSOLUTELY VITAL
PICKUP BE MADE BY *AMITY*.

VICE-ADMIRAL MARCOSA, COMBOREX, PREPYAT
CODE/VER *@7882//53

8:22 GMT///ESD 3 APRIL 2335

"Commander, contact the station and get us that data
feed," Roman ordered, feeling the knots in his stomach
begin to relax a bit. Heading into a system on the brink
of stellar explosion was hardly cause for joy, but it was a
far cry from the call to arms he'd envisioned. "And alert
the Tampies; I want Pegasus ready to Jump just as soon
as we know where it is we're Jumping to."
"Yes, sir," Ferrol said, his voice still tight. "Shall I
secure from yellow alert?"
"Yes, you'd better," Roman agreed. The warbling
siren had probably driven most of the crewers to the
same conclusion that he and Ferrol had already jumped
to, and things were likely pretty tense back there. "Go
ahead and read the message over the general intercom,
too—if the star is really this close to going critical,
we're going to want everyone running at top efficiency."
"Acknowledged."

Roman keyed off the intercom and unstrapped, and as his feet found the nearest velgrip patch the warbling faded and was replaced by Ferrol's voice announcing the sudden change in *Amity*'s planned schedule.

And for a moment Roman paused beside his desk, frowning at the stars outside. 8:22 GMT, the message datestamp had said, on Earth Standard Date 3 April 2335. Something over thirty hours ago . . . and in the time the message had sat around waiting for the *Amity* to make its appearance at Solomon, Marcosa could have sent the message to the Tampies via a space horse-equipped courier and had a rescue ship already in the 1148 system, possibly even at the research station itself.

So why hadn't they?

Politics, he thought darkly. Politics and pride, and a hell/highwater unwillingness to ask the Tampies for help. Damn foolishness, by any reasonable standard; and if the survey team lost their lives because of it—

It would be *Amity* that would get the blame.

Ferrol had skimmed through the entire data feed, distributed the appropriate sections to the appropriate people, and had started a more careful reading when Roman finally arrived. "The team consists of roughly fifty people, under the direction of Dr. Jamen Lowry of Cambridge," he told the captain as the latter floated to his command chair and strapped in. "They set up there because the star was thought to be in a pre-nova stage and they wanted to study it. Apparently, the thing's going off sooner than theory predicted."

Roman nodded and keyed himself a copy of the data. "What about their own ship?"

"They haven't got one," Ferrol said. "They had to hire a Tampy ship to give them transport—the system's a good thousand light-years outside Mitsuushi range."

"And that ship isn't available to them?"

"I'd say that's almost irrelevant at the moment, sir," Ferrol said. It wasn't, really, but with luck the captain wouldn't notice that. "They called Earth; Earth called us. It's in our laps now."

"So it would seem," Roman grunted. "Do we have the system located yet?"

"Yes, sir," MacKaig spoke up from the helm. She tapped a key, and the relevant page of the New Cygni Listing appeared on Ferrol's helm repeater display. "Eleven hundred sixty-five light-years away, longitude minus 2.6 degrees, latitude 5.9 degrees," she said. "We can't Jump directly to it from here—not visible enough—but Pegasus *can* see Deneb from here, and it ought to be able to see 1148 from there."

Roman studied the listing for a moment before nodding. "Should work. Feed the direction and maps down to Hhom-jee and tell him to Jump as soon as Pegasus is ready."

"Yes, sir," she said, and busied herself with her intercom.

Beside Ferrol, the computer signaled that the problem he'd set for it a minute ago had been completed. He turned back as a map of the 1148 system appeared on the display, framed by four-decimal numerical listings of current planetary locations. Adjusting the scale, he took a good look.

The system consisted of two stars—a smallish red giant and a white dwarf—plus three planets of the usual variety of sizes and orbits. The two stars were so close together, the dwarf circling perilously close to the giant's outer atmosphere, that there was little or no room for a stable planetary orbit between them. All the planets revolved around both stars, an arrangement with enough perturbations to make hash out of a standard orbit calculation, and Ferrol gave silent thanks that the team out there had been thinking straight enough to include updated numbers with their tachyon distress call. The base was on the innermost planet, which the team had dubbed Shadrach: a roughly Mars-sized chunk of lifeless rock with a pair of moons, orbiting some five hundred million kilometers out from the center of the giant.

"We're starting to come around," MacKaig announced. "Lining up for the Jump to Deneb."

"Good," Roman said. "Commander Ferrol?"

"Sir?" Ferrol said, eyes still on the display.

"Do you know this Admiral Marcosa?"

Ferrol felt his back go abruptly stiff. He forced the muscles to relax, glad his face was away from the captain. "I've heard of him, sir, but never met him," he said. It was more or less true.

"Anti-Tampy?"

Ferrol suppressed a grim smile. Certainly he was anti-Tampy—rabidly so, in fact. Marcosa was one of the Senator's closest friends within the Admiralty, a quiet ally in everything from the *Scapa Flow*'s poaching runs to the backstairs maneuvering that had gotten Ferrol aboard *Amity* . . . and the fact that the new orders had come in over Marcosa's name was almost certainly not a coincidence. "I'd guess so, sir," he said aloud. "Why do you ask?"

He could feel Roman's eyes on the back of his neck. "I wondered why he took the chance of waiting for us," Roman said, almost offhandedly, "instead of asking the Tampies to send one of their ships."

There was opportunity here for a dig at the whole question of Tampy speed and efficiency, but there were too many other things on Ferrol's mind for him to be bothered. "I've got a suggestion, Captain, about our approach." Without waiting for permission, he sent the planetary schematic to Roman's station. "If we Jump to 1148 directly from Deneb we'll arrive someplace along this line—" he traced a line from the double star outward with a mousepen—"depending on how the gravitational equipotential surfaces work out. That'll put us a minimum of a hundred million kilometers away from the planet itself."

"Whereas if we shuttle back and forth between appropriately positioned stars we should be able to come in considerably closer?"

Ferrol nodded, impressed in spite of himself. Maybe Roman was smarter than his blind pro-Tampy sentiments would indicate. "Yes, sir," he acknowledged. "I've found a couple of good possibilities, but I'm not sure which one would be the best."

"Ensign?" Roman invited.

MacKaig was frowning at Ferrol's schematics and preliminary numbers, fingers skating across her own keys. "Looks like the second one will get us closer," she said slowly. "Not by much, though—maybe half a million kilometers at the most."

"We'll take anything we can get at this point," Roman said, a grim edge to his voice. "Put it into visual format and send it down to Hhom-jee. We'll want to do the Jumps one-two-three, as fast as we can get in position for each one."

"Yes, sir." She hesitated. "That assumes, of course, that Pegasus can *do* three Jumps in a row."

"A fair question," Roman agreed, reaching for his intercom. "Let's find out, shall we?"

Ferrol keyed himself into the circuit just as a Tampy face appeared. "Rro-maa, yes?" he grated.

"Yes," Roman nodded. "The *Amity*'s just been called on for an emergency rescue mission, Rrin-saa. Had you been informed?"

"Ffe-rho has told us, yes," Rrin-saa confirmed.

"All right. We'll be doing three Jumps in a row, and I need quick answers to two questions. First: will Pegasus need to rest between the Jumps?"

"I do not know," the Tampy whined. "I know space horses have Jumped twice without rest; that is all."

"I see," Roman said, with no sign of impatience at yet another example of Tampy waffling. Perhaps, Ferrol thought cynically, he was to the point of considering that an adequate answer. "I guess we'll find out together," the captain continued. "So: second question. Given that space horses absorb a high percentage of the solar energy that hits them, will a nova or pre-nova star be too bright for Pegasus to handle?"

Ferrol swallowed. That thought hadn't even occurred to him, and he found himself holding his breath as he waited for the answer.

He needn't have bothered. "I do not know, Rromaa," the other said. "I know that they come close to normal stars; that is all."

"Yes, well . . . thank you. Captain out."

Ferrol keyed off his intercom with a snort of disgust. "You didn't really expect to get anything useful from them, did you?" he growled.

Roman sent him a thoughtful look, turned to the helm. "Status, Ensign?"

"We're in line for Deneb," MacKaig reported. "Hhom-jee signals Pegasus is ready."

Roman nodded. "Jump."

The Jump to Deneb went off without a hitch, and from the new location MacKaig was able to refine her numbers for the remaining two Jumps. A half-hour's drive through normal space put *Amity* in position for the second Jump, to a dim and unnamed star.

It seemed to Ferrol that it took longer for Hhom-jee to get Pegasus ready for that one. By the time they were ready for the third Jump, to 1148 itself, there was no doubt.

For the first time in the voyage, Pegasus was showing signs of fatigue.

"Rrin-saa, we've been in position for the past five minutes," Roman said into the intercom, his voice carefully showing no signs of either irritation or nervousness. "What seems to be the trouble?"

"There is not trouble," the Tampy's reply came faintly. "Pegasunninni is in mild *perasiata*—it will be only another few moments."

Roman hissed quietly between his teeth. "Have Hhom-jee push it as much as he can. There's no guarantee as to how much time we've got."

"Your wishes are ours."

Roman broke the connection and turned to Ferrol. "Any word from below on the latest dust sweat analysis?"

"The composition's definitely changing," Ferrol told him, the sour taste of irony in his mouth. He'd argued—loudly, in fact—against all of the dust sweat work; now, suddenly, it was turning out to be of more than academic curiosity, after all. It left Roman looking brilliantly foresighted; and it left him, Ferrol, looking wrong. It was a toss-up as to which part of that he hated more. "Overall output is up, but at the same time there's been a sharp drop in several of the trace elements."

Roman nodded. So far he'd passed up any snide comments on the demise of Ferrol's side of the dust sweat argument. Not that anyone on the brige really needed reminding. "Sounds like a buildup of fatigue wastes," he suggested.

"Dr. Tenzing says that's one of the possibilities."

"Mm. Well, we'll just have to wait and see how fast it clears up."

"Yes, sir. So what's this *perasiata* scam, anyway?"

"It's hardly a scam," Roman said, his voice a little stiff. "It's a kind of withdrawal of consciousness the space horses sometimes experience. Something like the way the Tampies sleep, or so they've described it."

Ferrol nodded to himself. So there *was* a limit to how hard you could push a space horse. Interesting. Even more interesting that no one had discovered it before now.

"Captain?" MacKaig spoke up. "Hhom-jee signals we're finally ready to Jump."

"Very good. Execute."

The words were barely out of Roman's mouth when the sunlight did its abrupt and instantaneous change . . . and they were there.

To the naked eye, 1148 was merely a bright reddish star; seen through *Amity*'s sunscope, it was a truly awesome sight. Shrouded in a brightly lit haze, seemingly meshed together by roiling tendrils of colored

vapor, the twin stars seemed to project both the ultimate in unity and the ultimate in conflict. A child in its
mother's arms; or two fighters literally tearing the life
from each other.

With a shiver, Ferrol forced the images down. The
last thing he needed going into a pre-nova system was
an overactive imagination.

"Interesting view," Roman remarked from behind
him. "Ensign, do we have Shadrach on the scope yet?"

"Yes, sir," MacKaig told him. "About three degrees
off a direct line to the stars, range approximately forty
million kilometers."

"About as close as we were likely to get," Roman
said. "Good job. Feed the numbers to Hhom-jee and
have him get us going." He tapped his intercom, indicating to Ferrol to join the circuit. "Dr. Tenzing? Have
your people come up with any theories as to what's
going on out there?"

"Guesses only at this stage, Captain," Tenzing grunted.
The scientist's expression, Ferrol thought, seemed to
be hovering midway between scientific eagerness and a
very unscientific desire to be several light-years away.
"Two things seem pretty certain, though. One: both
stars, especially B—the dwarf—are much hotter than
they should be; and two, B is also cooling down fairly
rapidly. That suggests we're looking at some variant of a
classical Anselm Cycle, either gravitationally or ther-
mally driven."

"The Anselm Cycle being . . . ?"

"Well, it's never actually been observed, as far as I
know, but the scenerio goes something like this. Some
of the gas envelope material from A—the giant—falls
past the gravitational equipoint onto B and triggers a
burst of energy, which both heats B's surface and blows
off a shell of material. The extra radiant energy from
that burp heats up A slightly, causing it to expand a bit
more and therefore dump even more material onto B.
Eventually—or so the theory goes—one of these cycles
will dump enough matter onto B to trigger a proton-

proton nuclear reaction in the surface. At that point, B goes nova, increases its brightness a factor of fifty thousand or so, and fries everything in the system."

Roman seemed to digest that. "Seems reasonable enough. When can we expect the next of these burps?"

"We don't know," Tenzing admitted. "Best estimate is that the last one happened sixty to eighty hours ago, which turns out to be roughly two-thirds of what the theory would predict for the cycle. That would indicate the next one should come within thirty or forty hours, but I really can't say for certain."

"How much warning will it give us before it goes?"

Tenzing's eyes flicked to the side. "Again, none of my people can say for certain. Probably a few minutes at the most."

"I see. Any idea as to which of these burps will trigger the nova itself?"

Tenzing's face tightened. "Not really. We don't have the equipment to take accurate readings on the plasma dynamics going on out there, and without a better feel for the Lagrange surfaces and expansion coefficients all we can really do is guess. It could go on the very next burp, or it could hold off for a couple of weeks."

Roman nodded grimly. "Thank you, Doctor," he said. Cutting the circuit, he swiveled to face the engineering monitor. "How's the ship taking this?"

"Hull temperature's going up, but not dangerously," the ensign manning the station reported. Dangerous or not, he wasn't taking his eyes off the readouts. "As long as B continues to cool down we should be all right. Particle radiation is marginal, but within safety limits."

Which was all right, Ferrol knew. Spaceship hulls were built to take a lot of that kind of abuse; and if worse came to worse they could move into Pegasus' shadow—

He spun around to face Roman; and in the captain's face he could see that they'd both caught it at the same time. Roman got to the intercom first. "Rrin-saa? This is the captain. Why aren't we moving?"

Ferrol keyed himself into the circuit, and for a long moment the display remained blank. Then, abruptly, it cleared to show a contact-helmeted Tampy wearing a green/purple neckerchief. "Rro-maa, yes," he grated.

"Hhom-jee, why aren't we moving?" Roman demanded again. "Ensign MacKaig sent you the direction several minutes ago."

"Pegasunninni will not move."

Roman swore under his breath. "Hhom-jee, we have *got* to get in there. Is Pegasus worried about getting closer to the hot star?—if so, we may be able to shield it from—"

"Pegasunninni is not worried about star," Hhom-jee said. "He will not move. Any direction. He does not seem to be well."

Roman looked up at Ferrol, his eyes abruptly tight . . . and Ferrol felt his stomach twist into a hard knot. Without Pegasus, *Amity* was trapped in this system.

With a star preparing itself to explode.

Chapter 9

It was odd, Roman thought distantly. Over the years he'd spent hours on end in cramped deep-space shuttlecraft and powered worksuits, all without the slightest hint of trouble. Now, with billions of cubic kilometers of open space around him, he was suddenly feeling the unpleasant stirrings of claustrophobia.

Trapped in a pre-nova system . . . "What do you mean, he's not well?" he demanded. "You mean he's sick, or fatigued, or what?"

"I do not know," was the all-too predictable reply. "I know that I have never seen a space horse like this; that is all."

Roman gritted his teeth. "Where's Sso-ngii? Let me talk to him."

"He is resting."

"Well, wake him *up*," Ferrol growled.

"He cannot be disturbed," Hhom-jee said.

Ferrol started to say something else, stopped as Roman threw him a warning look. "I'm coming down there," he told Hhom-jee. "Keep trying."

He broke the connection and unstrapped. "Commander, light a small fire under Tenzing's people," he ordered over his shoulder as he launched himself toward the door. "I want their best guess as to what's wrong with Pegasus, and some suggestions on how to cure it, by the time I get back."

"Yes, sir," Ferrol called after him.

The Tampy section looked the same as it had the first time Roman had gone there, but this time he hardly even noticed the alien beauty of it. Fingers searching out the handholds half-buried in the moss, he pulled himself along the corridors as quickly as he could.

He reached the Handler room door and pushed himself through the opening, to find three of the aliens waiting quietly there for him. Though to be more accurate, only Rrin-saa and Hhom-jee were actually waiting for *him*: floating alone over in a far corner, humming dreamily to himself, Sso-ngii wasn't in any shape to be expecting Roman or anyone else.

"Rro-maa," Rrin-saa said gravely as Roman found one of the few patches of velgrip the Tampies had allowed in their section and planted his feet onto it. "Hhom-jee informed me you were coming."

"Hhom-jee informed *me* that Pegasus was sick," Roman returned, breathing heavily through his filter mask as he threw a glance at Hhom-jee. Beneath the amplifier helmet, the Handler's eyes were turned upward, toward the viewport and Pegasus.

"We do not know if he is sick," Rrin-saa said. "Perhaps he is simply disturbed by the changing light of the star and does not yet wish to move."

"Well, why *don't* we know?" Roman demanded. "Hhom-jee is in contact with it—why can't he just ask it what's wrong?"

Rrin-saa looked at Hhom-jee, back at Roman. "It is not like that, Rro-maa," he said. "There are no *questions* or *answers*. There merely *is*."

Roman took a deep breath, forced down the sudden rush of anger. "This isn't the time or place for philosophic discussions, Rrin-saa," he told the Tampy. "There are fifty humans on that planet who are going to be vaporized if we can't get Pegasus moving again. Not to mention everyone aboard *Amity*."

Rrin-saa looked at him, an odd intensity in his lop-sided face. "We share your feelings, Rro-maa. The Tamplissta also have an observery on that world."

Roman felt his eyebrows lifting. There wasn't any particular reason, of course, why there shouldn't be Tampies down there—Shadrach was large enough to accomodate all the research teams anyone could want. But it felt somehow out of character for them to be interested in a non-living part of nature. "Why didn't you say something about this earlier?" he asked.

Rrin-saa touched fingers to ear: the Tampy shrug. "I was not asked."

Roman pursed his lips. "All the more reason for us not to hang around out here." He nodded toward the humming Sso-ngii. "And if Hhom-jee can't get Pegasus to move, perhaps Sso-ngii can."

Rrin-saa looked at Hhom-jee, at Sso-ngii, back at Roman. "I do not think so. He will not wish to use compulsion; and I do not think compulsion will be effective, regardless."

"Try it anyway."

Rrin-saa looked again at Sso-ngii. "He is resting now and cannot be disturbed."

Roman bit down hard on the inside of his cheek, forcing his mind to remain calm. "Rrin-saa . . . I understand that these rest periods are as important to you as sleep is to us. But we're in a crisis situation here; and I know full well that waking him up won't harm him. So *wake him up.*"

"It will not be good for him," Rrin-saa insisted. "And there is no need. If Hhom-jee cannot move Pegasunninni, then Sso-ngii will not be able to do so."

For a long moment Roman was sorely tempted to go over there and personally shake Sso-ngii awake. But there was a principle at stake here; a principle, and a reminder of why they were all on *Amity* in the first place. "Rrin-saa. When we began this voyage you acknowledged that I was in command of *Amity*, that for the sake of this experiment you and the others would agree to follow my leadership. I accept your assessment that Sso-ngii's chances are probably very slim; but we humans thrive on slim odds—and when we win them it's precisely *because* we don't give up until we're forced to." He nodded toward Sso-ngii. "We haven't hit that point; not yet. Consider it a lesson in human thought patterns, or even just a lesson in human stubbornness, whichever you'd prefer.

"But also consider it an order."

For a handful of heartbeats Rrin-saa remained silent and motionless. Then, slowly, he floated over to Sso-ngii and touched him on the arm, speaking softly in the high-pitched Tampy language. The humming stopped; Sso-ngii shook himself like a wet terrier and rubbed his neck. Rrin-saa said something else. Sso-ngii gazed at Roman for a moment, then went to where Hhom-jee floated, relieving him of the helmet.

"He will try now," Rrin-saa said. There was no trace of any emotion in his voice that Roman could detect.

For a few minutes the room was silent. Then Sso-ngii turned from the viewport. "Pegasunninni will not move," he said. The words were clear and flat, with no room for argument.

It had still been worth a try. "Keep trying," Roman told Sso-ngii. Kicking himself over to the repeater instrument panel, he found the intercom and keyed for the bridge. "Commander? Anything from the survey section?"

"Nothing of any use," Ferrol said grimly. "They've come up with four or five theories, everything from radiation sickness to malnutrition, and not a shred of real evidence to support any of them. A cure is completely out of the question, of course."

That, too, had been worth a try . . . and it left *Amity* with just exactly one option left. "All right, then, I guess it's time for some serious improvisation," he told Ferrol. "Call engineering and have Stolt start running the fusion drive back up to power. Then tell Tenzing that he's to collect the equipment he'll need to continue analyzing Pegasus' condition and get it to the lander."

Ferrol's forehead creased. "I trust, sir, that you're not going to try to drag Pegasus all the way to Shadrach." It was a statement, not a question.

"That's correct," Roman confirmed. "We're going to cut *Amity* loose and go in alone. Pegasus will stay here, along with most of the survey section and enough Tampies to make sure it doesn't suddenly get well and Jump on us."

"And what if—?" Ferrol broke off abruptly. "I'd like to discuss this with you privately, Captain, if I may."

Roman eyed him. "I'll be back on the bridge in a minute. Will that be soon enough?"

Ferrol nodded. "Yes, sir. I'll get Stolt started on the drive."

"Very good. Out."

He turned back to the Tampies. "You heard, Rrin-saa?"

"I heard, Rro-maa."

"All right. Figure out who you'll need to come to Shadrach with *Amity*; the rest should start getting the lifeboats ready to fly. All three of your Handlers should stay with Pegasus, of course."

Rrin-saa hesitated. "Your wishes are ours," he whined.

"Keep trying to get Pegasus moving," Roman said, heading for the door. "If you succeed, head out immediately. I'll be on the bridge if you need me."

Amity's corridors were already beginning to hum with activity as Roman emerged from the Tampy section and headed forward. Ferrol was waiting for him when he arrived at the bridge. "Stolt says it'll take about an hour to bring the drive up," he told Roman. "I told him not to cut any corners, that it would take that long for us to get the lander and lifeboats ready, anyway."

"Good." Roman took a moment to run a quick status check, then cocked an eyebrow at his exec. "So what is it you need a private moment to discuss?"

Ferrol's eyes bored into his. "To put it bluntly, Captain, I don't trust the Tampies."

"You mean as in they may be faking Pegasus' illness?"

"No, sir. I mean as in making a run for it once Pegasus is well again . . . whether *Amity*'s back yet or not."

For a moment Roman studied the younger man. The ghosts of Prometheus seemed to swirl behind those eyes . . . and Roman thought about those ninety-seven unfavorable questionnaires. "I think that highly unlikely," he said at last, "but there's no particular need to take even that small a chance. We certainly can't leave the bulk of the survey section out here without a contingent of ship's crew along to look after them . . . so you'll have plenty of people to watch the Tampies, too."

It took a second to register; and then Ferrol's eyes widened. "*Me*, sir?"

"You, Commander," Roman confirmed. "I'll need a list of the people you'll be taking with you within half an hour. Make sure it's a compatible bunch—*Amity*'s got her share of intercrew squabbles, and there won't be room for any friction on the boats."

"Yes, sir." Ferrol's tongue swiped briefly across his upper lip. "Sir . . . with all due respect, I'd prefer to stay with the *Amity*."

"I know you would, Commander," Roman said, "but I don't have any other choice. Someone with command authority has to stay with Pegasus, and I'm going to need both Kennedy and Stolt here with me. That leaves you."

Ferrol took a deep breath. "Yes, sir," he said, his voice stiff with protest. He turned back to his station without further comment.

Roman watched the other's back for a moment, then turned to his own console. There were orders to be given; but before he got enmeshed in that, there was a crucial question that still had to be settled.

The computer's opinion, delivered a minute later, was clear but ominous: *Amity* could survive the trip to Shadrach, even without using Pegasus as a shield . . .

but only as long as B's energy output stayed at or below current levels. At a two-gee acceleration—the maximum that Tampies could handle for long periods—it would take them over twenty-five hours each way.

And the white dwarf's next burp could come at any time. If it happened in the next fifty hours, *Amity* was going to fry.

We humans thrive on slim odds, he'd told Rrin-saa. He could only hope that hadn't been all bravado. Clearing his screen, he keyed for the computer's pager. "Call Lieutenants Kennedy and Marlowe to the bridge," he instructed it.

The blazing plumes of superheated plasma from *Amity*'s fusion drive were visible long after the ship itself was too far away to be seen. Ferrol watched through the lander's rear viewport as they grew steadily fainter; and after a few minutes, they too were lost in the glare of the twin stars.

Amity was gone.

Ferrol gazed after them a moment longer, conflicting emotions churning within him. Roman had played the danger down, but Ferrol had run all the numbers on his own before leaving the ship, and he knew the dimensions of the razor-edge monorail Roman had sent *Amity* skating along. If the star gave off with one of its burps before they reached Shadrach, the ship was most likely gone.

Leaving him in command.

He grimaced. In command of a disorganized mob of scientists, few of whom had any idea which end of the lander was which, most of whom were likely to be far more trouble than help if push came to shove. In command of a group of ship's crewers who knew damn well what was going on, and were edgy as hell because of it.

In command of a group of Tampies.

Ferrol turned away from the viewport and sent a sour look around the lander interior. Surrounding him on all sides was a three-dimensional chaos of people and equipment, a hell designed for the terminally fastidious. Near the middle of the storm floated Dr. Tenzing, bellowing out instructions to his people as best he could through a filter mask; a little ways away Weapons Chief Garin was doing similarly with the crewers.

And beyond them, in a little pocket of calm at the lander's nose, were the Tampies.

Sitting together in their compact little group—and even in zero-gee Ferrol's mind insisted on defining their odd cross-legged stances as *sitting*—they remained for the most part silent and motionless. Occasionally they spoke quietly together, or touched each other, or ducked their misshapen heads to peer out past the cluster of lifeboats at the dark shape of Pegasus floating a kilometer away. One of them moved slightly, giving Ferrol a brief glimpse of Sso-ngii, his eyes unblinking beneath the bulky amplifier helmet, and an even briefer glimpse of the disgusting animal tied in to that helmet.

They were planning something—of that much Ferrol was certain. The only question was . . . what?

Kicking off the wall, he headed forward, and with unexpected luck managed to intercept Tenzing between orders. "Doctor," he nodded. "How are your people doing?"

"We're almost set up," the other said, his voice sounding a little hoarse. "We should be able to get going in, say, ten or fifteen minutes."

"Good. I presume I don't have to tell you to push it."

Tenzing's face wrinkled, and Ferrol guessed that beneath the filter mask the other was probably giving him a tight smile. "I hold a minor degree in astrophysics, Commander," the scientist said. "I know considerably better than you do just exactly what a nova does to its immediate neighborhood."

"I don't want to see it close up, either," Ferrol agreed. "Let's make sure we don't have to."

He gave his handhold a push and floated over to the port side, where Garin was hovering at the midship viewport. "How's everything look?" he asked.

"As good as can be expected," Garin grunted. "I was just giving the lifeboat tethers a visual inspection. They seem solid enough."

"All right. When you've got a minute I want you to go find Yamoto and have her move us around into Pegasus' shadow. No particular rush, but make it soon—we don't have *Amity*'s shielding, and there's no point in sitting out here picking up heat and radiation when we don't have to."

"Yes, sir," Garin nodded. "And after that?"

Ferrol pursed his lips. "After that . . . I want you to keep an eye on the Tampies for me."

Garin's eyebrow twitched. "Anything in particular I'm supposed to watch for?"

"Something underhanded. Attempting to Jump without the *Amity*, if and when we get Pegasus back to normal. Maybe some kind of crazy sabotage scheme—for all we know, Rrin-saa may have saddled us with a suicide squad here. I don't know what they're up to—but they're up to *something*. I can feel it."

Garin looked at the group of Tampies. "Me, too, sir. Don't worry; I'll watch them."

"Good. And if you catch them at anything—" Ferrol hesitated. "Well, just let me know. Privately."

"Yes, sir," Garin said softly. "I'll do that."

Ferrol nodded and pushed away. In his inner tunic pocket, the tiny needle gun felt very large.

Chapter 10

Amity was still four hundred thousand kilometers from Shadrach, and Roman was catnapping in his chair, when B burped.

"You're sure?" he frowned, studying his displays as he fought to brush the cobwebs from his brain. B's energy output curve didn't seem to have changed significantly.

"Yes, sir." Marlowe touched a key, and a velocity plot appeared on Roman's scanner repeater display. "The dwarf's blown off a thin shell of plasma, and it's expanding outwards at nearly four hundred kilometers per second. For the moment the shell's blocking off the extra radiant energy, but that won't last long. As soon as it spreads itself thin enough for the light to get through . . . well, we'll be in a little trouble."

"How long?" Roman asked, punching for course status.

"A few minutes at the most."

Roman nodded grimly. *Amity* was already decelerating toward Shadrach, but at the two gees she was pulling it would take them an hour and forty-six minutes to reach the safety of the planet's umbra. "Kennedy?"

Her fingers were already moving across the helm keys. "We could turn the ship, sir, and accelerate for a few minutes before turning again and decelerating," she offered doubtfully. "But flipping over twice would almost certainly eat anything we gained in the process."

And simply increasing their deceleration rate wouldn't do any good, either, Roman knew: it would bring *Amity* to a stop sooner, but leave them stranded far short of the planet.

Unless . . .

He keyed for a large-scale position plot, holding his breath . . . and the gods were indeed kind. The larger of Shadrach's two moons was almost directly on *Amity*'s heading, and was a good three hundred thousand kilometers closer to them than Shadrach itself. "Course change, Kennedy," he ordered. "We're going to try for the dark side of Shadrach's moon. Execute as soon as you've got the numbers, then compute deceleration and ETA and see how much time that'll buy us. Marlowe, get me an estimate of B's brightness behind that expanding shell and send the numbers back to Stolt—I want to know how long the hull will be able to take it. Then check Kennedy's ETA and see if it's going to be enough."

He felt a slight sideways tilt as *Amity* began the task of changing its direction the required few degrees. The bridge creaked a bit as it rotated slightly to accomodate; and then the straight-line motion came back, and Roman fought against the opposite tilt until the bridge finished the inverse correction. "Course change executed," Kennedy reported. "If we run a constant eight-gee deceleration from here we'll reach the moon in just under twenty-seven minutes."

"Marlowe?"

"It'll be damned tight, sir," Marlowe grunted. "The drive nozzles will take the brunt of it, and they're a lot more heat-resistant than the hull itself. But we're not exactly dead-on to the star; and even if we rotate slowly so that each section of the hull gets equal exposure, we'll still reach the theoretical danger point in fifteen to twenty minutes."

Roman nodded. "What else have you got, Kennedy?"

"Not much, sir," she shook her head. "We can cut it to twenty minutes by shutting down the drive and maintaining our current speed for nine minutes, but that'll mean doing the last eleven at twelve gees."

Eleven minutes of twelve gees. Eleven minutes of hell for the ship and its human crew . . . and maybe far worse for the Tampies still aboard. *Could* Tampies even survive twelve gees? Roman keyed his intercom. "Rrin-saa?"

The alien's face appeared. "I hear, Rro-maa."

"Rrin-saa, we're in a crisis situation here," Roman told him. "We're going to have to pull eleven minutes at twelve gees or *Amity* isn't going to make it. Can your people take that?"

A shadow of emotion might have crossed Rrin-saa's face; Roman couldn't tell for sure. "I do not know," he said. "I know Tamplissta have survived eight gees for short times; that is all." He paused. "Your wishes are ours, Rro-maa. You must do what is necessary."

Roman gritted his teeth. "Lay in your course, Kennedy. Signal for dangerous acceleration. Rrin-saa . . . good luck."

The drive cut off; and as the warning alarm began to hoot, Roman's chair unfolded into its acceleration couch mode. He snuggled down into it as best he could in zero-gee, feeling the contour cushions adjust to his body, and watched the displays. He'd done everything he could, and now there was nothing to do but wait as the laws of physics played themselves out.

A minute later, right on schedule, the expanding plasma shell broke.

The hull temperature numbers skittered upward, higher than Roman had ever seen them, before falling abruptly as all sunside sensors either cut out or flared into uselessness. The pattern of destruction repeated itself around the entire circumference as the slow rotation Kennedy had put *Amity* into gave each section of hull the same deadly exposure in its turn. Within minutes the outer reflective layer was beginning to show signs of blistering, and the temperature within the ship was rising faster than the cooling system could dump it.

And then the fusion drive kicked back in . . . and Roman gasped for breath as the giant invisible hand jammed him hard into his couch. Jammed him, held him down, did its damnedest to crush the life out of him . . .

The last thought to flicker through his mind before the blackness overtook him was that putting his ship and crew through this high-pressure volcano was a hell of a way to run a rescue mission.

Slowly, as if in disbelief at her survival, *Amity* began to pull herself together.

"—Damage control reports over twenty buckled hull plates. Repair crews are working on the worst of it."

"—Breakage of improperly stowed gear is pretty high, Captain, but nothing vital seems to be lost. We're cleaning it up."

"—The landing was a little rough, but didn't cause any damage to the drive nozzles. We're a few kilometers southeast of the center of the moon's dark side. Rotation period is about nine days, so we can stay put for as long as we'll need."

"—Casualties, Captain. The Tampies report eight dead during deceleration. No deaths on our side, but a number of broken bones and minor internal injuries. A medical team's gone portside to assist the Tampy doctors."

Eight dead. Roman swore, uselessly, under his breath. Eight dead . . . and the fact that they were Tampies almost made it worse. He would have to call Rrin-saa and give his official condolences, of course—

"Captain?" Marlowe called. "I've managed to punch a laser carrier through all that ion-soup static out there. We've got Dr. Lowry's group."

Roman jabbed at his intercom. "This is Captain Haml Roman of the Cordonale Research Ship *Amity*. Dr. Lowry?"

"Here, Captain." The static cleared slightly, giving Roman a glimpse of a snowy-haired man in full pressure suit. His face—what could be seen of it through the helmet—looked haggard. "You can't know how happy we are you're here."

"I'm glad we made it. Where are you?"

"Dark side of the planet. I can give you our latitude and longitude, but that won't help you much—Shadrach rotates once every forty-two hours and we have to keep moving to stay out of the light."

"Yeah." Roman had looked through the viewport at the planet only once. Low in the sky, showing about half a disk, and shining only by light reflected from fairly dark rock, it had still damn near blinded him. "I assume you have some sort of lander down there?"

"Yes—a Sinor-Grayback TL-1. A little cozy for all fifty of us at once, but we can manage."

"Kennedy?" Roman murmured.

"A bit on the large side, sir," she said promptly, "but with our own lander gone there'll be enough room for it in the hangar."

"Thank you. We can handle that, Doctor. How's your fuel situation?"

"We had to abandon a lot of it at the base, and we've used some since then to keep out of the sunlight, but we've got enough left to meet you in orbit whenever you're ready. Assuming it's not too high an orbit, that is."

"I think we'll be able to accomodate you," Roman said. "Now, I understand there's a Tampy group down there, too. Are they with you?"

Lowry shook his head. "I'm afraid they're beyond help, Captain," he said tiredly. "Their encampment was on the sunside when the dwarf first flared up. They're all dead."

Roman felt his stomach tighten into a hard knot. "You're certain?"

Lowry's sigh was just barely audible, and even through the static and pressure suit Roman could swear he saw the other shudder. "We're certain. We went to their encampment as soon as it had rotated to the dark side. They had no warning whatsoever, no chance to escape. If the flare hadn't blown off Shadrach's minuscule atmosphere and sent shock waves through the ground we'd have been caught the same way ourselves." Lowry's hand reached up, as if to run his fingers through his hair, then dropped in obvious embarrassment. "We don't know why the dwarf triggered so soon; it should have been all right for at least another month—"

"We can sift through the details later, Doctor. Are the rest of your people all right?"

Lowry visibly drew himself together. "We're fine—or we will be as soon as we can get out of here. Just tell us when we should lift to meet you."

"It'll be a while yet, I'm afraid," Roman told him, glancing at his scanner repeater display. "We'll have to wait until the light intensity goes down enough for us to get across to you. We're presently on your larger moon's dark side."

Lowry stared. "You're not over Shadrach itself? Captain—" He swallowed and took a deep breath. "Captain, you can't wait that long. Our calculations show that the next flare-up will be the final one."

Roman's mouth felt suddenly dry. "The nova?"

Lowry nodded. "And the intensity won't decrease more than a magnitude or so before that."

The bridge had gone very quiet. "How long have we got?" Roman asked.

"As best as we can estimate, between sixty and seventy hours."

Sixty hours. And it would take a minimum of twenty-five of those to get back to Pegasus . . . "All right, Doctor, we'll see what we can do. *Amity* out."

He tapped the disconnect key, and the static abruptly shut off. It made the silence in the bridge that much more noticeable. Turning carefully—the twelve-gee run had left aches in every muscle—he looked at Marlowe. "You heard all that," he said. "You and Stolt get your heads together and find out how much more the hull can take."

"We've already done that, Captain," Marlowe said. The light-intensity curve on Roman's repeater display disappeared and was replaced by a second curve and a column of numbers. "Commander Stolt estimates the drive nozzles could handle another fifteen hours or so without damage," Marlowe continued, indicating the appropriate part of the curve with his mousepen. "Unfortunately, we can't go from here to Shadrach's shadow in that position—the maneuvering jets don't generate enough thrust."

"How about the rest of the hull?"

Marlowe's cheek twitched. "In twenty minutes she'd start popping seams."

Roman pursed his lips. "What about it, Kennedy?"

"No good, sir," she replied, shaking her head carefully. "If I stay below eight gees we can't make it in less than an hour. And any higher acceleration will just kill more of the Tampies."

Which reminded him, he had some unpleasant news to break to the aliens. He'd have to make time for that soon. "What about putting extra shielding on the hull?" he asked Marlowe. "I know we've got some spare drive plates."

Marlowe's lips compressed briefly. "I doubt we've got enough spares to do any real good, sir, but I'll check." He hesitated, his eyes flicking to Kennedy, and for a moment he seemed to be teetering on the brink of saying something else. The uncertainty won, and he started to turn away—

"You worried about the nova, Lieutenant Marlowe?" Roman asked mildly.

The other seemed to stiffen, and the wince that crossed his face was probably not entirely due to sore muscles. Again his eyes went to Kennedy, a hint of pleading in them.

"I believe, sir," Kennedy spoke up, "that the lieutenant wished to point out that the higher resistance of the drive section means we can head *away* from B anytime we wish to. We have adequate fuel left to do a straight-line drive all the way back to Pegasus, provided we don't waste any of it on the way."

Roman locked eyes with her. "That would leave fifty people stranded on Shadrach, of course," he said. "Are you recommending that we abort the mission? Either of you?"

Just inside Roman's peripheral vision, Marlowe looked thoroughly uncomfortable. Kennedy, directly under his gaze, didn't flinch. "Not at this point, sir," she said evenly. "But if we can't get to them in thirty hours that *will* have to be my recommendation."

The bridge had gone quiet again. "Consider it noted, Lieutenant," Roman told her. "Let's just hope it doesn't come to that."

"Yes, sir."

She and Marlowe turned back to their consoles, and the background hum of conversation resumed . . . and Roman found himself studying the back of Kennedy's head. Wishing her file had spelled out her previous military service a little more explicitly. She'd served on mainline warships, certainly; probably seen actual combat in one of the plethora of interplanet squabbles that had popped up with depressing regularity all over the Cordonale before the Tampy problem had taken everyone's attention away from all such minor disagreements.

It was entirely possible she'd had to abandon people to death before.

He shivered. *Yes, let's hope it doesn't come to that,* he told himself fervently. So far he'd never been forced to send men to die, and he had no real interest in starting now.

And then memory hit him like a splash of ice water, and he felt his face warm with embarrassment and shame.

No, he hadn't sent men to die. Just Tampies.

For a long moment he stared at his intercom, stomach muscles knotting painfully. But the call was long overdue, and putting it off any longer would only make it worse.

As usual, it was Rrin-saa who answered. "Rro-maa, yes?"

"Yes, Rrin-saa," Roman nodded. "I wanted to offer my condolences on the deaths of eight of your people."

"Eleven. Three more have died of internal injuries. We mourn them."

Eleven. "I'm sorry; I didn't know." He hesitated. "I'm afraid there's more bad news from the planet. It appears your research base here was completely destroyed by the first great flare."

Rrin-saa gave the Tampy equivalent of a nod. "This is as expected."

Roman frowned. "You already knew?"

Rrin-saa closed his eyes briefly. "If the Tamplissta had survived there would have been no need for a rescue, Rro-maa. They would have transported themselves and the humans alike to safety."

"Oh. Of course." Which meant, Roman realized, Rrin-saa and the others must have known or at least suspected as soon as the distress call came through. But he hadn't bothered to ask their thoughts on the matter . . . and Tampies seldom volunteered such information. "Again, I'm sorry. I wish things had gone differently."

"As do we. I must leave now, Rro-maa. The mourning continues." The screen went dark.

Stolt's face on the intercom screen looked haggard and vaguely uncertain—the face of a man juggling a dozen crises, all of them clamoring for immediate attention. But there was nothing vague or uncertain about his words. "There's no way, Captain," he said, shaking his head carefully. "Between the spare drive plates, shielding sections, and spray-on ablative material we've got maybe enough stuff to add two extra centimeters to the outer hull. Assuming, that is, that we could spread it all out evenly, which of course we can't."

Roman nodded heavily. "I didn't think we'd have

enough, but it seemed worth checking. Any progress on that reflector umbrella you proposed earlier?"

"We're still doing simulations, but it's not looking especially hopeful," Stolt admitted. "Every material we try can handle either the light *or* the radiation, but not both. Woller's setting up a trial with a multi-sandwiched sort of layering, but I'm not optimistic."

"Captain?" Kennedy spoke up, turning to face him. "Would there be enough spare shielding to adequately cover a lifeboat?"

And then fly it across to Shadrach, cram the scientists in somehow and fly back . . . "How about it, Stolt?"

The answer was prompt enough to show that Stolt had already considered that approach. "No good," he said. "It'd be a mess to fly, for starters—we could only shield one side of the boat, which would throw the center of mass 'way to hell and gone. And even then, you'd only have enough shielding for a one-way trip— too much of the stuff would boil off on the way for you to make it back."

"Unless Lowry's group has something they could use to protect it on the return trip," Kennedy persisted.

Stolt snorted. "If they had, don't you think it would have occurred to them to use the stuff on their own lander?"

"Maybe not," Kennedy countered. "They're astrophysicists, not engineers. Maybe they've got something that would work but don't realize it."

"It wouldn't hurt to suggest it," Roman agreed. "Have one of your people call down to Lowry and get a complete list of the materials they have on hand."

"Yes, sir," Stolt said.

Roman keyed the intercom off and turned to Marlowe. "The radiation going down at all out there, Lieutenant?"

"Ah . . . yes, sir, a little," Marlowe said distractedly, his eyes steady on one of his screens. "Not fast enough, though. Captain, I've just picked up something in orbit around Shadrach. I think you'd better take a look."

Roman frowned at his scanner repeater. A flashing circle marked the spot . . . "A space horse?"

"That's what I thought," Marlowe agreed. "Probably the one the Tampy expedition brought with them—you can just barely see what's left of a ship trailing behind it. The question is, why is the thing still here?"

Roman chewed the back of his lip. For an instant a crazy image flashed through his mind, that of the space horse standing faithfully by like a pet dog, protecting its departed masters . . . "It's probably dead," he said aloud, shaking the picture away. "Killed the same time as the Tampies."

"Or else there's someone still alive on that ship Handling it," Kennedy murmured.

It wasn't impossible, Roman knew. The attached ship looked to be half melted, but if it had been lucky enough to be in the space horse's shadow when the star blew, one or more of the Tampies *could* indeed still be alive in there.

Which led immediately to the question of why any such theoretical survivors hadn't either rescued Lowry's group or ignored them and gotten the hell out of the system. "Have you tried contacting the ship yet?" he asked.

"Been transmitting since it first came out from around the planet's limb," Marlowe said. "No response yet."

Roman grimaced. Rrin-saa and the rest of *Amity*'s Tampies would still be mourning their comrades' deaths, and he'd already interrupted them once. But something told him that this couldn't wait.

Rrin-saa wasn't in the Handler room, but the intercom monitor made quick work of tracking him down. "Rro-maa, yes?" he whined. If he was annoyed at being again taken away from the funeral service, he didn't show it.

"We've found your expedition's space horse," Roman told him. "It's still in orbit around Shadrach. Any ideas as to why it hasn't Jumped?"

For a long moment the alien just stood there, his

lopsided face running through a series of subtle and—to
Roman, at least—unreadable changes. "There is a possibility," he said at last. "The space horse would have
been set in stationary orbit above the ground observers,
with six or fewer Tamplissta as Handlers. When all died
. . ." He paused, and his expression again altered. "You
must know that we feel more deeply toward life than
humans seem to. The sudden deaths of their companions may have caused a *perasiata* reaction in the Handlers and, through them, in the space horse."

Catatonia, in the middle of a dying system. So the
vaunted Tampy empathy could occasionally be a handicap. "When will they all come out of it?"

"The Tamplissta will not. They will be dead now."

Roman hissed between his teeth. For a moment he'd
dared to hope they'd found their ticket out of this mess.
"I'm sorry," he told the Tampy. "I suppose the space
horse is dead, too?"

"I do not know. I know he may be dead or still in
perasiata; that is all."

Roman glanced at Marlowe, pointed at the other's
displays. The other nodded understanding and got to
work. "Suppose the space horse *is* indeed in *perasiata*,"
he said to Rrin-saa. "How could we get it to wake up?"

"I did not say he was in *perasiata*," the Tampy reminded Roman. "I do not know."

Roman clenched his jaw against a flash of anger. This
was not the time for Tampy verbal reticence. "Pretend
just for argument's sake that it is," he growled. "Tell
me how we would wake it up."

"There are methods," Rrin-saa said. "Handlers are
taught them."

Terrific. Handlers could do it . . . except that *Amity*'s
Handlers were all back with Pegasus. "I don't suppose
any of your people here have had any of that training."

Rrin-saa hesitated. "Even if the space horse could be
made to move, he would not have the strength to pull
Amity any great distance."

"It won't need to," Roman shook his head. "All we

need is its shadow to hide in—we have more than enough fuel to fly to Shadrach under our own power. All we'd need is someone with Handler training who'd be willing to ride a heavily shielded lifeboat over there and try to wake the space horse up."

Again, Rrin-saa's face went through its subtle contortions. "Very well," he said at last. "Prepare your lifeboat. I will go."

Roman blinked. "You?"

"I have had Handler training. It is my task."

Roman gazed at him. A short, ugly creature whose features hovered midway between the macabre and the thoroughly ridiculous . . . calmly volunteering to risk his life to save what was, to him, a group of semi-dangerous aliens. "I can't order you to go out there, you know," he reminded the other, moved by some vaguely insistent impulse to make sure the Tampy understood fully what he was letting himself in for. "It'll be dangerous—possibly fatal—"

Something in Rrin-saa's face made him stop. "Do you still not understand us, Rro-maa?" the Tampy said softly. "Our duty is to all living things; to respect them, and the balances and natural hierarchies within which they exist. As sentient creatures we have great power to alter these balances. With such power comes equally great responsibility. We do not choose the role of caretaker. It is, instead, thrust upon us as the price paid for the gift of sentience."

It was a philosophy Roman had heard many times before. But always from Tampy apologists and supporters, never from one of the Tampies themselves. "And so you risk your life to help save a group of humans?"

Rrin-saa touched fingers to ear: a shrug. "You are neither creature nor caretaker, Rro-maa; and yet are both. We do not yet fully understand you. But we are learning."

Unbidden, a shiver ran up Roman's back. He'd often wondered just what the Tampies' motivation had been in agreeing to join the *Amity* project. Dimly, he wondered what sort of report Rrin-saa would be bringing back. "I appreciate your willingness to go," he told the other. "Let's hope it works."

"For the space horse's sake, as well as the humans'," Rrin-saa said. "He, too, is worth saving, if such is possible."

"Agreed," Roman nodded. And if it wasn't possible to save it, the creature might still have enough strength left in it for one last Jump. If it did, *Amity* might not have to run that perilous gauntlet all the way back to Pegasus.

Assuming, of course, that Pegasus had recovered from whatever was bothering it. For a moment his thoughts went back to Ferrol and the others waiting for them . . .

Resolutely, he forced his mind away. Whatever was happening back there was far beyond either his control or his assistance. "We'll get the lifeboat ready," he told Rrin-saa. "It'll take an hour or so—we'll let you know."

"I will be ready," Rrin-saa said.

Roman blanked the screen and looked up at Marlowe. "Anything?"

"There's no way to tell, sir," the other said, shaking his head in obvious frustration. "All the readings I can get through that plasma soup out there come up ambiguous. It could be alive; it could be dead."

"All right. Call Stolt and have them get started on the lifeboat." Bracing himself, he turned to Kennedy. Now came the sticky part. "We're going to need a volunteer to fly this thing," he told her. "A pilot who can handle something as lopsided as the boat's likely to turn out."

"MacKaig's the one you want," Kennedy said promptly. "She's had experience with both tugboats and mine-sweepers. I'll call her up here."

Roman stopped her with an upraised hand. "Make it crystal clear to her that if the space horse out there is dead this is a suicide mission."

Kennedy smiled tightly. "She'll go," she said. "She's

not exactly what you'd call trusting when it comes to Tampies."

It was a long time before Roman understood the logic behind that last cryptic comment. It wasn't until the lifeboat was ready to launch, in fact, that it and Rrinsaa's reference to saving the space horse finally clicked together.

There was no simpler way for the Tampies to save the space horse, after all, than to wake it up and let it Jump.

Chapter 11

The tiny speck of brilliant light was like a lost diamond floating against the background of icy-cold stars. "Well?" Ferrol demanded as Tenzing pulled back from the telescope panel, blinking as his eyes adjusted from the dazzle of the distant asteroid to the relative darkness of the lander.

"It's definitely getting dimmer," the other reported, sounding even wearier than he looked. "I don't think it would be safe to leave Pegasus' shadow yet, though."

"I wasn't planning on doing that," Ferrol told him, listening to the frustration rumbling in his stomach as he gazed out at the pinprick of light. Without any tethered instrument packs available aboard the lander—and with the radiation flood from B's last burp far too intense for anyone to go out from Pegasus' shadow for a direct measurement—they'd been forced to improvise. Analyzing the reflected light from the asteroid out there was crude, but it was the best they'd been able to come up with. Unfortunately, of all the scientists aboard only Tenzing had ever had actual field experience in estimating stellar magnitudes without instruments, and those days were far in his past.

Not that accuracy was really needed. A single glance at the asteroid was all it took to know that B was still too blazingly hot to risk direct exposure to it.

And if the light and radiation this far out was this bad . . .

"You think *Amity* could have survived?" Tenzing asked quietly.

Ferrol shook his head, the movement generating a quick flicker of light-headedness. It had been almost thirty hours since *Amity*'s departure, and he'd had barely five hours of sleep in that time. Not that staying awake to run things had made any appreciable difference. "There's no way to know until we can move out around Pegasus and try raising them on the radio or laser," he told Tenzing. "If the captain pushed their acceleration above the two-gee mark for any of the trip, they ought to have had time to get into the planet's umbra before the balloon went up."

And if they hadn't . . . but there was no need to spell that scenerio out. Tenzing and everyone else on the lander and lifeboats had by now run that one out to its logical conclusion.

"Yeah," Tenzing breathed. "Well . . ." He shivered.

"What's the latest on Pegasus?" Ferrol asked, more to change the subject than for any other reason.

"No appreciable change," Tenzing told him with a sigh. "The dust sweat chemistry is still way off all our standard benchmarks, though it seems like it might be coming back just a little."

"Anything dramatic happen when the big burst came?"

"No. Not even anything *un*dramatic, as far as we could tell. The Tampies said the same thing regarding its mental condition, by the way."

"Yes, I'd heard," Ferrol grunted, passing up the chance to tell Tenzing just how much trust he had in the Tampies' word. Still, it was looking more and more likely that whatever was bothering Pegasus wasn't related to the extreme conditions outside. "So that leaves us back where we started: fatigue or illness."

"Looks that way," Tenzing agreed soberly. "Unfortunately, without any way to treat either condition, the diagnosis seems more or less academic."

"And of course the Tampies don't know anything that could help."

Tenzing gave him an odd look—the words must have come out with more venom than Ferrol had intended. "They're doing what they can, Commander," he said. "You have to realize that none of *them* has ever seen a space horse in this condition, either."

"Sure." *Or at least*, Ferrol thought sourly, *they won't admit to it*. The thought still nagged at the back of his mind that *Amity*'s Tampy contingent had been selected as a suicide crew, though what the Tampies could hope to gain by *Amity*'s destruction he couldn't guess. "I gather nothing ever came of the vanadium test?"

"Not a whisper," Tenzing said with a grimace. "As far as the dust sweat goes, the stuff just disappeared."

Ferrol nodded. Vanadium had been one of the trace elements in Pegasus' normal dust sweat that hadn't been seen since the Jump to this system. On Dr. Sanderson's recommendation Ferrol had ordered some instruments and tools rich in vanadium to be dumped overboard. Pegasus had promptly telekened them into a feeding orifice, but there had been no other reaction from the huge creature. Then, or in the six hours since. "Maybe we should try again with a different trace element," he suggested. "Pegasus has stopped passing, what, eight of them?"

Tenzing shrugged. "We could try, but I really think we'd be wasting our time. Nutritional deficiencies just don't come on that quickly."

"Maybe not with normal animals," Ferrol growled. "With space horses, who can tell? Besides, it's as good a way to waste our time as any, at least until we find out the real problem."

"There's that," Tenzing conceded. "Though if the Tampies can't figure it out, I doubt that we—"

He broke off in midsentence as Ferrol's hand lashed out to clamp hard around his upper arm. "I don't want to hear that again," Ferrol told him icily. "Not from you, not from any of your people. The Tampies aren't omniscient, they aren't supermen, and you damn well will *not* behave or think otherwise. So they commune with nature and love all the humble creatures of the universe?—fine. *We* bend nature, and do what we like with it; and if Pegasus doesn't want to Jump, we will damn well find a way to *make* it Jump. With or without the Tampies' help."

"Understood, Commander," Tenzing muttered, his eyes wary.

"Make sure you do," Ferrol said, releasing his arm. "Now get back there and find me a cure."

Tenzing swallowed. "Yes, sir," he said. Without another word, he turned and kicked off back to the impromptu laboratory.

I shouldn't have chewed his head off, Ferrol thought, a touch of embarrassment seeping through the frustration and fatigue and worry. But Tenzing had more than once shown a quiet awe toward Tampy opinions that occasionally flirted with hero worship, and Ferrol had no intention of letting the aliens' passive wait-and-see-what-happens attitude soak into the only people who could get a handle on Pegasus' mysterious ailment.

His eyes strayed to the bow of the lander and the Tampies . . . and abruptly he forgot about both embarrassment and the subtle dangers of defeatism.

The aliens were no longer merely sitting cross-legged in a rough three-dimensional circle around the Handler. Instead, they were clumped tightly together, each with a solid-looking grip on one of the Handler's arms or legs. The Handler himself was rigid, distorted face contorted into something even stranger.

And on the amplifier helmet, half the indicator lights had gone red.

"Garin!" Ferrol snapped, launching himself toward the bow; but he was too late. Without warning Pegasus gave a violent lurch, throwing the lander sideways and pitching Ferrol headlong into the back of one of the couches.

He was still scrambling for a handhold when the

space horse lurched again, throwing him back into the air. The warble of the acceleration warning cut through the sudden confused babble, and Ferrol had barely enough time to get a grip on a couch headrest before a burst from the lander's engines shoved the craft forward. Yamoto, on pilot duty, was fighting to keep the lander in Pegasus' shadow. "Everyone strap in!" Ferrol bellowed over the dull roar. Not that anyone needed to be told. The burst lasted perhaps three seconds before cutting off, returning them to zero-gee. "Garin!" Ferrol barked again.

"Here, sir," Garin's voice snapped from right behind him. "What the hell's happening?"

"I don't know," Ferrol returned, pulling hard on the headrest and hoping fervently that there wouldn't be any more bumps until he reached the bow and could strap into one of the seats there. "Come on—let's find out."

Pegasus lurched again before he got there, but this time Yamoto was ready for it and was able to use the maneuvering jets to smooth most of the jolt out. Reaching the row of command chairs, Ferrol jammed himself into one and grabbed for the straps. "Sso-ngii?" he called, eyes searching the freshly jumbled tangle of Tampy bodies for the chief Handler's red-white tartan neckerchief. "Sso-ngii, where the hell are you?"

"I hear, Ffe-rho," the grating voice came from near the middle as the Tampies took advantage of the momentary lull to untangle themselves.

"Glad to hear it," Ferrol snarled. "What the *hell* was that all about?"

"Pegasunnninni is not . . . well," Sso-ngii said, hesitating noticeably on the last word.

"Oh, really," Ferrol snorted. "It seems a damn sight healthier than it's been for the past day and a half."

"You do not understand, Ffe-rho," Sso-ngii said. "Pegasunninni is not well. We must release him."

Ferrol felt something cold run up his back. "We must *what*?"

"We must release—"

"Yes, I heard you," Ferrol cut him off. "I just didn't believe it—not even from Tampies. What do you mean, release it? Release it where?"

"Release him to—release him to be free," Sso-ngii said, uncharacteristically stumbling over the words. His slight form seemed unnaturally tense, but whether from fear or something else Ferrol couldn't tell. "He must be made free or he will die."

At Ferrol's side, Garin snorted. "Oh, *right*," he said. "Let it go, just like that? What kind of scitte-headed idiots do you think—"

Ferrol waved a hand in front of Garin to shut him up. "*Why* must Pegasus be freed?" he demanded, forcing his voice to remain calm. Sso-ngii's tension was strangely contagious.

For a moment Sso-ngii hesitated. Then, almost reluctantly, he opened his mouth wide behind his filter mask—the Tampy equivalent of a shaking head. "I do not know," he said.

"What do you mean, you don't know?"

"I cannot explain it, Ffe-rho—" The Tampy broke off as Pegasus again lunged and Yamoto again fought to keep the lander and attached lifeboats in the space horse's protective shadow. "I do not know why he will die. Only that he will."

Ferrol twisted to look over the chair back. "Tenzing!" he called. "What're you getting on Pegasus' dust sweat?"

"There wasn't anything new in the last sample," Tenzing called back, his voice trembling against obvious efforts to control it. "But that was nearly an hour ago. What's happening?"

"We don't know," Ferrol told him shortly, thinking hard. The way Pegasus was lurching around, Tenzing's usual collection method was probably out of the question. "Garin, get an EVA team suited up," he told the man beside him. "I want them to get over to Pegasus and take a fresh sample."

"Yes, sir," Garin said. Ducking his head once to

glance out the forward viewport at Pegasus, he un-strapped and kicked off aft, collecting a pair of crewers on the way.

"You must allow Pegasunninni to be freed, Ffe-rho."

Ferrol turned back to face him. In his pocket, the little needle gun was a hard lump against his side. "Do you know what'll happen if we unweb the space horse?" he asked quietly. "It'll Jump, that's what. Leaving us here to fry in the light and radiation out there."

Sso-ngii floated silently for a moment. "I do not believe Pegasunninni will Jump," he said at last. "Not immediately. He does not yet have the strength and ability to do so."

"It's got more than enough strength to whip us around like a kid's pull-toy," Ferrol countered. "What makes you think it can't Jump?"

"I do not know," Sso-ngii answered, a trace of some-thing that sounded almost like frustration in his voice. "I know he must be freed; that is all."

"And you'd stand by that recommendation?" Ferrol demanded. "Even if it means you yourself will die? And I mean right *now*, and in considerable pain."

The Tampy's face twisted even further than usual, into something that could have been interpreted as a vaguely sardonic smile. "You waste time, Ffe-rho," he whined. "There are no threats. If I am wrong, and Pegasunninni Jumps, then all of us will die."

Ferrol glared at him . . . and for a handful of heart-beats all of his anger and contempt for the Tampy race seemed to narrow itself into laser-focus on the single individual floating before him. Calmly devious, unreadably tight-lipped, blandly unconcerned with risks—Sso-ngii was for that instant everything Ferrol hated about Tampies. His hand hovered beside his pocket, and the needle gun hidden there, and he had the almost over-whelming urge to draw it. To draw it, to see if that lopsided face would show any fear before he shredded it beyond recognition.

But he resisted the urge . . . because in the midst of

all the churning emotion within him he knew that he had no real choice. Releasing Pegasus was a hell of a risk to take, but if they didn't do so one of the space horse's twitches would be violent enough to throw the lander and lifeboats out into full sunlight.

And if remaining webbed did indeed somehow kill the space horse, then everyone in the system was dead. Themselves, the *Amity*, the trapped scientists; everyone. Guaranteed.

Sso-ngii was right . . . and Ferrol hated that the most.

"Garin!" Ferrol called, twisting to look over his shoulder, the bitter taste of defeat in his mouth. "Suit up three more crewers—people with EVA-work experience. We're going to loosen the webbing around Pegasus, see if that helps any."

"And if it does not?" Sso-ngii asked.

Ferrol grimaced. "Then I guess we'll have to try taking it off entirely," he said without turning around. "For now, you just concentrate on getting the damn beast back under control."

"Your wishes are ours," Sso-ngii said, and fell silent.

Ferrol ground his teeth together, his eyes on Garin and his EVA crew. *Given your feelings about the Tampies*, Roman had asked him at the beginning of this voyage, *are you certain you're willing to trust your life to them?*

Ferrol hadn't been sure of the answer then. Now he was.

And if Sso-ngii was lying—if Pegasus Jumped and left the men and women under his command to die—then it was as sure as hell that the Tampies would be the first to go. In as much agony as Ferrol could arrange.

Guaranteed.

Chapter 12

"Contact in one minute," Marlowe announced, and Roman shifted his attention from the hull repair work to the lifeboat monitors. There was little to see; MacKaig was coming in on the space horse's dark side, and the low-level lighting she was using disappeared into the creature's energy-absorbent surface without a glimmer. Only the thin strands of the Tampy harness were visible, floating somewhat loosely against the creature.

"I'm approaching a rein line," MacKaig's voice said, just audible above the static. "Rrin-saa has gone into his trance or whatever, and Hill and Sievers are waiting to link us up."

"Marlowe?" Roman murmured.

The other shook his head. "Still no way to tell if it's alive or not."

The bridge's background of quiet conversation faded into silence. *It* has *to be alive*, Roman repeated to himself. Space horses were theorized to have evolved in the energy-rich accretion disk of a black hole—surely a few days in B's enhanced sunlight couldn't have killed it already.

On the display, the space horse twitched violently, taking Roman's heart with it. "MacKaig?" he snapped.

"I'm on it, sir," her voice came amid the static as she

matched the motion. "They're getting the line connected . . ."

"Got it," Sievers's voice cut in. "Take it, Rrin-saa."

Roman held his breath; but there was nothing but static from the lifeboat. "Rrin-saa? What's happening?"

Something like a wheezy sigh penetrated the crackle. "He is alive, but is very weak," the Tampy said in a voice Roman could hardly recognize as his. "He has suffered badly from the radiation."

"Can it make the round-trip flight out here and back?"

"I do not know. It may be too much for him." Another sigh. "But we will try."

"Captain, we're moving," MacKaig announced.

"Confirmed," Marlowe said a moment later. "ETA . . . oh, at least ten hours at the acceleration they're pulling."

"Good enough," Roman nodded. It *was* a bit slow; but on the other hand, Lowry's calculations indicated they had the time to spare, and pushing the space horse for more speed at this point might be dangerous. "Stay on them, Marlowe. Keep a sharp eye for any problems."

"Yes, sir."

He gave the display one last look, then keyed for a status readout. *Amity*'s repairs were progressing well; with luck, the ship would be ready by the time the space horse reached them. "Kennedy, when you've got your course plottings ready, I'd like you to throw together a status summary and shoot it out to Commander Ferrol's position. Laser only, and put it on indefinite repeater. Tell him to expect us in about fifty hours." He hesitated; but it had to be said. "Also tell him that if we haven't arrived by the time the star starts blasting again that he's to take off *immediately* and make his own way back to Solomon."

"Yes, sir," Kennedy acknowledged, as glacially calm as if he'd just given her his dinner order. "May I remind the captain that they're almost certainly sheltering behind Pegasus and out of reception range?"

"I realize that," Roman told her. "But we have to try.

They don't know that the next burp will be the nova, and by the time they figure it out it's likely to be too late."

"Understood, sir." For a moment her eyes locked with his, and it wasn't hard to read the thought there: if the space horse limping in from Shadrach had indeed been crippled by overexposure to the double star's radiation, what was that same radiation doing to Pegasus?

It was a question Roman didn't really want to think about.

Twelve hours later the space horse dipped briefly into the moon's shadow, keeping well back from the body itself. *Amity* was waiting, and together they headed back into the deadly passage.

"Getting a little radiation spillover from the space horse's side," Marlowe reported as they left the moon's penumbra. "Not as bad as the simulations had thought it might be, though."

"Is the umbrella helping any?" Roman asked him.

"Definitely," Marlowe replied. "Particularly against the visible light, but it's absorbing a decent fraction of the neutron flux, too."

Roman nodded. The "umbrella" had been the inspiration of someone in Stolt's engineering section: a thin layer of silvered plastic held a couple of meters out from *Amity*'s hull by a central strut and stiffened by ribs of memory plastic. The latter had been the big obstacle to the operation—*Amity*'s synthesizers could generate the stuff only so quickly—until someone had thought to check the survey section's records. The organic memory bones and muscles that had so startled everyone on that first planetary survey two months ago had turned out to be not only easier and faster to synthesize than the standard varieties, but also had a significantly larger neutron-capture cross section, as well. "Keep an eye on it," he instructed Marlowe. "We'll want to jettison it if and when it becomes more trouble than it's worth." He keyed for the lifeboat. "Rrin-saa? This is the captain. How's the space horse doing?"

There was a long pause. "His condition is worsening," Rrin-saa said, the words coming out with difficulty. On the display his eyes seemed flat and oddly glazed. "I do not know if he will survive the trip."

Roman rubbed his thumb and forefinger together. "MacKaig?"

"I have to agree, Captain," she said grimly. "We started with an acceleration of barely 0.1 gee; our deceleration at rendezvous was three-quarters that. The way things are going, we'll be lucky to reach Shadrach in eighteen hours."

Eighteen hours to Shadrach, and then twenty-five back to the *Amity* . . . with the nova possibly going off as early as forty-six hours from now. Their leeway was getting thinner by the minute. "Marlowe? Radiation status?"

"Still too hot out there for a solo trip to Shadrach," the other shook his head. "The hull plates would last maybe an hour or two."

And they would need to keep some of that strength in reserve for the twenty-five-hour trip back to Pegasus. "That's it, then," Roman said. "We stay with the space horse as long as possible and keep our fingers crossed. Kennedy, you'd better start updating the ETA every fifteen minutes and feeding the numbers to Lowry's group—I want them ready to make orbit as soon as we're in position to pick them up."

"Yes, sir."

MacKaig was right: the space horse was definitely losing strength. There were periods when it simply drifted, allowing itself to be pulled by Shadrach's gravity; and as the hours dragged by those periods began to stretch ever longer.

And finally, with Shadrach's disk filling the displays, the creature gave up.

"I'm sure it's dead, Captain," MacKaig said, her voice under tight control. "It hasn't done anything but fall

planetward for the past twenty minutes. And Rrin-saa
. . . he doesn't look right."

Roman frowned at the appropriate display. Rrin-saa's
face beneath the amplifier helmet was strangely blank.
"Rrin-saa?" he called. "Rrin-saa, what's happening?"

There was no response. "Sievers, get that helmet off
him," Roman ordered, already keying his intercom for
Amity's Tampy section. "I'll find out from the Tampies
how to break him out of this." He leaned toward the
intercom—

"There is no need."

Roman jerked his eyes back to the display, throat
muscles tightening reflexively. Rrin-saa's whiny voice
was very alien; dry and brittle and almost animalistic—a
voice that Roman had never heard before. And yet,
behind the alienness there was at the same time a rich
and very human sadness. It was an unnerving combination, and it sent a chill up Roman's back. "Are you all
right?" he asked when he could get his tongue moving
again.

"Yes, Rro-maa," the Tampy assured him. Already his
voice was returning to normal. "He is dead."

Roman took a careful breath. "I'm sorry," he said.
"MacKaig? That's it, then. Pop your tether line and get
back here. We'll stay in the shadow until you're aboard,
then probably have to make a run for it. Kennedy?"

"The space horse will enter Shadrach's shadow before
it hits," Kennedy said promptly, "but if we stay with it
the whole way we'll go too deep into the planet's gravity well."

"Plot us a compromise," Roman told her. "Something
that'll expose us to minimum sunlight without using up
large amounts of fuel."

"Already plotted, sir. We'll leave the space horse's
shadow in exactly eighteen minutes."

"Good. Stand by to execute as soon as the boat is
aboard. And inform Dr. Lowry that this is it."

Thirty-seven minutes later, securely planted in a stable orbit, *Amity* waited as the dagger of blue flame that marked Lowry's lander rose to meet it.

The rendezvous was an anticlimax, but a distinctly welcome one. Roman had worried that the smaller craft wouldn't be able to match *Amity*'s horizontal velocity and would crash violently into the forward hangar at bulkhead-smashing speed. But Lowry's pilot had planned correctly, spending the last of his fuel in a burst of acceleration as *Amity* swept down on him. The meeting was accompanied by a great deal of noise and a considerable jolt, but nothing vital was broken.

"Welcome aboard," Roman called via intercom to the hangar. "You'll be shown to acceleration couches; strap into them immediately. Acceleration in five minutes."

He switched off and turned to Kennedy. "You ready?"

"Yes, sir," she said, her course plot appearing on Roman's helm repeater display. "We break orbit and drive straight away from Shadrach, staying in its umbra as long as we can. Then we blast laterally to get back to Pegasus. That gives B more time to cool down and also puts us farther out before the hull gets any direct sunlight."

"Even then," Marlowe put in, "we'll probably still have to shut down the drive occasionally and rotate sternward to B to let the hull cool."

Kennedy nodded. "I've figured that in. We should reach Pegasus in approximately twenty-seven hours."

Trimming their leeway time down to just about an hour. "How's the radiation look out there?" Roman asked Marlowe.

"Dropping off nicely," the other said. "We shouldn't have any real problem with that." He craned his neck to look at Roman. "It should be safe enough now for Commander Ferrol to sneak a quick look now and then from around Pegasus' side."

Roman had already come to that conclusion. In fact, his own calculations indicated that that safety level had been reached nearly an hour ago.

Without bringing any message from Ferrol.

"He may decide to play it safe, though," Kennedy said into his quiet fears. "Or his laser may not be able to cut through the interference out there—it wasn't designed for this kind of soup."

Or perhaps Pegasus had gotten well, and had already Jumped. If Sso-ngii and the other Tampies hadn't been able to adequately control it . . . "There's no point in speculating about it," he said. "Whatever's going on out there, we'll know all about it in twenty-seven hours . . . and until then, there's not a damn thing we can do about it anyway. Sound your warnings, Kennedy, and let's get out of here."

Chapter 13

"Commander?"

The voice was little more than a husky whisper, and for a long moment Ferrol wasn't sure whether it was real or merely another of the surrealistic dreams that skittered continually through the deadly twilight consciousness that seemed to be suffocating the life out of him. But, "Commander?" the voice came again; and this time the dream also contained a gentle shaking of his arm. Wearily, resentfully, he dragged his eyes open.

It was Yamoto, her face drawn and shiny with sweat. "Commander, it's my turn on duty," she croaked.

"Ah," Ferrol said. He took a careful breath, and immediately wished he hadn't: the air was even more like the residue of a blast furnace than he remembered. "How're things back there?" he asked, licking parched lips.

Yamoto shrugged. Like everyone else on the lander, she'd long since taken off her tunic, but Ferrol hardly noticed the view. "About the same as an hour ago," she said. "People keep drifting in and out of consciousness."

"Like me, for instance," Ferrol nodded, fumbling with the straps pinning him to the helm chair. For some reason of shape or focus, the lander's bow was about five degrees hotter than its stern, and he'd had to order that command duty up here be limited to an hour at a stretch.

That order not including the Tampies, of course. For a moment he gazed at them, huddled together at the very tip of the bow, and not for the first time it occurred to him that nothing he could have done with his needle gun could possibly have been worse than what they were going through at the moment.

Visible out the forward viewport beyond the Tampies, sheltering together in what there was of the lander's shadow, were the lifeboats, looking for all the world like baby ducks beneath their mother's wing. Briefly, Ferrol wondered how they were faring, then put it out of his mind. Exposed to slightly less of the godawful sunlight, and with a larger surface-to-volume ratio for dumping their excess heat, the lifeboats were probably doing at least as well as the lander. And even if they weren't, there wasn't anything he could do about it until the *Amity* returned.

If it ever did.

"Radiation counter's gone out again," Yamoto said.

Ferrol focused on the control panel, and with some effort found the proper display. Sure enough, it was blank, its electronics having given up the ghost. "Last time I checked it we were way below any danger level," he assured her, trying to remember exactly when he'd made that check. "That shell of matter the star blew off way back when was the worst of it—the levels started dropping as soon as that passed." He gave the rest of the instruments a cursory check, noting that despite having rigged extra heat radiators the lander's interior temperature had still risen another half degree in the past hour.

"Nothing more from the *Amity*?"

Ferrol waved his hands, the gesture half frustration and half resignation. "As long as they stick with the laser exclusively, how could there be? We were lucky to have picked up the one transmission from Shadrach's moon."

"I suppose so. Are we still broadcasting a homing—? Oh, there it is," she broke off her question as her eyes found the radio display board.

"For all the range it's got out there," Ferrol grimaced. "They've probably got as good a chance of picking us up visually as they do of finding a beacon signal in all that static."

Assuming, of course, that there would actually be someone out there to look for them . . .

"Commander?"

With an effort, Ferrol brought his attention back to her. "Sorry," he muttered, reaching for the straps before remembering he'd already loosened them. "Never thought growing up in a planet's temperate zone would someday turn out to be a handicap." He got a grip on the chair arm, eased himself out of the squishy clutch of the molded contours—

He had just about worked himself free when there was a quiet beep from the radio display.

The panel beeped again before his numbed mind even registered the sound; and it wasn't until the fourth beep that he realized that it was coming from the beacon's transponder.

The *Amity* had arrived.

He dived for the panel, fingers fumbling with the main transceiver switch. "Lander to *Amity*," he called toward the microphone, hoping fervently that the visual display was still operational. "Lander to *Amity*."

"*Amity* to lander," Roman's voice boomed out of the speaker. "Commander Ferrol?"

"Yes, Captain," Ferrol said. Behind him, he could hear a sudden stirring as crewers on the brink of heatstroke dragged themselves awake to the realization that the long ordeal was almost over. "It's good to hear your voice, sir."

"Same here," Roman said. Belatedly, the visual came on; and through the static Ferrol could see the frown on the captain's face. "We have visual contact with you now . . ." His voice hesitated, and the frown deepened noticeably.

"You're wondering about Pegasus?" Ferrol prompted.

Roman looked briefly to the side, to where Marlowe was probably saying something. "We seem to be having some problem with our scale program," he told Ferrol.

Ferrol shook his head. "No, sir, it's not the scale," he assured the other. "Pegasus is gone, all right. Jumped about fifty-three hours ago."

Roman's frown shifted a fraction, toward what was probably the scanner repeater display. "Then what—?"

"—is that thing out there?" Ferrol finished for him. "A farewell gift from Pegasus, actually." He looked at the aft-camera display, at the short cylindrical shape framed aura-style by the sunlight behind it. "Captain; meet Junior. Pegasus' calf."

He looked back at Roman . . . and thanked whichever gods had permitted the visual display to function. The expression on the captain's face was all he could have hoped for.

For the tenth time—Ferrol had kept track—the tiny needle poked not quite unobstrusively into his skin; and then, thankfully, it was all over.

"That's the last of them," *Amity*'s medical officer said briskly, throwing the release lever and swinging up the top of the automed. "Ten precancerous growths, Commander. Not bad, really, considering all the radiation exposure you had out there. We got them all, of course."

"Glad to hear it," Ferrol said, getting gingerly out of the shiny box and pulling on his pants. The worst thing about automeds, he'd often thought—aside from their resemblance to high tech coffins—was the way the damn things demanded the total surrender of one's dignity. "I'd hate to have put up with those needles for nothing. I gather there wasn't anything deeper?"

"Not that we could detect," the doctor assured him. "Though we'll be doing follow-up tests on you for the next few weeks, just to be sure. Or, rather, *someone* will be doing them," he amended, a bit wistfully.

"Right," Ferrol grunted, busying himself with the fasteners on his tunic. Of course the other would be sorry that the *Amity*'s mission was nearly over—he'd always been one of the more simpering pro-Tampy types aboard. "You'll excuse me; the captain left orders I was to report to him as soon as I was finished here."

He escaped to the corridor, and air not quite so thick with maudlin sentiment, and made his way forward to Roman's office.

"Commander," the other nodded gravely as Ferrol entered. "I don't suppose I have to tell you that you've made it into the history books."

"*Amity* has, anyway," Ferrol demurred politely. "I don't expect to be more than a referenced footnote, myself."

"You're too modest," Roman said. His eyes seemed to search Ferrol's face. "The man in charge of the first captive breeding of a space horse will certainly rate more than just a footnote."

Ferrol forced himself to match the other's gaze. "May I assume Sso-ngii told you I threatened to kill them before the calving?"

Roman's face didn't change. "Not in so many words, but I'm slowly learning how to read between Tampy lines. You want to tell me why?"

"You mean why I threatened them? As in, why would I threaten creatures who blandly told me to, in effect, destroy our exit ticket out of hell, but who then wouldn't offer the slightest explanation as to why I should do so?"

"They wouldn't because they couldn't," Roman interjected mildly. "The Tampies have never been able to breed their space horses."

Ferrol shrugged. Perhaps; but on the other hand, he wasn't yet willing to believe that the Tampies hadn't had at least an inkling of what was happening before the bulge in Pegasus' side had made it obvious. After all, the term "calving" came directly from the Tampies—a reference to the similarity between space horse reproduction and glacial splitting—and to Ferrol that implied strongly that, somewhere along the line, the aliens had witnessed the entire birth process. Possibly even including the parent space horse's physiological distress . . . which Rrin-saa had also denied having any knowledge of.

None of which was provable, of course, at least not from aboard the *Amity*. "The fact remains, sir," he said instead, "that I had no way of knowing whether they were right, wrong, or lying through their teeth. Going for some sort of ritual mass suicide, maybe, and inviting us along for the ride."

"Though it turned out that they *were* right," Roman pointed out.

"*This* time, yes," Ferrol countered. "And even then, some of us damn near died."

"Yes, I've read the preliminary medical report," Roman said soberly. "In hindsight it would have been nice if we'd thought to leave you some extra shielding or reflector material. But of course we had no way of knowing you were going to trade in an eight-hundred-meter space horse for a hundred-meter calf."

Ferrol felt his hackles smoothing back down. Apparently Roman had been merely interested in his side of the incident, not spoiling for a confrontation. "Yes, sir," he said. "It was just dumb luck that we were able to free Pegasus and get Junior webbed up before they oriented themselves and Jumped off somewhere together."

"Yes, Sso-ngii was impressed with your crew's speed." Again Roman seemed to search Ferrol's face. "He said you seemed to know exactly what you were doing."

"As I said, dumb luck," Ferrol told him evenly. "And a good EVA crew." If the captain was hoping for some guilty confession of Ferrol's past poaching activities, he was going to be disappointed.

Though if he was, he didn't show it. "And you kept Junior instead of Pegasus because . . . ?"

"I thought that Pegasus' pre-nova problems might not all have been related to the calving process," Ferrol said. It wasn't the whole truth, but it was plausible enough to pass as such. "If so, we'd have a better chance of getting Junior to Jump us out of there when the time came."

"A gamble," Roman agreed. "That's the way of life, it seems. We stack the odds as best we can, then just throw the dice and see what happens." He glanced up and out his viewport, toward the netting and Junior. "In this case, we seem to have broken the bank."

Ferrol nodded. They had indeed. "By the way, where exactly are we?"

"Oh, just a minor midway system," Roman told him. "It was the fastest and easiest place to Jump to after we linked back up with you. A red dwarf star, a couple of frozen planets—nothing of any real interest. We'll spend a couple of days swinging around it to get into position, then do what Kennedy says will be a quick double Jump to first Sirius and then Solomon."

"Good." Ferrol got to his feet, balancing carefully in the half-gee Junior's acceleration was giving the ship. "Then with your permission, I'll get started on the debriefing."

Roman frowned. "What debriefing is that?"

"Dr. Lowry's team, of course," Ferrol said. "I assumed it would be standard procedure in a case like this to get their verbal reports down on tape as soon as possible. And since you *did* assign me to be ship's science liaison, it seems to me that I should be the one handling it."

"That's not exactly what I had in mind when I gave you the assignment," Roman pointed out, still frowning. "And anyway, after what you've been through you probably ought to spend the rest of the trip either in sick bay or in your own bed."

"I appreciate your concern, sir," Ferrol said stiffly, giving his voice what he hoped was just the right touch of professional pride. "May I remind the captain that everyone else aboard—himself included—has had an equally rough time of it the past four days?"

A faint smile touched the captain's lips. "Point noted," he conceded dryly, easing what Ferrol guessed were probably still rather stiff shoulder muscles. That twelve-gee race to Shadrach's moon he'd heard stories about was one for the books. "Very well, Commander. The last thing I want right now is any more heat—from *any*where. If you want to do the debriefings, you're welcome to them."

It took until nearly the end of the debriefing interviews, but eventually Ferrol found the man he knew had to be there.

His name was Kheslav, and he was one of Lowry's equipment technicians. "I was afraid the Senator would just throw me to the lions," he muttered, his face twitching as he looked around the conference room for at least the fifth time since Ferrol had shut off the recorder. "Abandon me to face whatever happened alone."

"Well, obviously he didn't," Ferrol told him. "Almost too obviously, as a matter of fact. The message about your predicament came in over Admiral Marcosa's signature, with a thirty-hour time delay to boot. He might as well have put neons all over it and officially invited a backtrack."

Kheslav's head jerked back around, his eyes wide with nervous guilt. "You think anyone will do that?" he breathed.

"Probably not," Ferrol growled, sorry he'd even mentioned it. Kheslav was rapidly showing himself to be a mixture of all the personality characteristics that Ferrol hated most in people: lack of any real conviction or commitment to whatever it was the Senator had sent him out here to do, lack of any courage whatsoever, and a blathering tongue on top of it. "So tell me why Marcosa wanted the *Amity*—and presumably that means he wanted *me*—to be here when you were picked up."

Kheslav licked his lips. "I have a datapack in my cabin," he said, his voice lowering conspiratorily. "Lowry never knew, but my real job on Shadrach was to study the Tampies' space horse. It was going to be there for several months, you know—day in and day out, in the same place, where we could monitor it continuously—"

"Yes, I understand," Ferrol cut him off. "Part of the *Amity*'s job was to do the same sort of thing."

"Right." Kheslav looked around the room again. "The thing is, we had some monitors attached to the space horse's webbing—without the Tampies knowing, of course—with everything funneled back to a receiver either direct or through a pair of tight-beam relay satellites. When B blew the first time—and all the Tampies died?—well, I have a complete record of the light intensitites and types of radiation the space horse took, as well as a lot of the stuff going up and down the rein lines." He lowered his voice still further. "And since some of the instruments were on the shielded side, away from the light, and you were in line of sight with us when you came over in the space horse's shadow . . . some of that data goes right up until the end." He fixed Ferrol with a suddenly intense stare. "You understand what that means?"

Ferrol did indeed. It meant that, for the first time ever, humanity would know exactly how to kill a space horse.

It was like a moment of truth, a moment that should have been filled with a deep and profound silence. Typically, Kheslav babbled right on through it. "You see the problem, then, with me trying to take the datapack home myself," he said, waving his hands helplessly. "With all the publicity and attention—especially now with this calving thing—I'm not going to be able to just walk past the university people with a private datapack I'm not letting anyone see—"

"So I gather you want me to take charge of it?" Ferrol cut through the flood.

"If you would," Kheslav said, obvious relief on his

face. "I figure you can just hide it somewhere aboard the ship for now, and then later get it to the Senator—"

"Yes, thank you, I think I can handle it," Ferrol growled. "When I've finished interviewing the rest of your party I'll come by your cabin and pick it up." He let his gaze harden, just a bit. "And after that I don't expect to see or talk to you for the rest of the trip."

"Sure." Kheslav nodded with puppy dog eagerness. "Sure, I understand. I really appreciate this, Commander—"

"Good-*bye*, Kheslav."

"Yeah." Awkwardly, Kheslav got to his feet. "Uh . . . yeah. Good-bye."

For a wonder, he was silent as he left the room.

Two hours later Ferrol was back in his cabin, wedging the datapack with only moderate difficulty alongside the needle gun in his lockbox. Alongside the gun, on top of the Senator's envelope . . . and for a moment Ferrol paused, staring at the bulkhead separating him from the Tampy section as he savored the bittersweet taste of irony. The Senator had placed him aboard the *Amity* for the express purpose of sabotaging the ship's mission; of making sure that, with or without his direct intervention, this experiment in human-Tampy cooperation was a total and embarrassing disaster.

Instead, it had succeeded in doing something no human or even Tampy had ever done before . . . and with that event, Ferrol's task had turned on its head.

Now, he was going to have to do his damnedest to make sure that the *Amity* experiment was allowed to continue.

He smiled tightly as one more irony of it struck him. He'd had a space horse calf within his grasp once before— had seen then the possibilities such a creature presented —and it had been Roman who snatched it from him. Now, it was that same man whose ship had given humanity this second shot at building its own space horse fleet.

And even if space horse calves proved uncontrollable by human handlers . . . Ferrol's gaze dropped once more to the datapack. It would be unfortunate, but it wouldn't be a total disaster. With the Pegasus calving, and now Kheslav's data, the Tampy domination of space travel had come to an end.

One way or another, it had come to an end.

Sealing the lockbox, he replaced it in its underbed storage drawer, and returned to his duties.

Chapter 14

The shuttle's engines gave one final burp and cut off, and for a few seconds Ferrol fought the usual brief battle with nausea as his system made its adjustment back to free-fall. The adjustment seemed to take longer than usual . . . but then, he was seldom this weary during such transitions.

He sighed, and looked around him. A shuttle, the Senate crewers had called it; but they might as well have labeled it a yacht and been done with it. A rich man's yacht, drafted into allegedly public service with a few rows of seats bolted into what had probably once been a dining room or conference room or something. Not that the alterations had done much to dent the atmosphere—infinitely-adjustable seats with individual built-in entertainment systems were hardly likely to be mistaken for standard Starforce-issue acceleration couches. Listening to the rumbling in his stomach, Ferrol wondered sourly if having someone throw up all over their flying glitter-room would do anything to bring the visiting senators back into the real world. From the evidence to date, he doubted it.

"Commander Ferrol?"

Ferrol looked up before he realized the voice was coming from the seatback behind him. "Yes?" he said.

"Captain Mendez's compliments, sir; he'd like to see you on the bridge at your earliest convenience."

Ferrol frowned. Some kind of trouble? "On my way."

He found the release and pulled it, staying where he was for the couple of seconds it took the safety harness to remold itself and retract smoothly into the seat again. The bridge, he'd seen when they entered, was three compartments forward, just ahead of a ready room and a closet-sized box the yacht's downgrade renovation had left apparently unused. Easing to the aisle, he gave himself a push forward and headed for the door.

It opened as he reached it, closing behind him almost before he'd gotten fully inside. A flicker of light—identity scan, possibly—and then the inner door slid open and he floated through into the ready room.

"Good evening, Chayne."

Ferrol reached out a hand to steady himself on one of the nearby seats, relief that there wasn't an emergency mixing with annoyance that he'd jumped to that conclusion in the first place. In retrospect, he should have expected something like this. "Good evening, Senator," he replied, coolly polite. "Been promoted to captain, have you?"

The Senator's lip twitched in a momentary smile. "It seemed safer to have the call put in the captain's name. Personal entertainment systems aren't supposed to leak over, but there's no reason to take unnecessary risks."

Ferrol pulled himself down into a seat, his eyes flicking to the bridge door a couple of meters away as he strapped himself in. "I'd have thought your being here at all would come under that heading, sir."

"They're all my people in there," the Senator assured him, raising one hand to study a fingernail. "You know, Chayne—forgive my bluntness—you seem rather less than satisfied with the way the hearings went today."

Ferrol snorted. "You noticed that, did you?"

Deliberately, the Senator raised his eyes from his examination. "We've noticed. Believe me. All of us."

Ferrol felt his face growing warm. "Sorry," he muttered.

For a long moment the Senator eyed him without speaking. "I'm sure you'll understand," he said at last, "that you're the last person we would have expected to see passionately arguing a Tampy point of view. I'm sure you'll also understand how such an abrupt change in attitude is likely to make our friends nervous."

"I am *not* arguing a Tampy point of view," Ferrol growled. "I'm arguing that, in this particular case, we happen to have as much to gain from an extension of *Amity*'s mission as do the Tampies. I don't know how to make that any clearer than I already have."

"Oh, your position is clear enough," the Senator shrugged. "It's your judgment that's in question."

Ferrol's annoyance was starting to simmer into anger. "This isn't some half-assed idea I came up with on the spur of the moment, Senator," he reminded the other stiffly. "I've thought that space horse calves were humanity's best bet since long before you put me aboard the *Amity*."

"Indeed," the Senator said dryly. "Yes, your warhorse concept is quite well known among our group. Some of us feel it almost qualifies as an obsession, in fact—which is a major part of our concern. What evidence do you have that space horse calves would be more responsive to human control than the adults are?"

"Absolutely none," Ferrol said. "What evidence do *you* have to the contrary?"

The Senator's lip twisted in a way that always made Ferrol feel like a stubborn and not very bright child. "Let me spell it out for you, Chayne, in terms you apparently haven't thought of. Assume for a moment that Junior wasn't a fluke, that there really *was* some factor in *Amity*'s mission or crew that induced the breeding. Assume further that we can reproduce the results at will and are at some point able to make off with one of the calves. What do you think the Tampy reaction will be?"

"They won't be exactly happy about it—"

" 'Won't be happy' doesn't even begin to cover it," the Senator cut him off sharply. "In case it's escaped your notice, Chayne, the Tampies see themselves as the guardians of nature in general and of space horses in particular. Stealing a calf out from under their noses for research purposes could well trigger a full-scale war that we're emphatically *not* ready for."

With an effort Ferrol unclenched his teeth. "Then we don't steal the calf," he said. "We find some way to experiment on it without the Tampies knowing what we're doing."

The Senator raised his eyebrows. "And how do you suggest we do that?"

"I don't know," Ferrol shot back. "You have the idea people—ask *them*. Assuming *they* haven't lost their nerve, too."

The Senator's face darkened. "Such things take time, Ferrol. Time, and money, and planning. You'd probably have to stay on the *Amity* for several more months, possibly as much as a year."

"Whatever it—what?" Ferrol stared at him. "What do you mean, *I'd* have to stay on the *Amity*?"

The Senator gazed at him. "The only way the committee will authorize a breeding mission for the *Amity* is if at least fifty percent of the original crewers and *all* of the senior officers agree to stay with it. Until we know what—if anything—the actual trigger mechanism is."

Ferrol stared at the other, his anger turning into something icy. "Is that what all this was about?" he demanded. "Getting me worked up so that I wouldn't have time to think about signing away another year of my life for you?"

"Consider it a test of your nerve," the Senator countered coolly. "This is *your* vision, after all. If you don't have the commitment to see it through . . . ?" He shrugged.

It was emotional manipulation of the most blatant sort—deep within him, Ferrol could see that clearly. But the knowledge of what the Senator was doing to him didn't help in the slightest. As the Senator had undoubtedly known it wouldn't. "I'll stay with the *Amity* as long as it takes," he gritted out. "Just be damn sure you find a way to get one of the calves."

"Assuming there are calves to be gotten," the Senator agreed. His goal achieved, all the challenge in his voice and manner was gone again, leaving behind the slightly cynical detachment that Ferrol had always associated with the man. "I suppose we'll just have to wait and see."

"Yes," Ferrol said shortly, fumbling for the release with a hand that still shook slightly with emotion. *Just like a damn clockwork robot,* he thought bitterly. *He just flips a switch, and I do a little dance.* "If that's all, I'll be getting back to my seat."

"One more thing, Chayne." The Senator paused, and Ferrol thought he saw the lines around the other's mouth tighten, just a bit. "Keeping all of *Amity's* senior officers aboard means that Erin Kennedy will be staying, too."

Ferrol cocked his head. "You say that as if it should bother me."

The Senator snorted under his breath. "Perhaps it should. Are you aware that she took a reduction in rank to join the *Amity's* original mission?"

"I'd heard that, yes," Ferrol said slowly, forehead wrinkling in thought. He'd never had much social contact with Kennedy, but she'd never struck him as anything but highly competent in her bridge duties.

Perhaps *too* competent? Or was the Senator just jumping at shadows? "You think she's some kind of plant?" he asked. "Military Intelligence, maybe?"

"Could be," the Senator admitted. "So far we haven't been able to dig out just why she's there . . . but we *do* know she was originally slated to be executive officer, and that implies strongly she's a darling of the pro-Tampy side. So watch her, Chayne. Watch her very closely. Especially if . . ." He raised his eyebrows significantly.

Especially if and when it came time to use the envelope. "I'll watch her, sir," Ferrol nodded grimly. "I still have the gun you gave me."

"Good," the Senator said. "I don't doubt you'll be able to deal with her if and when it becomes necessary. But bear in mind always that, as far as you're concerned, she's the most dangerous person on the *Amity*." He nodded once, briskly. "Now; I understand you have a package for me."

With an effort, Ferrol switched gears. "Yes, sir: Kheslav's datapack. I'll bring it to the hearings tomorrow morning."

"You'll get it for me now."

Ferrol paused, floating above his seat. "What, while the shuttle's running its pre-return checks? Won't it look a little odd for me to dash off *Amity's* hangar deck and then come charging right back again?"

"I don't especially care what it looks like," the Senator said, his voice abruptly icy with command. "I want the datapack, and I want it now."

For a long minute Ferrol locked eyes with him . . . but it was no contest. "Yes, sir," he growled. "With your *permission*, Senator, I'll return to my seat now."

"Just one more thing, Chayne." The Senator's eyes bored hard into his. "I didn't much care for the way you spoke to me a few minutes ago. I don't want you to ever again suggest that I've lost my nerve—in fact, I don't want you to ever even *think* it. Do I make myself clear?"

Ferrol swallowed. "Perfectly clear. Sir."

Which was not to say, he thought darkly as he returned to his seat, that it wasn't true. . . .

The shuttle docked with the *Amity* half an hour later, and the preparations for its return planetside were still being carried out when Ferrol returned from his stateroom with Kheslav's datapack.

The Senator accepted it without a word, though with what Ferrol imagined to be a suspicious set to his mouth. But if he wondered why the errand had taken Ferrol so long, he didn't ask about it.

Perhaps he didn't have to ask. Ferrol wasn't worried about it one way or the other. Twice in a single brief discussion he'd gotten the uneasy feeling that the Senator and his friends were starting to lose it . . . and if they were, it would be all too easy for their copy of the Kheslav data to be somehow mislaid.

And even if they weren't, it was just good sense for there to be an extra copy of the data. Somewhere no one would think of looking for it.

One month later, with much the same crew but a new space horse, *Amity* left Solomon and headed again into deep space. Its mission this time was a laserstat copy of its first: the preliminary investigation of four Tampy-discovered planets. There was no way to duplicate the pre-nova experience, even if anyone had been damnfool enough to risk it; as a substitute, Roman took the ship into the expanding gas cloud of a planetary nebula.

Three months later they returned to Solomon with datapacks full of scientifically exciting numbers and a new space horse calf towing their lander.

On its third mission the *Amity* investigated a pulsar and a nearby Wolf-Rayet system. On its fourth, it did nothing but examine various sections of the interstellar medium.

By then it was clear to even the most cautious members of the Senate and Admiralty that the actual content of the mission didn't seem to matter. Nor, apparently, did the fact that interpersonal conflicts forced a large turnover of crewers and scientific personnel each time. At the end of each voyage, the *Amity* returned with a new calf.

And on the last day of the preparations for its fifth mission the Senator finally—finally—made his move.

Chapter 15

The man standing beside Ferrol was tall and gangling, with the sort of faraway look in his eyes that Roman had always associated with heavy drug use. That drugs were not involved, though, was clear from the orders the man had brought aboard the *Amity* with him.

In a way, Roman thought as he skimmed the orders, that almost made it worse. It meant that that look was a normal part of the man and would probably be with him for the entire mission.

Flipping off the reader, Roman turned his full attention to his visitor. "Well, Mr. Demothi," he said. "An intriguing experiment, to be sure. You'll forgive me if I remain skeptical."

Nodin Demothi's expression remained serene. "The Senate was skeptical, too, Captain," he said. "As was the Starforce Admiralty before them, and the Sinshahli Psych Sciences Institute before them, and the University before them." He nodded toward the orders. "None of them remained so for long."

"Perhaps," Roman said. "On the other hand, dolphins and whales share a home planet and a great deal of history with humanity. Space horses are totally alien."

Demothi shrugged minutely. "So are Tampies, but I

was able to communicate with several of them during my time on Traklee-Kyn."

"Which may mean even less than your cetacean studies," Roman pointed out. "Your Tampy partner at the other end of the amplifier helmet could have been doing all the work."

Deep down, Roman realized, part of him was trying to spark a reaction—any reaction—from the man. He'd have done better with a lump of concrete. "I understand your disbelief, Captain," Demothi said, his face and body language remaining totally placid. "I've run into the same hostility a thousand times, from a thousand different people, and my detractors have always come away silenced. All I ask is the chance to prove myself."

And unfortunately, Roman had no choice but to give him that chance. The orders Demothi had brought with him were clear, explicit, and without any latitude whatsoever. "My orders guarantee you that chance, Mr. Demothi," he told the other, a sour taste in his mouth. "But understand this: if I find any reason to suspect that your contract is endangering the life or well-being of the calf, that one chance will be all you get. Is that clear?"

Demothi pulled himself to his full height, a gesture that would have been a lot more impressive in a man half again his weight. "One chance will be all I'll need."

"Fine." Roman glanced at Ferrol, who after making the introductions had stayed carefully out of the conversation. "I presume you've made arrangements for Mr. Demothi's quarters?"

"Yes, sir," Ferrol said, his voice and face neutral. He needn't have bothered; it didn't take any of Demothi's alleged psychic powers to see Ferrol's anti-Tampy friends moving in this. "I've assigned him to the number four cabin in D section. The one vacated when the Starforce shuffled the organizational table and decided we really didn't need four geologists anymore."

"Such convenient timing," Roman commented dryly.

He watched Ferrol's rigid lack of reaction for a moment, then turned back to Demothi. "You ever been on a military spaceship before?"

"I spent a few days on one during my Starforce tests," Demothi said. "I've also flown several times on passenger liners. Lately, much of my travel has been with Tampy ships."

"Well, you're going to be in for some adjustment, then," Roman said, pressing a button on his desk console. "Life aboard *Amity* doesn't resemble a passenger cruise much—more scheduled and less private, for starters. We'll be in free-fall a fair amount of the time, too."

Demothi's eyes flicked to the viewport, where the stars were tumbling past in time to *Amity's* axial rotation, and quickly looked away. "I understand. I can handle it."

"We'll also probably be in deep space for several months," Roman added. The door buzzed and slid open to reveal a young crewer. "The mean time of our mission has been ninety-eight days, the longest having been 134."

"I understand," Demothi said again.

Roman pursed his lips. He hadn't really expected to scare Demothi off his ship, but it had still been worth a try. "As long as you know what you're getting into." He gestured to the waiting crewer. "Kliment here will escort you to your quarters and help you stow your gear. We'll be staying in orbit around Solomon for another five hours."

Demothi ducked his head in an abbreviated bow. "Thank you, Captain. I'll do my best to stay out of everyone's way." Turning, he and Kliment left, the door sliding shut behind them.

Roman turned his attention to Ferrol. "So. Opinion, Commander?"

"About what, sir?" Ferrol asked.

"Demothi, of course. You think he has any chance?"

Ferrol cocked an eyebrow. "The Senate must think

he has," he said. "I can't see them going this far out on a limb on wishful thinking alone."

"True," Roman agreed. "Unless, of course, he's here for some other purpose entirely."

Ferrol might have twitched. Roman couldn't tell for sure. "What other purpose could there be?" the other asked. "A secret inspection of some sort?"

"I'd think that highly unlikely," Roman shook his head. "The only thing *Amity* does of any real interest these days is to midwife space horse calvings, and all except that first one have been fully recorded. What would an observer see that the cameras haven't?"

"The crew's performance, maybe," Ferrol suggested. "Or possibly the Senate's still interested in human/ Tampy interactions. That *was* the original reason for putting this ship into space, after all."

It was indeed . . . and with only four voyages under *Amity*'s belt, the most optimistic of the pro-Tampies had probably already conceded defeat on that point. Not even the excitement of being part of something as rare and awesome as a space horse calving was enough to dampen the anti-Tampy feelings that invariably grew among the human crewers; and despite the prestige and public attention the *Amity* was starting to attract, less than thirty percent of any given crew signed up for the following mission. Aside from the senior officers and the Tampies themselves, only ten of *Amity*'s original crew had made it through all four of its voyages. "I seriously doubt that anyone still thinks of us in those terms anymore," Roman told Ferrol. "No—whatever Demothi's here for, it has to involve the calving. If all he needed was a space horse he could go to the corral at Kialinninni and take his pick." He eyed the other. "And that includes this so-called contact experiment."

Ferrol shrugged. "Perhaps. On the other hand, I can think of at least two reasons why you'd want to try this kind of contact with a calf first. One, because a calf might not have the same aversion to humans that they seem to develop later in life; and, two, because the calf wouldn't be nearly as strong as a full-grown space horse. And, of course, completely unable to Jump."

"That last being a major point," Roman conceded, the uncomfortable feeling in the pit of his stomach growing stronger. It all made sense . . . but Ferrol had the arguments just a little bit too down pat. Which meant . . . what? That his friends in the Senate had briefed him on Demothi's true mission? Or merely that he'd been thinking lately about space horse calves and their possibilities? "I suppose we'll just have to wait and see."

"Yes, sir. I really don't think there's any cause for worry, though. I expect he's really just here to try and contact the calf."

Roman sighed. "Well, if he is, good luck to him. I'm sure we'd both agree that human control of space horses is the key to further expansion of the Cordonale—and with an eye to that, it's probably just as well that Kennedy will be handling the lander on this calving."

Ferrol's poker face cracked, just a little. But enough. "Kennedy, sir?" he asked carefully.

Roman nodded. "She's been wanting to have a shot at handling the webbing maneuvers anyway; and with the Senate so hot on "Demothi the Boy Wonder" we'll certainly want our best people out on the lander with him. Just in case any problems crop up."

"Of course, sir," Ferrol said between stiff lips. "I had, however, hoped to ask you to let me be in charge of the webbing this time around."

Roman felt an unpleasant chill run up his back. So his vague suspicions had been right, after all. Demothi *was* up to something, Ferrol knew what it was . . . and it was something he very much wanted to be on hand to participate in.

Or else, he just *didn't* want Kennedy to be there alone. Fleetingly, Roman wondered just what Ferrol's friends had told him about Kennedy. "Well, that shouldn't be a problem," he said, forcing his voice to remain casual. "There's no reason why you can't both go."

For a moment Ferrol seemed to be studying him, and Roman had the odd sense that his own thoughts, mirror-imaged, were running a parallel track through the other's mind. "That should work," Ferrol said at last. "Provided Kennedy won't feel her capabilities are being called into question, that is."

Roman shook his head. "She'll be there for the helm experience," he said. "You'll be there because of your interest in space horse calves. That's all there is to it."

Another brief flicker of reaction. "Yes, sir," Ferrol said. "Thank you, Captain."

"Good. That's settled, then," Roman said, pretending he hadn't seen anything. "You'd best get back to the bridge now, Commander. There's still a lot of work to do before we leave orbit."

"Yes, sir." Nodding, Ferrol turned and left.

For a moment afterward Roman gazed darkly at the door. So it had come at last; the anti-Tampies' response to *Amity*'s unexpected breakthrough. Ferrol, Roman felt sure, he could handle if it became necessary . . . but Ferrol plus Demothi was another matter entirely. And if push came to shove . . .

Involuntarily, he shivered. What, he wondered, *had* Ferrol's friends told him about Kennedy?

New faces were hardly a novelty aboard the *Amity*; but even so Roman expected Demothi to make something of a splash, a prediction that was borne out with a swiftness beyond his most pessimistic fears. Within an hour the news about Demothi and his—possibly—historic experiment was all over the ship; within two hours, it was the major topic of conversation in the lounges and workrooms. By the time Sso-ngii had their new space horse, Man o' War, ease the ship out of Solomon orbit everyone seemed to have formed an opinion about the chances of success, and the arguments began to appear.

And by the time *Amity* made its first Jump, the man had become the punch line of at least two jokes.

It followed immediately that Demothi was going to be a major pain in the neck for all involved; but here, Roman's expectations proved wrong. Demothi wasn't a great deal of trouble; he was, in fact, almost exactly the opposite. Much of his time was spent on the Tampy side of the ship, discussing his upcoming contact attempt with Sso-ngii and the other Handlers and practicing with the spare amplifier helmet. He returned to the human side only for meals and sleep, and since he often ate in the solitude of his own cabin, Roman could often go days at a time without so much as passing him in a corridor. There was no particular reason Roman could see for the other's self-imposed isolation—certainly the psych profile that had accompanied him aboard gave no hint of antisocial tendencies. The most plausible suggestion Roman heard came from Kennedy, who pointed out that Demothi might think he would stand a better chance of making a successful contact if he stayed as aloof as possible from the other humans. Given how little was really known about space horse senses, it was as good a theory as any.

Still, Demothi's space-hermit act didn't help his reputation among the more heavy-handed humorists aboard, and Roman was therefore not at all disappointed when Man o' War began to show the telltale lethargy a mere sixty days into the mission.

"It's started, all right," Marlowe reported, fingers dancing across his keys as he ran comparisons against the data from the previous calvings. "I'd say one more Jump and a few hours' rest and Man o' War will be ready to become a mother."

Roman nodded. "Good. Give Demothi a call—he may need some time to prepare. Commander?—how's the delivery room search going?"

Ferrol had a section of the New Cygni List on his screen; from his chair Roman could see that several of the lines were highlighted in yellow. "Working on it, sir," Ferrol told him. "I think . . . yes, here we go. NCL 11612. Little K-type about four light-years away from here. Couple of gas-giant planets, no known life, completely uninteresting." He turned to face Roman, eyebrows raised questioningly.

"Sounds good," Roman agreed, shifting his eyes to the helm. "Yamoto?"

"Vector worked out, Captain," she reported promptly. "Ready to transmit to the Tampies."

Roman nodded, feeling his stomach muscles beginning to tighten. "Do so," he instructed her. He shifted his attention back to Ferrol, who was still watching him, and the muscles tightened a little more. "You'd best get below, Commander," he told the other. "You'll want to supervise the webbing team's preflight preparations."

"Yes, sir." Unstrapping, Ferrol kicked off for the bridge door.

To supervise the team's preparations, Roman thought after him, *and to make your own.*

Whatever those preparations would include.

Most of the physical arrangements for the calving had been completed far in advance, and the few that required waiting until the last minute were over with in less than an hour. Ferrol's own personal last-minute checklist—consisting mainly of getting the needle gun and envelope from his cabin and slipping them into his EVA pack—took even less time.

Which left him several hours with nothing at all to do. Except think. And worry.

He'd spoken with Demothi perhaps half a dozen times since the voyage began, and had come away from each conversation progressively less certain as to what the hell the senator was up to. Was Demothi really nothing more than what he seemed, a rather fog-bound dreamtype who the senator had found and inveigled onto the *Amity* in response to Ferrol's demands for action? Or was he, in fact, a quiet agent of the anti-

Tampy forces, with some mission above and beyond the contact experiment?

None of Ferrol's delicate conversational probes had gotten him any nearer to finding out. And the uncertainty made him nervous.

They had made the Jump to their target system, and Man o' War had been quiescent for nearly an hour, when the call finally came. "Captain to ready room; Commander Ferrol?"

"Yes, sir," Ferrol called toward the intercom. "Is it time?"

"It seems so, yes," Roman told him. "The dust sweat analysis indicates that you've got perhaps two hours before the calf comes."

Definitely time to get into position. "On our way, sir."

With Kennedy and Demothi following, he led the way to the hangar deck, wondering sourly how long he'd have to wait for the two Tampies who'd be accompanying them to make their leisurely way aft. The cynicism was, for a change, wasted: even as he ducked his head and maneuvered his way through the door he saw that they were already there.

"Ffe-rho?" one grated as both turned.

"Yes," Ferrol acknowledged. Beneath the filter mask covering half the misshapen face a corner of red and white cloth was visible . . . "Sso-ngii?" he tentatively identified the other.

"Yes." The Tampy indicated his companion. "Wwis-khaa will assist."

"Fine," Ferrol said shortly, moving forward to take his place at the command station and keying for status readouts. It was, he realized, a revealing choice of assistants for Sso-ngii to have chosen: Wwis-khaa, according to the crew profiles, was the only Handler aboard *Amity* who'd had any experience with soothing space horses freshly captured in the wild. None of the previous calvings had required any such soft-touch Handling . . . but then, none of them had had Demothi poking around with an amplifier helmet, either. To the best of Ferrol's knowledge none of the Tampies had raised any objections to Demothi's experiment; but it was clear that they weren't interested in taking any chances with him, either.

"Ready to go, Commander," Kennedy reported into his thoughts.

Ferrol shifted his attention back to his own readouts and nodded. "Looks good," he agreed. "Let's do it."

Deftly, Kennedy eased them out of the hangar, swung away from the hull, and headed up the shimmering rein lines toward the patch of starless sky that was Man o' War.

They reached the space horse's curved side to find a stockfloor of activity already in progress. Floodlights from three outlying lifeboats illuminated the area where a hundred-meter-long cylinder was already pushing outward from the dark gray skin. Surrounding it, spacesuited Tampies were snipping carefully through the tight-fitting webbing, giving the bulge room to expand. Fifty meters away, two more lifeboats stood by, the shimmer of slack webbing between them. It was to this group that Kennedy directed their boat, where they would have both a bird's-eye view of the final stages of the calving and would be in position to link up with the brand-new space horse as soon as it was secured.

As yet there was hardly enough data to define a "textbook" space horse calving; but if one was ever written, Ferrol decided, Man o' War's would probably be close to the mark. Two and a half hours after the bulge first appeared the space horse's skin abruptly split, opening like a long toothless zipper along the calf's entire hundred-meter length. Seconds later the new space horse drifted free, a shiver rippling through its lighter-colored skin the only sign of life. In theory even such a young space horse had enough telekinetic strength to play havoc with the web boats, but in practice it had never happened and this time was no exception. The calf floated docilely as the boats completed their capture; swinging in right behind them, Kennedy caught the bundle of rein lines in the lander's forward grapple. Seated to Ferrol's left and a row behind him, Sso-ngii stiffened and then relaxed as the rows of tiny indicator lights on the amplifier helmet flicked to green. "That's it, *Amity*," Ferrol said into the mike. "Contact's made. Looks solid."

"Very good, Commander," Roman's voice came back. "Better pull it back a little, as soon as you can. Hhom-jee? Any sign of trouble with Man o' War?"

"Manawanninni is fine," the Tampy's voice cut in. "His recovery is nearly complete, and he shows no sign of stress."

Ferrol snorted under his breath. "Glad to hear it," he said dryly. Their third calving run had resulted in what Hhom-jee had described as "mild stress," and it had taken him and Sso-ngii half an hour to calm the space horse down. He had no desire to be out in a flimsy lander the next time something like that happened. "So. I guess we're ready to try this."

"I guess we are," Roman agreed, with only a slight hesitation. "We'll move a few kilometers away from you first, give you plenty of room. Just in case there's a problem."

Ferrol stole a glance at Demothi. There were lines of tension showing through the placid serenity in his face. "Good idea," he agreed. "By the way, have you picked a name for the calf yet?"

"I thought we'd just go with 'Quentin,' since this is our fifth calving."

"Not particularly inventive."

"Our files fail to list the original Man o' War's progeny," Roman said, just a bit tartly.

Ferrol grimaced. In the excitement of the calving, he'd almost forgotten that he and Roman were on opposite sides of war here; that the captain would almost certainly see a success by Demothi as a dangerous destabilization of the fragile truce *Amity*'s breeding program had provided to human/Tampy relations. "Quentin it is, sir," he said.

For a few minutes there was silence, and Ferrol felt occasional tugs as the calf began its first, tentative movements. Most of that motion was away from the lander, and Ferrol watched as Kennedy carefully played out the rein lines to their full half-kilometer length. As if she'd hooked a rare and giant fish . . . He shook the image from his mind. "Better get on with it," he told her.

"Right." Kennedy gave the instruments a leisurely scan. "Okay. Rein lines all the way out and tight; *Amity's* just passed the five-kilometer mark. They're slowing now to zero-vee relative . . . all our cameras are on and transmitting."

"We're in position, Commander," Roman's voice confirmed. "Whenever you're ready."

"Yes, sir." Ferrol turned to Demothi, sitting quietly there between Sso-ngii and Wwis-khaa, and braced himself. "Go ahead."

Sso-ngii removed the amplifier helmet and offered it to Demothi; with only the slightest hesitation, the other took it and placed it carefully over his head. Ferrol held his breath . . . and his brain had just enough time to register the indicators' abrupt switch to red—

And he was slammed hard into his seat as Quentin bolted.

"Sso-ngii!" he snapped, his body automatically gauging the acceleration at about a gee. The calf's full strength, probably—whatever Demothi had done, he'd done a damn good job of it. An instant later Quentin changed to a sideways motion, hurling Ferrol against his harness. The roar of maneuvering jets filled the lander; clamping his jaw tightly to protect his teeth, Ferrol watched as the two Tampies and Demothi fought to retrieve the helmet as it swayed erratically around them on its supporting cables. Quentin changed direction four more times before Wwis-khaa finally got a firm grip on the helmet and jammed it over his head. The lights changed, and the wild run began to ease up.

"Kennedy, figure out our course," Ferrol ordered as soon as he could safely open his mouth again. "We'll want to curve back to the *Amity*—"

"Ferrol—the *Amity*," Kennedy cut him off. "It's *gone*."

"It's *what?*" Ferrol stabbed at his display controls. A complete steradian sweep showed nothing the size of a spaceship out there. "It can't be gone," he said, immediately cursing himself for making such an asinine statement. *Relax*, he ordered himself harshly. *They wouldn't just Jump off and leave us. There's a good and proper explanation here. Somewhere.* "Are we still in the 11612 system?"

"Quentin's supposed to be too young to Jump," Kennedy reminded him, hands playing over keys.

"I *know* what he's supposed to be—"

"And anyway, the spectrum matches," Kennedy added as the computer finished its analysis.

Ferrol pursed his lips. The shock was fading, and he could feel his brain starting to work again. "Did you hear anything on the radio or laser?" he asked her.

She shook her head. "I was running the jets most of the time to try and smooth some of that out," she reminded him, already keying the recorder rewind. "A short transmission could easily have been lost in the noise . . . here we are." She listened a moment on her own headset, then keyed for speaker.

Roman's message was indeed brief. "Lander—Ferrol— Man o' War's spooking. Hhom-jee can't hold it—we'll be back—" The voice and hum of *Amity*'s carrier cut off simultaneously.

Kennedy looked at Ferrol. "I think," she said dryly, "we've just made a brand new discovery about space horses. Isn't science wonderful?"

"Just terrific," he agreed. "How about it, Sso-ngii?" he asked, turning to face Demothi and the Tampies. "You want to tell me why Man o' War would suddenly spook and Jump when *Quentin* was the one who was scared?"

Demothi frowned. "What makes you think he would know—?"

Ferrol silenced him with a look. "Sso-ngii?"

"I do not know," Sso-gnii replied. "I know that sometimes emotions can be communicated between nearby space horses; that is all."

"Telepathy?"

Sso-ngii gave the short fingers-to-ear gesture that was the Tampy shrug. "What is telepathy?"

Kennedy chuckled. "Telepathy: any method of communication we don't yet understand."

Ferrol snorted; but she was right. And anyway, the method hardly mattered at this point. "All right, then, try this one," he said to Sso-ngii. "Assuming Quentin's panic was somehow transmitted to Man o' War, why did Man o' War Jump instead of coming to Quentin's aid?"

"You're anthropomorphizing," Demothi said stiffly. "You can't expect a space horse to act like a human mother."

"Mmo-thee is correct," Sso-ngii said. "Perhaps Manawanninni heard only the calf's fear and Jumped as the calf wished to do." His face twisted even more than usual. "Humans do not understand such complete sharing of feelings."

"No, I think the noble Tampy empathy is probably beyond us," Ferrol grunted. Something on Kennedy's board beeped. "Is that the *Amity*?" he asked, turning to scan his own displays.

Kennedy shook her head. "No—one of the outrider boats has found us with a comm laser. Basically repeating the captain's message."

Ferrol hadn't thought about the fact that the three outriders would have been left behind, too. "Might as well head back to join them," he told her. "Figure a course for Wwis-khaa to follow—I'll get our laser set up and tell them we're on our way."

"Assuming Wwis-khaa can get Quentin to obey," Kennedy reminded him.

Ferrol glanced at the Tampy, noted the glowing rows of tiny green lights on the helmet. "I think anyone who can manage a wild space horse should have no problems with Quentin," he assured her. He turned back—

"But Wwis-khaa won't be Handling Quentin," Demothi said. "I will be."

Slowly, deliberately, Ferrol turned back again. Demothi had drawn himself up to his full height, an affectation which looked even more ridiculous while strapped into a lander seat than it had when standing upright in the captain's office. "What was that?" he asked mildly.

"I said I'll be Handling the calf," Demothi repeated. "My orders from the Senate and the Admiralty—"

"You had your chance," Ferrol cut him off, a flash of anger boiling through him. With all that had happened since Quentin bolted, he'd almost forgotten that Demothi's failure to control the calf was the end of a dream. The end of *his* dream . . . "You had your chance, and it's over."

"It wasn't a fair trial." Demothi's usual passive expression had vanished, replaced by an odd combination of determination and pleading. "It was a new experience, both for me and for Quentin, and neither of us had a chance to adjust. I've been thinking it through, and I believe I know what I did wrong." He took a deep breath. "Please, Commander. Just one more chance."

"In twenty-four hours or so," Kennedy murmured, "Quentin'll be fully capable of Jumping."

Ferrol looked sharply at her, the Senator's veiled warnings about her flooding back. She looked back at him, nothing but mild questioning on her face . . .

And she did, unfortunately, have a damn good point. If Demothi was ever to have a second chance, it had to be while the calf was still too young to Jump. "All right," he ground out, giving an extra tightening tug on his harness. "*One* more chance, and that's it. Wwis-khaa, give him the helmet. Demothi, you concentrate on setting up a stable contact before you try anything fancy like moving—and if you feel Quentin panicking you take the helmet off damn quick. Got that?"

"Yes." Demothi gave him a lopsided smile. "I won't fail."

Right, Ferrol thought sourly. Demothi accepted the helmet from Wwis-khaa and slid it over his head. The indicator lights blinked uncertainly, each flicking between red, orange, and green several times before finally settling down to green. The lander rocked gently once, but nothing worse happened; and as the lights continued their progression Ferrol had the eerie sense of watching history in the making. Demothi was going to make it . . . and then Ferrol dropped his eyes a fraction and focused on Demothi's face.

The man looked like he was going to explode.

"Sso-ngii!" Ferrol shouted . . . but he was too late. With another spine-wrenching tug the lander pulled sharply to the left. Ferrol's eyes came back to focus to find Sso-ngii reaching for the helmet, pulling against the lander's acceleration to try and get it off Demothi's head. The maneuvering jets kicked in again, and as they did so another lurch twisted the lander around, throwing Ferrol's head to face the side viewport and the dim red star visible there.

He was still facing that direction when the star vanished.

Chapter 16

Quentin subsided, and the maneuvering jets cut off, and for a long minute the lander was silent. A hundred curses chased each other through Ferrol's mind, none of them strong enough to adequately cover the impossibility that had just happened. Ahead, the edge of a brilliant blue-white star blazed painfully at them around Quentin's bulk; slowly, Ferrol turned from it to focus on Kennedy's profile. Perhaps sensing his movement, she turned to face him, and for a moment they just gazed at each other in silence. Apparently, a small section of Ferrol's mind decided, Kennedy's repertoire of curses didn't cover this situation, either.

"Well," he said to her at last, "shall we see what we've got here?"

She took a deep breath. "Right. Okay." Slowly, as if still half paralyzed by the shock of it, her fingers began to move across her keys. Ferrol watched them a moment, then turned around.

The two Tampies were sitting quietly, the helmet on Sso-ngii's head showing all green. Between them, Demothi had the expression over his filter mask of a small child who has insisted on carrying the family heirloom crystal and then dropped it. "We'll dispense with any spilled-milk recriminations for now," Ferrol

174

said, fighting to keep his voice calm and controlled. "Wwis-khaa, I want to know how Quentin managed that Jump."

"I do not know—"

"Yes, you do," Ferrol cut him off harshly. "You know, or at least have a good idea. What is it, that space horse calves *can* Jump at birth, but just can't see well enough to lock onto a target star?"

Wwis-khaa tilted his head. "It is possible."

"But it is only a thought," Sso-ngii cautioned. "The Tamplissta do not know for certain."

"I'll settle for good half-assed theories at this point," Ferrol countered. "So. How well could Quentin see? Wwis-khaa?"

The Tampy hesitated. "I do not believe he could see very well," he said at last, mouthing the speculation with obvious reluctance.

Ferrol carefully unclenched his teeth. "Look," he said, fighting hard against a sudden urge to wrap his fingers around someone's neck. "I understand how you hate to repeat anything you don't personally know to be a fact. But try and get it through your heads that we are *lost*; and the only way we're going to find our way back is if we have some answers."

Silence. "Demothi, keep working on them," Ferrol growled, the rage turning into disgust. "Do something useful for a change." Turning away, he focused on Kennedy. "Got anything yet?"

"Not really." Her voice, he noted with relief, was back to its usual iron control. "The computer's still checking the brightest stars, but I doubt the nav program's complete enough to have any real chance of locating us. If this was the *Amity* I could get it for you in three minutes; as it is, all I can say is that we're in a system with a B4 star, we're more than eight hundred light-years from where we started, and we're almost certainly still in the Milky Way."

Eight hundred light years. Ferrol shivered. "Okay," he said. "So. Assume you're Captain Roman, and you come back to find us gone. What do you do?"

Kennedy pursed her lips. "Well . . . if you're right, that it's the calf's vision that limits its Jumping ability, then it should be pretty straightforward. All the *Amity* has to do is pick out the brightest stars visible from the 11612 system and start Jumping until they find the right one."

Ferrol gritted his teeth. Straightforward enough . . . unless Roman decided that this was all some elaborate scheme he, Ferrol, had cooked up with Demothi to steal a space horse calf. If the captain thought *that*, he might try some other response entirely. Such as starting his search with the Cordonale and nearby stars . . .

With an effort he shook the thought from his mind. They were in enough trouble already without going shopping for more. "If that's the case," he said, "I guess our logical response is to conserve our resources and wait." Off in a far corner of his panel, out of the way, was the red-rimmed emergency beacon switch. Reaching over, he flipped it on. "Let's just hope the captain's smart enough to figure it out."

"He is," Kennedy said.

Ferrol winced at the conviction in her voice. Roman was smart enough, all right. The only question was whether he was too smart to waste time with obvious red herrings.

But there was no point in mentioning that to Kennedy. "Well," he said, trying to sound as calm as she did, "as long as we're just sitting here, we might as well get something useful done. I'm going to go back and get the telescope set up; you load the survey program into the computer and get it running. Let's see if this system has anything worth looking at."

Roman watched the outrider recording twice, a cold knot settling all the harder into the pit of his stomach. Gone. A space horse calf, three humans and two Tampies—all impossibly vanished. "Marlowe?" he asked.

He looked up to see the other straighten from his console and shake his head. "Sorry, Captain. The image is just too distant for the computer to scrub it any cleaner."

"So there's no way you can tell me which way Quentin was pointing when they Jumped."

He hadn't meant the words to sound like an accusation, but Marlowe winced anyway. "No, sir," he admitted. "I'm sorry."

Roman looked back at his display, the taste of defeat souring his mouth. So Demothi had been an agent of the anti-Tampies, after all. With a mission of stealing a space horse calf . . . and Roman had sat idly by and let him do it.

But how in hell's name had he gotten Man o' War to Jump? For that matter, how had he gotten *Quentin* to Jump?

Shutting off the useless outrider recording, he keyed for the Tampy section. A moment later Rrin-saa's face and yellow-orange neckerchief appeared. "Rro-maa, yes?" the other grated.

"Rrin-saa, I need some information," Roman said. "Everything we thought we knew about space horse calves said that one as young as Quentin couldn't Jump. How did it do that?"

"I do not know," came the all-too-predictable response.

Roman gritted his teeth. "Is Hhom-jee there? Hhom-jee, can you hear me?"

"I hear," a voice came from the background.

"Hhom-jee, how was Quentin able to Jump?" Roman repeated his question.

"I do not know," the other said. "I know only that the space horse calves I have touched have not felt ready to Jump, even though their fear was at first great. That is all."

Roman glowered at Rrin-saa's silent image. "Thank you," he managed, switching off.

"Lot of help *they* are," Marlowe murmured.

"They could have been more informative," Roman agreed grimly. "Looks like we're on our own here, people. Spin me a theory, Lieutenant."

"The simplest explanation, it seems to me, is that new calves don't Jump because they can't see where they'd be Jumping to," Marlowe suggested. "If so, all we need to do is make a list of the brightest stars visible from here and start checking them out."

Roman nodded. It was in many ways a default hypothesis; but it was the only one where the logical response was both obvious and at the same time something they could handle. "Lieutenant Yamoto?" he invited.

"I agree with Marlowe, sir," she said, tapping a key. "Here's the list of stars, in order of decreasing brightness, down to about first magnitude."

For a moment Roman studied the list. There were fifteen entries, topped by three B-class stars: a B1, a B4, and a B6. Halfway down the list . . .

"Shall I have Hhome-jee set course for number one, Captain?" Yamoto asked into his thoughts.

Roman pursed his lips. "No," he said slowly. "We'll start with number six."

Marlowe turned to frown at him. "Vega?"

"Yes," Roman told him. "If they're not there I want to be close enough to the Cordonale to Jump back and get the alert out on tachyon."

Marlowe's forehead furrowed. "Yes, sir," he said, a little uncertainly.

"Yes," Roman said quietly, answering the unspoken question he could read in the other's face and voice. "I think it's entirely possible the whole thing was an attempt by Demothi to steal the calf . . . and if so, chances are he'll be heading back to the Cordonale to deliver it."

Marlowe's face hardened. "I understand, sir. We'll want to get after him as fast as we can, try and cut him off."

"Right." Roman shifted his eyes back to the helm. "Alert Hhom-jee, Lieutenant. I want to Jump as soon as he can get Man o' War lined up properly."

"Yes, Captain." Yamoto hesitated. "Sir . . . what if it

really *was* just an accident, though? They'll be stuck out there somewhere, waiting for us to come find them."

"And we will," Roman told her shortly. "After we've checked out the other possibilities."

She colored slightly. "Yes, sir," she said, and turned back to her console.

Roman regarded the back of her head, a slight twinge of conscience poking through the high-speed mental shuffling of plans and possibilities and contingencies. She was right, of course; if it *had* been just an accident Ferrol and the others were in for a few tense hours. But the lander was routinely kept well stocked, and with only five of them aboard they could hold out a couple of weeks if absolutely necessary.

They would survive just fine. Bored, certainly; but boredom, contrary to popular belief, was seldom fatal.

"Ffe-rho?"

Ferrol made one last adjustment on the telescope's remote hookup and floated above it to look forward. "What is it, Sso-ngii?"

"Quentinninni has found a food supply and wishes to feed. May he?"

Ferrol frowned. "Where does it want to go?"

"Approximately fifty thousand kilometers in—" the Tampy paused, and then raised a hand—"that direction."

"Kennedy?"

"It's an asteroid belt," she answered promptly. "Reflection data implies high metal content, as asteroids go."

Good feeding for a space horse, then. "What kind of rock density are we talking about?" he asked her. "Bearing in mind the limited amount of shielding this teacup has."

"Shouldn't be dangerous," Kennedy assured him. "Provided Quentin doesn't go twitchy again and try to drag us through it retrograde. It's as good a place as any to wait for the *Amity*."

"Okay," Ferrol said, giving himself a push forward.

"Give me a minute to strap in, Sso-ngii, and we'll go and feed the baby."

They had arrived nearly twenty degrees off the ecliptic plane and with a slight retrograde motion that had them drifting leisurely toward the central star. A potentially deadly situation for a normal ship with a normal fuel supply; not even worth comment for a craft tethered to a space horse. Under Sso-ngii's guidance Quentin pulled them toward the asteroid belt at a steady 0.5 gee for just under an hour, turned around and decelerated for the same length of time, and finally accelerated again to match speeds with the drifting stream of rocks.

Floating at one of the side viewports, Ferrol watched as Quentin telekened a small boulder into one of its rear feeding orifices. He'd never before been this close to a feeding space horse, and it was one hell of an impressive sight. "You gotten a first-order analysis on those rocks yet?" he asked Kennedy.

He turned to look as Kennedy fiddled with her keyboard. "Should be just about finished . . . yes, here it is. Um. *Very* interesting—no wonder Quentin was panting to get here. Unusually high percentages of iron and nickel; *exceptionally* high concentrations of bismuth, tellurium, thallium, and a dozen other trace metals. Especially right here—the stuff we passed while Quentin was matching speeds didn't register as nearly this good."

And exceptionally high concentrations of trace metals meant . . . Craning his neck, Ferrol looked over at the Tampies. Even with filter masks plastered across their faces he could still see the sudden interest there. "A *yishyar* system?" he suggested.

"Certainly by textbook definitions," Kennedy agreed, turning to look at the Tampies too. "Sso-ngii?"

"Yes," the Tampy murmured. His raspy voice was dry and very alien, as if surprise or excitement had driven all attempts at human overtones from it.

Ferrol could well understand their interest; his own

mind was already simmering with the possibilities. A brand-new *yishyar* system—more to the point, a *yishyar* system eight hundred light-years outside of Tampy-claimed space. If the Senator could keep the Cordonale from meekly handing it over to the aliens—and if he could figure out a way to get back to the damned place himself—then maybe Demothi's idiot experiment might yield something useful, after all.

"Ferrol?"

He blinked the grand schemes out of his mind and focused on Kennedy. "Sorry. You said . . . ?"

"I said I think we've got a space horse locator program aboard," she repeated. "A simple one, probably: an anomalous-motion program coupled with a shape-recognition package. You want me to get it up?"

And look for any other space horses that might be feeding here? "Good idea," he nodded. "And don't forget to tie in the recorders. Sso-ngii, let's have Quentin boost speed a little—a few kilometers an hour shouldn't affect the feeding any, and it'll let us survey more of the belt."

"Your wishes are ours." The Tampy paused. "Ffe-rho, Quentinninni is not happy. Something is disturbing him."

Ferrol pushed himself away from the viewport. "Something from in here?" he asked, bringing himself to a halt in front of them.

"No," Sso-ngii said. He hesitated, then removed the helmet and handed it past Demothi to Wwis-khaa. "It is something outside, something that causes . . ." He stopped again and made a gesture Ferrol had never seen before.

"Uneasiness," Wwis-khaa supplied, the word seeming to come out with difficulty. "Quentinninni is uneasy. Perhaps . . . fearful."

Something hard settled into the base of Ferrol's throat. He'd seen space horses get skittish, spooked, and stressed . . . but never before had he seen one afraid. Or heard of one being afraid.

What the hell out there could scare even a baby space horse?

The lander was suddenly very quiet. Everyone else, apparently, was wondering the same thing. And perhaps coming to the same conclusion. "All right," he said as Wwis-khaa handed the helmet back. "Stay on that feeling, Sso-ngii, and let me know the minute it changes or gets any clearer. Kennedy, get that locator going, but alternate it with the regular scan program. I don't want us to miss something important just because it's not shaped like a space horse."

"Right," Kennedy said, and got to work. Her voice was still calm, but there was a hardness beneath it.

They traveled for a time in silence, with questions and replies delivered in low tones. Outside the viewports several hundred asteroids could be seen at any given time, the nearest handful as irregular lumps, the rest as pinpoints of reflected light from the distant sun.

Ferrol had spent more time than he cared to remember sitting around asteroid belts exactly like this one without the slightest touch of claustrophobia; but as the minutes dragged into hours he found the white dots on the monitor seeming to press ever closer and more oppressively around the lander. The air coming in through his filter mask felt to be growing ever hotter, and he found himself continually plotting updated escape routes through the moving boulders. A side effect of having to wear the mask for so long, he tried to tell himself; but down deep he knew better.

And four hours after they began their search, they found the space horse.

"It doesn't seem to be moving at all," Kennedy said, gazing closely at the readouts. "Just drifting with the asteroids."

Ferrol nodded, keying the enhancement program one more time. Again the fuzzy image of the distant creature sharpened just a bit; again, the computer was unable to resolve a section of its outline.

He wasn't sure exactly what that meant. But he knew already he didn't like it. "Sso-ngii, has Quentin detected the other space horse yet?" he asked over his shoulder.

"Yes. His uneasiness is increasing."

Ferrol chewed hard at his lip, uncertainty twisting at his stomach. The last thing he wanted to do was to take the lander any closer to that thing out there than he had to . . . but on the other hand, if the space horse was merely injured and not dead, there was every chance in the world it would detect them and Jump before *Amity* and its remote probes could arrive to study it. And if that happened, their chance of finding out what had done such damage to it would be gone. Probably forever.

"All right," he told Sso-ngii between dry lips. "Let's get a little closer. Just a little, and take us in slowly. And let me know if Quentin shows any signs of spooking. *Any* signs—if we Jump out of this system *Amity*'ll never be able to track us down."

"Oh, God, we'd be lost forever," Demothi murmured, his voice more muffled than usual by his filter mask. Ferrol half turned to tell him to shut up—

"Movement!" Kennedy snapped suddenly. "Small objects—lots of them—moving toward us from the other space horse."

Ferrol spun back, a curse catching in his throat. Under attack—? "How small?" he demanded, shaking hands fumbling with his controls.

"Five to ten meters across," Kennedy told him. "Way too small to be space horses themselves."

Ferrol had the proper display centered now, and for a long, horrifying moment he thought the approaching dots were somehow multiplying before his eyes . . . "What are they doing, collecting boulders?"

"Looks like it," Kennedy agreed. "Telekening them as they come."

Ferrol nodded, his hands curling into fists as he watched. Like a starburst skyrocket the dots spread apart; and then, to his surprise, they began to coalesce again. "Coming together about thirty kilometers ahead of us," Kennedy read off the numbers.

And there was no longer any choice left. A Jump, no matter how carefully planned, was damned risky, and could very well leave them lost for good. But it was less risky than sitting here and maybe getting slaughtered. "Get Quentin ready to move, Sso-ngii," Ferrol ordered, keying for an astronomical display. If he could find a small, nearby star—

"Hang on, Ferrol, they're not attacking," Kennedy told him. "Or at least the edge we can see around Quentin isn't. They're holding position relative to us, about twenty-seven kilometers out."

Ferrol switched back to the tactical display. Sure enough, the rangefinder showed them to be clustered together in front of Quentin, their speed perfectly matched with the calf's.

So it was not, in fact, an attack. Or at least it wasn't an attack yet. "Any idea what those things are? Anybody?" he added, looking back at the Tampies.

"I do not know," Wwis-khaa answered for both of them.

Ferrol turned back in disgust, wondering why he'd even bothered to ask. "They're probably related to the space horses, anyway," Kennedy offered. "Motive power seems the same, not to mention the telekening of those rocks."

"And they must understand space horses," Demothi said quietly.

Ferrol twisted his head to look at the other. "Why must they?" he demanded.

Demothi gazed back without flinching. "Adult space horse telekene range is usually twenty kilometers, occasionally extending to twenty-five." He nodded toward Quentin. "You said those creatures were staying twenty-seven kilometers away."

A cold shiver ran up Ferrol's back. "They're staying out of telekene range," he said. "Deliberately."

For a moment the lander was silent. Then Kennedy stirred. "On the other hand," she reminded them, "if they're out of Quentin's range, then we're probably outside of theirs, too."

"Point," Ferrol admitted. "Well, then . . . let's keep going toward that space horse out there and see what happens. Sso-ngii?"

"Your wishes are ours," the Tampy replied.

A thought occurred to Ferrol as a mild surge of acceleration pushed him slightly into his seat: that if the creatures out there couldn't recognize that Quentin was a calf with only a fraction of an adult's telekene range, then they couldn't be very intelligent. It was something to keep in mind.

"We're moving," Kennedy reported unnecessarily. "The creatures out there . . . moving with us."

Ferrol frowned at his displays. He'd expected the creatures to hold their current position and try to prevent the lander's approach. But Kennedy was right: they were sticking like paste, moving like slaved machines exactly twenty-seven kilometers in front of Quentin.

Directly in front of Quentin . . .

"Kennedy," he said slowly, "give us a little boost, will you?—forward and starboard. I want to move around Quentin a bit."

"Sure." The lander's drive hissed briefly, and as the rein lines slackened and they moved around Quentin Ferrol kept his eyes on the tactical display.

No mistake. The creatures and their attendant boulders didn't care at all about the lander's position.

He turned, to find Kennedy's eyes on him. "They're staying with Quentin," he told her.

She nodded, her lips compressed together into a pale line. "I think," she said, "that we'd better run a check on just how opaque that clump of stuff out there is."

"There is no need," Sso-ngii said softly. "You are correct. Quentin cannot see through them."

"*What?*" Demothi demanded, his voice halfway between a gasp and a snarl. It was, Ferrol thought, the most emotion he'd ever heard in the man's voice. "Why the bloody hell didn't you say so before?"

"To what purpose?" the Tampy asked reasonably. "We could not have Jumped—it is here that the *Amity* will come to search for us."

Demothi took a shuddering breath, clearly fighting for control. "We could have kept them from getting in front of Quentin in the first place," he bit out. "We could have turned around and tried to get away. Instead, we've got—" He waved vaguely forward and sputtered to a halt.

"All right, calm down," Ferrol told him. "It might have been nice to know what was going on a little earlier, but once the things out there were in place it was too late to do anything about it. And Sso-ngii's right; it would have been dangerous to try to Jump." Dimly, a part of his mind noted the irony of him having to take the Tampies' side of an argument, but it wasn't something he had time to dwell on. "When the *Amity* gets here it shouldn't have any trouble getting rid of the things; until then, there doesn't seem to be anything immediately dangerous about them."

"I'm not so sure about that," Kennedy said suddenly, her voice taut. "You'd better have a look at this, Ferrol."

Ferrol swiveled back to his console. In the past few minutes, while his attention had been on the creatures ahead, they'd covered a fair amount of the distance to the quiescent space horse. Enough so that the computer enhancement program could finally provide a reasonably sharp picture of the creature.

Or rather, of the two-thirds of it that remained. Where the rest should have been was a ragged-edged hole.

Chapter 17

Kennedy swore gently under her breath. "Recommendation, Ferrol: let's get the hell out of here."

"No argument," Ferrol said grimly. "Sso-ngii, turn Quentin around and ease us away. Take it slow and gentle—we don't want to provoke those things with any sudden movements."

"Your wishes are ours."

Quentin began a leisurely turn, and Ferrol felt himself pushed gently against his chair's side restraints. He watched the tactical display just long enough to confirm the cloud ahead was matching their maneuver, then turned to face the Tampies. An idea was tugging at the back of his brain . . . "Wwis-khaa," he said, choosing his words carefully, "you told me you didn't know anything about these creatures. Correct?"

"It is correct," the Tampy replied.

"All right. Can you tell me, then, if *other* Tampies know anything about these creatures?"

The alien hesitated. "I do not know for sure," he said slowly. "I know that some have claimed to; that is all."

Ferrol grinned humorlessly to himself. "So what would one of those Tampies tell me about the creatures, if they were here?"

There was a long silence, as if Wwis-khaa was trying to decide whether or not that came under the dreaded name of speculation. "I'll remind you," Ferrol said into the silence, "that our lives could depend on knowing what we're facing." A flash of inspiration—"Quentin's life, too, of course."

Wwis-khaa exhaled, teeth chattering together. "They are spoken of as . . . carrion-eaters. As—" He fumbled for words.

"Vultures," Kennedy supplied. "Terran carrion birds."

"Yes," Wwis-khaa said. "They were said to be observed beside a dead space horse in the asteroids of a distant system. No recordings were made."

"Did these vultures make any move against the Tampy ship?" Ferrol asked.

"They moved toward it, but the space horse Jumped before they came near. The Handler afterward reported fear."

Ferrol thought a minute. "Did the Tampies actually see the dead space horse die?"

"No. He was dead and being consumed when they arrived."

"Have there been any other sightings?" Kennedy asked. "Has anyone witnessed a space horse dying before the vultures showed up?"

"I do not know," Wwis-khaa said.

"I also do not know," Sso-ngii put in. "I know I have heard of no such reports; that is all."

"You think they're more than just carrion-eaters?" Ferrol asked Kennedy.

"They're small, but there are a hell of a lot of them," Kennedy pointed out thoughtfully. "The literature says that the Tampies have had some of their space horses in captivity for seven hundred years now; no one even *knows* what their natural life span is. To assume the vultures just *happen* to show up at the exact place and time a space horse dies is stretching things a little far."

"But we don't know that's the case," Demothi spoke up, his voice uneasy. "This space horse could have been dead hundreds of years before the vultures found it. Or perhaps they exist in huge numbers all over the galaxy, drifting in suspended animation like spores until a space horse dies nearby. Or maybe a dying space horse gives out a telepathic pulse or something that attracts them. We just don't *know*."

Kennedy threw Ferrol a look. He nodded agreement; Demothi was trying just a little too hard to talk himself into believing the vultures were harmless. And under the circumstances, wishful thinking wasn't a luxury they could afford to put up with. "You're talking like a Tampy thinks," Ferrol told him, taking surprisingly little pleasure in popping the other's bubble. "Before you get all misty-eyed over the infinite variety of the universe and the need to refrain from preconceived ideas, let me remind you that these allegedly passive carrion-eaters have very effectively locked us into this system."

"Looking us over, probably," Kennedy said.

"Or else waiting for Quentin to tire," Ferrol said. "Though trying to starve a space horse in a *yishyar* system strikes me as pretty stupid." Quentin had completed its turn now, and Ferrol felt himself being pushed back into his seat as the calf began to pick up speed. "The vultures stay with us the whole time?" he asked Kennedy.

"Like they were welded there," she confirmed. "Quentin's just too slow on turns to get ahead of them. Even with them having to lug that optical net of boulders along with them."

An optical net. An odd term . . . but that was exactly what it was. A semisolid disk that had them trapped as thoroughly as if they were inside the webbing back at the Tampies' Kialinninni corral.

Trapped . . . but why?

"Kennedy," he said slowly, "is that locator program still running?"

She checked. "Yes. Still nothing registering."

"Can the anomalous-motion section be extracted and run alone?"

Kennedy gave him a hard look. "You think," she said, dropping her voice, "that the vultures might be holding us here for something else?"

"I can't see them breaking off a good meal just for the fun of it," Ferrol told her, matching his volume to hers.

She nodded and got to work; and a second later Ferrol was slammed briefly into his seat as Quentin jerked. "What was that?" he snapped, twisting his head to look at the Tampies.

Sso-ngii's mouth moved soundlessly for a handful of heartbeats before any words came out. "I do not know," he said. "I know that I have never felt such intensity of feeling in a space horse before; that is all."

"Well, what's it *like*?" Ferrol snarled. "Is it like fear, or concern, or happiness—?"

"Movement!" Kennedy snapped. "One object, very large; bearing one hundred starboard, thirty nadir, range 170 kilometers. Closing!"

Ferrol had the object on his own display now; the scale clicked on—

"Ffe-rho!—Quentinninni is afraid—I cannot hold him—"

"Give it its head!" Ferrol barked. "Just don't let it Jump—"

The rest of his words were blown out with his wind as Quentin shot forward, ramming him two gee's-worth back into his seat. "Kennedy!" he managed as his body struggled to adjust to weight again.

"No contest," she said, her voice tight. "The thing's doing at least seven gees toward us."

Ferrol got a hand to his display, keyed for tactical. Two gees or not, the vultures were still staying with them. And the scale on the intruder— "My God," he said. "Damn thing's almost two kilometers long."

"I'd say we've found our space horse killer," Kennedy agreed. "That thing's bearing down on us like a hungry shark."

"Yeah, well, let's see if we can discourage it a little."

Fighting the extra weight in his arms, Ferrol keyed the comm laser for a full-intensity unmodulated pulse and set it to tracking the shark, wishing to hell he had some real weaponry to work with. "We got anything aboard this teacup besides the laser?" he asked.

"Not that I know of," Kennedy said. "But we're running directly away from it now, which means the main drive's pointing straight down its throat."

"Good." The tactical showed the laser locked firmly on the elongated mass overtaking them. "Be sure to balance with the forward jets—we don't want to ram Quentin."

"Right. Range, forty-five kilometers—"

And without warning the weight was abruptly lifted from them. An instant later Ferrol was jammed painfully against his harness, the hiss of the forward jets in his ears. He caught just a glimpse of Quentin's dark bulk as it rushed toward the forward viewport—

And with a grinding of metal the lander caromed off the calf's side.

It took a second for Ferrol to shake off the shock. "Kennedy—what the hell—?"

"Shark reached out and grabbed Quentin, I think," she said, her voice a bit slurred. Ferrol looked sharply at her; but her next words were clear enough. "I couldn't stop us in time."

From behind them came a low moan—fear or anger or something else, coming from Demothi. "Sso-ngii, is Quentin hurt badly?" Ferrol called, glancing back.

"He is not injured." The words were barely understandable, as if the Tampy could spare only a tiny fraction of his mind for the task of speaking English. His eyes were bright; his twisted face preternaturally alert and very alien. "He is being drawn toward the other. Who will consume him."

Demothi moaned again. "Kennedy, give the shark a full-power spurt from the drive," Ferrol gritted. "See if we can distract it."

"Damn far away for that."

"Yeah, but the telekene grip will just get stronger as it reels us in. We've got to try it."

"Right."

Ferrol braced himself; and was slammed again into his seat for an instant as the roar of the lander's fusion drive filled the boat. Lost in the noise was the *crack* of capacitors as his jabbing finger fired the laser. The sound and acceleration cut off simultaneously. "Ssongii? Are we free?"

"The hold remains," the Tampy said.

"But we're not moving backwards any more," Kennedy put in. "Could be we've confused or startled it."

"Hit it again," Ferrol ordered. On the visual he could see what looked like one of the shark's feeding orifices rotating into view, and he'd just focused the laser on it when Kennedy fired the drive again. He rode it out, clenching his teeth firmly together; and she'd just cut off the power when the capacitor blinked ready. This time, the *crack* was clearly audible. "Again," he snapped. If the tactical numbers were right, they'd actually gained a little distance on their attacker. The roar and acceleration came—

And the lander leaped forward, swaying wildly back and forth like a pendulum. "Sso-ngii!" Ferrol snapped, fighting both the two-gee weight and a sudden surge of nausea.

"Quentinninni is free," Sso-ngii said. "He is running toward an asteroid where he hopes to hide."

Ferrol took a shuddering breath, eyes on the tactical. The shark was falling back, apparently not pursuing. Fifty kilometers . . . fifty-five . . . sixty—probably out of telekene range now . . .

"The vultures are still with us," Kennedy said.

Ferrol nodded grimly. "I'll settle for half a victory at this point," he told her. "Sso-ngii, what're the chances we've discouraged the shark permanently? After all, Quentin's a pretty small mouthful for a predator that size."

"I do not know," was the predictable reply. "But you

humans are a predator species yourself. Can you not form an accurate idea within yourself?"

Ferrol swallowed. Indeed he could . . . and the idea he formed wasn't an especially encouraging one.

They fled at a full two gees' acceleration for nearly ten minutes before Quentin could be persuaded to ease up. Under Sso-ngii's guidance the calf modified its speed and heading until it was paralleling a particularly dense section of the asteroid belt. "Maybe we should try weaving in and out, see if we can throw the vultures off," Ferrol suggested.

"Probably a waste of time," Kennedy shook her head. "However they hold station in front of Quentin, I don't think they're doing it strictly by visual means."

Ferrol frowned. "What makes you think that?"

"When they first moved in on us they were nearly a hundred kilometers away," she reminded him, fingers skating across keys. "Quentin's only about a hundred meters long, with a maximum width maybe twenty-five. The difference between head-on view and complete broadside would have been only sixteen minutes of an arc. That's . . . let's see; a thumbnail at seventeen meters. Yet they *immediately* settled in directly in front of Quentin. I find it hard to believe their eyesight is *that* good."

"I don't see what difference it makes *how* they do it," Demothi growled impatiently.

For a man who'd spent two months trying to suppress human emotions, Ferrol thought sourly, Demothi was certainly making up for lost time. "How it matters," he told the other, "is that whatever they're locking onto is very likely the same thing the shark's going to use to track us if and when it decides on a rematch." At least, that was what he *thought* the point was. He glanced at Kennedy, got a small confirming nod, and focused on the Tampies. "Sso-ngii, Wwis-khaa: do either of you know of any long-range senses space horses have that the shark and vultures may be duplicating?"

"It is thought that the internal source of telekinetic power is detectable," Wwis-khaa said. Apparently, having been verbally maneuvered once already into revealing something he didn't know personally made it easier the second time. Either that, or even Tampies could give up their silly philosophic games when their own deaths were on the line. "In addition, it is thought that much of a space horse's energy is produced by small fusion and fission reactions within his body."

"That'll give off neutrinos, among other things," Kennedy commented thoughtfully. "Maybe in a recognizable pattern."

"I'd vote for the telekene-detector, myself," Ferrol said. "The direction or distribution of the ability is clearly asymmetric; otherwise, space horses could back up better than they do. A neutrino distribution ought to be more uniform."

Kennedy shrugged. "Maybe. Either way, though, it means we've got at least one very obvious solution." She gave him a significant look, gave a slight nod forward.

"What's that?" Demothi demanded, his voice heavy with suspicion. "What's she talking about?"

"She's talking about cutting Quentin loose and letting it run," Ferrol told him.

He was prepared for objections. But not prepared enough. "*What?*" Demothi all but yelped. "You can't do that—Quentin wouldn't have a chance."

"It might," Kennedy put in. "Either way, if it's a choice between the space horse or us—"

"You can't *do* that," Demothi repeated. "Damn it all, Ferrol, you might as well just kill Quentin here and now."

"Mmo-thee," Sso-ngii said, reaching an awkward hand to Demothi's shoulder.

Demothi shrugged off the touch. "That's a calf, damn it—a *baby.*"

"It's survival of the fittest," Ferrol snapped, suddenly tired of having to argue about everything he said. "Ecology, Demothi—space horses eat rocks, sharks eat space horses, and vultures eat what's left. You're so keen on Tampies and Tampy philosophy?—well, that's it in a nutshell. Letting nature take its course."

Demothi's face was red; but it was Sso-ngii who spoke up. "We respect all living things and the systems in which they live, yes," the alien said. "Yet, in accepting a space horse's service, we in return offer him our protection. We cannot turn Quentinninni free under such dangerous conditions, Ffe-rho. Not even to save ourselves."

"It doesn't really matter whether you like it or not," Ferrol told them shortly. "I'm in command here, and I'll do what I think necessary." He took a deep breath. "As it happens, though, turning Quentin loose now would only postpone the problem. The minute the *Amity* gets here they're going to be in the same fix we're in now, and the more data we can collect between now and then, the better everyone's chances of getting out of here alive."

He turned to Kennedy. "So. First thing, I suppose, is to call up the record of the fight, see if we did any real damage to the shark."

He hadn't expected to find evidence of any; and in this he was right. "Just not enough energy in either the laser or the drive to overload its natural absorption capabilities," Kennedy shook her head as she frowned at the analysis. "At least not at the distance we had to work from."

Ferrol nodded. "So what we need is a way to concentrate a lot of energy into either a smaller area or a shorter time."

"You speak of attacking the shark," Sso-ngii said quietly. "Perhaps you intend to kill it. It would be preferable if another way could be found."

Ferrol felt his lip twist. The shark had been out of sight for several minutes, so of course the Tampies were going all soft and mushy again. So much for survival instincts. "You might want to take a minute right

now," he threw over his shoulder, "and decide whether
it's Quentin or the shark you really want to protect."

"Why may we not protect both?" the Tampy persisted. "If we can simply evade the shark until the
Amity arrives, then disrupt the optical net which prevents our escape—"

"And how do you expect us to do anything to the
vultures when they stay on Quentin's far side and thirty
kilometers away?" Demothi asked dully.

"As a matter of fact," Kennedy put in. "Sso-ngii's
right. We can't hope to kill the shark—neither we nor
the *Amity* is equipped with the sub-nuke torpedos or
military lasers we'd need to do that. All we can go for is
escape; and the vultures are our best breakpoint."

"I don't suppose you'd have any ideas how we'd *do*
that," Demothi growled.

"Maybe," she said. "Anyway, now's the time to try."
She tapped a spot on the tactical display. "The shark's
moving away from us."

Doing 1.4 gee, Ferrol read off, on a course that
would take it back to the dead space horse. "It'll be
back," he murmured to Kennedy. "The advantages of
eating a space horse are the same as feeding at a *yishyar*,
only more so: all the trace and rare elements it needs,
all in the right porportions and concentrated in a single
package."

"Why all predators exist, in other words," Kennedy
nodded. "Which means we have to come up with something now, before it finishes out there and heads back
for dessert."

"Right. You have any idea?"

"Possibly." She tapped some keys, and a schematic of
the lander appeared on her display, together with an
inventory list. "It'll depend on how much spare webbing we've got aboard, and on what sort of miracles we
can do with the engines."

She began describing her plan . . . and as she talked,
Ferrol found himself studying her face. Seeing, as if for
the first time, the cool eyes and the small age lines

around them. Kennedy's file, he remembered, had listed her age as forty-six—not quite twice Ferrol's own—with a military record that had been left deliberately and disturbingly vague. The Senator had hinted that that hidden record was an impressive one; he'd out-and-out warned Ferrol that she was highly dangerous.

And dangerous was exactly what they needed right now. He hoped like hell the Senator hadn't been exaggerating.

Chapter 18

The B1 star had been big and almost viciously bright, and even though its dim white-dwarf companion had orbited well outside the larger star's photosphere, the whole thing had still evoked unpleasant memories of the *Amity*'s fun-filled tour through Dr. Lowry's pre-nova system. Not in his mind alone, Roman had noted; it was reasonably clear from their quiet and hurried efficiency that Yamoto and Marlowe felt it, too, and had set themselves the mutual goal of doing their search as quickly as possible and getting out.

The B4 star that was second on their list wasn't a lot dimmer, but at least it had no companion. No companion, but something considerably more surprising.

It was, according to Rrin-saa, a *yishyar* system.

"Interesting indeed, Rrin-saa," Roman agreed. The alien face centered in his intercom seemed more twisted than usual, he noticed. Excitement? Probably. "Would Quentin have been able to detect that from the 11612 system?—maybe come here deliberately so that it could feed?"

"I do not know, Rro-maa."

"Captain," Marlowe spoke up, an odd tone in his voice. "Anomalous-motion program just triggered."

"Quentin?" Roman asked, keying for the proper screen.

There was a long pause. "No, sir. It's . . . I'll be damned. Captain, there's more than one—my God, it's a whole *bunch* of them." He swiveled around, his eyes shining. "Captain, this is something absolutely new— another species of space-going creatures."

Roman shook his head in wonderment. First the space horse calvings, and now this. *Amity* was indeed a charmed ship. "Rrin-saa, take a look at your display. Have the Tampies ever run into these things before?"

"I . . . do not know."

Roman looked back at the intercom. There'd been an uncharacteristic hesitation there. "Rrin-saa?"

Another hesitation. "I know that others have claimed to have seen them; that is all."

Roman glanced at Marlowe. "And what would those others say about them?" he asked Rrin-saa.

"They are said to be carrion eaters."

Something hard settled into Roman's stomach. "Quentin?"

"I do not know."

Roman gritted his teeth. "Marlowe?"

"No sign of their emergency beacon yet," the other said. "But their range here will be pretty restricted, with the solar wind that star's blasting out and all."

Roman nodded, forcing the fears back. Chances were that Quentin and the lander were perfectly safe. "Okay, Yamoto, you know where their theoretical entry point was. Figure us a spiral search path in toward it and feed the numbers to the Handler."

"Yes, sir," she said. "Suggestion, Captain: instead of aiming for their Jump point, perhaps we should focus on the nearest section of the asteroid belt to that point."

"The assumption being that all that exercise would have made Quentin hungry?" It was, Roman decided, a fair assumption. "Very good. Figure your course and let's get started. Marlowe, you getting anything on our visitors yet?"

"It's starting to come in, sir," Marlowe told him. "Survey section computers are working on a—ah; here it is." A fairly undetailed computer rendition of top, side, and bottom views appeared on Roman's display.

Roman hunched forward to study them. Approximately eight meters across, the creatures were generally disk-shaped, with flat, roughly triangular wing-like appendages pointing outward in four directions from the edge, and with what looked like a single large feeding orifice and sensory ring taking up much of the flat underside. "Reminds me of a tailless manta ray," he commented to no one in particular. "Rotated through ninety degrees to give it those other two wings. Odd that a creature that size has such a large feeding orifice."

"I noticed that, too," Marlowe nodded. "And you'll note they're staying solidly with us."

Roman felt his forehead wrinkle as he called up a tactical display. Man o' War had started its turn toward the asteroid belt now, and the creatures out there were indeed matching the maneuver. Staying directly in front of them, some twenty-seven kilometers out.

The hairs on the back of Roman's neck began to tingle, just a little. Calling back the computer's schematic of the creatures, he keyed his intercom for the survey section. A moment later Tenzing's face appeared. "Yes, what is it?" he asked, sounding distracted.

"I wondered what you made of our visitors, Doctor," Roman said.

"They're beautiful," Tenzing replied, his eyes watching something outside the range of the intercom camera. "A brand-new species of space-going creature. What else would you like to know?"

"I'm interested mainly if they could be predators."

Tenzing looked back at the intercom camera, his expression a combination of impatience and a slightly supercilious amusement. "I'd say that was highly unlikely, Captain. What on earth would have given you that impression?"

"The relative size of the feeding orifice, for one thing," Roman said, determined not to let the other make him feel like an idiot. "That, plus the fact that they're sitting out there as if poised for attack."

Tenzing shrugged. "I doubt the positioning's significant," he said, his shoulders shifting as he fiddled with his keyboard. "As to the size of the orifice, my guess is that the creature's a sifter-type of feeder; floats through space and either just lets gravel and dust flow in or else telekenes it the last few centimeters from close range. That would explain those triangular body extentions, too: they could reach out and help scoop material in toward the center."

"They could also be used to hold the thing against a space horse while it eats its way in," Marlowe put in. "Captain, we're reading some extra structure on those extensions now. Could be a cluster of octopus-type suction cups."

Roman frowned at the revised schematic. "Dr. Tenzing? Comments?"

With an almost visible effort—a slightly resentful effort, at that—Tenzing tore his attention from his displays again. "Yes, they could be suction cups," he conceded, a touch of professorial pique coloring his voice. "*Or* they could be any of a hundred other things. Maybe these creatures are the space-going version of remoras—hitchhiking fish that attach themselves to turtles or sharks or whatever for easy transport. But they're most definitely, emphatically *not* predators, Captain—certain not on the level you're obviously worried about. They're far too small and fragile to even think of taking on anything as big as a space horse. Man o' War could telekene them to shreds before they got halfway in."

Roman rubbed his thumb and forefinger together thoughtfully. He had to admit the other's arguments sounded reasonable enough. And yet . . . "But if they're hoping to hitch a ride," he asked slowly, "then why are they hanging so far back?"

"Maybe they're not," Tenzing countered impatiently. "Maybe it's Man o' War who's holding them away. Captain, we're really very busy down here, collecting data and all, so unless you have something else to discuss with me, I'd like to get back."

"Of course, Doctor," Roman said, forcing down his own annoyance. "Enjoy yourselves."

The image vanished, and for a moment Roman glowered at the place where it had been. The size of *Amity's* scientific section had been steadily shrinking as the ship's missions had gradually shifted from straight survey work to survey-plus-breeding to straight breeding, and Tenzing's resentment of the Starforce's tinkering had risen with every cut. Roman could sympathize, but it didn't make the man any easier to put up with.

His eyes drifted back to the visual display. There were at least twenty of the creatures out there; more, possibly, hidden in among the boulders that the group seemed to be lugging along with them. Tenzing's last comment . . . Reaching over, he keyed the intercom for the Tampy section. "Rrin-saa?"

"I hear," the alien said.

"Rrin-saa, is Man o' War holding those things out there away from us?"

"He is not," an off-camera voice answered. Hhomjee, probably—he was on Handler duty at the moment.

So much for Tenzing's ramora theory. "Thank you," Roman told him. He was just reaching for the off-switch—

"Rro-maa?"

"Yes, Hhom-jee?"

There was a long pause. "Rro-maa, Manawanninni is afraid."

Roman stared at Rrin-saa's unreadable alien face in the intercom screen. "What do you mean, afraid?" he asked carefully. "Afraid of what?"

Another pause. "I do not know."

Roman pursed his lips, his eyes flicking to the visual display. Ramoras, Tenzing had called them. Harmless to a space horse . . . "Try and find out," he told Hhom-jee. "Or see if you can get a location or direction or something."

"Your wishes are ours," Rrin-saa said.

Roman keyed off and looked over at Marlowe. "Full scan," he ordered quietly. "I want you to take a good look at everything within ten thousand kilometers of us."

"Yes, sir," Marlowe nodded grimly, and turned to his task.

Roman shifted his gaze to Yamoto. "There's a combat-operations file in the helm library," he told her. "Dig it out and put it into standby." He hesitated; but if the ramoras were interested in Man o' War . . . "And have engineering start the drive activation sequence."

"Yes, sir." If she understood the implications of that order, she hid it well.

And for the moment, Roman decided, that was all *Amity* could do. Until and unless they found Quentin and the lander here—

And right on cue, Marlowe's console emitted a loud beep. "Captain!" the other called. "Picking up an emergency beacon; bearing inside the asteroid belt.

"We've found them."

It turned out not to require any miracles, after all; Ferrol hadn't realized just how readily the lander's equipment could be disassembled and recombined, though in retrospect that wasn't unreasonable for a craft that would often serve as a large-capacity lifeboat. The necessary technical data was stored on one of the datapacks in the survival library kit, and Kennedy's plan was relatively straightforward besides. But with only two of them available to work on it—the Tampies were useless, of course, and Ferrol flatly refused to let Demothi anywhere near the equipment—the job took nearly three hours to complete. It was a good thing, Ferrol thought more than once, that the shark wasn't in any hurry.

But finally the oddly shaped missile was finished and mounted to the outer hull. "Now what?" Demothi asked as Ferrol struggled to strip off his EVA skinsuit in zero-gee.

"What do you think?" Ferrol snorted, tugging at a pant leg that didn't want to come off. "We wait, that's what. If this works we'll have a clear Jump window for only a few seconds, and it would be awfully handy to have some idea where we were Jumping to before we start. Wouldn't you say?"

"And if the shark attacks before the *Amity* arrives?" Demothi countered.

"We'll worry about that if and when it happens," Ferrol growled, stuffing the EVA gear into its locker and closing the door. "Until then—"

And beyond Demothi, a blue light suddenly began flashing on the control board. "Ferrol—they're here," Kennedy called.

Ferrol kicked off the locker and shot forward, slapping his hands against successive rows of seats to slow himself down. "Where are they?" he asked, grabbing his seat and shoving himself down into it. From the speaker he could hear Marlowe's voice hailing them.

"Bearing twenty-four port, thirty zenith," she read off the numbers. "Haven't got a range yet. Laser's tracking them now . . . there; on target."

Ferrol jabbed the *transmit* button. "This is Commander Ferrol aboard *Amity* lander," he called toward the microphone. "Come in, *Amity*." Eyes on the clock, he counted seconds: four . . . five . . .

Marlowe's voice abruptly vanished. "Ahoy, lander," Roman said. Even with the distorting crackle of charged-particle static, Ferrol could hear the relief in the captain's voice. "I gather you've never heard it's impolite to leave a party while the host is out of the room."

"Sorry, but we didn't have much choice—our ride was leaving," Ferrol countered. A six-second round-trip delay—three seconds each direction—put *Amity* about nine hundred thousand kilometers away. Timewise, that meant . . .

"A good four hours away at a two-gee acc/dec course," Kennedy murmured from beside him.

He nodded his thanks. "Can you tell us where we are?" he called into the mike.

"We've got a complete nav dump ready for you," Roman said six seconds later. "Here it comes." A light on Kennedy's console came on, indicating incoming data. "As a matter of interest," Roman continued, "Quentin made almost 1120 light-years in that Jump. Not bad for a beginner."

"We'll contact the record books later," Ferrol said. "Right now, we all have to get the hell out of this system. Do you have a clear Jump window?"

The delay was longer than six seconds this time. Considerably longer. "No," Roman said at last, his voice grim. "We've picked up an advance guard of small space-going creatures. They seem to be blocking Man o' War's Jump vision."

Ferrol swore under his breath. *Amity* was far enough from the dead space horse that the vultures shouldn't have found the larger ship nearly this soon. Was the whole system swarming with the damn things?

Or had the shark abandoned its prey . . . ?

"Marlowe, key in a full sweep with your anomalous motion program," he ordered tightly. "Right now. Captain, recommend you get moving, at whatever gees you can pull. If the vultures found you this quickly, there's a good chance the shark is somewhere nearb—"

"Motion, Captain," Marlowe interrupted. "Bearing eighty-seven port, sixty nadir. It's . . . my *God.*"

"Hhom-jee, go to four-gee acceleration," Roman's voice came, glacially calm. "Yamoto, are we still on course for the lander?"

"Yes, sir," Yamoto answered, her voice changing midway through with the unmistakable strains of high-gee acceleration. "We'll need to correct later for the higher acceleration, but it'll be close enough."

"Marlowe?"

"The monster just went to four gees, too, Captain," the other reported. "At current course . . . intercept in just over two hours."

"Don't get overconfident—we've seen it do seven gees," Ferrol warned them. "I'd guess it's taking its time because it's not very hungry."

"We'll take any small favors we can get," Roman said. "I take it the—shark?—is a predator?"

Ferrol snorted. "In capital letters, underlined. We got a look at the space horse it'd been feeding on. Or what was left of it."

"We've got some recordings, Captain," Kennedy added. "They're not very good, but they'll give you some idea of what you're up against."

"Good. Transmit whenever you're ready."

The indicator light went on, then off, and for a few minutes there was silence. "I see what you mean," Roman acknowledged at last. "I'll send it down to the survey section, see what they can dig out of it. You have any other recommendations?"

Ferrol licked at his upper lip. "We almost certainly can't kill the shark, sir," he said. "The *Amity* hasn't got anything that could take out even another spacecraft, let alone something that kills and eats space horses for a living. Our only chance is to try and get rid of these vultures and their optical nets long enough to Jump." He glanced at Kennedy. "Kennedy's come up with one possible method. Now that we know where we are and how to get back, I think it's time we gave it a try."

"The rough design specs are in the package I just sent you," Kennedy added.

"Hang on, let me take a look."

For a minute the carrier was silent. Kennedy took the opportunity to finish the last details of programming for her missile. Ferrol sat and watched her, wishing he had something useful to do, too. "Interesting idea," Roman grunted at last. "Yes, I agree there's no point in waiting. Let's see . . . if it works, try for Deneb. Give us two hours to catch up with you; if we don't show, your new nav pack should have enough to get you back to Solomon."

"Kennedy?" Ferrol murmured.

She nodded. "Deneb it is, Captain," she called.

"Give us a continual helm dump," Roman instructed. "If it works, we'll want to see how. Good luck."

"Right." Ferrol took a careful breath. "Let's do it, Kennedy."

She nodded. "Move us out," she ordered Wwis-khaa, who had taken Sso-ngii's place under the helmet. "Turn Quentin about thirty degrees port, seventeen nadir—big bluish star standing all alone."

"Your wishes are ours."

A minute later Quentin was in position, at least as well as Wwis-khaa could tell with the vultures' interference. "Missile ready," Ferrol read off, mentally crossing his fingers. "Okay, Kennedy: *fire*."

With a flash of maneuvering fire their creation crawled away from the lander. A minute later, the low-level fusion drive kicked in, sending the missile leaping outward like a scalded bat. It streaked past Quentin as Wwis-khaa twitched the calf aside; then, with the delicacy of a surgeon, the Tampy turned Quentin back again until the optical net was directly in line with the oncoming missile. Ferrol held his breath . . . and a second before impact the miniature star suddenly blossomed into a filigree of space horse webbing. At five hundred meters per second the human-rigged net collided with the vultures' optical one—

"Wwis-khaa!" Ferrol snapped, his eyes on the displays. "Do it!"

"Quentinninni cannot yet see the star," the Tampy said.

"Damn!" Ferrol slammed an impotent fist onto the edge of the console, watching helplessly as the webbing swept through the mess of vultures without obvious effect. "It's not working. It's not *working*."

"I see the problem," Kennedy told him. "The webbing caught a bunch of them, all right, but before it could drag them clear the rest filled in the hole."

Ferrol hissed between his teeth. "Yeah. Damn. And now they're wriggling out the open end and going back to the main swarm. We need three or four missiles, or one really big one, to make this work."

"And a way to seal the end after it's collected them," Kennedy added. "You copying all this, *Amity*?"

"We got it all," Roman acknowledged. "I think you've got the right idea; we'll see if engineering and Tenzing's people can improve on the model. Hopefully before the shark catches up with us."

Which would be fine for the *Amity*, Ferrol thought. But for them . . . "We've already used all the webbing we had aboard, Captain," he told Roman.

"I assumed that," the other said. "We'll think of something."

"For starters," Kennedy said, "there's no real point any more in our skulking around out here. Recommend we head in and meet you halfway."

Roman seemed to ponder that. "That'll bring Quentin in uncomfortably close to the shark," he pointed out. "Are you sure you want to risk that?"

"It's a damn sight better risk than hoping you can outrun the shark the whole way here," Ferrol countered.

"Point," the other conceded. "Yamoto?"

"Ready, sir," was Yamoto's prompt reply. "Lieutenant?"

"Go," Kennedy told her. Again the incoming-data light flicked on and off. "Got it."

"Good," Roman said. "Looks like a rendezvous of . . . an hour fifty minutes."

With the projected shark intercept at just under two hours away. "Pretty tight," Ferrol grunted. "Especially if the shark decides to speed up."

"Yes, well, Man o' War can do six gees if necessary," Roman reminded him.

And the shark could do seven . . . "There's one more thing you should do, Captain," Ferrol said, the words coming out with difficulty. "In the underbed storage of my cabin is a lockbox—combination seven-two-seven-three-three. In it is a datapack—" he braced himself— "that shows the effects of excessive radiation and heat on space horses. If the shark's physiology is similar enough, the data may give you a handle on how to fight it."

He held his breath, waiting with dread for the obvious question. But Roman had a better sense of priorities than that. "Thank you, Commander; I'll get it to the survey section right away," he said. "Let's hope it helps."

Ferrol nodded silently at the console, a hollow sensation in the pit of his stomach. *So much for secret politics and secret weapons,* he thought blackly. But this was a matter of survival—his and *Amity's* both. Just for once, politics could go to hell.

And if the Senator didn't like it, he could go to hell, too.

Chapter 19

Four gees meant four times normal weight, which meant *Amity*'s scientists had to work from acceleration couches, which in the past had usually prompted bitter complaints and long delays. But for once there were no complaints; and in less than half an hour the preliminary reports began coming in.

"It's two thousand fifteen meters long," Tenzing told Roman, the intercom screen showing a familiar tapered-cylinder shape. "About two and a half times the length of the average space horse, with similar proportions. Sensory clusters are arranged in similar axial rings fore and aft, though from the diameter of each cluster it appears that the feeding orifices are proportionally much larger than those of space horses." The diagram vanished, replaced by Tenzing's drawn face.

Roman grimaced. "So if current theory is right about telekene strength scaling with volume, we're talking a creature fifteen times stronger than Man o' War."

Tenzing nodded heavily. "We can hope it's not that bad, but it's certainly bad enough. The lander's data proves that much."

"Agreed. What about the vultures?"

Tenzing shrugged as best he could in four gees. "The

shark seems to be covered with the things," he said. "It appears my ramora theory was at least partly right."

"Except that in this case the scavengers play an active part in the hunt."

"Right," Tenzing agreed. "And that's going to give us some trouble. We estimate the shark's carrying about four times as many vultures as we've got sitting in front of Man o' War right now. That's considerably more than the net missile we're building will be able to web up, particularly if they come at us in waves."

Roman rubbed his chin thoughtfully. "Though as long as the waves come in far enough apart to give us a Jump window, the trick should still work."

"Maybe," Tenzing said. "Depends some on how close the shark is to us at the time—and on what, if anything, it can do to counter the web missile."

And that was, indeed, what it all ultimately came down to: whether the shark was instinct-controlled, or whether it possessed a genuine, creative intelligence. "You think it can reason that way?" he asked Tenzing.

"Professional opinion?" Again, Tenzing shrugged. "I don't know, Captain, I really don't. Intelligence generally scales upward with brain size, but there's no rule that says it has to, and there are some major exceptions." He nodded toward the display. "Your shark, here, retreated back to the dead space horse after its encounter with the lander; but then it must have left again right away to have been where it was when we first spotted it. So: did it fall back, do a little feeding, and then wander around licking its wounds? Or did it go back to collect the rest of the vultures so as to have its full attack force ready for the unknown thing that had fought back so strangely?" He shook his head. "Your guess is as good as mine."

Roman looked at the tactical display. Still an hour and twenty minutes to go till their rendezvous with the lander . . . and the shark was still closing. "What about the information in Commander Ferrol's datapack?" he asked Tenzing. "Anything there we can use?"

"Oh, there's plenty there," Tenzing snorted. "Whether *we* can use it is something else entirely. It seems clear that heavy dosages—and I mean *heavy* dosages—of ionizing radiation and dense relativistic-particle fluxes can disable or kill space horses, with the sensory clusters being especially vulnerable. But *Amity* didn't come equiped with X-ray lasers and fine-tune particle accelerators."

Roman nodded. "Lander? You getting all this?"

"Yes, sir," Ferrol said a few seconds later, his voice grim. "Doesn't sound especially hopeful, does it?"

"We're not dead yet," Roman reminded him. "Engineering will have the drive at full power well before the shark reaches us, and there's enough particle radiation in there to give it at least a hefty slap in the face. And we're trying to build an X-ray laser from parts of the aft comm laser—theoretically, that's supposed to be possible."

"I've seen it done," Kennedy put in. "But even if *Amity* has all the necessary equipment, you almost certainly don't have the time that kind of conversion will take. Recommend you concentrate on rebuilding the laser for multi-pulse capability, and then use it to fire on the shark's sensory clusters."

"We're already doing that with the spare comm laser," Roman told her. "You have anything else, Dr. Tenzing?"

"As a matter of fact, I do," the scientist said. "And for a change, this tidbit may actually turn out to be useful. It seems that our shark is a sprinter."

Roman frowned. "Come again?"

"A sprinter," Tenzing repeated. "As opposed to a long-distance runner. Here, I'll show you." Tenzing's face vanished from the intercom again, to be replaced by a graph superimposed on a tactical diagram. "This is an analysis of the lander's scuffle with the shark," he continued. "You'll note that the thing waited until the lander reached the closest approach to its position before attacking; and, furthermore, that tremendous seven-gee acceleration it chased them with was already dropping

a minute or so before it grabbed Quentin. Even now—"
the diagram changed—"you can see that the shark seems
to be deliberately pacing itself, pulling just enough gees
to keep gaining on us."

"Interesting," Roman said slowly as the display cleared
and Tenzing's face came back on. "What you're saying
is that, even though the shark is faster, there's actually
a chance we can outrun it?"

"I'm not sure I'm saying *that*," Tenzing cautioned.
"Remember that we're talking about a predator here,
Captain. Any predator that could be easily outrun by its
prey wouldn't be a predator for very long."

"Um," Roman grunted. "Point. On the other hand, a
predator might not expect its prey to slow down while
being pursued, either. We've got a turnover and deceleration coming up; maybe that'll confuse it."

"Maybe," Tenzing said doubtfully. "I wouldn't count
on it, though."

"I don't intend to," Roman told him. "I'm hoping we
can get clear from our optical nets before the shark runs
us to ground. Lander, is your vulture squad still holding at twenty-seven kilometers?"

"Like it was nailed there," Ferrol said.

"Same with ours," Roman said. "Sitting just outside
Man o' War's telekene range. So. Yamoto came up with
this one a few minutes ago: what happens if we run
Man o' War and Quentin nose to nose with each other?"

For a long moment the laser carrier hummed with
silence. "What happens," Ferrol said, his voice thoughtful, "is that, at fifty-four kilometers, the two optical nets
intersect. Closer than that . . . the nets either have to
pass through each other or else have to pull closer in to
their individual targets. Either way, both sets have to
eventually wind up inside somebody's telekene range."

Roman nodded. "That was the same conclusion we
came to," he told Ferrol. "We'll find out for sure in . . .
just under seventy-five minutes."

"Unless, of course," Tenzing warned, "the shark is

smart enough to see what we're planning and moves in to cut us off before we get close enough."

Roman grimaced. That was, indeed, the crucial question. "If so," he said, "we'll find *that* out somewhat sooner."

Privately, Roman still held on to the hope that the shark would be confused by *Amity*'s turnover and deceleration; but it was a hope that died a quick and quiet death. Within thirty seconds of Man o' War's turnover, the shark had duplicated the maneuver, decelerating into a slightly altered course that *Amity*'s computers indicated would bring it to zero-gee relative at almost exactly their own projected rendezvous point.

And thus it was down to a race. Sitting at his station, squeezed into his chair by four gees' worth of weight, Roman watched his displays, listened to the running commentary from the engineering and survey sections, and ran endless calculations. From all indications, the race was going to be very, very close.

"Got the lander on visual," Marlowe announced, hunched over his displays. "Range, fifty-five kilometers. Our respective optical nets should pass each other any time now."

As yet, the mass of vultures on Roman's tactical display showed no change. "Yamoto?—what's your reading on the shark?"

"Coming in fast," she said, her voice fighting to be calm but not succeeding very well. "Range, two thousand kilometers; decelerating at five gees. We've got under five minutes if it holds that."

"Lander?" Roman called.

"We're ready," Ferrol said.

Roman tapped his intercom. "Hhom-jee?—*now*."

Almost immediately there was a pull to the side as Man o' War began a gentle starboard turn. A minute later *Amity* straightened out again and continued on toward Quentin, who the tactical display showed had

performed a similar circling maneuver. "Marlowe?
—what's the lander's heading?"

"Projected as being dead-on to Deneb," the other
confirmed.

"Good. Ferrol, as soon as you get a clear window, go.
If we're not there in two hours, continue on home."

"Yes, sir."

And this was it. Clenching his teeth, Roman returned
his attention to the tactical display. "Optical nets inter-
secting," he told Ferrol. "Starting to pass each other
. . . no . . . no, cancel that—they're sticking together.
Holding position in a single mass between us."

"Shouldn't matter, as long as both sets are forced into
telekene range," Kennedy reminded him.

"And as long as Man o' War can hold onto them,"
Marlowe muttered.

Roman nodded grimly. As matters stood right now,
Man o' War and Quentin were acting as optical nets for
each other. Only if the space horses could grab the
vultures and hold them off to the side while they themselves got out of each other's way—

"Nets separating!" Marlowe barked suddenly. "Quentin's vultures are moving back toward the lander."

"Damn," Roman swore under his breath, keying the
tactical for scale. Moving in toward Quentin and the
lander . . . and staying just out of Man o' War's telekene
range. "Ferrol! Can Quentin telekene them yet?"

A pause—"Not a chance," Ferrol said tightly. "Wwis-
khaa says Quentin's range is only about four kilometers."

"Captain, the shark's accelerating," Yamoto cut in.
"And it's launching more vultures."

"They're coming in fast," Marlowe added. "ETA about
two minutes."

"The shark seems to have caught on to what we're
trying," Roman told Ferrol. "Give Quentin a kick in
the rear—you've got to get that net cleared out before
the next wave gets here."

"We won't make it." Ferrol's voice was under icy

control. "Quentin's just not fast enough. You'll have to go without us."

"Rro-maa, Manawanninni is holding the vultures," Rrin-saa's voice came from the intercom.

And the Jump window was open. For the next ninety seconds.

"Captain?" Yamoto prompted.

Roman hissed between his teeth. "Secure from Jump," he ordered. "Stand by for balanced thrust from main drive toward the shark. Laser crew, lock onto the shark—aim for one of the forward sensory clusters. Missile crew—"

"Captain, what the hell do you think you're doing?" Ferrol snarled. "You've got your window—get going."

"We're not leaving you here alone," Roman told him flatly. "Missile crew, shift your aim aft to—"

"Don't be a damn fool," Ferrol cut him off. "Sir. You can't beat the shark, and you know it. Get back to the Cordonale and bring back a warship or something useful."

Roman glared at the tactical display. The hell of it was, Ferrol had a damn good point—if *Amity* didn't get back, neither the Tampies nor the Cordonale might ever find out about this threat until it was too late to do anything about it. But to deliberately abandon his own crewers—"Sorry, Ferrol, but we're not taking applications for martyr today," he said. "The shark isn't going to get either of us."

"The shark doesn't give a damn about *us*," Ferrol shot back. "It's the space horses it wants. We cut Quentin loose and let it run, and we'll be perfectly safe."

"Maybe. But maybe not; and we can't take the chance." An insert appeared in Roman's tactical display: a close-up of the shark, with the aft laser's tracking circle searching for a sensory ring. Searching with some difficulty; the approaching cloud of vultures obscured much of the view. "Most of the elements a space horse needs are present in that lander and its equipment," he reminded Ferrol. "In different compounds and alloys, but the shark may not care." The cloud of vultures between the

Amity and its pursuer wasn't clearing—if anything, it was getting thicker. How many of the damn things, Roman wondered uneasily, had the shark *sent*? "Regardless, the subject is closed. Turn Quentin around and start hauling gees away from here while we slow down the shark a little."

For a long second he thought Ferrol was going to argue. But— "Yes, sir," the other gritted out. "Wwiskhaa, you heard the captain."

"Main drive ready," Yamoto announced. "Laser crew reports difficulty in aiming through the vultures."

"Acknowledged," Roman said. "All crewers; stand by." The alert warning warbled, and for a brief moment Roman's mind flashed back to the *Dryden*. A genuine fighting ship, the *Dryden,* with genuine weapons and a trained crew to handle them.

The moment passed. He was on the *Amity*, with jury-rigged weapons and an unskilled crew, facing an enemy the Starforce's planners had never dreamed of.

All they could do was their best.

The shark had closed to fifty-five kilometers now, its vulture escort some ten kilometers closer. Ferrol's records had shown the predator had grabbed Quentin from almost forty-five kilometers away . . .

He took a deep breath. This was it. "Drive and laser: *fire.*"

The fusion drive roared to life, jamming Roman deeper into his seat as Man o' War's acceleration was briefly doubled. Almost instantly the lighter hiss of the forward maneuvering jets joined in, their thrust fighting against that of the drive, and a second later the extra acceleration was gone. Roman stole a glance at the helm display. The rein line tension registered zero: *Amity*'s drive was now matching Man o' War's own acceleration. "Yamoto? Lander's acceleration?"

"Two point six gees," she called back.

"Hhom-jee, bring Man o' War up to 2.2 gees," he ordered into the intercom. "Yamoto, get ready to match it."

"Yes, sir."

Another brief moment of adjustment, and Roman could give his attention back to the tactical display. The shark was almost to the forty-kilometer mark and still closing. "Laser crew: report."

"We can't get through!" Even muffled by the engine roar, the young crewer's voice sounded on the edge of frantic. "The vultures won't get out of the way—they're blocking the laser."

"Steady," Roman snapped, a cold feeling settling into his stomach. So the shark had learned something from its encounter with the lander, after all. Briefly, he wondered if it had learned too much. "Focus your shots on individual vultures," he ordered. "See if you can kill or disable them. Missile crew: launch."

The edge of the rear camera view went black as the sunscreens edited out the flare of the net missile's drive tube. Roman shifted his attention back and forth between the visual and tactical displays; and a handful of heartbeats later, the missile cracked open into a silent explosion of silvery space horse webbing. The flood swung up and over the nearest group of vultures . . . "Tenzing, it's not working."

"Give it another second, Captain," the other's voice came tensely. "—*There!*"

And, abruptly, the explosion reversed itself, Tenzing's framework of artificial Alphan memory muscle closing the net in on the vultures like a giant fist. Another burst from the missile's drive knocked the bunched vultures to the side—

"Laser crew!—you've got your opening!" Roman barked. Even as he spoke, a faint line of ionized hydrogen flickered on the visual, targeting the shark's side. The predator seemed to twitch—

And a second later the beam was again blocked as a second swarm of vultures came up from below to fill the gap.

"Damn," Marlowe snarled. "Laser's blocked again."

"What did we hit?" Roman asked him.

"Looked like the beam caught the edge of a sensory cluster," the other said. "But it didn't stay there long enough to do any real damage."

"Still, we're clearly on the right track," Roman pointed out. "It wouldn't have reacted so strongly to what wasn't much better than a near miss unless we'd genuinely hurt it. Missile crew—status?"

"Second missile's almost ready to go, Captain." The crewer must have been facing away from the mike; Roman could hardly hear him over the drive. "As soon as we set the launch timer—"

And without warning Roman was thrown against his restraint straps as *Amity* suddenly was yanked backward.

"Yamoto!—full thrust," Roman shouted. The order was pure reflex; already the roar of the drive was changing pitch as Yamoto kicked out all the stops. For a second the ship seemed to teeter on the verge of breaking free . . . and then, slowly, the pressure on the rein lines increased, and the inertial indicators began to show backwards movement.

They were caught. Caught, and being reeled in.

Chapter 20

A dozen frantic voices shouted for Roman's attention. He ignored them all, eyes flicking across displays for information, mind furiously sifting possibilities. The shark was only thirty-two kilometers away— apparently it had opted not to risk grabbing them until they were well within its telekene range—and closing fast. The drive was at full power, and even though it wasn't strong enough to pull them away, all the extra heat and radiation had to be doing *something* to the vulture cloud. The question was whether it would do enough, and do it before the shark got close enough to rip the ship apart.

And if it didn't . . .

"Missile crew: I want a fast reprogramming," he ordered, shouting over the roar of the drive. "Shut down the proximity fusing and send the missile ahead, toward the lander's vultures. Ferrol, you copying?—you're to let the missile pass you and then use a standard 460 codex radio signal to trigger it when it's in position."

Ferrol's voice was almost inaudible over the noise. "Captain, we can't just leave you—"

"Shut up, Ferrol, that's an order. Laser crew: concentrate on the vultures that are in the most direct line with the drive emissions—maybe we can blast a hole there and get through to the shark."

"Captain, Man o' War's panicking," Yamoto shouted back at him. "Hhom-jee's having trouble holding contact."

Roman clenched his teeth, Ferrol's suggestion about cutting Quentin loose flashing through his mind. Was the shark really interested in *Amity* itself, or had it simply grabbed the ship because it recognized that *Amity* and Man o' War were linked together? "Hhom-jee, is Man o' War itself being held?" he called into his intercom.

The roar of the drive was his only answer. "Hhom-jee?—*answer* me!"

"He cannot reply," came another Tampy voice. "His full speaking must be with Manawannnini."

Roman swore under his breath. "Yamoto, what's the strain on the tether lines?"

"Approaching critical," she told him. "We hold this level much longer and they'll snap."

So the shark was indeed only holding *Amity* itself. Recognizing, perhaps, that taking the ship gained it the space horse, too?

But if the tether lines were cut, forcing the predator to choose between them . . .

A set of numbers on the tactical screen abruptly turned red. The *Amity*'s internal stress indicators, starting to go crazy—"Stolt?"

"Laser still useless," the other reported. "Drive's making a hash of the vultures, the the shark's moved just enough off centerline that those vultures aren't the ones directly between us any more."

Demonstrating once again the creature's ability to learn. It had recognized *Amity* as being the more dangerous of its two targets and was exerting all its force in the ship's direction.

Apparently ignoring Man o' War entirely . . .

"What about structural integrity?" Roman asked, his eyes flicking again to the red stress numbers.

"Getting some stretching," Stolt said tightly. "Both linear and transverse—like tidal effects, only stronger. Probably the shark trying to pull us apart."

And given the fight *Amity* was putting up, the shark could reasonably be expected to put as much effort into the job as it could spare. "Estimated time to damage?"

"At this strength, we'll start popping seams in maybe thirty minutes," Stolt said. "But the strain will probably go up as the shark gets closer."

Roman nodded grimly, indecision tearing at him. If Tenzing was right about the shark being a low-stamina sprinter, then it might still be possible to hold to the current status quo and try to wear the predator out.

But if Tenzing was wrong, any delay might well forfeit them their only other chance to get away.

It was a gamble they had to take. "Laser crew, cease firing," he ordered. "Charge all pulse capacitors and stand by. Yamoto, ease up on the drive, just a little. Rrin-saa, I need to get a message in to Hhom-jee—can that be done?"

"He can hear you, Rro-maa," the Tampy's voice came faintly.

"Good. Hhom-jee, when I give you the word, I want you to have Man o' War reach back and telekene away as many of the vultures between us and the shark that it can."

"Your wishes are ours," Rrin-saa replied.

"Yeah," Roman muttered under his breath. "Yamoto? Range?"

"To the shark, twenty-four kilometers, Captain," she said promptly. "The leading edge of vulture cloud is just over eighteen."

At least two kilometers inside Man o' War's telekene range; maybe more. "Laser crew, stand by," he ordered, shifting his attention to the internal stress indicators. They would have exactly one shot at this. A little closer; just a little closer . . .

"Captain, tether stress is redlining," Yamoto said abruptly. "Another minute and we're going to lose Man o' War."

Roman's hands curled into fists. This was it. "Hhom-jee: *now*."

For a single, awful second he thought the gamble had
failed. And then, as if by magic, a circle of black suddenly appeared in the hazy white cloud of vultures and
rocks behind them. The hole spread outward like the
negative of an explosion—

And behind it, clearly visible in the reflected light of
the drive emissions, was the shark.

"Laser: *fire!*" Roman snapped. The faint line lanced
out—

And without any warning at all Roman was slammed
hard back into his chair.

There was no time to shout warnings or orders; but
Yamoto was ready. A split-instant of weightlessness as
she cut the drive was followed by a second back-
wrenching slam of high acceleration as Man o' War took
up the slack in the rein lines and leaped forward.

And they were free.

"Keep firing," Roman managed to shout.

"Shark falling back," Marlowe called: "Range, fifty
kilometers . . . sixty . . . seventy . . . I don't think it's
even trying to follow us, Captain."

"It doesn't have to," Yamoto put in. "The optical net
is back with us."

Roman pushed against the acceleration to take a deep
breath. "Laser crew: cease fire. As soon as you can, I
want a maintenance check started on your equipment
—we may need to use it again." Leaden hands fought
unsuccessfully to switch displays— "Marlowe, did the
lander get away?"

"Negative," the other said. "They're about 230 kilometers ahead of us; bearing twenty port, five nadir."

With an effort, Roman reached up and keyed into the
comm laser circuit. "*Amity* to lander: report."

"Lander here," Ferrol's voice came back. "You do
believe in cutting things close, don't you?"

"We didn't have much choice," Roman told him,
giving the tactical display a quick check. The shark still
didn't seem to be giving chase. "I take it from your

presence here that the net missile we sent out to you didn't work?"

"It didn't get even that much chance," Ferrol said grimly. "The shark stopped it about a kilometer out from you."

"I've got the recording queued, Captain, if you want to see it," Marlowe put in.

Roman nodded. "Go ahead."

Stopped was an understatement; or else that was all Ferrol had been able to see from his distance. From *Amity's* closer perspective, it was far more spectacular. "It was stopped, all right," Roman told Ferrol. "Also torn into small pieces and dispersed. Here, take a look."

He sent a copy of the tape down the laser, and for a minute there was silence. "Looks pretty deliberate, doesn't it?" Ferrol commented at last.

"I'd say so, yes," Roman agreed. "It saw what the first missile did and didn't care for it much."

"And so the next time it saw one, it shredded it."

Roman nodded. "More evidence that the shark can learn. As if we needed it." The acceleration was beginning to slacken: Man o' War tiring or else Hhom-jee getting it back under control. Mentally crossing his fingers, Roman turned toward the intercom. "Hhom-jee, can you talk to me yet?"

A pause. "I hear, Rro-maa."

Roman let out a quiet sigh of relief—the prospect of trying to find a way out of the system with a fear-crazed space horse wasn't something he'd wanted to contemplate. "Is Man o' War back under control again?"

"He is still . . . frightened."

"It's got plenty of company. As soon as you've got it calm enough to steer I want to rendezvous with the lander—Yamoto will give you the direction."

"Your wish is ours."

"Good." Roman turned to Yamoto. "Run up a rendezvous plot with a continual update," he instructed her. "No telling how long it'll take for him to get Man o' War functional again."

"It had better be damn quick," Ferrol growled. "Whatever finagling you did to get away from the shark isn't going to work a second time. The business with the net missile pretty well proves that."

"I'm afraid you're probably right," Roman agreed. "Which sends us straight back to square one."

"Getting rid of the vultures?"

"Right. And with the shark more or less on alert now, it'll have to be something we can do *fast*, before the shark has time to react to it."

"A pretty tall order," Ferrol grunted.

"We'll think of something."

Leaning against Quentin's 2.4 gee acceleration, Ferrol flipped off the *transmit* switch. For a moment he glowered at the panel, feeling the knot of tension in his stomach tighten another few turns. " 'We'll think of something,' " he muttered under his breath. "Famous last words."

"Could be worse," Kennedy pointed out calmly. "We damn near lost *Amity* and Man o' War there, you know."

Ferrol threw her a glare. Her face, like her voice, was as unperturbed as ever, and for a moment he wondered if she'd felt even a twinge of panic during any of the last few hours. "Some day," he told her, "*something* in this universe is going to throw you for a skid. I just hope I'm alive to see it."

A smile twitched at the corners of her mouth. "Much better," she nodded approvingly. "Anger's a lot less paralyzing than fear. More conducive to constructive thought, too."

"How would *you* know?" he snorted; but the swipe lacked any real force. Even while resenting the motherly tone he had to admit she was right.

He took a deep breath and gave the instruments a quick scan. For the first few minutes of that mad dash away from the *Amity* and the pursuing shark, Quentin's acceleration had been slowly but steadily increasing;

but for the last few minutes it had been just as steadily dropping. "Wwis-khaa, Quentin's slowing down," he called over his shoulder. "What's the trouble?"

"Quentinninni is growing tired," the Tampy said. His tone was odd . . .

Ferrol twisted to look at the other. One look was all he needed. "Sso-ngii, take over," he snapped. "Wwis-khaa's losing it."

Sso-ngii stirred, and for a moment looked around as if orienting himself. Then, shaking once like a wet dog, he reached past Demothi to take the helmet from Wwis-khaa. He gazed at the device, then slowly lowered it onto his head.

"We're losing both of them," Kennedy murmured from beside him.

Ferrol hissed between his teeth. "I know. What's *Amity's* ETA?"

"About fifteen minutes. You want me to call over and have another Handler standing by in a lifeboat?"

He nodded. "I just hope they've got someone to spare. That fight with the shark may have wiped out some of their Handlers, too."

Kennedy nodded and turned back to her console. Ferrol listened with half an ear, his eyes drifting to the forward viewport. Half a kilometer away, Quentin was a dark blot against the stars. Far beyond it, invisible at their distance, the vultures and their damned optical net would be holding position.

Twenty-seven kilometers away . . . and Roman wanted a way to take them out *quickly*.

"One of the other Tampies will be ready when we match velocities," Kennedy reported into his thoughts. "Captain Roman says they're hurting a little for Handlers, too, but can spare us one."

Ferrol snorted gently. "Terrific. We may wind up having to cut Quentin loose, after all. By default." On his helm display the *Amity's* projected course and intercept point appeared . . .

He frowned suddenly. "You set this intercept up yourself?" he asked Kennedy.

She shook her head. "No, Yamoto and the Tampies did," she told him. "Trouble?"

"I don't know." He gestured at the plot. "Why is *Amity* going to hang so far out?"

Kennedy shrugged. "Why not? There's no real need to run the two ships too closely together. Especially not with the space horses already skittish from the shark."

Skittish. For a dozen heartbeats Ferrol stared at the display, listening to the word ricochet around his brain. *Skittish.* "Is that why we need a half-kilometer of rein line between us and Quentin?" he asked. "Because if we don't the calf will get skittish?"

He turned to find Kennedy frowning at him. "I'm not sure I understand what you mean," she said.

"Sure you do," he said. "Maybe you've never thought of it at a conscious level, but you *know* it just the same." A picture from his old grade-school biology text flashed through his mind: a group of sea birds standing on a fence, spaced apart with almost military precision— "Don't you see?—space horses aren't social animals. They don't travel in groups, not even family or clan groups. More to the immediate point, when they come across each other, *they don't clump up.*"

Kennedy's eyes defocused a bit. "You're right," she said slowly. "Every time we midwife a calf, the first thing the mother does is pull away from it. And the first thing the *calf* does is pull away from the net boat." Her eyes came back to focus, and she glanced at the black starless circle that was Quentin. "Interesting, but so what?"

Ferrol grinned tightly. "So this. The captain's wrong; we don't need to actually outfly or outshoot the vultures. All we really need to do is to confuse them." He nodded toward Quentin. "And I think I know how to do it."

She cocked an eyebrow. "I'm listening," she invited.

Chapter 21

The rain lines were softly glowing strands brushing across the lander's ports, impossible to focus on even at such close range. Ferrol's eyes stubbornly tried to do so anyway, even as the rest of his body braced for the wrenching jolt that would mean Quentin had lost control and panicked. But the surge the Tampies had more or less predicted didn't come . . . and eventually Roman's confirmation did. "All set, lander," he said. "Web boats are coming back in now. We'll keep firing the comm laser until they're back in the hangar—the longer we keep the vultures distracted, the better chance we've got. Presumably."

Ferrol clamped his teeth against the retort that wanted to come out. Roman had been noticeably less than enthusiastic about the plan—not, Ferrol suspected, because of any flaw the other could see in it, but simply because all the Tampies seemed likewise quietly opposed. Not for any reason *they* were willing to put into words, either, but for Tampies broad hints of vague uncertainties always seemed to be enough.

"We're drifting a little," Kennedy said into his thoughts.

With an effort, Ferrol shook the resentment from his mind. This was no time to let himself be distracted by

Tampy coyness. "Ppla-zii, Quentin needs to ease a little to port," he called to the Tampy behind them.

"Your . . . wish is mine."

Ferrol threw a quick look over his shoulder at their replacement Handler, who'd taken up position between Demothi and a sleep-humming Wwis-khaa. He immediately wished he hadn't; the Tampy's face was twisted into a painful-looking expression Ferrol wouldn't have thought even such lopsided features capable of. "Pplazii? What's the problem?"

"Quentinnninni is . . . troubled," the Tampy said thickly.

Ferrol glanced at Kennedy. "How troubled?" he demanded.

Ppla-zii tried twice before any words came out. "He . . . will endure . . . as necessary."

"We'd better get this thing off the ground, and fast," Kennedy murmured.

Ferrol nodded and turned back to his console. Maybe the Tampies' worries hadn't been totally unfounded after all. "Lander to *Amity*: better scorch with those boats, Captain."

"How's Quentin doing?" Roman asked.

"Ppla-zii says it's troubled," Ferrol told him. "Whatever the hell *that* means."

"Probably just what it says: trouble. Especially since Bbri-hwoo's telling me the same about Man o' War." Roman paused. "All right, web boats' ETA for the hangar is two minutes. Let's go ahead and get started—they'll be in before we're ready."

"Right." Ferrol leaned forward to peer out the viewport. Ahead and to their left, paralleling Quentin barely a hundred meters away, Man o' War was a ghostly gray-white wall in the light of the distant sun. "You heard the captain, Ppla-zii," he called. "Let's do it."

"Your wish is . . . mine."

Ferrol settled into his seat and keyed for a tactical display. Twenty-eight kilometers ahead, the two optical nets were a pair of blobs sitting next to each other, each exactly in front of its chosen space horse. "Quentin's starting to rotate," Kennedy reported.

"Confirmed," Roman said. "The vultures are matching it."

Ferrol nodded silently. Reacting to the calf's slow rotation, they were indeed moving, sliding over toward the group that was blocking Man o' War's Jump vision. Just a little further . . .

"Mark!" Kennedy called. "Okay, Ppla-zii: ease it back again."

Ferrol held his breath . . . and as Quentin rotated away from Man o' War, its attending vultures also reversed their motion

Damn. "We're going to have to move Quentin closer in."

"I'm afraid you're right," Roman agreed reluctantly. "I don't know, though. Rrin-saa?"

"It is dangerous," the Tampy's voice came faintly. Manawanninni already shows signs of stress."

"What kind of stress is getting eaten going to give it?" Ferrol retorted.

"That's enough, Commander," Roman said sharply. "Escaping the shark at the cost of losing all control of Man o' War isn't going to gain us much."

Ferrol ground his teeth. "Captain, with all due respect—"

"Ffe-rho is right," Rrin-saa put in. "For Manawanninni's sake, as well as that of ourselves, we must try."

"Not to mention all the helpless test mice in the lab," Ferrol muttered under his breath. "Ppla-zii? Let's go— move us another twenty-five meters or so toward Man o' War."

It took nearly five minutes for the calf to be coaxed in that close . . . and in the end all of Ppla-zii's work proved to have been for nothing. Again, the vultures had no problem keeping optical nets in front of both space horses.

"But we're on the right track," Kennedy pointed out. "The vultures were measurably slower this time in their reaction to Quentin's movement."

"For all the good *that* does us," Ferrol growled. "We're at the end of the line here—we're never going to get them any closer together." He could feel his face warming with anger and frustration. It had seemed like such a *good* idea—

"Let's not be quite so hasty to give up," Roman admonished him thoughtfully. "Agreed, if the vultures can still resolve two side-by-side space horses at this separation, it's almost certainly a waste of time to try and push them any closer. But then, maybe side-by-side isn't really our best approach, anyway."

Ferrol frowned. "What, you mean fore-and-aft?"

"Exactly. We'll send another, longer rein line out to you, cut the one that's tethering you to Man o' War at the moment, and have Quentin slide into line directly *behind* us."

Ferrol looked sharply at Kennedy, got a similarly sharp look in response. "Captain, even with Quentin in front to shield us, *Amity*'s drive hasn't had nearly enough time to cool down."

"No, of course not," Roman agreed. "Once the rein line's in place and we've got it rigged to an amplifier helmet in here, you'll cut loose from Quentin and bring the lander in. If we can get Quentin right in line with Man o' War, we may just be able to fool the vultures into thinking there's only one—"

"Captain!" Marlowe's voice interrupted. "Shark's on the move again. Heading toward us on an intercept course at—good God, it's pulling almost eight gees."

Kennedy swore quietly, her fingers skating over her console. "Must have finally figured out what we're doing," she said grimly. "ETA . . . Captain, there's not going to be nearly enough time to send the web boats out again."

Ferrol looked at the tactical, did a quick calculation

of his own. She was right . . . and it left them with
exactly one option. "We'll have to swing back in line
with you from here," he told Roman. "Squeeze ourselves and Quentin in between Man o' War and *Amity*."

"It won't work," Roman said, with a promptness that
showed he'd already anticipated that suggestion. "The
way your line is tethered, you'd wind up bringing Quentin another twenty meters or so closer to Man o' War.
You'll never push the calf in that close."

"We won't have to," Ferrol said, his eyes tracing
the lines on the tethering schematic. The angles, and
fulcrum points . . . "All we need is for you to give
Man o' War a kick forward. That should make us fall
back to the end of the tether and swing right into
position."

"Only if Quentin doesn't panic," Roman said.

"Have we got another choice?" Ferrol countered.

"Not really," the other agreed tightly. "Rrin-saa?—
you heard. Tell Bbri-hwoo to give Man o' War a nudge."

For a moment, nothing. Then, as Ferrol stared at
Man o' War's bulk, he saw it begin to move. "Here we
go," he murmured.

"Tether line tightening," Kennedy reported. "Man o'
War's starting to pull away and ahead."

A slight tremor went through the lander, and Ferrol
braced himself. But Quentin didn't bolt; and a minute
later the calf and lander had swung neatly into place
inside the kilometer-long gap between Man o' War and
Amity.

Ferrol let out a breath he hadn't realized he'd been
holding. "*Amity*? We're blocked back here—what's happening with the vultures?"

"Holding position ahead," Roman told him. "But they
seem to be in a fairly amorphous mass, and not as
clearly in two groups as they were before. We may
have finally done it."

"We'll find out soon enough," Ferrol said. "Okay,
Ppla-zii: give Quentin a small rotation."

There was no reply. "Ppla-zii?" Ferrol said, twisting around. "—Oh, *hell*."

"What?" Roman snapped.

"I'm not sure," Ferrol growled. "But—Demothi, take a look."

Demothi was already leaning forward to peer at the Tampy's face. "No doubt," he said, his voice trembling noticeably. "It's *perasiata*—a sort of deep sleep or coma state."

"Yeah, we know what *perasiata* is," Ferrol gritted. And if the Handler had it, then Quentin was almost certainly out of commission, too. And if Quentin was gone—

Roman had apparently followed the same line of reasoning. "Rrin-saa," he called. "Rrin-*saa*! What's happening down there? Is Man o' War still conscious?"

"No." Rrin-saa's voice was quiet, almost calm. "It is the end. The cycle of life closes—"

"We're not giving up yet," Roman cut him off harshly. "Marlowe, give Man o' War a shot from the comm laser—see if that'll jolt it back to consciousness."

"Waste of time," Demothi murmured, more to himself than to anyone else.

"So give us an alternative," Ferrol told him. "You're the expert on Tampies here—how do they snap someone out of *perasiata*?"

"They don't," Demothi said bitterly. "They just sit back and let nature take its course."

Ferrol snorted. Of course. What else would Tampies do?

"In this case nature being a predator bearing down on us at eight gees," Kennedy put in. "What about an electric shock, transmitted along the rein lines? Any chance that could do it?"

Ferrol shook his head. "I doubt it. A massive enough shock can knock them out, but anything less than that doesn't seem to have any effect at all."

Kennedy tapped a fingernail gently against her teeth.

"Maybe a physical jolt, then," she suggested. "Ramming the lander into Quentin's hide, for instance."

Ferrol glanced behind him. Barely two hundred meters behind the lander he could see the gleam of *Amity*'s nose. "We're a little close for firing the drive, aren't we?"

"Never mind *Amity*'s paint job," Roman said. "Give it a try."

"Yes, sir." Kennedy's hands brushed across the panel, flicking on all ten pre-fire switches in what appeared to be a single motion. "Hang on."

The lander lunged forward, gathered speed . . . and ten seconds later rammed full into Quentin's smoothly curved end.

The shock threw Ferrol hard against his restraints. "Ppla-zii?" he snapped, twisting his neck to look behind him.

The Tampy's face hadn't changed . . . and peering intently into that face, Demothi shook his head. "No good. He's still under."

Ferrol swore and turned back to the tactical display. The shark had stopped accelerating now, and was turning ponderously over for the deceleration phase of its attack. If it decelerated at the same eight gees it had been doing earlier, it would be within telekene range of them in perhaps three minutes.

"Ferrol—look at the vultures," Kennedy said suddenly.

Ferrol shifted his attention to that part of the display. The lander's impact with Quentin had angled the calf a couple of degrees out of line with Man o' War . . .

And for the first time since they'd appeared, the vultures had failed to match the motion.

Ferrol hissed frustration between his teeth. It was, perhaps, the ultimate irony: the barrier finally lifting just as the engine died. "Great," he said. "Hooray for us. Too bad there won't be time to break out the champagne."

"Knock it off," Kennedy snarled. "We've got two and

a half minutes left to snap them out of it—let's *use* those minutes."

Ferrol clenched his jaw tightly enough to hurt. She was right . . . but the seconds ticked by, and no inspiration came.

And the shark was two minutes away. "There's a predator bearing down on us," Kennedy muttered under her breath, her face tight with concentration. Still not ready to give up. "Self-preservation ought to come into play *some*time here."

"Unless they're like the Tampies," Ferrol grunted. "Ready to roll over and die whenever—"

He broke off, head jerking around as it suddenly hit him. "That's *it*. They *are* like the Tampies—they're both nonpredator species."

"I don't see—"

"Demothi!" Ferrol cut her off. "Get that helmet on— *now*."

"Lander?" Roman's voice came sharply. "What's going on?"

"Maybe a chance to wake Quentin up," Ferrol shouted over his shoulder. Demothi was fumbling with the helmet—fumbling far too slowly—there; it was off Pplazii's head, and he was easing it over his own. "I think that's why Quentin originally spooked and Jumped, Captain—it sensed Demothi as being a predator and tried to get away. If he can spook it again—"

Without warning, the lander lurched violently, slamming Ferrol's teeth down on his tongue. He had just enough time to taste blood—

And suddenly a blue-white star blazed in front of them, a faint luminescent haze outlining Quentin like a halo.

They'd done it.

It took Kennedy and her people an hour to plot their position and figure out a route back to the Cordonale. It took Rrin-saa and his people almost as long to decide what to do with Quentin.

"I don't understand," Roman said. His eyes flicked past Rrin-saa, to where Sso-ngii and Hhom-jee sat quietly together under the twin amplifier helmets that now were wired into the Handler room. "I thought it was *you* who were so dead-set against abandoning Quentin the first place."

"We could not leave him to the shark," the Tampy said. "But the danger is now gone."

"So why release him?" Roman persisted.

"Because he is damaged," Rrin-saa said. "Not in body, but in his deeper self."

"All the more reason to bring it back," Roman countered. "Surely your people can do something to help."

"It is not a matter of helping," Rrin-saa said, and Roman could almost hear a note of sadness in the whiny alien inflections. "It is a matter of betrayed trust."

Roman frowned. "I'm sorry, but I just don't understand. What happened wasn't your fault."

"We brought Quentinnnini into our service, Rromaa. We attached him to a ship, spoke deeply into his mind. In exchange for such service, we promised him care and protection. Instead, we exposed him to great danger. Further, we forced him into such trauma that he entered *perasiata* as the only way to endure it." The Tampy gave a wheezing sigh. "How can we now pretend nothing has happened?"

Roman pursed his lips. "It seems to me that circumstances warrant giving yourselves a second chance."

"We made a promise," Rrin-saa said simply.

Roman sighed. The Starforce and Senate weren't going to like this at all . . . but *Amity*'s charter specifically stated the Tampies had final say in any decision concerning space horse health. This was close enough. "All right. There's probably no advantage in sending Quentin off wrapped up in space horse webbing. If you'll allow me another hour, I'll send a boat out to remove the stuff properly."

"That will be acceptable," Rrin-saa agreed. "Thank you, Rro-maa."

An hour later, Roman watched from the bridge as Quentin drove swiftly away into the black of space . . . and wondered if perhaps the Tampies really were too alien for human beings to ever truly understand.

Chapter 22

The hearings convened forty-eight hours later—not in the relative luxury of the Solomon state house this time, but in Earth orbit in the grim starkness of the warship C.S.S. *Defiance*. At Solomon, the Starforce and Senate had been more or less evenly represented; here, such balance was summarily dispensed with. Military men and women dominated the sessions, with the handful of civilians present participating mainly through intent listening.

The Senator, of course, was one of those civilians. As Ferrol had expected he would be.

But for the first three days they had literally no chance to speak privately. Ferrol's days were filled to the brim with debriefings; sometimes alone, other times with Roman or Kennedy or Tenzing sharing the stand with him. Nights were likewise filled, with fatigued sleep punctuated by disturbed dreams of sharks and vultures.

And of Prometheus. It had been this same *Defiance* which had taken him and the other evicted colonists away from their world. More than once, he wondered if choosing this particular ship for the hearings had been someone's twisted idea of a joke.

Awake, he talked; asleep, he dreamed . . . and at all

times he waited with growing impatience for the Senator to finally draw him aside. On the fourth day, the last one scheduled, he got tired of waiting.

"I'm sorry," Stefain Reese said, his tone a combination of firm and bland, "but the Senator is really *very* busy at the moment."

"He'll see me," Ferrol told him, craning his neck to see past the half-closed door into the other part of the office suite. The Senator was there, all right, in deep conversation with another civilian and two military men in heavily decorated dress uniforms. "Tell him who it is."

The other hesitated just a second, then picked up his phone and murmured into it. Straining, Ferrol could hear the tone of the Senator's speech change— "He says for you to go back to your room, Ferrol, that he'll call you later."

A quiet alarm bell went off in the back of Ferrol's brain. The scheduled return to *Amity* was barely two hours away. "There isn't going to be any 'later,' " he told Reese. "Tell the Senator I'll give him one minute to get rid of his guests. After that, I'll go on in and state my business in front of all of them."

Reese gave him a long, thoughtful look, as if weighing the feasibility of calling Security. Ferrol countered with a stare of his own; and after a moment Reese dropped his eyes and spoke again into the phone. A short pause— "He'll be right with you," he muttered.

Ferrol nodded and, for no particular reason, began counting off the seconds. Fifty-five of them later, the Senator's visitors got to their feet and, with only casual glances in Ferrol's direction, filed out of the suite.

The Senator remained standing in the inner doorway; and as the last of his guests left, his gaze shifted deliberately to Ferrol. A calm gaze, even and totally devoid of emotion. "Commander," he nodded in a voice that matched the gaze. "Do come in."

Silently, Ferrol eased past him into the room. This

time, the Senator closed the door all the way. "You interrupted an important meeting," he told Ferrol, crossing to an ornate metal desk in the corner and seating himself behind it.

"I'll be leaving the *Defiance* in two hours," Ferrol told him, successfully fighting the automatic urge to apologize. For once he wasn't going to let the Senator put him on the defensive right from word one. "Sometime in the next twelve hours *Amity*'ll get her orders, and it'll be off to God knows where, for God knows how long. Breaking up a meeting was the only way I was ever going to get to talk to you."

The Senator lifted an eyebrow. "And what makes you think we have anything to talk about?"

For a long minute Ferrol stared at him. "I don't understand."

The Senator's lip twisted. "Then let me spell it out in block letters: you, Chayne, are no longer in my service."

Ferrol felt his mouth fall open. "What?" he whispered. "But . . . why not?"

"Does it matter?" the other asked.

Ferrol swallowed hard, moisture in his eyes making the room swim. The air around him had turned abruptly cold, filled with ice and disapproval and contempt. Suddenly he was a child again, facing his father's anger. . . .

He fought the feeling back. He was not a child, and the man facing him was not his father. "Yes," he gritted out between clenched teeth—clenched so that they wouldn't chatter with emotion. "It matters. For years now I've been one of your best agents—"

" 'Best'?" The Senator snorted in a genteel sort of way. "Oh, come now, Chayne, you don't even fool yourself on *that* one. You were useful, certainly, but hardly one of the best. That status takes far more years of experience than you've even been alive."

"And I won't be having any more of that experience now, will I?" Ferrol countered. The helpless childlike feeling was fading, leaving behind a growing anger. "Why?"

"For one thing, there's a little matter of confidence," the Senator said, his manner shifting abruptly from daunting to idly offhanded. Perhaps he'd recognized the other approach wasn't working. "When an agent of mine freely offers classified information to an opponent—well, I'm sure you can see how that could make me reluctant to keep such an agent on."

It took Ferrol a second to realize just what the hell the other was talking about. "Senator, we were facing a life and death situation out there," he growled. "Would you rather I have played dumb with Kheslav's data and let the shark eat *Amity* and me both?"

"From what Captain Roman has testified, Kheslav's data didn't really seem to help him much."

"No, it didn't," Ferrol conceded. "But that was hardly something I could have known in advance."

"Perhaps. The fact remains that the datapack was private information, and that you had no business possessing a copy of it in the first place."

"And that's the *real* issue here, isn't it," Ferrol said. "The fact that I had illegally obtained information that could be traced to you."

He expected a reaction of some sort—anger, caution; *something* that would give him a glimpse into what the other was thinking. But as usual, the Senator denied him even that much. "Illegally obtained?" he asked mildly. "Come now, Chayne—how on Earth can information about a creature orbiting an unclaimed planet be illegally obtained? And as for tracing it back to me, don't be absurd. I cover my tracks better than *that*." The Senator shook his head. "No, Chayne, the real issue here, as you put it, is not whether you and your past activities—any of them—can be linked to me. It's not even whether or not I can still trust you to function on my behalf; I really only brought up the Kheslav thing to air my disappointment with how you handled the situation. The *real* issue—" he paused dramatically —"is that we've won."

Ferrol frowned. "What do you mean, we've won? Won what?"

"Our undeclared, non-shooting war with the Tempies, of course," the other said. "Come now; surely the implications of these sharks on space horse transport haven't been lost on you."

"There are implications there, all right," Ferrol nodded, "but not the ones you seem to be thinking of. The sharks didn't just spring up last week out of sawdust somewhere, and if the Tampies have been running space horses all these centuries without bumping into them, they must be pretty rare. At least around here."

"Agreed; but their abundance or lack of it may not be the important factor. According to Captain Roman's testimony, the Tampies have a rather lopsided sense of almost contractual responsibility toward their space horses, to the extent that they'll let the animals go free if they feel their side of the bargain has been violated. Whatever the hell kind of bargain you can make with a non-intelligent animal, that is," he added with thinly veiled contempt.

So that was why Roman and Rrin-saa had turned Quentin loose . . . and perhaps why Roman had been so evasive to Ferrol about his reasons. If the mere existence of the sharks could really induce the Tampies to dismantle their space-going capability . . . "So what are you going to do?" he asked. "Web a shark and drag it to the Tampies' Kialinninni corral system?"

The Senator smiled thinly. "Give me credit for a *little* common sense, Chayne," he said dryly. "Besides which, I don't think anything that drastic or dangerous will be necessary. The sharks are predators, after all, and predators must have *some* way of locating their prey. In time, they'll find Kialinninni on their own."

"At which point we settle for a draw."

The Senator lifted an eyebrow. "Meaning . . . ?"

"Meaning no space horses for us *or* for the Tampies.

They'll be stuck inside their systems, and we'll be stuck with our Mitsuushi snaildrive."

The Senator's face darkened. "At least we'll have the stars."

"Some of them. Not very many."

"We'll have enough," the other said firmly. "All the planets we'll ever need are within our reach right now. Provided, that is, we don't have the Tampies standing over us telling us what we can and cannot do with them."

Ferrol's thoughts flashed back to the discoveries *Amity* had brought back from its first voyage—discoveries that had been overshadowed in both public and official minds by the excitement of Pegasus' calving. "Oh, we'll have enough room, all right," he snorted. "But we'll be giving up the rest of the universe in the process. And maybe for nothing. Now that we know about sharks, the problems Demothi and everyone before him has had trying to control space horses make sense."

"Yes; your 'predator invading a non-predator's mind' theory," the Senator said. "You brought that up about every third question. So what do you suggest we do? —web a shark and offer Demothi a chance to ride it?"

Ferrol clamped his mouth shut, the presentation he'd so carefully prepared and rehearsed over the past two days dying in his throat. The Senator was truly and totally uninterested in obtaining space horse capabilities for the Cordonale; his only interest was in robbing the Tampies of theirs. Period.

Had that always been his goal? Probably. Dimly, Ferrol wondered why he'd never recognized that. "Given your obvious disinterest," he said tightly, "I suppose there's really nothing to discuss."

"As I said when you came in," the Senator reminded him, standing up. "Now if you'll excuse me—"

"I presume my commission with the *Amity* is still valid," Ferrol continued, not moving. "If only because dropping me out now might attract unwelcome attention. So. What about my ship?"

The Senator frowned. "What ship is—? Oh, you mean the *Scapa Flow*. What about it?"

"You told me when I signed onto the *Amity* that you'd be using it for private courier work," he reminded the other. "Is that agreement still valid, or are all of my crewers officially off the payroll now, too?"

The other favored him with a long, speculative look. "I've never been impressed by people who try to keep their foot in the door on their way out," he said coldly.

"I have no interest whatsoever in keeping my foot in with you," Ferrol countered, matching the Senator's tone. "I'm interested solely in the well-being of my crew. You owe them some measure of financial security, at least as long as I'm still watching out for your interests aboard the *Amity*."

The Senator's lip twisted, but he nodded. "I *owe* them nothing; but I suppose I can go ahead and buy out their contract. If that will be satisfactory . . . ?" he added with thinly veiled sarcasm.

"Quite satisfactory," Ferrol nodded in return, getting to his feet. "Thank you, Senator; and for your time, as well." He turned to go—

"Chayne?"

He turned back. "Yes?"

"If I were you," the other said quietly, "I wouldn't count on the *Amity* remaining in service for too much longer."

Ferrol stared at him. "I don't understand."

The Senator smiled faintly. "You will."

Two hours later Ferrol left the *Defiance* with the others and headed back toward the *Amity*. It was a long shuttle ride, which was fine with him. It gave him time to think.

An hour after arriving at the *Amity*, he was in the ship's main communications room with a short, laboriously hand-coded message.

Even with their skyhook prices, the Cordonale's tachyon transceivers were normally so jammed with messages that delays of twenty-four to forty-eight hours were not uncommon. But Ferrol's status as exec of a major Starforce ship gave him an impressive priority factor, and barely thirty minutes later the central Earth transceiver relayed an acknowledgment of the message from the *Scapa Flow*.

The Senator might be willing to settle for a draw. Ferrol wasn't . . . and if no one else was interested, then he and the *Scapa Flow* would just have to do it on their own.

Chapter 23

For the next four days the *Amity* remained in Earth orbit, waiting for orders, while conflicting rumors as to what those orders might be swept through the ship like a sequential set of gas leaks. When they finally came, it was a distinct anticlimax: *Amity* would return to Solomon to trade Man o' War for its next space horse. The breeding program, apparently, would continue.

They were back in Solomon system an hour later, and within a few more had made orbit around the planet. There they were met by a Tampy ship and the cumbersome but reasonably straightforward process of switching space horses was performed. Man o' War and the Tampy ship left, leaving Sso-ngii and the other Handlers to settle in for a few hours of taking turns under the amplifier helmet—introducing themselves to the newcomer, Rrin-saa had once tried to explain it. The same hours on *Amity*'s human half were considerably less filled, with activities consisting mainly of last minute checks, idle conversation, and practice in saying "Sleipnir" instead of "Man o' War" when referring to the source of the ship's main motive power.

Several days were normally allotted for the welcoming/acclimation procedure. But Sleipnir was a quick study; or else the extensive practice *Amity*'s assembly-line schedule had forced on its Handlers was beginning to pay off. Whichever, within a single day—less than forty-eight hours after leaving Earth—*Amity* was ready.

And for the next six weeks, as per orders, that was how it remained. In Solomon orbit, and ready.

"Sorry to wake you, sir," the bridge officer said apologetically. "But the overcode on this was marked 'urgent.'"

"That's all right," Roman assured her, rubbing the last bits of sleep from his eyes and shrugging on a robe before switching on the intercom's visual. He keyed in to the laser comm circuit— "Solomon tachyon station, this is Captain Roman," he identified himself. "Acceptance code follows." He keyed the sequence into his terminal.

"Acknowledged," the station said a few seconds later. "Beginning transmission."

Roman leaned forward, mentally crossing his fingers. If this wasn't, in fact, some kind of orders—

TO RESEARCH SHIP *AMITY*, SOLOMON: FROM COMMANDER STARFORCE BORDERSHIPS EXTENSION, PREPYAT:

:::URGENT-ONE:::URGENT-ONE:::URGENT-ONE:::

HUMAN/TAMPLISSTA STUDY TEAM AT NCL 9862 OVERDUE. *AMITY* TO PROCEED IMMEDIATELY PREPYAT; CONTINUE ON TO 9862 WITH RESEARCH SHIPS *ATLANTIS*, *STARSEEKER*, AND *JNANA* IN TOW.

FURTHER INFORMATION AVAILABLE FROM RESEARCH SHIPS.

VICE-ADMIRAL MARCOSA, COMBOREX, PREPYAT CODE/ VER *@7882//53

2:16 GMT///ESD 6 MAY 2336

Roman read the message twice, a cold chill settling

into his stomach. There was something wrong here. Something *very* wrong . . .

"Any orders, sir?" the bridge officer's voice prompted. From her tone, it was clear she was desperately hoping there were some.

Roman took a deep breath. "Alert the Handler," he told her. "We're Jumping to Prepyat as soon as he and Sleipnir are ready. Number One web crew to start prepping their equipment—we'll be taking three ships in tow, and we'll need to run tether lines to them." He hesitated. "And wake Lieutenant Kennedy. Tell her I want her dressed and on the bridge in fifteen minutes."

The three ships were grouped tightly together a hundred meters away from the *Amity*, holding to an almost perfect zero-vee-relative as the two web boats moved among them fixing tether lines. Standing on the velgrip beside the command station, Kennedy studied the activity on Roman's display. "Opinion, Lieutenant?" Roman asked her quietly.

"I'd say no doubt, sir," she shook her head. "Even at this distance you can see that the missile tubes haven't been sealed. And that ion projector just under the main sensor bulge on the *Atlantis* would never have been left on a surplused ship. Legalities aside, the things are just too expensive to give away."

Roman nodded. Her conclusions, unfortunately, jibed with his own. "So what we really have here is an unmarked military task force."

"Yes, sir. If I had to guess, I'd say the *Atlantis* is either a destroyer or light cruiser, and the other two are converted and possibly beefed-up corvettes."

Firepower, and to spare. "What about the 9862 system itself? Dug up anything on that yet?"

"Yes, sir," she said, leaning over his shoulder to tap a few keys on his console. A chart appeared on Roman's helm display, with the star marked in flashing brackets. "It's a blue-white giant, about six hundred light-years from the Cordonale. Pretty undistinguished, as far as I can see from what little we've got on it. No mention of any visits to the system; no indication, for that matter, that anybody's ever so much as had a passing interest in the place."

"Until now," Roman said, tapping the data listing on the display. "I note the star's very similar in size and magnitude to the one the shark chased us away from. Coincidence?"

"It could be a *yishyar*," Kennedy agreed. "I guess we'll know for sure in a couple of hours."

Roman's radio crackled. "Web One to *Amity*. All finished here; we're coming in."

"Acknowledged," Roman said, and switched to the comm laser. "*Amity* to *Atlantis*; come in."

"*Atlantis*; Captain Lekander," the calm—and very military—voice came back promptly. The face on the screen was an excellent match to the voice. "What's our status, *Amity*?"

"My web boats will be back in about ten minutes," Roman told him. "At that point we'll be ready whenever you are."

"Good," Lekander said briskly. "I'm not sure what you were told, Captain, but here's the scenerio. A research team running on a *very* precise schedule has come up almost six hours overdue. We're going in to find out what happened to them."

"Pretending to be a civilian research team?" Roman asked mildly.

Lekander's face didn't change. "It was thought your Tampies might balk at ferrying military ships," he said. "That's not important. What *is* important is that you understand you're here strictly as transport; you will not—repeat *not*—get involved in whatever happens once we reach the system. You will sit tight until we're ready to go, observe everything that happens, and stay *out* of it. For the observing part, we'll be sending over a boat containing a high-power telescope/recorder when we reach 9862. The sitting-tight part is your responsibility."

Roman locked eyes with him. "And if there turn out to be vultures in the system?" he asked bluntly.

"If you feel you're in immediate danger," Lekander said stolidly, "you're authorized to Jump to the 66802 system—about two light-years away—and wait for us to rendezvous with you on Mitsuushi. Otherwise, we should have no problem clearing the vultures off you before we leave."

Roman nodded, a hollow feeling in the pit of his stomach. "That assumes," he said quietly, "that you *will* be leaving."

Lekander's face cracked, just slightly, into a tight smile. "Don't worry," he said. "We'll be leaving, all right." He paused. "But the boat I'll be sending you will also have an AA-26 midrange sub-nuke torpedo aboard. Just in case."

Sleipnir Jumped, the task force disengaged from their tether lines and headed off, and *Amity*'s crew set about unpacking Lekander's telescope/recorder from the boat *Atlantis* had sent across.

They also unpacked the sub-nuke torpedo and mounted it and its launcher to the outer hull. Just in case.

And when that was done, and the telescope was tracking the departing fusion tracks, there was nothing to do but wait. For hours and hours . . .

"They certainly seem to know where they're going," Kennedy said, leaning back in the helm chair and watching the task force's progress. "There's nothing of a search pattern about their course—they're just heading straight across into the asteroids."

"Must have a beacon on the missing ship," Marlowe agreed, studying his own displays. "Damned if I can pick up the signal, though."

"Probably a split-wave," Kennedy told him. "Or something equally private. I'd guess they're doing a minimum-time course, Captain; as soon as they make turnover we'll be able to figure their endpoint."

"Can't we do that now?" Ferrol asked. "We should at least be able to track along their projected path."

"I'm already doing that," Marlowe said. "So far, I haven't found anything that could be a ship."

For a moment the bridge was silent. Roman thought about how the shark had tried to tear *Amity* apart . . . "They could be behind an asteroid," he reminded them. "Let's not assume the worst until—"

"Movement!" Marlowe snapped. "Portside of the task force, maybe four hundred kilometers away."

"They see it," Kennedy added. "They're altering course—blasting lateral to swing around toward it. Breaking formation . . . they're going for it."

"Give me some more power on this scope, Marlowe," Roman ordered, straining to make out the form that was now definitely picking up speed toward the circling task force. "I can't tell if that's a shark or a space horse."

"One second, Captain—these damned controls are twitchy." The view shimmered, gave an eye-wrenching jerk, steadied and enlarged—

"Holy mother," someone murmured.

Roman found his voice. "What's the scale on that?"

"Measures out to almost twenty-six hundred meters," Marlowe said grimly. "About thirty percent longer than the one we fought, with just over twice its volume."

And if telekinetic strength indeed scaled with volume . . . Roman clamped down hard on the almost overpowering urge to send out a comm laser warning. A waste of time, or worse: Lekander would certainly know what his force was up against, and the last thing he needed was extra distractions. "Any sign of vultures?" he asked instead.

"Not that I can see," Marlowe said. "Definitely no optical nets, anyway, at least not so far. Must recognize that they're not space horses."

"Or else the lack of telekinetic abilities leaves the vultures nothing to lock onto," Roman nodded. "Either way—"

"Got laser fire," Marlowe cut in. "All three ships."

Roman peered at the scope screen. The pale lines of ionized gas were just barely visible as they tracked along the shark's surface. "Any idea what power they're using?"

"Hard to say at this distance," Marlowe said. "Though if they're standard combat lasers—yowp; there goes the shark."

The huge predator swerved violently as one of the beams raked up toward its forward end. The laser corrected; but even as it found its target again, a cloud seemed to detach itself from the shark's body and flow forward. "There go the vultures," Ferrol muttered under his breath.

"The lasers must have hit a sensory ring," Kennedy said. "—Firing again."

Again, the pale lines lanced out . . . but this time they stopped far short of their intended target, disappearing into the cloud that had coalesced in their path. "Is that the vultures doing that?" Roman asked Marlowe.

"Affirmative," the other nodded. "Looks like they've got a screen of rocks set up, a sort of heavy-duty optical net. Though against military lasers—there; got a punch-through."

One of the pale lines had pierced the barrier, and once again the shark twitched away from its touch. But almost instantly the beam was cut off again. "They got the hole filled in," Marlowe reported grimly. "Those sharks learn fast, don't they?"

"It can't keep that up forever, though," Ferrol shook his head. "Eventually it's got to run out of vultures."

"Yeah, but maybe not before the ships get within grabbing range," Marlowe pointed out. "If enough of that barrier is rock and not vulture, they may be able to hold it together long enough."

A tiny flare sparked at the *Jnana*'s hull— "Missile away," Kennedy identified it. "Heading for the vultures. Make that two," she amended as a second flicker appeared beside the *Starseeker*.

Roman frowned as the two flares swung into alignment, the second crowding the tail of the first. The lead missile reached the laser barrier—

"Missile breaking up," Marlowe announced. "Must be a net missile; yes, there's a glint from the filaments. Spreading around the vultures—*damn.*"

"What?" Roman snapped.

"Plasma discharge from the net," Marlowe said, sounding stunned. "Absolutely massive. Must have had a thousand amps and at least that many volts on it."

"*That* got the barrier open, all right," Kennedy said. "Second missile going straight through the hole. Shark's telekening it to the side—must think it's another net missile—"

And an instant later the center of the screen went black as sunscreens kicked in. "Sub-nuke explosion, Captain," Marlowe said. "Shaped blast, about a twenty-megaton rating, triggered approximately fifty kilometers out from the shark."

Roman hissed between his teeth. Even at *Amity's* distance . . . "Ferrol, call down to Tenzing's people and have them put a real-time monitor on the radiation," Roman ordered. "And have the Tampies watch for signs of stress in Sleipnir. We should be well clear of any trouble, but there's no point in taking chances."

"Yes, sir," Ferrol said, and turned to his intercom. On the scope screen the black dot was shrinking and fading—

And the shark was still moving. Sluggish, but clearly alive.

Roman shook his head in wonderment . . . in wonderment, and with the first stirrings of real fear. Even at fifty kilometers away a blast that size should have delivered a thunderclap of heat and particle radiation directly into the shark's surface and sensory clusters. If it could shrug off something that powerful—

"Missile away," Kennedy announced into his thoughts; clenching his teeth, Roman shifted his attention back to the ships. A flare had appeared beside the *Atlantis*; and beside the *Starseeker*, and beside the *Jnana*, and beside the *Atlantis* again— "Correction: barrage away," Kennedy amended. "Looks like they're throwing everything they have at it." The first missile flare erupted in a dim pinprick of light—

"They've gone to chemical warheads," Marlowe said, sounding stunned.

"Must be trying to kill it without excessive damage," Kennedy suggested. "Probably figured the first subnuke had taken enough of the fight out of it."

"Damn fool risky," Marlowe muttered. "There it goes, though. Turning around and . . . wait a minute. What the *hell*?"

The shark had veered ponderously away from the incoming missiles; but instead of turning a full 180 degrees and running, it proceded to trace out a convoluted path that seemed to be part helix, part spiral, and part random. Through it all the pinpricks of exploding warheads continued to flare across the middle of the display, looking for all the world like some strange space-going species of firefly.

And then, even as the task force launched a fresh barrage of missiles, the shark finally turned tail and fled.

"Only pulling about two gees," Kennedy reported. "It's hurt, all right."

"Hurt, and gone crazy both," Ferrol snorted gently. "What the hell *was* that, anyway?—the dying-swan version of a mating dance?"

"Or else an attempt at evasive maneuvers," Marlowe offered. "It was still doing a fair job of telekening those missiles away from it the whole time, even though they were getting closer there at the end."

"It's slowing down," Kennedy said, peering intently at her helm display. "Acceleration dropping toward zero . . . make that *at* zero."

Roman held his breath. Again the firefly flashes dotted the screen—

But this time, directly against the shark's surface.

"They've got it," Kennedy grunted. "—There go the lasers again."

"Ion beams, too," Marlowe reported. "And they're getting through—the explosions must have scattered the vultures. God, those lasers are actually cutting into the shark's hide. Cutting *deep* into it."

Between the lasers, ion beams, and warheads the light show went on for another twenty minutes . . . and when it was finally over, there was no doubt whatsoever that the shark was dead.

Or, to be more precise, what was *left* of the shark was dead.

"Well," Marlowe said to no one in particular, "that'll certainly give them a head start on dissecting the thing."

With an effort, Roman unclamped his jaw. "A head start, and then some." He reached for the comm laser control, set for tracking. The indicator flashed— "*Amity* to *Atlantis*," he called. "Come in, *Atlantis*."

"*Atlantis*; Captain Lekander," the reply came a few seconds later. "You enjoy the show, *Amity*?"

"It's just nice to know the things *can* be killed," Roman told him dryly. "We'd had our doubts."

"Anything alive can be killed," Lekander countered. "It's just a matter of having the right tools for the job."

"I imagine. So what happens now?"

"We'll give the area a few hours to cool off, then send a team over to do some dissection," Lekander said. "Assuming there's enough of it left by then—I don't know if you can see it from there, but the vultures have gone ahead and started lunch already. So much for honor among thieves, I guess."

"Um." Roman's helm display changed to show Kennedy's projection of the shark's drift. "How much time were you planning to spend studying the carcass, Captain?" he asked.

"That's fairly open-ended," Lekander said. "Why?"

"Our projection shows you'll be passing within a few hundred thousand kilometers of our current position,"

Roman explained. "We could rendezvous out there with you and take the whole carcass back with us."

"That's tempting, but no," the other said. "Like I said, you're supposed to sit there where we left you and not get involved."

Roman nodded. "Understood. Just thought I'd ask."

"Rro-maa?"

Roman jumped at the voice; he hadn't realized anyone from the Tampy section was listening. "Yes?"

"May we ask Lle-kann if the missing space horse has been located?"

Roman's face warmed with embarrassment. Concentrating on the shark, he'd totally forgotten the ship they'd come here to rescue in the first place. "Good question," he agreed. "How about it, Captain?"

"There's no sign of either the ship or the space horse," Lekander said, his tone just a shade too casual. "But I wouldn't worry too much about that. My guess is that they spotted the shark, dropped their beacon, and got out before the vultures could catch them."

Roman stared at the intercom, a nasty suspicion beginning to knot his stomach. "You told me they were six hours overdue at port," he reminded Lekander. "Even if they had had to Jump to a different star first, it wouldn't have taken them an extra six hours to find their way home."

"Maybe they had mechanical difficulty," Lekander said tartly. "Or stopped to calve or something."

"Or maybe they got home fine," Roman countered, "and all this rush was just to get out here before the shark left?"

"I don't really see," Lekander said, a noticeable edge to his voice, "how any of this could possibly matter."

Roman grimaced. No, Lekander probably didn't see. But someone above him surely had . . . and that someone had apparently realized that persuading Tampies to participate in a rescue mission would be a hell of a lot easier than talking them into joining a shark hunt.

And that same someone had obviously decided that keeping Roman in the dark would help sell the story.

"Rro-maa?"

Roman braced himself. "Yes, Rrin-saa?"

"Is it true that there was no one in danger here?"

He hesitated. "I don't know, Rrin-saa," he told the alien truthfully. "I really don't."

For a long moment the Tampy was silent. "We are not predators, Rro-maa," he said at last. "We do not kill without reason, nor interfere with the patterns of nature without cause."

"Rrin-saa, it's necessary that we learn as much about these sharks as we can," Roman said, cursing whoever the mallet-head was who'd put him in the middle like this. "As much for your benefit as for ours. If there are sharks moving into this region, your space horses will be in danger."

"When it becomes necessary, we will do what we can to protect them," Rrin-saa said. "You have lied to us, Rro-maa."

"The lie was to both of us, Rrin-saa," Roman said quietly. "I'm sorry."

"I am sorry, too," the Tampy said. "The *Amity* experiment has been built on trust. That trust is now gone."

Roman's stomach tightened. "Perhaps the trust can be rebuilt."

"No. The *Amity* experiment is at an end."

Rrin-saa's words seemed to echo through the bridge. Roman stared at the intercom without really seeing it, head spinning with disbelief. The last fragile diplomatic link between human and Tampy; and it was going to be lost over *this*? "What about the space horse breeding program? Surely that's worth something."

"It is worth more than you can imagine," Rrin-saa said, his voice almost sad. "And we will sorely regret its loss. But we have no choice. Our first duty is to honor the patterns of nature, and you have forced us through deceit to violate that duty." He paused. "I do not expect you to understand."

Roman sighed. "We have ethics, too, Rrin-saa. It's just that pragmatism is too often considered the most important of them."

"And duty is only to yourselves." Roman winced, but there was no bitterness he could hear in the Tampy's voice. Only more sadness. "I do not believe you will ever learn otherwise. We will return you and the others to Solomon when you are ready. We will then return Sleipnninni to Kialinninni."

"Rhin-saa—"

The intercom screen went blank.

Slowly, Roman looked up . . . to find Ferrol watching him. "You have a comment, Commander?"

Ferrol's face was hard. "I think he's bluffing, Captain."

Roman eyed him. "You think so, do you?"

"Yes, sir, I do," Ferrol said doggedly. "They aren't going to just throw away the breeding program—certainly not on the whim of a single Tampy. Their leaders will turn it around; and in the meantime, they'll have taken the opportunity to load a little more of that wonderful Tampy guilt onto our backs. It's emotional manipulation, pure and simple . . . and I think everyone else here can see that."

"Perhaps everyone else can," Roman said. Suddenly, he was very tired. "But then, general agreement has always been an unreliable indicator for truth." Unstrapping, he pushed out of his seat. "Continue with the observation and recording; I'll be in my cabin." He gripped the back of his headrest, aimed himself toward the bridge door—

"Captain, we're getting movement," Kennedy spoke up. "About two hundred thousand kilometers beyond the task force."

"Heading straight for them," Marlowe cut in. "Picking up speed now—" he turned to look at Roman, his face rigid. "Captain, it's another shark."

Roman twisted in midair and shoved himself back into his chair, grabbing for his restraints with one hand and keying the comm laser with the other. "*Amity* to

Atlantis; emergency. You've got another shark on your tails."

"We see it," Lekander's voice came back calmly. "Relax, *Amity*—we know how to handle these things now."

"I sure as hell hope so," Roman muttered under his breath, his eyes on the shark now centered in the scope screen. Still accelerating . . . "Marlowe, find out where that thing came from," he ordered. "Specifically, whether it just Jumped in or whether it's been lurking there watching the whole time."

"Yes, sir."

The task force was pulling away from the carcass, coming around and spreading out for battle. The pale laser tracks lanced out . . . and disappeared into the cloud of vultures running before the shark. "Marlowe? Snap it up," Roman gritted, a sudden surge of dread curdling through his stomach. If the shark had been watching—if all that intelligence and learning ability had already seen the ships' weapons in action . . .

"Got it, Captain," Marlowe announced. "The record shows a definite Jump point. It just got here, less than two minutes ago."

So it hadn't been there for the earlier battle; which meant it was sheer dumb luck that its vulture cloud had just happened to block the first laser salvo. Dumb luck, and nothing more.

But the sinking feeling refused to go away.

"It's not turning over," Kennedy said abruptly. "Captain, it's not doing a turnover for a zero-vee rendezvous with the task force. And it's still accelerating."

"It's going to ram them," Ferrol breathed.

Roman felt his hands curling into fists. "*Amity* to *Atlantis*—Captain, get your force out of there."

"Shut up, Roman," Lekander's voice snarled. "We're busy. Ready; *fire*."

On the screen, half a dozen flares suddenly flickered from the sides of the three ships. The missiles skittered away toward the shark—

And abruptly stopped.

Roman stared in disbelief. The missiles, their drives still flaring impotently away, sat frozen in space perhaps a third of the way to the shark

"The shark's stopped accelerating," Kennedy said, her voice very quiet. "It's holding the missiles back— putting that as its top priority." She looked back at Roman. "Which means it recognizes that the missiles are its chief danger."

"But it *can't*," Marlowe protested. "It just *got* here—it can't possibly know about the missiles."

Ferrol swore, suddenly, under his breath. "It's the vultures," he said. "It has to be. The first shark's vultures must have recorded the battle and then relayed it to the other one."

Roman gritted his teeth. The shark was continuing to move toward the task force; but the missiles, frozen in its telekene grip, were still hanging midway between ships and predator. "It's holding them, but isn't strong enough to push them back," he said. "Marlowe: assuming those are sub-nukes, how much closer do they have to get before triggering them will damage the shark?"

"They can't trigger them," Kennedy put in before Marlowe could answer. "The ships are way too close now themselves for that. If they tried it—"

She broke off as, on the screen, the missile flares abruptly and simultaneously vanished. "Marlowe?" Roman snapped.

"It broke them up," Marlowe murmured, a horrified awe in his voice. "Just . . . tore them to shreds."

And if there had been any doubt left, it was gone now. The shark knew exactly what it was up against . . . and exactly how to fight back.

And Lekander knew it. On the screen the three ships were veering away, blasting lateral to the shark's momentum. Roman held his breath— "*Atlantis* to *Amity*," Lekander's icy voice came suddenly, making him jump. "We track some vultures heading your way; better get out while you can."

"Never mind *us*—get yourselves out," Roman retorted. "You can't possibly defeat the shark now."

"We'd figured that out, thank you," Lekander growled. "Get to the 66802 system—we'll be there when we can. *Atlantis* out."

The console pinged its loss of the laser signal. "Idiots," Ferrol bit out. "What the hell are they waiting for?"

"They can't leave," Kennedy said quietly. "That subnuke explosion—the one they used on the first shark—will have fully ionized their Mitsuushi rings. It'll be at least another ten minutes before they can use them."

Ferrol stared at her, not saying anything. But then, Roman thought numbly, there really wasn't anything else to say.

On the screen the ships were still driving laterally, their accelerations up to eight gees. *They can do it*, Roman told himself, trying hard to believe it. *Just a few more minutes.*

And as he watched, the *Starseeker* faltered in its rush outward. Faltered, slowed to a stop . . . and began to fall back.

"Captain?" Marlowe said hesitantly. "I'm picking up those vultures now. They'll be in position to set up an optical net in maybe fifteen minutes."

Roman nodded. Of course the vultures would come for them; it was a pattern of nature out here, too inevitable for him to even feel anger about it. "Kennedy, send the vector for the 66802 system to the Tampy section," he ordered quietly. "Tell the Handler to prepare for an emergency Jump as soon as Sleipnir's in position. Ferrol . . . arm the torpedo. Target toward the vultures, close-in blast—I don't want them seeing which direction Sleipnir is pointing when we Jump."

A muscle in Ferrol's cheek twitched. "Understood, Captain," he said, and turned to his task. A moment later, "Torpedo armed and ready, sir."

"Fire."

Roman watched the flare streak off toward the approaching vultures. Then, with an effort, he turned his attention back to the scope screen.

The *Starseeker* was still falling back toward the shark. Falling through the vulture shield . . . and all at once, the ship seemed to expand and vanish. Its attention no longer divided, the shark began accelerating again; and at an unheard-of ten gees set off in pursuit of the *Jnana*.

"Handler reports Sleipnir in position," Captain," Kennedy said, her voice sounding distant in his ears.

"Set torpedo for five-second detonation." Roman took a deep breath. To run away now . . . but there was absolutely nothing they could do. "Jump."

The NCL 66802 system was just under two light-years away; two and a half days by Mitsuushi. Its collective fingers crossed, *Amity* settled down to wait.

Ten days later, neither the *Jnana* nor the *Atlantis* had joined them.

Chapter 24

"As executive officer," Ferrol said, working hard to keep his voice calm and formal, "one of my jobs is to inform the captain whenever I believe his course of action to be ill-advised or detrimental to the ship, the crew, or the best interests of the Cordonale. Therefore—"

"You'd like to know why we're still sitting out here?" Roman interrupted mildly. "Waiting for a task force that's ten days overdue on a two-day trip?"

Ferrol clenched his teeth. "Yes, sir, I do," he said firmly. The captain had evaded this meeting for two whole days now, and Ferrol was damned if Roman was going to undercut his arguments with that agreeable/civilized act of his. "Particularly when our delay prevents the Starforce from receiving information vital to the security of the Cordonale. Standing orders on that—"

"I take it, then, that you don't think there could still be survivors?"

Ferrol locked eyes with him. "Do you?" he asked bluntly.

Roman's expression didn't change. "There's always a chance," he pointed out calmly. "A damaged ship able to make a short Mitsuushi hop could be a few light-hours out from 9862 making repairs. How could we go off and abandon them?"

"We could send a ship back to wait for them," Ferrol told him. "Or drop our report and records at Solomon and then come back ourselves."

Roman's eyebrows went up. "And how would we do that? As soon as we reach the Cordonale, Rrin-saa and the Tampies will be taking Sleipnir back home."

Ferrol snorted. "And that's what this is *really* all about, isn't it? You're mad at the Starforce for their little verbal sleight of hand; and in return you're going to make them sweat a little."

Roman regarded him thoughtfully. "Tell me something, Commander. Back in the 9862 system, just before the second shark appeared, you said the Tampies' anger over being lied to was nothing more than emotional manipulation. Do you really believe that?"

Ferrol glared; but the reflexive answer caught in his throat. He *had* believed it at the time, certainly—it fit all too well with the standard Tampy pattern of shifting blame and guilt wherever possible. But now, with ten days of extra reflection behind him, the whole situation had muddied considerably. It still seemed slightly incredible to him that the Admiralty might have deliberately set up their shark hunt in such a way as to bring *Amity* down along the way . . . and yet, he couldn't shake from his mind that final, self-satisfied expression on the Senator's face. The expression, and the veiled warning that the *Amity* project would soon be ending. . .

And as matters stood now, the Senate could lay the blame for *Amity*'s cancellation squarely on the Tampies' shoulders. And most of the Cordonale would buy it.

"I think there was manipulation going on *some*where," he conceded reluctantly. "I'm not sure anymore which end of it the Tampies were on."

He braced himself for the inevitable sly smile or lift of eyebrows; to his intense relief Roman passed up the obvious comments on Ferrol's change of attitude. "All right," the captain said instead. "Let's assume, then, at least for the moment, that Rrin-saa's reaction was a true indication of how deeply he and the other Tampies felt about being along on the shark hunt. We already know how strongly they feel these things—their giving up of Quentin showed that much."

Or else, Ferrol thought sourly, it showed they'd realized such a deep and early trauma would make the calf useless, anyway. "Fine," he said aloud. "Let's assume that. So what's your point?"

Roman's face remained calm . . . but abruptly Ferrol noticed the hardness lying beneath the surface. "My point," the captain said quietly, "is that all of that was on the record, accessible to anyone who wanted to scuttle *Amity*. I think the verbal sleight of hand, as you put it, was done deliberately, and for that purpose."

Ferrol took a careful breath. "There is, of course, no way to prove it."

"I know. I was thinking more along the lines of offering the Tampies some sort of compensation."

Ferrol blinked. It wasn't what he'd been expecting. "What sort of compensation?"

Roman shrugged, deliberately casual. "You've lived with them for the past year. What could we on the *Amity* offer that they might be willing to accept?"

Ferrol frowned at him . . . and then he got it. "You mean a *calf*?"

"It would seem a suitable parting gift," Roman said. "Wouldn't you say?"

Abruptly, Ferrol realized his mouth was hanging open. "Are you suggesting," he asked carefully, "that we just sit out here—in the middle of *nowhere*—until Sleipnir is ready to have its damn calf?"

Roman smiled faintly. "Why do you think that after putting you off for two days I agreed to see you now?"

"Because you didn't—" Ferrol broke off, feeling his mouth fall open again. "You mean . . . *now*?"

Roman nodded. "All the indications are there," he said. "Rrin-saa tells me a Jump in about an hour will be just about optimum."

Ferrol's eyes drifted to the port, and the unfamiliar

star patterns beyond. "We're not going to do it here, then?"

"I thought we'd go ahead and Jump to Solomon first. That way the Tampies can take both Sleipnir and the new calf home with them immediately."

Ferrol nodded. The stars—the unfamiliar, distant stars—seemed to blur, and he could feel a lump form in his throat. So it was over. The Tampies had pulled the plug on *Amity*, and Roman was going to roll over for them . . . and if the Senator's reading of the aliens was right, space would soon belong to the Cordonale again.

And for want of a little daring, humanity would quietly settle for a draw.

For want of a little daring . . . "With the captain's permission," he said between stiff lips, "I'd like to request the web boat duty."

Roman cocked his head, and Ferrol held his breath. "Very well, Commander," Roman nodded. "You'd best get below, then, and start assembling your team." He paused, his eyes boring into Ferrol's. "Remember that it'll be *Amity*'s last calving," he added quietly. "Make it a memorable one."

A lump rose into Ferrol's throat. "Don't worry, sir. I will."

"Rein lines secure," Yamoto reported from the seat beside him, her voice sounding hollow behind her filter mask. "Calf's starting to pull away."

Ferrol nodded, feeling a tightness in his chest as he turned his head to look at the three Tampies sitting silently behind Yamoto. "Wwis-khaa?—We have control yet?"

"He is calming," the Tampy said, sounding vaguely distracted. Three of the lights on the amplifier helmet, Ferrol noted, were still red. "It will be soon."

"Good." Ferrol turned toward the mike. "Lander to *Amity*," he called. "Calf is secured; full control soon. Any problems with Sleipnir?"

"None at all," Roman told him. "Sso-ngii reports no stress or trauma. Any trouble at your end?"

"Not so far," Ferrol said, striving to sound casual. "At least nothing that Wwis-khaa will admit to. Looks like we aren't going to need extra help in the Handler department, after all."

"Murphy's Law," Roman said dryly. "Still, better to err on the side of caution than the other direction."

"Certainly after what happened with Quentin," Ferrol agreed, ears straining to pick up every nuance. But if the captain suspected Ferrol had had other reasons for bringing three Handlers along, it didn't show in his voice. "Have you decided on a name for the calf yet, sir? Or aren't we going to bother, given that the Tampies will be taking it straight home?"

"I thought perhaps we'd go with something like *Epilog*," Roman said. "Appropriate, and a little more subtle than, say, *Deathblow*."

Ferrol winced at the bitterness in the other's voice. On the other hand, the more of Roman's mind that was tied up with resentment toward the Senate and Starforce, the less he'd have left to wonder if Ferrol was up to anything. "Yes, sir," he said. "Do we have a plan yet on how we're turning Epilog and Sleipnir over to the Tampies?"

"I've already gotten a courier message through to the Kialinnini corral," Roman said. "The Tampies will be sending a pair of piggyback ships here to get them. Though it'll probably be a few more hours before they can leave Kialinnini, so perhaps it's just as well you took a full complement of Handlers out there with you."

Ferrol frowned. "A few *hours*? They have a party going on over there or something?"

Faintly, he heard the hiss of expelled breath. "Apparently the Tampies have decided to respond to the shark threat by pulling the bulk of their fleet back to the corral," he said. "What that gains them, I'm not really sure."

Behind his filter mask, Ferrol felt his lip twist with contempt. So the Senator had indeed been right. The Tampies weren't going to turn their space horses loose, but burying them all at Kialinninni wasn't really much different. Either way, they were effectively giving up. "Gains them some time," he grunted. "Maybe." He half-turned. "Wwis-khaa?"

"He is calm," the Tampy said. "We are speaking."

"Good." Ferrol swallowed hard. "Yamoto, there's a small datapack box strapped into one of the seats back near the entryway," he told her. "Go get it for me, would you?"

"Yes, sir." Yamoto slipped off her restraints and kicked her way aft.

And this was it. Keying the direction vector he'd so carefully worked out into the helm, Ferrol reached over and switched off the comm laser. "Wwis-khaa," he said quietly, "bring Epilog to the indicated direction. Nice and easy."

"Your wishes are ours," the Tampy said, and a moment later Ferrol felt a slight pressure on his side as the calf and lander came around. "It is done."

"All right. Now; the bright star directly ahead is Sirius. Can Epilog see it?"

There was a long pause. Above the background hum of the lander's systems, Ferrol could hear the pounding of his heart . . . "He can," Wwis-khaa said at last.

"Good." Ferrol took a deep breath. "Jump us there."

This time the pause was even longer. "Wwis-khaa? Did you you hear me?"

"Ffe-rho—"

"I said, did you hear me?" Ferrol cut him off, turning to face the other. Above the filter mask, the alien eyes were staring unblinkingly back at him.

"I hear."

"Then Jump. That's an order."

Wwis-khaa's eyes closed briefly; opened again. "Your wishes are ours," he seemed to sigh—

And an instant later blue-white light flooded in through the forward viewport.

"What the *hell*?" Yamoto snapped, shooting forward with the datapack box clutched in her hand. "Commander, we just Jumped!"

"I know," he assured her. "Don't worry; everything's under control. All right, Wwis-khaa," he added, keying the second vector into the helm, "now move Epilog to *this* heading. We'll want to Jump as soon as we're in position."

He confirmed that they were indeed turning the proper direction, then turned to face Yamoto. "Question, Lieutenant?" he asked mildly.

"Uh . . . yes, Commander," she said, her voice cautious. Over her filter mask, he could see tension lines around her eyes. "I wasn't informed we'd be leaving the *Amity*."

"No, you weren't," he agreed. "Wwis-khaa, how are we coming?"

"Epilonninni is almost ready," the Tampy said.

"Good. Keep it moving."

Yamoto dropped her eyes to her console. "We're going to Arachne, sir?"

"Briefly, yes," Ferrol nodded. "Or rather, for the Tampies and me it'll be briefly. We'll be dropping you off before we leave."

She looked up at him again. "Commander, whatever you're doing—"

"Is none of your concern," he cut her off, putting some steel into his voice. He had no intention of getting Yamoto entangled in this, and the simplest and safest way to do that was to keep her as totally in the dark as possible. "As I said, you'll be dropped off at Arachne, and your part will be over."

For a long minute she gazed at him, her eyes hard with suspicion. Ferrol returned the glare as calmly as he could, listening to his heart pounding in his ears and feeling the bulge of the needle pistol pressing into his side under his tunic. The last thing he wanted was to have to start waving the damn gun around . . .

Almost reluctantly, Yamoto let her eyes drift away. "Understood, Commander," she said with a sigh. "Here's your package," she added, holding out the datapack box she still held. "If you really want it, that is."

"Of course I want it," he growled, taking it. Opening it, he selected one of the slender cylinders and handed it back to her. "This is for you: all the navigational data on Arachne and the colony there. We'll be transferring you to a lifeboat once we reach the planet, and I'm afraid you'll have to make your own way down. Think you can manage it?"

"Of course," she said, professional pride momentarily eclipsing her misgivings.

"Good. Wwis-khaa, how are we doing?"

"Epilonninni is ready," the Tampy said.

"Can Epilog see the star all right?" he asked, double-checking. A blazing star like Sirius was a dead-simple target to Jump to; Arachne's sun was something else entirely.

"He can see the star," Wwis-khaa said.

Ferrol gave the scanners a quick check. Luck was with him; the *Amity* still hadn't caught up. His maneuver must have caught Roman completely flat-footed. "All right, then: Jump."

The blue Sirian light vanished from the side viewport; simultaneously, an unremarkable red-orange star popped into view directly in front of them. "We're here," Ferrol announced, striving for a confidence he didn't feel. *Here*; but if his direction vector had been wrong, *here* wouldn't be the Arachne system. And if his calculation of the planet's orbital position had been wrong . . . Feeling sweat breaking out on his forehead, he keyed for a proximity scan.

And found immediately that his fears had been for nothing. "Arachne, ho," Yamoto said, peering at her own displays. "Right on the nose, too—forty-eight thousand kilometers away, bearing six port, eighty-two nadir. Just slightly downslope."

Ferrol took a careful breath. "Make for the planet, Wwis-khaa," he ordered the Tampy. "Two gees acceleration, or as much as Epilog can handle."

"Your wishes are ours."

For a minute Ferrol's shoulders pushed against his restraints as Wwis-khaa turned Epilog nadir toward Arachne. The mottled blue-white crescent appeared in the forward viewport, the pressure eased and changed direction, and he was pushed back into his seat. "On our way," Yamoto said unnecessarily. "Two gees acceleration."

Ferrol nodded and keyed the lander's scope screen, his stomach beginning to knot up again. He'd ordered the *Scapa Flow* to wait for him here . . . but that had been nearly two months ago. If they'd gotten tired of waiting. . .

A brief glint of sunlight caught his eye. A ship, running in geosynchronous orbit, all the way around the planet from where the human and Tampy colonies were located.

Grinning tightly, Ferrol set the comm laser to track and keyed an intercept course into the helm. "Wwis-khaa, shift direction onto the vector indicated," he ordered. The laser signaled ready—"*Scapa Flow*, this is Chayne Ferrol," he called. "Identification: beta hopscotch. Come in." He held his breath—

"*Scapa Flow* here," Malraux Demarco's voice came. It sounded relieved. "Long time no hear, Chayne."

"Much too long," Ferrol agreed. "What's ship status?"

"Oh, pretty much ready to go whenever you are," the other replied. "You, uh, bringing us a gift there?"

"On loan only," Ferrol told him. "Listen closely, now. Our ETA is—" he scanned the helm display for the numbers—"about forty-five minutes. I want the cargo bay cleared—and I mean *cleared*—and one lifeboat prepped and stocked for a flight planetside. Also, dig a pair of mid-length rein lines out of storage—four hundred meters ought to do it—and get them attached to the forward grapple. Attached *good.*"

There was a short pause. "Sounds like we're not going to be going hunting, after all," Demarco said.

"Oh, we're going hunting, all right," Ferrol told him grimly. "Count on that. Now. Here's the plan: we're going to put the lander here into the cargo bay, with the rein lines hanging out the main hatchway. We'll pack the gap to make the bay airtight; but since any real tug on the lines would tear out the sealant, we'll run your set of reins between our space horse and the forward grapple to do the actual pulling, leaving the one from the lander slack. Clear?"

"Except for whether or not that lander will actually fit in our cargo bay," Demarco said. "Our rangefinder readout on you makes it pretty damn close."

"It's close, but it'll work," Ferrol assured him. "I've run the numbers twice, and it *can* be done."

"Well . . . if you say so," Demarco said, still sounding unconvinced.

"Trust me," Ferrol said. "Anyway, that's my problem. You just concentrate on making sure I've got room to get the thing in. That, and getting the rein lines hooked up. Oh, and you'd better run a cable from the bay intercom box so that we can link up to the lander's outside comm port." A stab of momentary guilt twinged at him; but without enough filter masks for the *Scapa Flow*'s entire crew, they really had no choice but to confine the Tampies to the lander and cargo bay.

"Got it. I presume we're rather in a hurry?"

Ferrol threw a sideways glance at Yamoto's profile. "There's enough time to do the job right," he told Demarco. "That doesn't mean you should stop for coffee, though."

"Right. We'll be ready when you get here."

"Good. Ferrol out."

He keyed off the laser and set the scanners for a full

radar and beacon search. Unlikely there would be any other ships in the vicinity, but there wasn't any point in taking chances.

"You going to do the docking yourself?" Yamoto asked.

Ferrol nodded. "I'd planned to, yes. Why?"

"Because I don't think you can do it," she said bluntly. "Not without wrecking either the lander or your cargo bay or both."

Ferrol had wondered about that himself. "I'll take it real slow," he told her. "Or else have the *Scapa Flow*'s chief helmer come out and take us in."

"With the *Amity* breathing down your neck?" she asked pointedly.

"Who said the *Amity* was breathing down my neck?" Ferrol countered.

She turned contemptuous eyes on him. "Oh, come on, Ferrol, let's cut through the snow," she said. "Whatever you're doing here, you're doing it on your own, without a scrap of authorization from anyone. We both know it; and we both know that if you take the time to EVA a helmer out here, you'll be crowding your timetable so much he's likely to rush the job."

"I can't let you do the docking," Ferrol told her quietly. "So far everything you've done comes under the heading of innocently obeying orders from a superior officer. I don't want you in any deeper than that."

"Your concern is touching," Yamoto growled. "But soothe your conscience—I'm not doing it for you." She jerked her head back toward the Tampies. "You've got three innocents at risk here—four, if you count me. I'm doing the docking, and that's final."

Behind the filter mask, Ferrol grimaced, glad the expression wasn't visible. Of course; it had to have been something like that. Not simply that she was willing to trust him or his judgment.

But then, no one seemed willing to trust his judgment these days. Why should Yamoto be different?

"In that case," he told her, "I accept."

*　　*　　*

"Sure as hell taking her time pulling away," Demarco growled, gazing at his displays. "You know, I don't think she's planning to head planetside at all."

Ferrol glanced at the screen. Demarco was right: Yamoto was just letting her lifeboat drift. "Probably decided she'd do as well to wait for the *Amity* to show up," he told Demarco. "Probably also figures that if she can record our Jump direction it'll give them a shot at tracking us down."

Demarco sent him a frown. "They can't do that, can they?"

"Don't worry about it," Ferrol advised him. "With the route we'll be taking they won't have a hope in hell of following us."

On his console the intercom pinged. "Chayne, we've got the intercom connection to the lander now," someone reported.

"Thank you." Ferrol keyed the proper switch. "Wwis-khaa? This is Commander Ferrol. Are you and the others doing all right?"

"We are well, Ffe-rho."

With Ferrol and Yamoto gone from the lander, the three aliens had removed their filter masks; briefly, Ferrol wished he was better at reading Tampy expressions. "I'm sorry we have to keep you back there in the lander," he apologized. "But without enough filter masks to go around we really can't let you into the main part of the ship."

"No scitte," Demarco muttered under his breath. "It'd take months to scrub the stench out of the air system."

Ferrol threw him a glare. "You should have received the next target star on your display by now," he continued to Wwis-khaa. "Can Epilog see it all right?"

"He can." Wwis-khaa paused. "Ffe-rho, I would like to know what it is you are asking us to do."

"A fair question," Ferrol agreed. "Very simply, I'm asking you to help your people. Your people, and your space horses. Have you ever heard of an Earth creature called the *dog*?"

"A domesticated carnivore of the *Canis* group," Wwis-khaa said promptly. "Its ecological position is usually as a companion or pet to humans."

"Right," Ferrol nodded, vaguely impressed that the alien would know that. "They're mostly pets now, but originally they were used by herders and shepherds to help guard food animals from dangerous predators. Still are, in some places."

He'd expected Wwis-khaa to catch his drift; and he wasn't disappointed. "You seek to find such creatures in space?" the Tampy asked, his head tilting to one side in a gesture Ferrol had never seen before. "Small predators to protect our space horses from sharks?"

"That's it," Ferrol nodded. "Granted, we don't know if such things even exist; but now that we know there are at least three species of space-going creatures, it seems reasonable that there should be others. True?"

"I do not know," Wwis-khaa said. "How do you presume to search for such creatures throughout the vastness of space?"

"I don't," Ferrol said. "We're going to leave space and normal star systems alone and concentrate instead on a much more select group of places: namely, the accretion disks around large black holes."

Demarco twisted his head around, a stunned look on his face. "I think it makes sense," Ferrol continued, ignoring the other. "That's where space horses are supposed to have originated; and if so, there must be some remnant of the ecology left. You game to take a look?"

For a long moment Wwis-khaa was silent. Ferrol held his breath, fully and painfully aware that if the Tampies refused the whole thing would die right here and now. "Your wishes are ours," the alien said. "When do you wish to leave?"

Quietly, Ferrol exhaled. "As soon as Epilog is in position," he told the other. "Let the helmer—Randall—know when you're ready."

"Your wishes are ours," Wwis-khaa repeated.

Feeling a little limp, Ferrol switched off the intercom. It had worked . . . and they were on their way. He looked up—

To find Demarco gazing hard at him. "I trust," the other said carefully, "that all of that was just so much spun sugar."

"Some of it was," Ferrol said. "Most of it wasn't. We *are* going to poke around a few black holes, and we *are* hunting for a scaled-down version of a shark. But not for the reason I gave Wwis-khaa—that was just to get his cooperation."

"You should have just told melt-face it was an order, and that you were his superior officer, and that was that," Demarco sniffed. "That's all the explanation the stupid plant-lovers deserve."

Ferrol frowned at the other, a strange feeling curling through his stomach. Somehow, he didn't remember Demarco as being quite this crude. "If I'm right," he said quietly, "we've probably got a good chance of running into some sharks along the way. Wwis-khaa and the others deserve to know what they're letting themselves in for."

Demarco raised his eyebrows. "I see some of the *Amity*'s heart-bleeding has rubbed off on you. Sir. So if we're not recruiting watchdogs for the melt-faces, what the hell *do* we want these miniature sharks for?"

"We want them for transport, of course," Ferrol growled. Demarco was teetering right on the edge of insubordination here. "We've been in a long, dead-end track here, trying to capture and train space horses. Human beings are predators, and the space horses can't or won't stand for that. But a space-going predator species might. Clear now?"

Demarco snorted. "If you say so. Sounds like the sort of wishy-wok stuff your melt-faced chummies would spout, though. If you ask me."

Quite suddenly, Ferrol decided he was tired of Demarco. "All right then; try this," he said coldly.

"We're going because I've given you an order, and I'm your captain, and that's that."

Demarco's lip twisted, but he nodded. "Yes, *sir*," he muttered, and turned back to his console.

"Chayne?" Randall spoke up tentatively. "Your melt-fa—your Tampy signals he's ready to go."

Ferrol took a deep breath, fighting for calm. "Tell him to go ahead and Jump," he ordered.

And wondered what had happened to his crew in the past year, to make them so harshly bigoted.

Chapter 25

"Arachne's director said they'd alerted Earth and Prepyat via tachyon," Yamoto's voice came over the comm laser. She sounded tired, and about as emotionally drained as Roman felt. Not really surprising, under the circumstances. "I guess the message didn't get through."

"It got through, all right," Roman told her. "Just not soon enough."

Yamoto sighed. "My fault, Captain. I should have alerted the colony as soon as we arrived in the system, and the hell with any consequences."

Roman shook his head. "It wouldn't have helped. Once we'd Jumped to Sirius and then back to Solomon system, we were already out of position to hit anywhere near Arachne itself. We couldn't have gotten here in time to stop Ferrol no matter when you blew the whistle. It wasn't in any way your fault."

"Yes, sir." She didn't sound like she believed it. "I'm ready to boost orbit whenever you're ready."

Roman gave his helm display a quick scan. After four hours of a hard three-gee acceleration/deceleration drive through Arachne system from their arrival Jump point, *Amity* had finally reached the planet itself. The tactical showed their course swinging close in to cut across

Yamoto's own geosynchronous orbit . . . "You might as
well just sit tight there," he decided. "It'll probably be
faster for us to catch up than for you to fiddle with your
orbit." Though what the hurry was for, Roman really
couldn't say—by Yamoto's numbers, Ferrol and the
Scapa Flow were a good six hours ahead of them already, and *Amity*'s chances of tracking them down at
this point were just fractionally above absolute zero.
"We'll be alongside in about ten minutes."

"Yes, sir."

At the helm, Kennedy half turned. "Captain? I've got
a probable vector for them now, if you'd like to take a
look."

"Thank you." For a minute Roman studied the tactical and visual maps she'd produced. In the direction
indicated—

Was, basically, nothing. "How probable *is* this?" he
asked.

"Only about seventy-five percent, actually," she admitted. "The tapes Yamoto made of Epilog's Jump are
good and sharp, but you can only be so accurate from
half a kilometer away. Computer gives a ninety-nine
percent probability for this area"—a small circle appeared on the visual, centered around the original
vector—"but there are at least fifteen stars in there that
ought to be visible to a space horse."

"Even one as young as Epilog?" Roman asked.

Kennedy shook her head. "I don't know. Neither do
the Tampies; I asked them."

And of course they wouldn't do anything so vulgar as
to speculate. . . Roman clenched his teeth, fighting
down a sudden surge of anger at the aliens. This wasn't
their fault, either. "Get me everything we have on
those stars," he directed Kennedy. "Let's see if we can
figure out what Ferrol's up to."

He hadn't expected there to be much; and there
wasn't. Estimated sizes, estimated distances, spectral
classes, estimated probabilities of solar systems—each
listing had barely half a dozen lines. "Not much there
anyone could want," Marlowe muttered.

"Unless Ferrol knows something about one of them we don't," Roman pointed out. "Kennedy, do you have a list yet of what those datapacks he had might have been?"

"Near as I can tell, all he accessed from the *Amity* were the navigational locator program and the full Cygni Telescope stellar mapping list," Kennedy said. "Plus the Arachne data he gave Yamoto. She told us he took six datapacks with him, which would be about right for dumps of the nav and Cygni packages." She eyed Roman. "Which implies to me that whichever of *these* stars he Jumped to was just a transition point to somewhere else."

Roman nodded, his throat tight with frustration and bitterness. He'd already come to the same depressing conclusion . . . and if Ferrol was doing a multi-stage Jump here, then he was gone. Period.

His console two-toned a proximity alert: the *Amity* was coming alongside Yamoto's lifeboat. "Kennedy, have the hangar doors opened; as soon as we've matched velocities Yamoto can go ahead and bring the boat in."

And when she was aboard, he knew, the decision would have to be made. Whether to fight the massive probabilities stacked against them and try and go after Ferrol, or to accept that any such attempt would be a useless gesture.

To accept that, whatever Ferrol was up to, he'd won.

I should have stopped him, Roman thought wearily. And he *could* have done it, too—that was what galled the most. He could have had Ferrol off his ship right from the very beginning, or at any point since then. It was his own damn fault—all of it.

The intercom pinged. "Rro-maa?"

Roman looked down at the lopsided alien face. *Here it comes,* he thought, bracing himself. The accusation—delivered, no doubt, in the usual quiet/polite Tampy manner—that through lack of foresight or simple plain stupidity he'd just lost them a priceless space horse calf . . . "Yes, Rrin-saa, what is it?" he said.

"Is it your wish that we follow Ffe-rho?"

"It's hardly a question of wishes at this point, Rrin-saa," he growled. So that was how the Tampies were going to play this. Nothing so crass as accusing the captain outright of negligence; Rrin-saa was simply going to throw out innocent-sounding questions until Roman wound up confessing the fact on his own. "Ferrol and Epilog are long gone." He raised his eyebrows. "Unless, of course, you'd happen to know where they went."

"I do not," Rrin-saa said. "But Sleipnninni does."

Roman stared at the screen. The question had been nothing but pure sarcasm . . . "Say again?"

"Sleipnninni knows where Epilog has gone," Rrin-saa said. "He can follow, if you wish."

Roman glanced up, caught Marlowe's disbelieving frown, looked back down again. "I don't understand," he told Rrin-saa. "Epilog Jumped six hours ago. How can Sleipnir possibly know where it went?"

"I do not know," Rrin-saa said. "I know that he knows; that is all."

Roman rubbed thumb and forefinger together, looked up again. "Marlowe? Opinion?"

The other shook his head. "You got me, sir. Sounds like pure voodoo."

"Does, doesn't it?" he agreed. "Kennedy?"

She shrugged. "I'd vote voodoo, too," she said. "But on the other hand, what have we got to lose?"

What, indeed? "All right, Rrin-saa, you're on. Get Sleipnir into position; as soon as Yamoto and the life-boat are aboard, we'll Jump."

The Tampy's face was, as usual, unreadable. "Your wishes," he said quietly, "are ours."

It took the *Scapa Flow* six Jumps over nearly eighteen hours to get to Cygnus X-1, the first black hole on Ferrol's list.

It was, for Ferrol, highly reminiscent of the pre-nova system *Amity* had gone into all those months ago. Blazing away to one side was the black hole's companion, a huge blue-white star of perhaps twenty solar masses; to the other side was the black hole itself, a pinprick of equally bright blue light. Surrounding both was a textured swirl of gas being ripped from the star by the black hole's gravity, thickest in a curved corridor directly between the two bodies, the entire mass of it fluorescing brilliantly under the steady blast of ionizing X-rays pouring from the black hole. The star was brighter on that side, and noticeably elongated as well. The cloud of gas enclosed the two masses like a free-form cage; and though most of it moved too slowly for human eyes to follow, right in close to the blue pinprick it could be seen visibly swirling in, falling from infinity to disappear from the universe, giving up its gravitational potential energy as it did so to feed the outward flow of radiation.

Impressive as hell. And just about as dangerous.

Earlier, in one of the systems they'd passed through on the way here, Ferrol had had Epilog pull the *Scapa Flow* an extra six million kilometers further out from that system's star, knowing that doing so would put them proportionally farther out along the X-1 system's gravity well when they finally arrived. Now, listening to the creaking of heat-stressed hull plates and watching as, one by one, the outside radiation detectors overloaded and burned out, he wondered if perhaps he should have taken the time to move them even further out.

They didn't stay long. A fifteen-minute run with the anomalous-motion program was enough to show that there was none of Ferrol's hoped-for life within a million kilometers of the ship, and it was already abundantly clear that even if they found something outside that radius the ship would never hold together long enough to go investigate it.

Four more Jumps took them to the next system on the list: a far quieter one, this, with the black hole's companion star too far away to lose such massive amounts of itself to the gravitational tugging and a correspondingly gentler flow of radiation. They stayed longer here; but again, there was no trace of life.

Nor was there in the third system. Or in the fourth, or in the fifth.

In the sixth . . . they found it.

"I'll be damned," Demarco breathed. "I'll be *damned*."

Ferrol nodded absently, a tingling thrill of excitement flooding through him as he alternated his attention between visual, tactical, and scanner-composite screens. Three flashing circles marked anomalous motion within the haze of gravel and rock that made up the black hole's accretion disk; even as he watched, two more circles appeared. "It's the rocks," he said. "Got to be. It's the only thing about this system that's different."

Demarco seemed to pull himself together. "Well, it's not the *only* thing," he countered. "The black hole itself is a hell of a lot quieter, radiation-wise, than any of the others we've seen. For starters."

Ferrol gritted his teeth momentarily, the flash of reflex anger breaking the spell and bringing him joltingly back to the real world. "That's true," he agreed, forcing his voice to remain calm. The thrill of excitement wasn't what was important right now; neither was the irritating—and possibly deliberate—habit Demarco had fallen into these past few days of challenging everything Ferrol said or did. What *was* important was that they not squabble this opportunity away . . . and what *that* meant was investigating the system and its life as carefully and thoroughly as possible. With a maximum of care, and a minimum of interpersonal conflict. "I'm sure the lower radiation makes the environment a lot more stable," he added. "Randall? You got a profile on the accretion disk yet?"

"Only first-order details so far," the other told him, "but it's looking pretty much like a normal asteroid belt. At least out this far; you start getting in too close and the radiation and gravitational effects start fouling things up good." He turned to look at Ferrol. "I think you're right, too, that it's the lumpiness of this particular disk that's the critical factor. At least two of the movements we've tracked so far definitely started out from the dark side of boulders. Probably helps to have a place to hide from the radiation when you're built smaller than a space horse—less shielding mass, and all that."

"Yeah," Ferrol nodded. "Take a look at the black hole itself; get me some idea what exactly we're dealing with."

"Right." Randall turned to his scanners, and Ferrol keyed for the cargo bay and lander. Speaking of space horses . . . "Wwis-khaa? You there?"

A Tampy face appeared on the screen, or what was visible of a face sandwiched between the amplifier helmet and a gold-blue neckerchief. "Ffe-rho?"

"Yes, Ppla-zii," Ferrol acknowledged. "Wwis-khaa resting, I take it?"

"He is," the Tampy replied. "He rests too much."

"You *all* rest too much," Demarco muttered.

Ferrol threw him a glare. "I know, Ppla-zii, and I'm sorry," he said to the Tampy. "I realize that what we've put Epilog through these last few days has been hard on the three of you, too. But it's paid off. We've found what looks very much to be the space-creature community we've been looking for."

"I know," Ppla-zii said. "Epilonninni has already seen."

Something that sounded like a snort of derision came from Demarco's direction. "I see," Ferrol growled, not even bothering with the glare this time. "Glad to hear it. What else does Epilog tell you?"

"I do not understand."

"I want to know what impressions Epilog has of this place," Ferrol amplified. "Does it feel uneasy or pained in any way by the black hole's radiation, for instance? Or is it bothered by the fact that the gravitational fields even at this distance are slightly warped?" He glanced at the flashing circles on the display. "More importantly, does it feel danger from any of the life-forms around us?"

"Epilonninni feels no danger," Ppla-zii said promptly.

"Good. You tell me *right away* if that changes—you got that?"

"Your wishes are ours."

"Yeah." But just in case . . . Ferrol glanced around the bridge. "Kohlhase, as of right now your only job is to watch for anomalous movement heading toward or across a line directly in front of Epilog," he instructed one of the crewers. "Randall?"

"The black hole weighs in at about a hundred solar masses," the other reported. "Only slightly charged, but it's rotating pretty fast. Figure the event horizon at about 150 kilometers; we're approximately three million kilometers out from that now."

Ferrol nodded, trying to remember everything he'd ever read about black holes. "We getting any relativistic effects yet?" he asked. "Frame dragging or other orbital anomalies?"

Randall shrugged. "Not at this distance, no." He cocked an eyebrow. " 'Course, we'll have to go a lot closer in if we want a real look at those beasties of yours."

"Right," Ferrol nodded. "And your job will be to make sure we don't get carried away by the thrill of it all. Pay especially close attention to radiation levels and gravitational gradients; but if you see *anything* going on outside the ship that bothers you, I want to hear about it. Clear?"

"Yes, sir."

And all was ready. Ferrol took a deep breath, shifted his gaze to the screen. Over twenty flashing circles marked anomalous motion now, the nearest of them twenty thousand kilometers further in toward the black hole. "Okay, Ppla-zii," he said. "Real slow and careful, now . . . take us in."

Chapter 26

The asteroid was large and craggy, its edges sheathed in a pale and ghostly blue light from the distant black hole. A spot of white from the *Scapa Flow*'s searchlight swept slowly over it, lingering on a handful of shadows before moving on. Staring at the display, Ferrol shook his head. "Okay, I give up," he said to no one in particular. "Where *did* the damn thing go?"

"To the left, I think," Demarco said. "Over there by the—there it goes!"

A black shadow had detached itself from the asteroid and was skittering off through space, reaching the edge of the display before the tracking system caught up and centered it again. Roughly half a meter across, with a tendency to make right-angle turns in mid-course, it had early on been dubbed a butterfly . . . and in Ferrol's opinion they'd learned just about all that twenty minutes of passive observation could teach them about it. "Let's bring it in, Mal," he said. "Whenever you've got a clear shot."

"Right." Demarco hissed gently between his teeth. "Here goes. . ."

The *Scapa Flow* jerked slightly as the net shot out. Ferrol held his breath . . . and at the last instant the butterfly swerved into a hairpin curve. Too late; the net swept around it and tightened—

In the pale blue light the brief flicker of coronal discharge from the net was clearly visible. The butterfly gave one last spasmodic twitch and went limp. "Townne: we've got it," Ferrol called into his intercom. "Reel it in."

"Right."

On the display the netted butterfly began moving back toward the ship. Ferrol arched his shoulders, stretching muscles stiff with tension, and listened to the growing sense of bitter emptiness rumbling through his stomach. In four hours of drifting through the accretion disk they'd spotted, identified, and filmed no fewer than fifteen different variants of space-going creatures. Four—five, now—had been netted, electrically stunned or killed, and brought aboard for further study.

And in that whole damn menagerie, they hadn't found a single solitary predator.

"Ffe-rho?"

With an effort, Ferrol shook the self-pity from his mind. "Yes, Wwis-khaa, what is it?"

"Is it your wish that we continue inward toward the black hole?"

Ferrol took a moment to check the external status readouts. He'd kept the ship moving with the general circular flow of the accretion disk since their arrival, moving only a few hundred kilometers further inward during that time. "Unless there's a problem, yes," he told Wwis-khaa. "Is the odd gravity bothering Epilog?"

"I do not know," the Tampy said. "I know that it is a troublesome place for him; that is all."

And a troubled space horse meant troubled and exhausted Handlers. A flash of anger flared up in the middle of Ferrol's frustration, but he clamped his teeth against it. There was no point in snapping the Tampies' heads off over this; for all their vaunted efficiency in hauling ships around, it was becoming painfully clear that space horses simply weren't up to operating under prolonged stress. "Can you estimate how long it'll be before we need to leave?" he asked Wwis-khaa. "Taking into account your own fatigue and that of the other Handlers?"

"I do not know," the other said. "I know only that I will be able to Handle Epilonninni for two more hours, and that Bbri-hwoo will not be able to take my place then; that is all."

Two hours . . . and they'd barely even scratched the surface of this system's potential. "Understood," he told the Tampy, a sour taste in his mouth. "All right, let's try this: as soon as Ppla-zii takes over for you, we'll find a nearby system to Jump to. Perhaps after you've all had a few days' rest we'll be able to come back."

"Perhaps. I do not know."

Ferrol looked up at Demarco. "Well," he said. "Looks like this is—"

"Ffe-rho?"

Ferrol looked back at the intercom. "Yes, Wwis-khaa, what is it now?"

"Epilonninni is . . . troubled." The alien eyes stared unblinking at Ferrol. "Something that troubles him is near."

Ferrol's mouth went suddenly dry. "Kohlhase? What have you got?"

"No motion anywhere near Epilog's bow," the other said promptly.

"Keep watching," Ferrol ordered. "Mal, Randall; I want a full scan of—"

"Motion!" Demarco cut in. "Bearing thirty-five degrees starboard, three zenith; range, eleven hundred meters."

"I'm on it," Ferrol gritted. His display locked and tracked; with fingers that were suddenly trembling he keyed for computer identification. The fifteen different species they'd listed ran past the image . . .

"It's a new one," Demarco confirmed. "Bigger than the others, too—almost four meters across."

A sidebar of Ferrol's display froze an image of the creature, scrubbed it . . . "Looks a little like a miniature vulture," he muttered, a shiver running up his back.

Demarco glanced over his shoulder. "Is that good or bad?"

Ferrol chewed at the back of his lower lip. The rest of the scan was still showing negative . . . "As long as there's just one of them it should be safe enough."

Demarco grunted. "Not your predator, then, I take it?"

Carefully, Ferrol forced down the momentary rush of panic. There was no danger here. Really. "Actually, I don't know," he told Demarco. Logical, scientific thinking—that was what he needed right now. "We've been calling them vultures this whole time because they were busy picking a dead space horse apart when we first spotted them . . . but on the other hand, they dived right into the fight on the shark's side when it attacked the *Amity*. Could be they're really more like jackals than vultures."

"Well, if the shark you described is anything to go by, these things sure don't fit the predator shape," Demarco pointed out. "For whatever that's worth."

"True," Ferrol nodded. "On the other hand, space horses are cylindrical, too. Maybe the shape has more to do with the ability to Jump than with any specific feeding or behavior pattern." He watched as the creature drifted along, just a little faster than the rocks around it, shifting direction slightly every few seconds. An odd hunting pattern, if that was what it was. "I wish we could get a good look at its underside," he commented under his breath. "The vultures we tangled with had really outsized feeding orifices down there."

Peripherally, he saw Demarco shrug. "Sure, why not? You've wanted one of everything else—might as well bag a junior vulture, too. Let me see if the secondary net gun is ready to fire yet." He turned to his intercom—

"Motion!" Randall snapped. "That rock just ahead of the vulture."

Ferrol's display skittered dizzyingly for an instant, locked on a blue-edged shape zigzagging between the rocks. "A butterfly?" he tentatively identified it.

"Looks like one," Randall confirmed. "In one hell of a hurry, too."

Ferrol keyed his display for a wide-screen overview, his heart starting to pound in his ears. If their junior vulture was indeed a predator . . .

But nothing. Even as the butterfly traced out its serrated path, the vulture continued on its slow meandering way, totally oblivious to the potential meal that had fled from practically under its nose.

"Off hand," Demarco said dryly, "I'd say your junior vulture has a lot to learn about the predator business."

Ferrol sighed. "Or else just brushed its teeth and doesn't want to eat yet," he countered, trying to match the other's tone. It was a wasted effort.

"So what now?" Demarco asked. "You still want me to net it?"

Ferrol shrugged. "Might as well, I suppose." The vulture was passing the asteroid the butterfly had fled from; the butterfly itself had long since vanished off the edge of the wide-screen display. Touching a switch, Ferrol keyed back to the vulture close-up again. "Like you said, we've got one of everything el— "

And without warning the vulture abruptly shot off the edge of the display.

"Track it!" Ferrol snapped. The wide-screen came back again, giving an even wider view this time—

"God Almighty!" Randall gasped. "Look at that thing *go!*"

Ferrol nodded, his full attention on the vulture. Zigzagging through the dust and gravel between the larger rocks at a speed Ferrol wouldn't have guessed it was capable of, it was almost like watching a repeat of the butterfly's flight.

Almost exactly like watching a repeat of the butterfly's flight . . . "Randall—run a comparison between the vulture's and butterfly's paths."

"Already done it, Chayne," Randall told him. "It's almost an exact match. The vulture's definitely tracking the butterfly."

"Cute," Demarco growled. "So what the hell is out there for it to *track?*"

Ferrol smiled tightly. "The butterfly's dust sweat, of course."

"The *what?*"

"Tell you later," Ferrol said. "I want to watch this."

The butterfly had appeared on the display again. Still running . . . but there was no doubt now that the vulture was going to catch it. Even as they watched, the predator came within a handful of meters—

And, abruptly, the zigzagging ceased, both creatures continuing on in tandem with the pursuer's last velocity. "The vulture's got it," Randall murmured. "Locked up solid in a telekene grip."

Demarco hissed between his teeth. "And reeling it in . . . there it goes."

The two creatures came together . . . and a moment later it was all over.

For a minute the bridge was silent. "All right," Ferrol said quietly. "Randall, give Wwis-khaa a call—tell him to ease us forward into net range of that vulture."

"Chayne!" Kohlhase cut in. "Movement ahead and port—something *big.*"

Ferrol slapped the intercom switch. "Wwis-khaa— emergency," he snapped. "Find a target star and Jump us out of here."

"Your wishes are ours."

"As soon as Epilog's ready," Ferrol told hm. "Demarco —computer ID scan; I want a size readout on it. Kohlhase, scan for anything that could be vultures coming off it."

And at that instant his console pinged. A comm laser had made contact—

"This is Captain Roman aboard the *Amity*," a familiar voice boomed out of the speaker. "Come in, *Scapa Flow.*"

*   *   *

Ferrol stared at the speaker, a rush of déjà vu flooding over him. The Tampies' *yishyar* system—the captured space horse colt—Roman's challenge from the *Dryden*, and the *Scapa Flow*'s chip-skin escape. . .

And it was only as the flashback faded and he was able to think again did the crucial question even occur to him.

How in bloody hell had Roman tracked them here?

He cleared his throat. "Tell Wwis-khaa to secure from that emergency Jump," he told Randall. Keying for vision, he tapped the *transmit* switch. "This is Ferrol," he said into the mike. "Bit far from home, aren't you, Captain?"

"I could say the same about you," Roman countered as his image appeared on the comm display. He looked tired; but at the same time, there was something grimly self-satisfied about his expression. "What's your status at the moment, Commander?"

"No problems, except that we have less than two hours before we'll have to leave," Ferrol told him. "Our space horse and Handlers are a little strained by the conditions here."

"I trust no one has been hurt."

Ferrol swallowed. There had been a very definite threat beneath the words. "Everyone's in perfect health," he assured the other. "And before you ask, there've been no threats, either. Wwis-khaa and the others came voluntarily."

"At least from Arachne," Roman said pointedly. "From what Yamoto said it didn't sound like you called for volunteers before then. So. Did you find what you came for?"

Ferrol curled a hand into a fist, wondering if Roman had somehow guessed his real motive. "Not really," he said evenly. "But along the way we've learned a fair amount about the space-going ecology of this place, and we've collected five samples for further study back at the Cordonale. We have a line on a sixth at the moment; with your permission, we'd like to try and get it."

"Go ahead." Roman cocked an eyebrow. "You don't seem especially surprised to see us."

"No, we were surprised enough," Ferrol admitted. "It's just that the surprise got covered over by relief—when we first spotted you I assumed you were a shark. I don't suppose you'd like to tell us how you managed to track us down."

Roman shook his head. "Actually, we're not absolutely sure ourselves," he said. "All the Tampies can tell us is that Sleipnir was able to follow you here. Marlowe's suggested that it's some kind of perturbations in some theoretical telekene field, but so far—"

"Damn," Ferrol breathed. Suddenly, so loudly he could almost hear the clicks, it had all fallen together. "It's the dust sweat, Captain. Sleipnir read our trail from Epilog's *dust sweat*."

Roman frowned. "I don't see—"

"Hang on," Ferrol cut him off, fumbling for the recorder keys. The junior vulture's attack on the butterfly . . . there. "Take a look at this," he said, keying for transmission. "We recorded it here, just before you showed up."

For a few moments the laser carrier hummed with silence as Roman's image frowned thoughtfully at something off camera. "Interesting," he said at last. "You're right, dust sweat clearly seems to be the space-going analog of a terrestrial animal's blood-scent. But that only works if the animal doesn't Jump."

"No," Ferrol shook his head, feeling the excitement of the revelation tingling through him. Why had no one ever *seen* this before—? "The dust sweat ends at a Jump, but the trail doesn't. Those complex silicon molecules in the dust, remember?—the ones everybody's looked at and never really seen? It's there. Somehow, the information on Jump direction is locked into those molecules."

"Oh, my God," Roman said, a sudden look of horror on his face. "You're right . . . but it's not just the Jump information. It's a record of *everything* the animal's gone through. Short-term, maybe even long-term memory—all of it."

Ferrol frowned. "I don't see how that follows."

"The second shark in the 9862 system," Roman said quietly. "The one that destroyed the *Atlantis'* task force. *It knew everything about their weapons and tactics.*"

Ferrol stared at the other, a cold knot tightening in the pit of his stomach. In his mind's eye he saw that horrible massacre: the second shark using its vulture cloud to block the lasers and ion beams, using its own telekening power to block the missiles and then to put death-grips on the ships themselves. . .

And the first shark's twisting, roiling dance of death. "It wasn't a death dance at all," he murmured. "The first shark was trying to spread its dust sweat around."

"I think you're right," Roman agreed. "Marlowe?"

"Confirmed, Captain," Marlowe's voice came from off-camera. "The second shark passed through that area, all right; and if you look closely, you can see that it pauses there for a couple of seconds before starting its charge."

Ferrol shivered suddenly. "And we sat in the 66802 system afterward . . . for *ten days.*"

"We did indeed," Roman nodded grimly. "And were sitting ducks the entire time. The only thing I can think of is that the missile we shot off to try and blind the incoming vultures did enough damage to Sleipnir's dust sweat residue to make it unreadable."

Ferrol gazed out the port at the eerie blue light edging the nearest asteroids and creating a sort of background haze from the distant ones. "It's crazy," he said, shaking his head. "The Tampies have been running space horses for over half a century now. How come they never figured this out?"

"Probably never had any reason to," Roman said "I doubt they've had someone steal a space horse out from under them before."

The bubble burst, and Ferrol abruptly remembered

where he was. And why. "Right," Ferrol said. "So. What now?"

For a moment Roman gazed off into infinity. "What now," he said, "is that we get back to the Cordonale with this as quickly as possible. Or perhaps to—"

He broke off suddenly, something blazing in his eyes. "Kennedy, get on your nav system—I want a minimum-time route to the space horse corral at Kialinninni. Ferrol, consider yourself as on parole: collect that animal you're chasing down and head back to the Cordonale —we'll sort out any charges against you later."

"Wait a minute," Ferrol protested. "What's the rush?"

"Don't you remember?" Roman ground out. "The Tampies have been pulling their space horses back to Kialinninni. *All* of them."

And abruptly, Ferrol got it. "Leaving dust sweat trails over the place," he breathed. "Every one of them pointing straight at the corral."

"Exactly," Roman said tightly. "We've got to warn them right away. Maybe we can do something to confuse the trail—send ships out to drop sub-nuke missiles at the original Jump points or something."

Ferrol chewed hard at his lower lip. The possibilities here . . . "I'd like to come along, captain," he said. "If we head toward you right now, we should be able to rendezvous in half an hour or so."

Roman had been looking away, presumably at Kennedy. Now, very deliberately, he looked back at Ferrol. "May I ask why?"

Ferrol forced himself to hold the other's gaze. "I'm still *Amity*'s exec," he reminded the other, aware for the first time in hours of the needler pressing against his side beneath his tunic. The needler, and the Senator's envelope. . . "It's where I belong. Even if you choose to confine me to quarters." A sudden thought occurred to him— "Besides, which, the *Amity* is far better equipped to handle these animal samples than we are. And since it'll probably take at least a few hours to get back, this would give Dr. Tenzing a head start on studying them."

Roman pursed his lips, frowning at Ferrol as if trying to read the motive behind the words. Ferrol held his breath . . . and at last, almost reluctantly, the other nodded. "Very well, Commander. Proceed with your capture, and prepare your samples for transfer. We'll rendezvous with you in an hour."

Ferrol exhaled quietly. "Yes, sir. Thank you, Captain."

"I'll talk to you then. *Amity* out."

The display went blank. For a long moment Ferrol stared at it, feeling his stomach knotting up within him. Once again, in the face of totally inexcusable actions, Roman was going to give him another chance . . . and once again, Ferrol was very likely going to betray that trust.

He'd known, from the beginning, that this would probably happen. What he hadn't expected was that it would hurt.

"First Jump completed, Captain," Kennedy reported from the bridge. "We'll be driving cross-system now for about twenty minutes to get into proper position for the second."

Roman nodded. "Good. Any problems with the *Scapa Flow*?"

"Not so far." She paused, her eyes flicking away from Roman's face for a quick scan of her displays. "No. The tether line's holding just fine, and Sleipnir doesn't seem to be having any trouble at all with the extra mass."

"Very good. Keep me informed."

The intercom screen blanked, and he looked back up. On the other side of his desk, Ferrol was sitting quietly, trying to exude respect and a sort of righteous dignity. Not that it was really coming off. "Probably a slightly bumpy ride for them back there," Roman told him. "We can still arrange to berth your men here, you know."

Ferrol shrugged. "I appreciate the offer, sir, but to

be perfectly honest, they've got better accomodations in the *Scapa Flow* than they'd have here."

"As well as a better chance of cutting the tether line and escaping once we're back within Mitsuushi distance of the Cordonale?" Roman asked pointedly.

Ferrol seemed to draw himself up. "I've given you the ship's parole, Captain," he said, his voice stiff. "They won't try to leave."

Roman thought about that. "No," he acknowledged, "I don't believe they will. My apologies, Commander."

"Thank you." Ferrol seemed to brace himself. "So. Do I get a formal hearing before I'm confined to quarters? Or are we going to hold off on such formalities until we get back to Earth?"

Roman studied him. The semi-genuine respect was still there, and the righteous innocence too . . . but there was no real worry. Which seemed just a little odd, considering how much a man in Ferrol's position should have to worry about. "You assume," he said, "that I'll be leveling charges."

Ferrol frowned, a touch of uncertainty flicking across his eyes. "Aren't you?"

"Depends partly on why you did it, I suppose," Roman said evenly. "Motivation *is* a relevant part of action, wouldn't you say?"

"Depends on whether you're talking ethics or legalities," Ferrol countered.

Roman shrugged. "Perhaps. At any rate, I had a chance to speak briefly to Wwis-khaa while you were helping transfer your specimens aboard, before he and the lander took Epilog and headed for home. He told me you were looking for some sort of flying sheep dog to help the Tampies protect their space horses." He cocked an eyebrow.

"And you, obviously, don't believe that," Ferrol said, an edge of challenge in his voice.

"You were talking to a Tampy," Roman reminded him.

"So naturally you assume I was lying through my teeth."

Roman just waited; and after a moment Ferrol snorted. "As it happens, I *was* more or less telling the truth," he growled. "Once we knew space horses weren't just some isolated evolutionary accident, it stood to reason that they had to be part of a complete space-going ecosystem. Any ecosystem worth its salt ought to have several different varieties of predators, so I went off to hunt for them."

"Without any scrap of discussion or authorization," Roman pointed out.

"True," Ferrol admitted. "On the other hand, Rrin-saa had already said he and the other Tampies were going to collect their marbles and go home when we got back to Solomon. If I hadn't taken the opportunity Epilog presented, we might never have gotten another chance." A half-smile twitched at the corners of his mouth. "Besides, if I'd told you in advance your head would be on the block beside mine now."

"Not if I'd simply locked you in your cabin in the first place," Roman said coldly.

Ferrol raised his hands, palms upward, all innocence again. "If you had, we'd never have found the black hole ecology."

For if it prosper, the old cynicism ran through Roman's mind, *none dare call it treason*. The politics of convenience and end result . . . the politics on which the Cordonale seemed to run these days. "You said what you'd told Wwis-khaa was more or less the truth. I presume from that that you had something other than guard duty in mind for these theoretical predators of yours?"

Ferrol leaned forward, a sudden earnestness in his face. "We can train them, Captain," he said, a quiet fire beneath the words. "Train them like the Tampies have trained space horses; only these would be ours. *Ours*. With our own space—whatever; wolves, maybe—with space-wolf ships the universe would be open to us. We could explore and colonize—we could do whatever we damn well pleased, and all of it without the Tampies interfering and hand-wringing us to death."

"Including the building of your warhorse fleet?" Roman asked.

"Including any—" Ferrol broke off, his eyes narrowing as his mind belatedly caught up with his ears. "What did you say?"

"Your warhorse fleet," Roman repeated quietly. "The one you've been trying to sell to your Senate backers for quite some time now. Since before *Amity's* first calving, anyway; possibly as far back as your escape from the *Dryden* and me in the Cemwanninni *yishyar* system."

Ferrol stared at him. "Where did—?" He swallowed visibly, took a deep breath. "I don't know what you're talking about," he said, clearly striving for an indignant tone.

"I'm talking about you," Roman said, watching the other carefully. "A man who lied under oath and misappropriated Senate funds for the purposes of poaching space horses from the Cemwanninni system. And who then—"

"I never appropriated anything," Ferrol protested. The dazed look was still there . . . but behind it was a growing sense of horror. "Ever. None of that was on my own—they *recruited* me for that, damn it."

"As a matter of fact, I believe you," Roman told him. "But the official story that's begun to make the rounds says otherwise. My guess is that your former supporters are laying the groundwork to discredit anything you might possibly say against them in the future."

Slowly, Ferrol's gaze slipped from Roman's face and drifted to the port, and for a long minute he stared silently out at the stars. Roman watched the play of emotions across the younger man's face, feeling a pang of guilt at having had to be the one to drop the hammer on Ferrol's head.

And yet, even as he watched, he found his gu

unexpectedly dissipating, replaced by interest and a growing sense of respect. Ferrol had always had a rather brash confidence in himself and his opinions, an arrogance Roman had put down to the combination of youth plus the heady political power unofficially backing him from the shadows. But now, with that power suddenly turned against him, Roman realized it hadn't been nearly as major a part of Ferrol's internal support as he'd thought. The shock of realizing he was being thrown to the wolves was already changing into a hard and icy anger . . . and when he again turned to face Roman he was back in control. "How long since this official story came out?" he asked.

"I heard it first during the *Defiance* debriefings," Roman told him. "I'd tried to dig into your record a few times before that, but your friends had done too good a job of burying it."

Ferrol nodded grimly. "And now it's suddenly accessible again," he growled. "Suitably modified, of course."

"So it would appear," Roman agreed. "So. What are you going to do now?"

Ferrol exhaled thoughtfully. "Try to interest someone else in the idea of taming space predators, I suppose. Maybe the Sinshahli Psych Institute—that place Demothi came out of."

"You may find it hard to get a hearing," Roman warned. "No telling how far afield they'll let the story circulate."

"They won't let it get too far," Ferrol shook his head. "If too many people heard it, they might wind up having to bring charges against me. The last thing they'll want is for me to tell my side of it in a public forum."

"So. Stalemate."

Ferrol shrugged uncomfortably. "Providing I don't do anything to shake the tree. Probably one reason they made sure you knew about it. A good way to deliver the message." He looked at Roman sharply, as if something had just registered. "But if you'd already heard the official version . . . why did you let me take the Epilog calving?"

Roman locked eyes with him. "As I said, I didn't believe the critical parts of it. You learn a great deal about a man when you spend a year serving with him, Ferrol—you learn about his character, and about his judgment, and which you can trust and under what circumstances."

Something might have passed over Ferrol's eyes; Roman wasn't sure. "Yes, sir," Ferrol said, his voice carefully neutral. "I . . . thank you for your trust, sir. If you'll excuse me now, it's been a very tiring few days. With your permission, I'd like to go to my cabin and rest."

"Certainly," Roman nodded. "Kennedy's projection puts us at Kialinninni in about twelve hours; I'll want you available for bridge duty then."

"Yes, sir," Ferrol said, getting to his feet.

"And Commander . . . ?"

Ferrol paused at the door. "Yes, sir?"

"Welcome home."

This time something did indeed pass over Ferrol's eyes. "Thank you, sir," he said, and left.

Something, it seemed to Roman, that had looked a great deal like pain.

Chapter 27

Kialinninni's sun was a dim red star marked on Roman's helm display by a flashing circle, moving with the rest of the stars across the screen as Sleipnir came around in a gentle arc to line up with it. For a moment, before the space horse blocked it, the star was visible in the forward port, and Roman threw a quick look out at it. It was even harder to see there than it was on the display. "Sso-ngii, are you sure Sleipnir can see the target star?" he asked into the intercom.

"He can," the Tampy replied.

Roman frowned again at the helm display; but Sso-ngii ought to know what he was talking about. "All right. Stand by to Jump at my command. And let me know immediately if this procedure startles or frightens Sleipnir." He keyed engineering into the circuit. "Commander Stolt; Dr. Tenzing—you ready?"

"Just waiting for the order, sir," Stolt replied. "The boats are all tanked up and ready to go, and Dr. Tenzing's double-checked the spray pattern."

"Very good. Launch."

"Yes, sir. Launching . . . now."

Roman shifted his attention to the tactical display. From *Amity*'s hanger came Stolt's two gimmicked boats, flying together in close formation as they came up *Ami-*

ty's hull. They passed the bow and began to split apart; and by the time they reached Sleipnir they were on opposite sides of the space horse's bulk.

"Starting the gas spray," Stolt announced.

On Roman's display the two boats, moving up opposite sides of Sleipnir's cylindrical mass now, began to trail what showed up on the screen as a cohesive-looking mist. Smoothly, and in perfect synch, the boats altered direction, and as Roman watched began tracing out a double-helix pattern a few meters above the space horse's surface. The mist spread slowly out behind them as they circled near Sleipnir's head and started back, and by the time they were once again traveling alongside the rein lines the mist had settled in around Sleipnir, circling and engulfing the creature like a halo from some strange medieval painting.

"Boats almost back," Stolt said. "ETA one minute."

Roman nodded. "Marlowe?"

"Cloud holding together nicely," the other reported. "Expanding just enough to fill in the whole gap around Sleipnir."

"Good." A thought occurred to him—"When you get a minute, you probably ought to let the *Scapa Flow* know what we're doing—we don't want them to be startled."

"Yes, sir." Marlowe turned to his intercom.

Roman returned his attention to the tactical. "Ssongii? Is Sleipnir bothered at all by the gas mixture?"

"He is not. He is facing the Kialinninni star, Rromaa, and is ready to Jump."

And was meanwhile busy exuding all the information any passing shark would ever need to find the Tampy corral. If this scheme Tenzing had dreamed up didn't work . . .

And the irony of it all was that if it *did* work they would probably never know it.

On the tactical, the boats hovering close beside *Amity*'s hull disappeared. "Boats aboard, Captain," Stolt announced. "Hangar door sealing . . . we're ready here."

"Sso-ngii?"

"I hear, Rro-maa."

Roman settled himself and shifted his eyes to the forward viewscreen. "All right, then. Everyone ready; fire, and Jump."

At the edge of the screen the comm laser lanced out, its passage marked just visibly by the flicker of ionized hydrogen atoms in its path. The dim line shifted inward, touched the edge of the gas cloud ahead—

And, abruptly, Sleipnir was sheathed in flame.

It wasn't a terribly hot fire, as fires went—Tenzing had made sure of that when preparing his mixture. The temperature at Sleipnir's skin would be no more than six hundred degrees Celsius, Roman knew—hardly worth a space horse's notice, but more than enough to char and scramble the complex molecules in the dust sweat beyond any possible reconstruction.

Or so the logic went. But for that first flaring instant, none of the chemistry or biology or logic really mattered. For that one single instant Sleipnir was a glimpse into semi-mythic racial memories of humanity's past: an echo of ancient Viking funeral pyres, or of the self-immolation of the Phoenix, or of the fiery horror of Dante's *Inferno*.

The flame flickered out, and the vision faded, and Roman took a deep breath, feeling vaguely foolish. He glanced around the bridge, wondering if anyone had noticed. But all were still huddled over their consoles, busy with the usual tasks of a Jump.

The Jump. Belatedly, Roman dropped his eyes back to his displays, giving them a quick scan. If the trick hadn't worked . . .

It had. Dead ahead on the nav display was the dim globe of Kialinninni's sun; and a check of the timeline showed that the Jump had taken place at virtually the height of the flash fire.

He looked up, to find Ferrol's eyes on him. "It seems to have worked," he commented to the other.

"Looks that way," Ferrol nodded. "So. Now what?"

"We find the corral," Roman told him, tapping keys on his console. If Kennedy's projections had been on the mark the corral ought to be somewhere off to starboard. . . .

"Got it, sir," Marlowe announced. "Bearing—well, the nearest edge of the enclosure's about thirty-nine starboard, ten nadir; range, ninety-five thousand kilometers."

Roman nodded as the corral—or, rather, the ovoid computer-enhanced shape marking its invisible boundaries—appeared, centered, on the scanner display. He tapped for a tenfold magnification; repeated the procedure—

"Good God," Kennedy murmured, peering at her own display. "When they say they're going to bring the space horses home, they don't fool around, do they?"

"No, they don't," Roman agreed, feeling just a little staggered himself. The last time he'd seen the corral, back when he'd arrived to take command of the *Amity*, there'd been perhaps a half-dozen space horses wandering around inside the enclosure; now, the place was almost literally packed with them. Moving restlessly about, visible only as pale slivers of reflected light from the system's star, it was oddly reminiscent of the view through a microscope at a drop of swamp water. Distantly, Roman wondered if the Tampies had ever noticed that; but almost certainly they had. The recurring and circular patterns of life and nature were, after all, the backbone of Tampy philosophy.

"Must be two hundred space horses in there," Marlowe commented, sounding awed.

With an effort, Roman shook the philosophic contemplations from his mind. There was work to be done. "It's supposed to be the bulk of the Tampy herd," he told Marlowe. "Or fleet; or whatever it is they call it.

Anyway. Get on the radio and contact that space station headquarters of theirs—we need to warn them about the dust sweat trails their space horses have been leaving." He tapped the intercom. "Dr. Tenzing?"

"Right here, Captain," the other said, sounding distracted. "Hang on a minute; the spectroscopic data from the fire is starting to come in."

Which would show—or perhaps only hint at—whether or not Sleipnir's own dust sweat trail had been adequately destroyed by the fire. Though even if it had. . .

Roman grimaced. Even if it had, the worst part of the job was still ahead. Tracking down and obliterating the trails from all the systems the Tampies had brought that many space horses in from would be a horrendous task, quite possibly beyond the aliens' own capabilities. But if the Starforce could be persuaded to help—in exchange, perhaps, for continued access to space horses—

"Captain?" Across the bridge Marlowe half-turned, a frown creasing his forehead. "I'm not getting any response from the corral station."

"Keep trying," Roman ordered, something cold settling into his stomach as he turned to his scanner display. The station's cylindrical shape was centered in the view, looking just about the way he remembered it from the last time.

Except . . .

"Kennedy," he said quietly, "start a full scan of the area. Anomalous motion, and tie in both the space horse and shark recognition programs."

"Yes, sir," she said, her voice grim.

Roman looked up, to find Ferrol frowning at him. "Trouble?" the other asked.

"I'm not sure." Roman nodded at his display. "The last time I was here there were three Tampy courier ships tethered near the station. Now, there aren't any."

Ferrol frowned at his own display. "It may not mean anything," he said slowly. "They could be off helping in the general round-up or something."

"Having left this batch all alone?"

Ferrol didn't answer. Roman turned back to his own displays, feeling the abrupt tightening of tension around the bridge. Kennedy was doing a three-dimensional spiral search, he saw, scanning outward to ever increasing distances from the ship. It was a standard military pattern, designed to quickly locate the most immediate dangers to the scanning ship. But if there was something happening far away . . . "Ferrol, call the *Scapa Flow*," he ordered the other. "Have them start a long-range search pattern with their anomalous-motion program."

Ferrol threw him an odd look, but nodded. "Yes, sir."

Roman keyed his intercom. "Sso-ngii? How's Sleipnir holding up?"

There was a pause. "He is . . . troubled, Rro-maa," the Tampy said at last.

"So are we," Roman told him, glancing at the visual. Still nothing showing but stars. "I want you to head us toward the corral enclosure; two gees acc/dec course."

Another pause. "Your wishes are ours."

He keyed off the intercom and returned his attention to his displays. Kennedy's scan was out to ten thousand kilometers now. Still showing nothing. A moment later he was pressed gently into the sides of his chair as Sleipnir turned toward the corral; felt the growing pressure backwards as the space horse began accelerating toward the two-gee goal he'd ordered—

And without warning was slammed with bone-jarring force deep into his chair. "Sso-ngii!" he shouted. "What in—?"

"Anomalous motion!" Kennedy snapped. "Coming up behind us—fast."

"Marlowe, get a reading on it," Roman ordered, his mouth suddenly dry.

"I'm on it, sir," Marlowe gritted. "Looks like a group of vultures . . . confirmed. Reading about fifty objects, some of which may be telekened boulders. Closing at approximately fifteen gees."

And according to the tactical display they were already swinging outward, far enough to stay clear of Sleipnir's telekene range as they passed. "Try the comm laser," Roman told him. "See if you can do some damage. Kennedy, backtrack their vector—see where they came from."

"I've got that, Captain," Ferrol cut in, his voice strained as he leaned against Sleipnir's panic acceleration toward his displays. "There're sharks out there, all right—the *Scapa Flow* reports at least six of them. Range of just over five hundred thousand kilometers."

Kennedy hissed something blasphemous. "Confirmed, Captain. Six sharks . . . and looks like three space horses, too."

The missing Tampy couriers? "Get me a clearer image."

"I'll try." The picture on Roman's display magnified, sharpened . . .

For a moment Roman just stared at the scene, a part of him not really believing it, the rest not wanting to. Six sharks, moving almost in formation, were flying toward the *Amity* and the corral; flying, according to the readout, with nearly five gees acceleration. A hundred kilometers ahead of them, just barely maintaining that distance, were the three space horses. From the small ships trailing behind them Roman could see a strangely flickering substance falling back toward the sharks. It took a second for him to identify it as space horse webbing, and another to realize what exactly the Tampies were up to. "They're trying to snare them," he murmured. "Snare them, or tangle them up."

"Webbing against sharks," Kennedy breathed. "They must be crazy."

With an effort, Roman shook off the mental paralysis. "Marlowe—report."

"Comm laser ineffective," the other said tightly. "The vultures are alongside the *Amity*—passing now.

And if they got in front of Sleipnir . . . "Sso-ngii: prepare for emergency Jump," Roman called toward the intercom. "Anywhere will do. Kennedy, we'll need a course from wherever we wind up back to the Cordonale." If the Starforce could throw together a task force quickly enough, the *Amity* might be able to Jump it here in time to help this from turning into a space horse slaughter—

"Rro-maa?"

Impatiently, he focused on the intercom. "Rrin-saa, didn't Sso-ngii hear me? Get him moving—we've got to get out of here—"

He broke off. The expression on Rrin-saa's face— "What's wrong?" he demanded.

"Sso-ngii is not able. Sleipnninni has become . . . he is in *perasiata*."

Roman felt his stomach tighten. "That's impossible," he said, hearing how stupid the words sounded even as he said them. "Sleipnir's *accelerating*, damn it—how can it be in a coma?"

"He is frightened of the vultures and the sharks," Rrin-saa said. "He is . . ." He seemed to grope for words.

"The word is *panicking*," Roman bit out, eyes flicking over his displays as his mind searched for a plan. The vultures were past the *Amity* now, heading for the point twenty-seven kilometers ahead where they'd be able to set up their optical net. Sso-ngii and the other Tampies had maybe a minute to snap Sleipnir out of this. . . .

"Marlowe, are there any more vultures closing on us?" Kennedy asked suddenly. "Or is this batch all of them?"

"Uh . . ." Marlowe frowned at his displays, fingers dancing over his console. "I don't track any more coming this way, no."

"Then I don't think we've got a problem." She swiveled around. "Captain, the *Scapa Flow*'s got netting equipment aboard. We can cut them loose, send them ahead to clear out the optical net, and link up with them again before we Jump."

Roman shifted his attention to Ferrol. "Possible?"

Ferrol hesitated, then nodded. "It should be, yes," he said slowly. "But not unless Sso-ngii can get Sleipnir to kill some of this acceleration."

Roman nodded, feeling the tension ease somewhat. The problem wasn't gone, but at least their deadline for action was extended somewhat. "Did you hear that, Rrin-saa?" he called. "You and Sso-ngii have got to get Sleipnir back under control."

"We will try, Rro-maa."

"Good. Ferrol, alert your people on the *Scapa Flow*; we'll want them to move as soon as they can."

"Yes, sir," Ferrol said, an odd expression flicking across his face before he turned back to his console.

Roman turned his attention back to the vultures. They were nearly in position now . . . and even as he watched the acceleration pressing him into his seat abruptly eased, and then vanished.

"Rro-maa? Sleipnninni is no longer in *perasiata*."

"Thank you, Sso-ngii." Roman looked at Ferrol. "Pop the tether line and tell the *Scapa Flow* to go," he ordered the other. "Kennedy, check and see if we're going to have any trouble Jumping from this deep in the gravity well."

"Already checked, sir," she said. "We're a little close, but shouldn't have any major problems. Our best bet will be the Torii system; recommend we Jump there and alert Prepyat and Earth via tachyon."

And while the Starforce scrambled a task force they would have time to get into position for the next Jump. "Sounds good," he nodded. He glanced at Ferrol—

And paused for a second look. The other was still sitting facing him, ignoring his console. "Ferrol? What's the trouble?"

Ferrol swallowed visibly, a strangely haunted look in his eyes. "No trouble, sir."

"Then get the *Scapa Flow* going." He turned back to Kennedy—

"No, sir."

Roman looked back. "No?" he asked, very quietly.

Ferrol's eyes flicked to Kennedy as his hand dipped into a pocket and withdrew an envelope. "Captain Roman," he said, his voice abruptly formal, "pursuant to the Senate carte blanche directive contained in this envelope—" He took a deep breath. "I hereby relieve you of command."

Chapter 28

It had been a moment Ferrol had thought about ever since coming aboard the *Amity*; a moment he'd thought about, and worried about, and occasionally dreamed about. A moment that had been part of the background of his mind for over a year now.

A moment that, with all that preparation, surely ought to have been easier.

The bridge was deathly silent, even the occasional clicks and beeps of recording and sensing instruments sounding muted to him. The crewers were silent, too, for the most part frozen in place like so many statues. Ferrol kept the bulk of his attention on Roman, forcing himself to meet the other's eyes as he fought back the strange sense of guilt and shame and waited tautly for the inevitable explosion of disbelief and rage.

The explosion never came. "May I see that?" the captain asked calmly, extending a hand toward Ferrol.

Swallowing hard, Ferrol unstrapped and floated across to the other, planting one foot into a velgrip patch. Roman took the envelope, glanced once at the Senator's handwriting on its face, and opened it. Withdrawing the paper inside, throwing a speculative look at Ferrol as he did so, he began to read.

Ferrol licked his upper lip, his eyes darting around

the bridge. This was the critical moment, the moment when the entire thing hung by a thread. If Roman refused to accept the Senate directive—if he refused to relinquish his command—

His darting glance touched Kennedy . . . and froze there.

He licked his lip again, the knot in his stomach tightening painfully as all of the Senator's veiled warnings about Kennedy flooded back at once. The most dangerous person on the *Amity*, he'd called her . . . and as Ferrol looked into those eyes—those rock-hard eyes, gazing unblinkingly straight back at him—he had no doubt whatsoever that the Senator had been right.

He took a careful breath, suddenly and acutely aware of the flat bulge of the needle gun pressing into his ribs beneath his tunic. *You'll be able to handle her*, the Senator had assured him; but gazing into those eyes, Ferrol wasn't nearly so sure of that. If she was indeed a trained professional, his only chance would be to make sure he shot first.

From Roman came a faint rustle of paper; with an odd combination of relief and reluctance, Ferrol broke his gaze from Kennedy and looked back at the captain. "I presume," the other said, almost conversationally, "that you have some explanation for this." He waved the paper gently.

"I believe the directive is self-explanatory," Ferrol told him.

"The directive itself is quite clear, yes," Roman agreed coolly. "I was referring to the reason you've chosen this particular moment to invoke it."

Ferrol took a deep breath. "I'm not here for a debate, Captain," he said, fighting against a quaver in his voice. This was hard enough without Roman dragging out the discussion. "The only question you need to consider at the moment is whether you're going to obey that directive. Yes or no."

Once again he braced himself for an explosion . . . and once again the explosion didn't come. Roman gazed expressionlessly at him for a long moment; then, with only a touch of hesitation, he keyed his intercom. "All crewers: this is Captain Roman," he said, his eyes steady on Ferrol. "As of this moment, per a Senate directive . . . I'm relinquishing command of the *Amity* to Commander Ferrol."

He keyed off and, releasing his restraints, pulled himself out of the command chair. "Your orders, Captain?" he asked Ferrol.

Ferrol looked down at the empty command chair, fighting back the acrid surge of shame rumbling through his stomach and wishing bitterly that Roman would at least show some resentment over what had just been done to him. To humiliate a captain in front of his crew this way was a horrible thing to do to any man; to do it to someone who accepted the blow uncomplainingly was absolute hell.

But on the other hand, that sense of guilt might be exactly what Roman was going for. Steeling himself, Ferrol pulled off the velgrip patch and eased himself into the command chair. It felt damned awkward; but if there was one thing he'd learned from the Senator, it was that appearances and symbols were important aspects of command. "Marlowe; status report on the sharks," he said, keying for scanner repeater.

"They're still coming," the other growled.

"Their ETA to the corral?"

"At current acceleration, and assuming a comparable deceleration phase, about two hours."

Two hours. For a moment Ferrol studied the tactical display. The three Tampy space horses were still giving ground; but the display now showed two more vectoring in toward the defenders from behind and upslope, and even as he watched a third Jumped into view. The rest of the Tampy empire, clearly alerted to the threat, throwing everything they had left into the Kialinninni system in a desperate effort to defend their corral.

Exposing the rest of their space horses to the attacking sharks . . . and in the process completing the total destruction of their space-going capabilities.

It was, perhaps, the last irony. For nine straight years now Ferrol had dreamed of playing a part in the Tampies' downfall; had hatched scheme after grandiose scheme designed to drive them from space and to pay them back in full for their cold-blooded theft of his world. And now, after all that planning, they were going to do the job all by themselves. By themselves, with a little help from the cycles of nature they professed such love for.

And all Ferrol had to do, quite literally, was nothing. Exactly nothing. For the next two hours.

"Commander, we're wasting time."

Ferrol looked up at Marlowe. "Your objections are noted," he said coolly. "Kennedy, do we still have that two-gee acc/dec course to the space horse corral on line?"

She was still facing him, that same rock-hard expression on her face. "We do."

"Good," Ferrol said. "Alert the Handler, then, and let's get going."

She didn't move. "And what exactly do you intend to do there?"

He met her gaze, determined not to be intimidated. "As I said before, I'm not here for a debate, Lieutenant," he said. "You have your orders; carry them out."

"You don't need to take us in to the corral to keep the Cordonale from sending help," Roman said quietly from beside him. "And the longer you hold us in this system, the more risk you're taking that the sharks or more vultures will reach us before the *Scapa Flow* can clear away the optical net."

"I'm aware of that," Ferrol growled, feeling a flash of annoyance that Roman had read his thoughts and plans so easily. "We're not going there to hide—we're going there to open the corral netting and let the space horses go."

It hadn't been what he'd intended to say; and judging from Roman's expression, it had come as a surprise to him, too. "We're *what*?" he asked carefully.

"You heard me," Ferrol told him curtly . . . and, actually, now that he thought about it, it wasn't such a bad idea. There was no particular reason why the space horses should have to suffer along with their Tampy masters, after all. Destroyed or scattered, the end result would be the same. "Unless," he added to Roman, "you'd rather see the sharks get them."

For a long moment Roman stared at him in silence. "So this is how you intend to get your revenge," he said, very quietly.

"They won't be hurt—just trapped on their own worlds, out of our way," Ferrol countered. "Would you rather we went to war and did the job more permanently?"

"You've seen space horses in action," Roman said, as if Ferrol hadn't spoken. "You know how poorly they handle stress situations. Do you *really* still believe the Tampies have a secret fleet of warhorses hidden off somewhere?"

Ferrol grimaced. No, not really. Not any more. "The mechanisms and methods aren't important," he told Roman shortly. "What's important is that the Tampies' very presence in and around human space is a threat to us . . . and that threat's going to end." He focused on Kennedy. "I gave you an order, Lieutenant."

For a moment he thought she was going to refuse. Then, without a word, she turned away from his gaze and swiveled back to her console. A brief, low conversation with the Handler, and a minute later *Amity* was moving again. "What's our ETA?" he asked as Sleipnir reached the indicated two gees.

"About seventy minutes," she said, not looking back.

Giving them just under an hour to destroy a section of webbing and get out of the way before the sharks arrived. Should be adequate. "Very good," he nodded.

"Rrin-saa also said they'd like to know why we're going there," she added.

"Tell them we're helping them do the honorable thing," he growled. "Let them figure it out from there."

Beside him, Roman stirred. "Commander, I wonder if I might see you in my office for a moment," he said quietly. "When you have the time, of course."

Ferrol frowned up at him, a ripple of suspicion running through him. "Anything you want to say to me you can say right here," he told the other.

Roman shook his head, his face unreadable. "What I have to say is strictly confidential."

Ferrol gnawed his lower lip. Confidential, hell—Roman was up to something, and they both knew it. But what? Some kind of attempt to overturn or get around the Senate directive? By having Kennedy secretly Jump them back to the Cordonale, perhaps, and getting someone there to countermand the directive via tachyon?

Or did Roman have something else in mind? Something more direct, perhaps?

"You realize, I trust," he said quietly, "that if anything happens to me, the *Amity* will be trapped here. I doubt very much the *Scapa Flow* will clear out the vultures' optical net unless the order to do so comes from me."

He held his breath, wondering if Roman would sense that the warning was at least fifty percent bluff. But the other merely cocked an eyebrow. "Are you suggesting," he asked mildly, "that I might engage in mutiny against a legally appointed commander?"

Ferrol glared at him, the uncertainty curdling in his stomach . . . but there was only one way to find out for sure what the other had in mind. "Kennedy, you have command of the bridge," he said, unstrapping himself and standing up carefully against two gees' worth of weight. "I'll be in the captain's office; continue our course, and alert me of any change in the situation with the sharks."

"Acknowledged," she said, not turning around.

Ferrol turned to Roman, and for a moment the two

men eyed each other. Then, Ferrol raised a hand, gestured toward the door. "After you, Captain."

And besides, nothing Roman could do now would make any real difference. Whatever happened to Ferrol or the *Amity*, the Tampies had already lost.

"You won't mind, I trust," Ferrol said as the office door buzzed and slid open, "if I sit at the desk."

Roman cocked an eyebrow at him. "So that you can watch the door?"

"So that I can watch the helm repeater," Ferrol corrected shortly, circling the desk and dropping into the chair. Keeping an eye on *Amity*'s progress really *was* his primary concern, he told himself firmly. The fact that this way Roman would be between him and any unannounced visitors was purely coincidental. "So. What's this confidential news you need to tell me?"

Roman sat down across from him, and for a moment studied Ferrol in silence. "That Senate directive of yours is dated over a year ago," he said at last. "You've had it ever since you first came aboard the *Amity*."

"That's right," Ferrol nodded. "It was my guarantee that you wouldn't rig things so as to snowdrift the data from our wonderful mixed-crew experiment."

"But you didn't use it then," Roman pointed out.

"There was no need," Ferrol snorted. "The experiment was a disaster, and everyone knew it. If Pegasus hadn't come out of left field with that calf, *Amity* would have been decommissioned and you'd have been sent back to the *Dryden*. We'd have become a footnote in some obscure Starforce report somewhere, and that would have been the end of it."

"Agreed; but that's my point. If the data so overwhelmingly supported the anti-Tampy viewpoint, and you were so afraid I'd hide it, why didn't you take command when we first returned to Solomon after our mission?"

Ferrol opened his mouth; closed it again. Somehow,

the question had never even occurred to him. "I don't know," he had to admit. "I suppose . . . well, I suppose I'd decided I could trust you to be honest."

Roman nodded, an oddly intense look on his face. "And that's what it ultimately boils down to, isn't it? Trust. None of us can ever truly *know* everything, at least not in the sense of personal, firsthand experience. Our knowledge, our opinions, even many of our deepest beliefs—all of them hinge on the reliability of other people."

"If you're wondering if my directive is valid—"

"Oh, I'm sure it is," Roman assured him. "Perhaps your former sponsors would repudiate it now, but by the time we're in a position to ask them our activities here will be a *fait accompli*. We both know that."

"Then if you have a point, I'd appreciate it if you'd get to it," Ferrol growled, the hairs on the back of his neck beginning to tingle. This was it: Roman was about to launch his countermove.

"The point," Roman said, "is in a black envelope in my desk. Bottom right-hand drawer."

"You have a Senate directive of your own?" Ferrol asked, trying for a sardonic tone even as a shiver ran up his back.

Roman shook his head silently.

For a moment Ferrol eyed him. Then, steeling himself, he reached down, making sure to keep Roman in his peripheral vision at all times, and keyed open the drawer. The envelope was large and thick and—especially in two gees—remarkably heavy.

And across its flap was plastered a blood-red TOP SECRET label.

He frowned at Roman. "What is this?" he demanded.

"Open it and find out," Roman told him.

Ferrol looked down at the envelope, wondering vaguely what the penalty was for unauthorized entry. But Roman was hardly the type to pull something so petty as trying to get him into minor bureaucratic trouble this way. With a quick slash of his hand, he broke open the seal and pulled out the folder inside.

And on its cover . . .

He looked sharply at Roman, a sudden pain shooting through his heart. "Yes," Roman said quietly. "It's the official report on the Prometheus colony. I thought it was time you knew the truth."

Chapter 29

Ferrol stared at the other across the desk, heart thudding painfully. "Where did you get this?" he demanded, his voice sounding strained and hoarse in his ears.

"From the Senate records," Roman said.

"From your pro-Tampy friends, you mean," Ferrol bit out. His hands were beginning to tremble; viciously, he jammed his palms against the edge of the desktop to silence them. "So what exactly is it?—just very heavily slanted in their favor, or a straight out-and-out forgery?"

Roman cocked an eyebrow. "You seem awfully vehement," he said calmly, "for someone who doesn't even know what's in the report."

Ferrol clenched his teeth, the ghosts and memories of Prometheus twisting through his mind and gut. "My parents' hopes are in there," he gritted. "Their hopes, and their dreams, and their lives. I *know* what happened on Prometheus, damn you."

"Then read it for my sake," Roman said. His voice was still calm, but there was a hard glint in his eyes. "So that you can enlighten me as to where I've been lied to."

Ferrol held the other's gaze a moment longer; then, slowly, lowered his eyes to the folder. What *was* he afraid of, anyway? He *knew* what the Tampies had done to his world, and no snowpile of propaganda—cleverly packaged or not—could ever change that.

Taking a deep breath, he opened the folder.

From its weight he'd known there was a lot of paper inside; what he hadn't expected was the sheer variety of types and forms that were represented. Depositions, official colony records, extracts from several of the C.S.S. *Defiance*'s logs, transcribed interrogations of some of the Tampies, logistics sheets, descriptions of the evacuation of the colonists, documents and memos written on fancy Senate alter-proof paper, and scientific and medical reports.

A *lot* of scientific and medical reports.

"There's an overall summary," Roman said, "at the beginning."

Ferrol nodded silently, fingering the pile of medical reports. The top one was for the colony's director, taken afterwards aboard the *Defiance*; and as he skimmed through it—

He looked up sharply. "Here's lie number one," he told Roman, jabbing his finger down on the report. "This medical report on Billingsham is a complete fraud. He couldn't possibly have been diagnosed with hive viruses—it's one of the first things they check for before they clear someone for a new colony."

"I know," Roman agreed soberly. "And you're right, he couldn't have brought anything like that to Prometheus. No one could have."

Ferrol stared at him, something hard and cold settling into his stomach. "No," he said. "No—just forget what you're thinking. There's no way he could have picked it up on Prometheus—we were totally clean of hive viruses."

"Are you sure?" Roman asked quietly.

"Of course I'm sure," he snapped. "I've read the survey team's report—"

The rest of the sentence stuck in his throat. "No," he

breathed. "No. It can't be. Prometheus was certified for colonization. It was *certified*, damn it."

Roman nodded, a flicker of pain crossing his face. "Certified, approved, and commissioned. And three thousand colonists sent there . . . over two hundred of whom have died since then from hive virus accumulation." He hesitated. "If the Tampies hadn't gotten you off when they did, it could have been all of you."

Ferrol's heart was starting to pound again. "I know what you're going for," he snarled. "What you and your pro-Tampy friends are trying to do. But it doesn't hold together. If there was a hive virus there that the original survey team didn't pick up on, how the hell could the Tampies have done it? They don't have any bio-analysis equipment worth dirt—damn it all, they'd been on Prometheus less than two months when they stole the planet and threw us off."

Roman held out his hands, palms upward. "I don't know how they figured it out," he admitted. "I'm not sure anyone does, really." He nodded toward the folder. "The follow-up committee's best guess was that their attunement with natural patterns somehow let them deduce the viruses' presence. Maybe something like the way Llos-tlaa knew that those creatures on Alpha weren't going to attack the landing party, even though he couldn't tell us why. And as for stealing the planet—" he shook his head. "They're just as susceptible to hive viruses as we are. Prometheus has been abandoned for the past nine years . . . and is likely to stay that way."

Ferrol bit hard at his lower lip, uncertainty twisting through him like a helical saw. No, it couldn't be. Couldn't be. A survey team couldn't foul up so badly as to miss something as long-term deadly as a hive virus. It had to be just another pro-Tampy lie. Even if Roman himself genuinely believed it, it still had to be a lie.

But if it wasn't . . .

And in the middle of his silent turmoil the door buzzer sounded.

For a single heartbeat Ferrol stared at the door . . .

and then, in a sudden blinding flash of insight, he saw at last what they'd done to him. Roman's invitation, designed to lure him off the bridge; the forged report, designed to keep him off it—

With the hiss of its released pressure lock the panel began to slide open; and with a single convulsive motion Ferrol jerked up half out of his chair, his right hand scrabbling beneath his tunic for the hidden needle gun. For an instant the barrel caught; then, as he slammed painfully down onto the chair again it came free. Swinging it up, banging it once on the edge of the desktop as he did so, he brought it to bear on the doorway, squeezing it tightly in a two-handed grip. The panel finished its retraction into the wall—

And standing there, framed in the opening, was Kennedy.

The most dangerous person aboard the *Amity*, the Senator had once called her; and in that first, heart-stopping second Ferrol knew he'd been right. Standing motionless in the doorway, her hands hanging loosely and apparently empty at her sides, he watched as her eyes flicked from his face to the gun and back again without losing any of their icy calm. She was calm, cold, and professional.

And she had come to kill him.

It was another moment Ferrol had tried to prepare himself for . . . another moment for which, he saw bitterly, the preparations had been utterly inadequate. *You'll be able to handle her*, the Senator had said with that infinite assurance of his; and Ferrol had nodded and believed him.

But no one had warned him what it would be like to look into someone's eyes as he pulled the trigger.

Roman cleared his throat. "If you're going to shoot her down in cold blood," he said, almost conversationally, "you really ought to get it over with. If you're not, perhaps you should put the gun down and invite her in."

Kennedy still hadn't moved. "You can't stop me,"

Ferrol warned her, his voice trembling with emotion, the taste of defeat in his mouth. If she would make just some move against him, something—*anything*—that he could justifiably consider an attack. But she just *stood* there. "Even if you kill me, you still can't get help to the Tampies in time."

Kennedy shot a quick glance at Roman. "I'm not here to kill anyone," she told Ferrol soothingly. "Really."

"Then why *are* you here?" he demanded. "I ordered you to stay on the bridge."

Her eyes hardened. "As it happens, I came to try and keep you from making a fool of yourself. Obviously, I'm too late."

Ferrol squeezed the gun tighter, determined not to be lulled. "I'm touched by your concern," he said sarcastically. "And how exactly did you intend to do that?"

Roman stirred in his chair. "I think," he said quietly, "that full introductions are in order." He held a hand out toward Kennedy. "May I present Commander Erin Kennedy . . . formerly executive officer of the C.S.S. *Defiance*."

Ferrol stared at her, the fingers wrapped around the gun gone suddenly numb. The *Defiance* . . . "I don't believe it," he heard himself say.

"Why not?" Kennedy asked. "Don't think I could handle the job, or what?"

"I was warned that you were dangerous—" He broke off.

Roman nodded, as if reading his mind. "Warned, no doubt, by your Senate supporters," he said grimly. "To whom the truth about Prometheus was indeed a touchy subject."

Ferrol licked at his upper lip, dimly aware as he did so that he'd lowered the gun to the desktop. "Who would have known that? That you'd been on the *Defiance*, I mean?"

She raised her eyebrows. "Everyone who read that report, for starters," she said, waving toward the folder lying open in front of him. "My name's on half those papers—I was the officer in charge of the depositions and follow-up survey debriefings."

Ferrol lowered his gaze to the folder, stomach tightening as he turned back a few pages to the stack of depositions. Interrogating officer's name . . .

He looked up at her again. "It can't be true," he said, the words more reflex now than genuine conviction. "The survey team certified Prometheus clean of hive viruses."

"They sure as hell did," she nodded, face darkening with remembered anger. "Certified it with such glowing recommendations that the Senate didn't even bother with the legally required backup survey. Why the hell do you think everyone was so damned anxious to snow-drift the whole fiasco?"

Ferrol dropped his eyes to the folder again. The Senate. The *whole* Senate . . . "You're telling me that they knew all along," he said. "That they . . . lied to me."

"Is that so hard to believe?" Roman asked. "You would have been useless to them without your hatred of the Tampies."

Ferrol threw him a sharp look. "If we're going to talk about manipulation, what about *you*?" he accused the other, a spike of anger poking through the numbness. "You knew about this all along—both of you did," he added, shifting the glare to Kennedy. "Why the hell didn't you tell me sooner?"

"Would you have believed us?" Kennedy asked.

"That's not the point."

"It's exactly the point," Roman said, his voice hard. "If I'd shown you this folder when you first came aboard, you'd have dismissed the whole thing as nothing more than a highly sophisticated scam by the pro-Tampy faction."

"So instead you played me like a puppet," Ferrol said bitterly. "Danced me around on wires, surrounded me with lots of pro-Tampy types, made me liaison with the survey section to make sure I got lots of exposure to the damn aliens. The exact same thing the Senator was doing to me, except in reverse. So why should I believe you instead of him.?"

"Because *we* have proof," Kennedy said, gesturing at the folder.

"And what if it's nothing more than a sophisticated scam, like the captain said?" Ferrol countered.

"Oh, come *on*, Ferrol—"

Roman raised a hand to silence her. "Chayne, we can't *prove* any of this to you," he said quietly. "We all know that. The indications are there, if you search your memory—the fact that the Tampies began the evacuation with the families of small children, for instance, who are classically the most vulnerable to hive virus accumulation. But that's not proof, at least not the kind you're looking for."

"So what do you suggest I do?"

"You do what all the rest of us have to," Roman told him. "In the absence of proof, you have to decide whose word you're going to trust."

Ferrol swallowed, his throat aching as he did so . . . but down deep he knew there was really no decision to be made. In his mind's eye he could see the Senator: the aloof eyes, the smugly arrogant voice, the endless manipulation of people and events. He could see a year of serving with Roman: the unashamed Tampy apologist, often irritatingly simplistic in his view of the universe, risking his life to try and save Ferrol and Kennedy from that first shark.

And he saw Kennedy: the calmness of temperament, the competence of long experience . . . and, according to her psych profile, an absolutely flat-neutral attitude toward Tampies. A woman with no axe to grind, for or against anyone.

A woman with no reason whatsoever to lie about Prometheus.

He focused on Roman's intercom, and for a brief moment it occurred to him that he was probably going to look and feel like a damn fool. But then, he'd never been much of one to care what other people thought of him. Tapping for general broadcast, he took a deep breath. "This is Commander Ferrol," he said, keeping his eyes on the console. "I'm returning command of the *Amity* to Captain Roman. That is all."

Keying off, bracing himself, he looked at Roman. Once again, the other passed up the opportunity to gloat. "Thank you, Commander," Roman said gravely.

Ferrol nodded acknowledgment. He'd been right: he did, indeed, feel like a damn fool. "With your permission, sir," he said, trying to keep his voice from trembling, "I'll confine myself to quarters until you're ready for the *Scapa Flow* to clear away the vultures."

He started to get to his feet; paused as Roman waved him back. "Lieutenant, what's the Jump situation?" the captain asked, turning to Kennedy. "Are we too deep in the gravity well to get out of the system?"

She shook her head. "Not really, though we'll scorch *Amity*'s hull pretty good no matter where we Jump to from here." She looked at Ferrol. "But Ferrol was right about one thing: if we ever had time to call up help from the Starforce, we don't any more."

Roman nodded slowly, his thumb and forefinger rubbing gently together as his eyes stared at nothing in particular. "In that case—" He stood up. "It's time we got back to the bridge. You included, Commander."

Ferrol got to his feet, feeling his stomach tighten up again. To have to face the rest of the bridge crew again . . . "Yes, sir," he said. "I'll have the *Scapa Flow* get ready."

"Thank you," Roman shook his head, "but I don't believe we'll be needing their services just yet. We still have an errand of mercy to carry out before we can leave."

Ferrol stared at him . . . and suddenly he understood. "You mean we're going to turn all the space horses loose anyway?"

Roman eyed him, a tight smile playing at the corners

of his mouth. "As I told you yesterday, Commander, I've learned a great deal about your character and judgment over the past year. You've hated the Tampies for a long time; but through all that you've never hated the space horses themselves." He nodded toward the viewport, and the distant corral beyond it. "Your instinct toward the space horses was one of mercy. I'm willing to trust instincts like that."

Ferrol nodded, as if he genuinely understood. For two whole minutes there he'd felt he knew exactly where he stood with respect to Roman, the Tampies, and the universe at large. Now, once again, he was totally lost. "I see, sir," was all he could think of to say.

"Good," Roman said, moving toward the door. "Let's get going, then. By my count we have about forty minutes until we reach the corral. You, Commander, have just that long to find us a way to punch a hole in it."

"Just about ready here," Demarco's voice came through the speaker on Ferrol's console. "Townne and Hlinka have the cables hooked up to the corral mesh, and they're coming back in. Main capacitors showing full charge, backups showing ninety-eight percent."

"Acknowledged." Ferrol looked over his shoulder at Roman. "It'll be just another minute, Captain."

Roman nodded and looked over at Marlowe. "ETA on the sharks?"

"Twenty-eight minutes for the leader," the other said tightly. "A few minutes later for the others."

Ferrol looked at his tactical display, feeling an odd mixture of frustration and melancholy. There were a total of ten Tampy ships harrassing the sharks now, but for all the effect they'd had on the predators' progress they might just as well have stayed away. The sharks were still coming, the Tampies' clumsy snare webbing hanging uselessly off their vulture vanguards or else simply vanished long behind them. Still coming . . . and on *Amity*'s other side, the corralled space horses

very clearly knew it. Their restless milling about the
enclosure had ceased; now, as if somehow divining
what the *Amity* and *Scapa Flow* had in mind, they were
pressed abnormally close together around the spot where,
if all went well, a section of their cage was about to be
vaporized.

And when that happened . . .

Ferrol bit at his lip, eyes suddenly brimming with
moisture. In the wake of his confrontation with Roman
and Kennedy everything he'd ever known or thought
he'd known about the Tampies had collapsed into chaos,
leaving his emotions far too tangled for him to really
know anymore how he felt about them. But amid all the
turmoil one fact stood out crystal clear.

The Senator, with all his cold-blooded conniving, had
won. And the thought of that made Ferrol ill.

"Backup at full," Demarco said. "All boards show
green."

Angrily, Ferrol blinked the moisture from his eyes.
"They're ready, Captain," he said, not turning around.

"Very good, Commander," the other said, his voice
steady. "You may give the order."

Ferrol gritted his teeth, shifting his attention to the
visual display. "All right, Mal. Get ready . . . fire."

From the radio came the faint *crack* of the *Scapa
Flow*'s capacitors; and on the visual a faint spiderweb of
brilliant blue coronal discharge abruptly appeared as
the massive jolt of current vaporized a half-dozen square
kilometers of webbing. For a second the blue light
illuminated the dark masses grouped silently behind it.
Then the spiderweb was gone . . . and in the dim red
light of the dwarf star Ferrol could see the masses
moving toward the opening.

At the helm, Kennedy exhaled audibly. "There it is,"
she murmured. "The end of an era."

Ferrol nodded. They were beginning to flow through
the gap now, the individual space horses making up the
mass angling off in all directions as soon as they were
clear of the webbing. He glanced at the tactical, won-

dering vaguely if the Tampies running before the sharks out there had noticed that their precious herd had been stampeded. Wondered if they would see it as a betrayal, or as a painful but necessary kindness.

He didn't know. For that matter, he didn't even know which way he'd originally meant it.

So much, he thought bitterly, *for trustworthy instincts.*

"They can come back," Marlowe said. But not as if he believed it. "They got to space once before without the space horses. Surely they can do it again."

Ferrol turned to see Kennedy shake her head. "Not without our help," she said. "The first time was a fluke—a space horse wandered into one of their systems and stayed there long enough for them to figure out how to catch it. They've never had any mechanical StarDrive of their own."

"We can hope they had enough foresight to keep a few of their space horses out of this fight," Roman said. "On the other hand . . ." He hesitated, a muscle in his cheek twitching once.

"Quentin?" Ferrol said quietly.

Almost reluctantly, Roman nodded. "It may not really matter how many they come out of this with," he agreed soberly. "The very fact that there are creatures out there they can't defend their space horses against may force them to turn the last ones loose anyway."

For a minute the bridge was silent. The logjam at the exit hole had cleared out now, Ferrol saw, and the fifty or so space horses that still remained inside were flowing smoothly and swiftly out. In seven hundred years, he'd heard once, none of the Tampies' space horses had ever died . . . which meant it had taken them all seven hundred of those years to assemble this stock.

And now they were all leaving; chunks of lumpy air from a punctured balloon. The end of an era, indeed.

"And speaking of ships without a mechanical StarDrive," Roman said into his thoughts, "it's time we cleared away those vultures and got out of here ourselves. Commander?"

"Yes, sir." Ferrol took a deep breath, watching the tactical as he keyed the radio. "*Amity* to *Scapa Flow*; Mal, we're pulling out. Get the net guns ready, and then—"

He broke off. Something on the tactical display . . .

"What is it?" Roman asked, his voice frowning.

Ferrol stared at the display, wondering if he was imagining things. But there was no mistake. The newly freed space horses, which had been angling sharply away from the approaching sharks' trajectory as they left the corral, had begun to curve back inward toward that vector again. "Captain, take a look at the tactical," he said carefully. "The escaping space horses . . . aren't escaping."

He turned to find Roman frowning at his own displays. For a moment their gazes locked— "Kennedy, are they still in too close to the star to Jump?"

Slowly, she shook her head. "I don't think so, sir," she said. "Not given what we now know about how much heat and radiation they can handle."

"They've each picked up an optical net," Marlowe pointed out doubtfully. "Maybe . . ." He trailed off.

"But they're not running away." Kennedy looked over her shoulder at Roman, a vaguely stunned expression on her face. "They're going to *attack*."

Roman looked at her a moment; then, abruptly, reached for his console. "*Amity* to Tampy ships," he called. "This is Captain Roman. Pull out of there, right now. You're about to be crushed by your own space horses."

His answer was a burst of unintelligible whinelike squeaks and moans. "Damn," he swore under his breath.

"Tie Rrin-saa into the line," Ferrol suggested. "He can translate for you."

Roman nodded, already keying for intercom. Ferrol shifted his attention back to the tactical; and a minute later the Tampy space horses began to veer away out of the sharks' path. Out of the sharks' path, and toward the loose sphere of space horses now closing in on the predators like a giant fist. "Make sure all recorders are on," he told Marlowe. "We're going to want to get all of this."

And the battle began.

It was, to Ferrol's mind, a surprisingly leisurely confrontation; but perhaps all the more awesome for its slow, inexorable pace. Even as the Tampy ships reached the contracting sphere of space horses the sharks were breaking their own flying formation, angling outward to face their attackers like the fingers of an opening hand. Between the two groups, the vultures swarmed about like smoke in random cross breezes, either unable to maintain their optical nets in the face of the assault or else simply being thrown about by conflicting telekinetic forces.

Without warning, the *Amity* jerked, jamming Ferrol back into his seat. "Rrin-saa!" Roman snapped. "What was that?"

"Sleipnninni wishes to join," the Tampy's voice came faintly over the intercom. "Sso-ngii is having trouble holding him."

"He has to," Roman told him. "We can't risk dragging the *Amity* into the middle of something like that. Change Handlers if Sso-ngii can't hold on—double up if you have to—but *keep Sleipnir here*. Is that understood?"

"Your wishes are ours."

Kennedy half turned. "We may be fighting a losing battle, Captain," she said tightly. "The other Tampy space horses have gone back in, too."

Ferrol swallowed hard. Kennedy was right: freed of the immediate threat of being the closest ones to the sharks, they'd now turned around to join the shrinking sphere, their tethered ships dragged helplessly along behind them like so much tinsel. Like Sleipnir, sensing somehow the group blood lust; unlike Sleipnir, too close to the center to have a hope of ignoring it.

The sphere continued to close . . . and then, moving in unison, the sharks abruptly veered off their vector, angling toward an edge of the sphere as if attempting to punch their way out. The space horses countered instantly, twenty or so of them shifting over toward the intersect point. Bolstering the forces at that flank . . . and as he watched the maneuver Ferrol felt a shiver run up his back at the irony of it all.

His dream, scoffed at by everyone from the Senator on down, of creating a fleet of warhorses . . .

On the tactical, the sharks again changed direction. "They're running," Kennedy said.

"Or trying to," Roman corrected grimly as the space horses again shifted to counter the move. "Marlowe, are you getting any indication as to what exactly they're fighting with?"

"No, sir," Marlowe shook his head. "I'd guess they're all trying to choke or bludgeon each other to death with telekinesis, but we haven't got any instruments that can confirm—"

He broke off as the *Amity* twitched again. "Rro-maa?"

"I'm here, Rrin-saa," Roman answered. "Still having trouble?"

"Sso-ngii and Hhom-jee cannot hold Sleipnninni for much longer," the Tampy said, his voice very alien. "He is driven, his mind closed to all else. As if, perhaps, in *perasiata*."

Ferrol hissed soundlessly between his teeth, throwing a glance at the intercom. The Tampies' first definition of *perasiata* had been as a sort of coma; two hours ago, they'd used the term for Sleipnir's panic reaction to the approaching sharks; and now it had become a berserker-type rage. The same word, for three entirely different reactions . . . Perhaps, he thought, the Tampies didn't know nearly as much about space horses as they thought they did.

He looked back at the tactical, at the sedate dance of death taking place out there. No; they really *didn't* know as much as they thought they did.

"Tell them they have to hold Sleipnir as long as they can," Roman was saying to Rrin-saa. "At least for another few minutes. Near as we can tell, the space horses are winning out there, but—"

"I'll be damned."

Ferrol twisted around. Kennedy's voice had been little more than a whisper, but there'd been something in her tone . . . "What is it?" Roman asked.

Kennedy took a deep breath. "I believe the battle's over, Captain," she said, the words coming out with—for Kennedy—unusual difficulty. "As good as over, anyway."

Ferrol glanced back to see Roman frown at his displays. "Explain."

She nodded toward her displays. "Look at the vultures," she said quietly. "It's hard to see—the space horses are blocking most of the view. But you can see enough."

"I'll be damned," Marlowe echoed. "She's right, sir. The vultures have grouped into optical nets again . . . in front of the *sharks*."

"They've switched sides," Kennedy said, shaking her head in obvious wonderment. "Seen which way the battle was going, and decided en masse to join with the winners."

On a hunch, Ferrol keyed for a forward visual scan. "Our optical net's gone, too, Captain," he told Roman. "The vultures are . . ." He paused, searching.

"They're heading for the battle," Marlowe put in.

"Interesting, indeed," Roman said thoughtfully. For a moment he stared at his displays . . . and then, as Ferrol watched, a tight smile tugged at his lips. Reaching over, he keyed his intercom. "Rrin-saa?"

"I hear, Rro-maa. We cannot hold Sleipnninni for much longer—"

"No need," Roman cut him off. "Tell Sso-ngii he can let Sleipnir go any time now, only to try and hold it down to a couple of gees."

"Your wishes are ours."

Roman keyed off the intercom; and as he did so the *Amity* abruptly lurched forward. Ferrol fought his stomach, and a moment later Sleipnir had settled down to a steady three gee acceleration. "I hope you've timed this right," he told Roman as the brief nausea faded away. "I really don't think we want to get there while the fight's still going on."

"I don't think that'll be a problem," Roman said. "I expect the sharks will have been beaten too far down to bother us by the time we arrive. And actually, it'll probably be better to get there a little early than to be too late."

Ferrol frowned at him. "Too late for what?"

"You'll see. Give the *Scapa Flow* a call; tell them to rendezvous with us at the nearest shark as soon as they're all dead." He gazed thoughtfully at the display. "If I'm right, we all have a lot of work ahead of us."

Chapter 30

"They're late."

Roman turned from his contemplation of the viewport and the scene outside it, and took a long look at Ferrol. Seated in the far corner of his office, as far from the desk and two guest chairs as possible, the other's face and body language were alive with low-level tension. "They'll be here," Roman assured him. "Being late is one of those qualities that make Tampies so darn endearing."

Ferrol snorted; but his tension seemed to ease a bit. "Right," he said dryly.

Roman studied him. "You sure you don't want a filter mask? Even with the air system going full blast some of their odors are going to get through."

Ferrol took a deep breath, as if trying to get all the air he could while it was still clean. "Thank you, but no," he said, glancing at the door. "I'm going to need to reprogram my reactions eventually, and this seems as good a time as any to start."

"All right." Roman cocked an eyebrow. "But no hitting then," he warned.

Ferrol flushed. Apparently, he'd forgotten that little incident, so long ago, in *Amity*'s hangar. "No hitting, sir," he promised.

337

The door buzzed. "Here there are," Roman said; and the panel slid open to reveal Rrin-saa and Sso-ngii, their twisted faces almost hidden behind their filter masks. "Come in," he invited them, gesturing to the two guest chairs facing him. "Please; sit down."

"We hear," Rrin-saa said, leading the way into the office.

The door slid shut behind them, and as they settled themselves in the chairs Roman threw a glance at Ferrol. Still tense, but clearly under solid control. He would be all right, Roman decided. "So," he said, turning his attention back to the Tampies. "Dr. Tenzing tells me his people have done about all the work on the dead sharks that they can for the moment, so we'll be ready to leave Kialinninni soon. I was hoping that you might have changed your mind about ending *Amity*'s charter once we've returned to the Cordonale."

"We cannot," Rrin-saa said. "We were lied to, Rromaa. Lied into taking part in an unneedful killing. I have stated the *Amity* experiment is over, and I must maintain that stating."

Roman nodded. "I understand," he said. "Certainly, consistency is an important part of policy decisions. I just thought that, given that we now know exactly why *Amity*'s space horse breeding program worked, the basis for that decision might have changed."

Rrin-saa's head tilted briefly to the side. "We do not *know* why the breeding was successful," he said, a note of firmness to his voice. "We know the presence of humans was necessary; that is all."

So the Tampy was determined not to give a single millimeter on this. Not that Roman had really expected him to; in their own sedate way, the Tampies could be just as mule-headed as humans. "Well, then," he told the other, "allow me to explain it to you. It worked because human beings, as you're so fond of pointing out, are predators . . . and because an accelerated breeding cycle is how space horses respond to the presence of predators."

"That is not yet proved," Rrin-saa said.

"Perhaps not to Tampy standards of proof," Roman countered, "but all the indications are there, and for us those indications are quite adequate. When two hundred space horses are not only willing but actually eager to attack a half dozen of their worst enemies, it's pretty clear that their ecological pattern of defense is to fight back with sheer brute-force weight of numbers. And there's only one way to get brute-force numbers."

Rrin-saa hesitated, then touched fingers to ear. "You may be correct," he allowed.

"You know I am," Roman said. "Whether you'll admit it or not. And that should be disturbing to you . . . because of all the aspects and patterns of nature which you've thought you understood, space horses have always been right up there near the top."

"We do not claim all knowledge, Rro-maa," Rrin-saa said. "We observe; we learn; we understand. Some understandings come swiftly, others only over centuries of study. The Tamplissta will ponder what we have observed, and will learn from it."

"Good." Roman flicked his gaze to Sso-ngii, back to Rrin-saa. "Then ponder this, as well, when you settle down to pondering things. You were wrong about space horses; I submit to you that you've been wrong about humanity, as well."

Rrin-saa gazed back unblinkingly, his head tilting again to the side. "We do not yet understand you fully, Rro-maa. Yet, we understand you better than you perhaps know."

Roman shook his head. "No," he said. "You think you do, but you really don't. You've gotten it into your heads that we're nothing more or less than tall, misshapen Tampies who can't or won't see the patterns of nature around us and who you're determined to raise to your level of sensitivity even if it kills us. You've held that picture for twenty years now, and refuse to let it go."

"You are sentient creatures, Rro-maa," Rrin-saa said.

"You have power over the balances of nature, and thus have responsibilities toward them."

"I understand what you're saying," Roman agreed. "And believe it or not, we *do* recognize and accept those responsibilities. But on *our* terms, not yours." He took a deep breath, feeling the weight of history pressing down on his shoulders. He'd joined the *Amity* in hopes of stopping a war neither side would really win. This was very likely the last chance he, personally, would have of doing that. "You see yourselves as the guardians and preservers of nature, Rrin-saa," he told the Tampy, speaking slowly and clearly. "You see the patterns and ecosystems, and you fit yourselves into them. Human beings are different. We see those same patterns, but then we mold them to our own needs."

"You use them," Rrin-saa corrected, his voice more whiny than usual. "And you then destroy them."

Roman shook his head. "Use, yes; but destroy, no. Of course there've been exceptions; some of them disastrous. But most of the time we haven't so much *destroyed* the patterns of nature as we've *changed* them. There's a difference, you know."

"But it is not your right to change them," Rrin-saa insisted.

"And that's exactly where you've been wrong all these years," Roman told him. "It *is* our right. It's our right because that's where we fit into the patterns of nature: as beings whose gift is to build and construct and recombine; to alter the faces of our worlds." He pointed his finger at Rrin-saa. "And what's more, as beings whose gift is to respect all such natural patterns, it's your responsibility to *allow* us that freedom."

The Tampies gazed back wordlessly, both with heads tilted sideways at nearly identical angles. Surprised, or deep in thought; Roman wasn't sure which the gesture indicated. "Do you understand what I'm saying?" he prompted.

Slowly, Rrin-saa's head returned to vertical. Pulling himself back together. "I cannot answer you, Rro-maa," he said. "But I will speak to the Tamplissta. This is a thought that must be pondered by all."

Roman breathed a quiet sigh of relief. "That's all I ask, Rrin-saa. And while you all ponder, consider this, as well." Picking up a small glass vial from the desktop, he offered it to Rrin-saa. "Do you have any idea what this is?"

Rrin-saa accepted the vial, peered cross-eyed at its contents. "It appears to be dust," he said.

"It is indeed," Roman nodded. "Dust sweat, to be exact, taken from one of the dead sharks out there. Dust sweat which, we believe, contains a complete record of its last few minutes of life. The record of six powerful sharks trying desperately to escape as they're telekened to death by two hundred maddened space horses."

"Such death is part of the pattern of nature," Rrin-saa said. "It is not the same as the hunt we were lied into assisting."

"I don't argue that," Roman said. "My point is something else entirely. What do you think a shark would do if it Jumped into a new star system and encountered a dust sweat record like that?"

For a long moment Rrin-saa stared at the dust. "I do not know," he said at last. "I know only that some predators would avoid a place where others had met death; that is all."

"It's enough," Roman told him, feeling a warm surge of victory. He'd feared that the Tampies wouldn't recognize the significance of the dust, or would deny it even if they did. But Rrin-saa had clearly chosen to be both honest and as open as Tampies ever were. "Because if the sharks follow that same pattern, then we've found our defense against them—a defense, please note, that doesn't require you to kill the sharks or in any other way interfere with their normal ecological patterns."

Rrin-saa peered over the vial at him. "Perhaps," he said. "But only if there were sufficient dust. There is not."

"No," Roman agreed, smiling tightly. "But there will be. You see, one of the ways we humans alter our environment is by breaking interesting things like dust sweat down to their component molecules . . . *and then duplicating them*. We'll be taking four hundred kilograms of the stuff back to the Cordonale with us; in a few weeks we can have tons of it made up, ready to scatter all through your systems." He nodded at the vial in Rrin-saa's hand. "So take that sample back to the other Tamplissta . . . and as you ponder the future of your relationship with humanity, consider that perhaps we were set here in space together for the express purpose of assisting each other. Each race complementing the other, each contributing talents and viewpoints the other lacks."

"We do not wish to be your enemies, Rro-maa," Rrin-saa said softly. "We never have wished that."

"I'm glad," Roman nodded. "We, too, don't wish to be your enemies . . . but we also can never be your duplicates."

For perhaps a dozen heartbeats the Tampies sat in silence. Then, shaking abruptly, Rrin-saa rose to his feet. "I will bring your words to the Tamplissta, Rro-maa," he said. "We will ponder them."

"That's all I ask," Roman nodded. "Then I will thank you for coming, and allow you to return to your preparations for departure."

Sso-ngii rose to stand silently beside Rrin-saa. "Farewell, Rro-maa," Rrin-saa said, the whiny voice oddly grave as, in unison, both Tampies traced a brief pattern in the air with their hands. "We have learned much aboard *Amity*. We trust you have learned, as well."

Roman nodded. "We have indeed, Rrin-saa. Farewell."

They turned to Ferrol, still sitting quietly in his corner, and repeated the hand-waving gesture. Then, without looking back, they left.

Roman looked at Ferrol, feeling himself sag with the release of tension he hadn't realized he was carrying. "I was starting to think that they weren't going to notice you at all," he commented.

Ferrol shrugged. "I wasn't particularly worried either way. That was a nice speech, Captain—probably the most eloquent I've ever heard actually delivered from memory."

"Thank you. Let's hope it does some good."

"It will, if they're honest with themselves," Ferrol said. "Misjudging their 'helpless' space horses that badly has got to have done *something* to that smug confidence of theirs. A good reappraisal of assumptions and prejudices ought to send a lot of them to the trash heap."

For a moment Roman was tempted to point out Ferrol's vast experience with reappraising prejudices. "It was worth a try, anyway," he said instead.

"Right." Ferrol hesitated. "So. We'll be leaving for Solomon in a few hours, you said?"

"The *Amity* will," Roman nodded. "I gather you won't?"

Ferrol blinked. "How did you know?"

"You've been spending a lot of time on the laser to the *Scapa Flow*," Roman reminded him, "which was at the time hanging around the Tampy ships. When couriers then started popping in and out, it was pretty obvious you were working a deal."

"To be more precise, a deal was being worked on me," Ferrol snorted. "It seems the Senate, in a burst of goodwill and friendship, has graciously offered the *Scapa Flow* and me to the Tampies to help round up their herd."

Roman whistled under his breath. "Now *there's* a job with steady employment."

"Tell me about it." Ferrol looked at the viewport. "I think even the Tampies were surprised that as many of the space horses hung around the system as did—more domesticated than anyone had realized, I guess. But they still lost nearly a hundred in those few hours after the battle, and the ones here that haven't been netted and taken back to the corral yet are starting to leave now, too."

"And the *Scapa Flow*, of course, just happened to have made records of the spots where each of them Jumped from?" Roman suggested blandly. "Just in case?"

"Just in case," Ferrol agreed. "Anyway. At the moment, the plan is for us to lead a Tampy ship to where one of the space horses Jumped from, let their own space horse sniff out the target system from the dust sweat, then piggyback out there with them and round the thing up. We'll bring it back, turn it in to the corral, and head out for the next one." He shook his head. "At probably something like a week or more per space horse—well, as you said: really steady employment."

"All of it, conveniently enough, at great distances from the Cordonale," Roman pointed out. "Convenient, at least, from the point of view of certain parties to whom you could be an embarrassment."

"The fact hadn't escaped my notice," Ferrol agreed sourly.

Roman eyed him. "The Senate is at least going to pay you for all this, aren't they?"

Ferrol smiled tightly. "They have some piddling sum in mind, yes. Fortunately, I've been able to do a little dealing of my own, directly with the Tampies. For each capture they'll be giving me—giving *me*, not the Senate—a credit of three weeks free use of a space horse and Handler team. And I mean *free* use, with no objections or handwringing or moralizing allowed."

Roman nodded. Somehow, neither the fee nor the conditions really surprised him. "You plan to go into the shipping business?"

"Hardly. I was thinking more along the lines of mid-distance planetary exploration, in the one- to two-hundred light-year range—survey stuff, like *Amity*'s first mission. Maybe keep an eye out for possible colony sites, too, for people who don't mind being a a little isolated." His lip twisted sardonically. "Who knows? I might even settle down somewhere out there myself. At a guess,

I'd say the Senate would probably offer lots of government assistance to help me relocate off to the backside of nowhere." He cocked an eyebrow. "What about you? Back to normal Starforce service again?"

"Unless the Senate taps me for the diplomatic corps," Roman said dryly. "No, I'll probably just be sent back to bordership duty once the *Amity*'s been decommissioned."

Ferrol eyed him. "Not a good place to be if it comes to war," he warned. "Especially for someone like you who would hate like crazy to have to blow Tampy ships out of the sky."

Roman shook his head. "It won't come to war. Not now."

Ferrol grimaced. "You'll forgive me if I don't put quite that much faith in this upcoming Tampy reassessment of humanity."

Roman shook his head again. "You miss the point, Commander. I'm not counting on any philosophical reassessment; I'm counting on a very practical enlightened self-interest."

Ferrol snorted. "I don't think Tampies believe in enlightened self-interest."

"Of course they do," Roman told him. "That's what species survival means: doing whatever is to the race's own best interests. For the Tampies that's always meant minimizing their impact on the environment while at the same time maximizing their benefit from that environment. I think that's been the crux of our conflict, in fact: they've seen our activities as being exactly the opposite of their approach, intrusive without being especially beneficial. Now that we and our technology are going to be of some practical use to them, they're almost certain to tone down on their criticism of our methods. Not stop entirely, mind you, but perhaps be more diplomatic in the way they present their complaints."

Ferrol shook his head. "You're reaching," he said. "The Tampies have never yet toned down their ethical posturing just because it cost them something."

Roman smiled. "Of course they have. Why else do you think the shared worlds' problems haven't exploded yet?"

Ferrol blinked. "You've lost me."

"Well, just think about what the situation was like out there when *Amity* was first launched," Roman reminded him. "A string of bombs, ready to go off—in fact, when that priority message came for us to get Lowry's group out of that pre-nova system we both assumed it was a notification of war. Now, over a year late, the explosion still hasn't come. So why not?"

Ferrol eyed him suspiciously. "You're not going to try and tell me that *Amity*'s space horse breeding program stopped a *war*, are you?"

"I am indeed," Roman said. "Because suddenly being overly loud and obnoxious toward us carried the risk of costing something very valuable: space horse calves that they didn't have to waste years going out and hunting down. And that's going to be even more the case with the shark repellent. The shark repellent, and the shark tranquilizers, and the vulture repellent, and the space horse calving-stimulator, and all the rest of the things we'll come up with once we've cracked the dust sweat molecular code. On our side of the balance, closer relations with the Tampies will give us increased access to space horses, and all the advantages that come with that."

His gaze drifted to the viewport. Outside, just visible in the dim red light, he could see one of *Amity*'s lifeboats carefully skimming along the surface of one of the dead sharks, busily harvesting more of the precious dust sweat. "The universe runs on economics, Chayne," he said quietly. "Not ethics, not rhetoric, not public opinion; but hard, cold economics. If there's clear profit to be made on both sides by ending a conflict, the politicians will find reasons to cool the conflict down. If one or both sides see more potential profit in war, then there'll be war. That's the way it's been throughout human history, and I don't see any reason why it should change now."

Ferrol exhaled audibly between his teeth. "You have a far more cynical view of the universe than I ever realized, Captain."

Roman shrugged. "Perhaps. But I've always felt that simply refusing to face unpleasant facts doesn't make you immune to their consequences, just powerless to make constructive use of them. Of course I'd prefer that our peace with the Tampies be built on something a little nobler than money . . . but I prefer it to having no peace at all. And the rest *will* follow eventually—the public opinion and political unity and all. It always does . . . if the economics can buy enough time." He cocked an eyebrow. "So don't be too quick to bury yourself away on some colony planet just as soon as you have enough space horse credits to get there. We're going to need people like you in the next few years—people who are willing to buck the inertia of public opinion to do what they believe in."

Ferrol smiled lopsidedly. "Even if what those people once believed in was war, warhorses, and genocide?"

Roman shrugged. "As Lieutenant Kennedy said," he reminded the other quietly, "it *is* the end of an era."

TIMOTHY ZAHN

CREATOR OF NEW WORLDS

"Timothy Zahn's specialty is technological intrigue—international and interstellar," says *The Christian Science Monitor*. Amen! For novels involving hard-edged conflict with alien races, world-building with a strong scientific basis, and storytelling excitement, turn to Hugo Award Winner Timothy Zahn!
